THE
HARROWING ESCAPE

THE HARROWING ESCAPE

THE QUEST OF DAN CLAY: BOOK TWO

T.J. SMITH

TATE PUBLISHING & Enterprises

Published by Tate Publishing & Enterprises, LLC
127 E. Trade Center Terrace | Mustang, Oklahoma 73064 USA
1.888.361.9473 | www.tatepublishing.com

Tate Publishing is committed to excellence in the publishing industry. The company reflects the philosophy established by the founders, based on Psalm 68:11,
"The Lord gave the word and great was the company of those who published it."

Book design copyright © 2008 by Tate Publishing, LLC. All rights reserved.
Cover design by Joey Garrett
Interior design by Kandi Evans

Published in the United States of America

ISBN: 978-1-60696-275-6
1. Fiction: Fantasy & Action
08.11.07

THIS BOOK IS GRATEFULLY DEDICATED TO:

the Holy Spirit for enlightenment,
my mother—Jean—may she rest in peace,
my father—Robert—for his inspiration,
my siblings and their spouses for their encouragement,
and
Celeste Thomas for her friendship over the years.

ACKNOWLEDGMENTS

My appreciation is extended to family members and friends who were influential in ensuring *The Harrowing Escape* became a reality. In particular, I acknowledge Reverend Joseph Blanco, Judy and Tim Keilman, Heather McDonald, Patricia and Michael McDonald, Nancy and Michael McKee, Anita, Deidre, and Trina Moog, Molly, Marty, and Chelsea Moore, Betty Jane Nelson, Rose Mary Nelson, Sharon Pitt, Caroline Rose, Reverend James Spahn, Daniel Vieira and Reverend Daniel Zimmerschied.

—T. J. Smith

TABLE OF CONTENTS

CHAPTER ONE

Salvus

SAM CLUTCHED THE HANDLE OF THE DUMBWAITER, DREADING the inevitable discovery of the travelers by the claw-man outside the kitchen entrance. He recalled the many adventures he and his friends had endured and the unearthly creatures they had encountered on their quest to the legendary fortress. To him, their detection in the castle kitchen seemed so unrewarding—so unjust.

With the creature's pincer inching closer inside the entryway from the right, Sam abandoned his flashbacks and focused on the safety of his teenage friends. *Where did I send Cindy and Dan in the dumbwaiter,* he thought, *and where can I hide Jimmy in the kitchen?*

Just then, the trapped travelers heard a thud; the dumbwaiter had returned. Sam, however, suspected it was too late; he presumed the creature near the entrance also heard the crashing arrival of the small elevator. Staring at the kitchen entryway, he raised his lance.

Without warning, the pincer slowly withdrew, as the claw-man round the kitchen's entrance was heard yelling, "Alright…alright, I'm coming!"

Jimmy was already pressed against a corner, inside the dumb-waiter, grasping his bag and lance. Sam quickly set his backpack and weapon alongside his teenage friend, climbed in, closed the door, and released the chain. After a twenty-second ride, the dumbwaiter came to a bumpy stop.

Slowly lifting the door, Sam was relieved to see Dan unscathed and sitting on a dirt floor with his back pressed against a wall and his lantern resting atop a wooden crate. Cindy was rummaging through a pile of garbage nearby.

"Where are we?" asked Jimmy, as he and Sam stepped from the dumbwaiter.

Still suffering from his wounds, inflicted by the troll when crossing the moat, Dan braced his hand against the wall and slowly rose to his feet. "Cindy and I think it's the dungeon," he replied. "See," as he pointed to a nearby wall that was adorned with chains and torturous devices.

"Cool," exclaimed Jimmy; he approached the musty wall.

After visually inspecting the group's new surroundings and detecting no presence of the claw-men, Sam speculated, "Well, I guess we'll be safe here for awhile." Noticing the layers of filth and grime, not to mention the atrocious odor, he added, "By the looks and smell of this place, I doubt anyone's visited this place in years."

With the aid of Dan's lantern, Sam gazed as far as the light would permit. From what he could tell, the room was enormous with wooden vertical beams and numerous passageways branching off in all directions from the main room. It reminded him of a maze.

As Jimmy examined the instruments of torture and Cindy scavenged through a junk pile and Sam snatched his gear from the dumbwaiter, Dan yelled, "What was that?"

Sam spun quickly and demanded, "What was what?"

Jimmy and Cindy rushed toward Dan.

"I saw something run by the fireplace and into that pile of trash," he informed, as he pointed to the left.

The fireplace was nearly centered in the dungeon, midway between the wall behind Dan and the far wall that housed the dumbwaiter. Obviously hundreds of years old, as the layers of ashes and soot confirmed, the fireplace boasted two opposite openings in which timbers—or possibly body parts, as Dan suspected—were placed to disperse the dampness of the dungeon.

With lances in hand, Sam and Jimmy crept around the side of the stone fireplace and neared a heap of trash; Cindy assisted Dan to the mound of garbage.

Sam extended the glowing lantern.

On seeing a wooden crate shift in the distance, Jimmy and Sam raised their weapons to shoulder height.

"Whatever or whoever you are," warned Sam, "you've got two lances aimed in your direction." There was a nerve-racking period of silence before he ordered, "Come out slowly."

With no response forthcoming from the poorly lit area ahead, the four trespassers advanced a few steps more.

Quite unintentionally, Jimmy knocked a crate on his approach, which forced a lightly clad creature to rise from the chest-deep trash with its hands raised, imploring, "Please, I mean you no harm."

The creature wore a gray toga, which the travelers suspected was white at one time; a frayed rope encircled its waist.

"Come out slowly," warned Sam again, "and don't do anything foolish or you'll be tasting the end of this lance."

As the creature cleared the pile of trash and was in full view of the travelers, Jimmy exclaimed, "What are you?"

In the lantern's dim glow, stood a man nearly six feet tall with shoulder-length brown hair, two small protuberances on either side of its forehead, pointed ears, a tail, and two mildly-deformed goat legs, complete with hoofs.

"I'm what your people call a satyr," answered the being, as he continued his advance toward the group.

"Slowly…nice and slowly," ordered Sam, with his weapon still poised for release.

Coming to a halt, the satyr introduced, "My name is Salvus; I live here in the dungeon."

"The dungeon," said Cindy. "Who forced you to live here?"

"Actually, I chose to live here years ago."

"Why on earth," she continued, "would you choose to live in this filthy, rat-infested place?"

"Let's just say it's safer than the forest," answered Salvus. "I don't know if you've confronted any of the forest dwellers, but if you have, then you would understand why I decided to live here."

"Oh, yeah," affirmed Jimmy, "we've met a few of your woodland neighbors."

Standing motionless, for only a few minutes, ushered in throbbing pain to Dan's leg. After limping to a nearby wall and gently lowering himself to the dirt floor, he asked, "So, what happened to you in the forest that made you take up residence in this place?"

Before beginning his story, Salvus insisted, "We must talk quietly. Virtually anything said in the dungeon can be heard throughout the castle, thanks to the acoustics of the tunnel network." In a softer voice, he recounted, "About two hundred years ago, when I was a child, my parents, along with an entire herd of nearly seventy-five satyrs, were slaughtered by a vast flock of Oswagis."

Two hundred years ago? thought Dan. *He doesn't look any older than thirty earth years.*

The satyr expounded, "I was spared because I had inadvertently wandered off to a lakeshore. The numbing death screams prevented me from immediately returning to the group. A couple hours later, after the cries had ceased, I mustered the courage and returned to the battlefield. As long as I live, I'll never forget the sight. Every satyr was massacred beyond recognition. I was able to identify the remains of a partially devoured body as my mother's, purely from the scent. The savage birds, on one foggy morning, ruthlessly annihilated every satyr. And why? Our species was the gentle kind that never threatened any forest creatures. Sadly, to this day and nearly two centuries later, I've never heard of another satyr roaming the forest. Granted, I never venture into the woods, but the Reclaimers, who do on occasion, have never mentioned seeing another of my kind."

Sam lowered his weapon and asked, "So, the Reclaimers took you in?"

"Yes," replied Salvus, with a trace of guilt in his voice. "Out of fear and desperation, not to mention my youthful age, I sought asylum here." Glancing from face to face, the satyr admitted, "While personally I can't stand the miserable beings, I do appreciate the security of the castle. Besides, I'm lucky, since I rarely see the snake creatures. In exchange for my safety and food, I pluck the lyre, here in the dungeon, during the twilight hours; the network of tunnels echoes my music throughout the castle. Believe me, I know the Reclaimers are evil men. I've witnessed their insane actions firsthand. However, even wicked men appreciate good music. For several decades now, I've wrestled with a haunting dilemma: do I continue living within the safety of the castle among the Reclaimers or die in the forest at the hands of a bloodthirsty beast?"

Sensing the satyr presented no threat to the travelers, Sam introduced, "Salvus, I'm Sam." Pointing to his co-travelers, he continued, "And this is Cindy, Dan, and Jimmy."

One at a time, the teenagers greeted Salvus. Jimmy and Cindy stepped forward to shake his hand. Dan, still on the dirt floor resting his leg, raised his hand to the satyr.

Shaking Salvus' huge hand, Dan asked, "So, what's the deal with the claw-men in the kitchen?"

Salvus squatted and seated himself on the floor alongside Dan. With his legs and hoofs fully extended, he clarified, "Actually, the claw-men and claw-women, as you refer to them, are called Pedwhips; their story is similar to mine. Eons ago, their species also was nearly obliterated by a rare and deadly plant predator called the scabbard tree, which lures its potential victims by its sweet-smelling sap. Once a Pedwhip placed its arms around a scabbard and its mouth to the sap, its lips were permanently sealed to the killer tree. Within a matter of only minutes, the Pedwhip was totally encased. Anyway, the extended longevity of the scabbard trees explains why there are great numbers of grotesquely-shaped tree trunks throughout the forest. Down through the centuries, in addition to the scabbards, vicious woodland creatures have also butchered countless Pedwhips. Finally, when their species was all but extinct, a group of Reclaimers approached the seven remaining claw-men and claw-women in the forest and offered their dwindling numbers food, safety, and shelter within the walls of the fortress, in exchange for their manual labor on the castle grounds and in the kitchen. Since that time, their offspring, again for the safety, food, and shelter of the castle, have assumed their ancestors' trades and have worked in the castle ever since. Twelve Pedwhips work in the kitchen—"

"Yeah," interrupted Jimmy, "we nearly met two of them fixing meals."

"And twenty-eight," continued Salvus, "work in the small orchard and garden in the open space, amid the castle walls, while also herding a few livestock around the perimeter of the fortress, in the grassy area near the forest's entrance. Granted, the courtyard isn't flooded with sunlight, but there's enough to grow fruits, vegetables, and a little wheat for the guests of the castle, the Pedwhips, and me. Since there are a number of Pedwhips, they will venture occasionally into the fringes of the forest—in groups, of course, for protection—but never into the deeper recesses of the woods. But I wouldn't worry about the Pedwhips; other than their stingers and pincers, they're pretty harmless."

"If it's all the same," remarked Jimmy, "I'd rather not meet them."

The satyr grinned.

"What about the Reclaimers?" asked Dan. "What do they eat?"

Salvus chuckled before answering, "They don't eat, Dan; heck, they don't even sleep. They're already dead; or as I refer to them, the living dead. As for me, the Pedwhips lower food through the dumb-waiter in exchange for my music, which they and the Reclaimers seem to enjoy. My music, by the way, was nurtured by my mother. She always said music was the universal language that all could enjoy and all should learn to communicate."

Cindy, who had recently joined Dan and Salvus on the floor, asked, "After nearly two hundred years in this place, are you ever tempted to leave?"

"Sometimes," he admitted, "but where would I go? I mean, the only thing outside the castle walls is death."

"Salvus," asked Dan, "are the Reclaimers afraid of light?"

"Not really."

Dan's facial expression revealed he was not pleased with Salvus' response.

"It's just that the Reclaimers prefer darkness," he explained. "That's why on the sixth floor where they spend most of their eternity, you'll find chandeliers with candle holders, but no candles. Light bothers them, but for only a short period of time. Eventually, their eyes adjust."

"But the Reclaimers have to be fearful of something," insisted Dan.

"No," replied the satyr, "I'm afraid…well, maybe . . ." He ended his speculation quite unexpectedly and declared, "If the Reclaimers knew we were having this discussion, they'd kill us all." Recalling the acoustics of the tunnels, he reminded his guests, "We mustn't take any chances; we must keep our voices low." In the softest of voices, he imparted, "Apparently, about two hundred years before my arrival at the castle, a young man is said to have overpowered the Reclaimers."

"Yeah," whispered Sam, "I've heard that story, too. But how did he escape?"

"The story is told," related Salvus, "that in the early 1600's, a boy who was suffering from paralysis was placed at the edge of the forest by his parents, hopeful a Reclaimer would deliver him to the castle. In their hearts, they felt a pain-free life in the castle for their son would be better than a physically-agonizing life in their home. After two months of extreme moral and personal anguish over their actions, the parents and their older son journeyed through the forest in search of the castle and the young boy. Unfortunately, the parents met their end at the jaws of a forest creature. But legends say the older son made it to the castle." Salvus raised himself and walked to a large trash heap.

Sam and Jimmy, who remained standing, raised their lances.

Noticing their obvious anxiety, the satyr pleaded, "You've got to trust me; I mean you no harm. If I did, don't you think I would have alerted the Reclaimers or the Pedwhips by now? Besides, I've waited a long time to entertain humans in my dungeon." After glancing around his living quarters, he acknowledged, "Granted, its appearance and smell may be less than desirable, but it is a dungeon." Kicking open a wooden crate with a hoof, he removed a silver shield, displayed the reflective armor to the group, and disclosed, "This was the young man's key to escape."

"What do you mean?" asked Dan.

"After learning his younger brother had died within weeks of his arrival at the castle," continued Salvus, "the older sibling sought revenge by passing himself off as an applicant for admission to the castle. Although the legends are sketchy on how the older brother learned of his sibling's death, I'd suspect the rescuing brother befriended one of the livestock Pedwhips, who had learned of the boy's fate, and revealed the tragic turn of events. After all, the Pedwhips, for the most part, are a fairly sociable species."

The satyr made a poor attempt at polishing the shield with his soiled toga, adding, "Anyway, after entering the Hall of Admittance with this shield concealed beneath a bulky cloak, the older brother dropped the outer garment revealing the silver shield. He quickly raised it within inches of the face of Spiritus Malus, who shrieked upon seeing his inner reflection in the armor. For I've been told when Reclaimers see their reflections, they see their souls. And when they glimpse their souls, they are reminded of their countless missed opportunities to inflict evil upon humanity. In absolute shame at seeing their demonic shortcomings, the Reclaimers attempt to gouge out their eyes so they never view their failures in wickedness again. But since they're already dead, their bodies—including their eyes—are indestructible."

Handing the shield to Dan, Salvus elaborated, "The Reclaimers are an odd bunch, I must say. For each one prides himself on being the perfect essence of pure evil. But when they see they could have been even more sinister, more sinful, well that's something they can't endure."

Taking two steps back and leaning one hoof against the wall, the satyr continued, "Back to the story. Anyway, this incident occurred in the Hall of Admittance on the main level. But since no other Reclaimers were nearby to foil the young man's revengeful act, he escaped. By the time his fellow Reclaimers descended the Grand Staircase from the sixth floor in response to Spiritus Malus' screams of torment, the young man and the shield were long gone. Sadly, he never made it safely through the forest. Legends say he met his death at the hands of a drunken centaur."

Dan, with a puzzled look, raised his sights to Salvus and asked, "If he took the shield with him, then how did it end up back in the castle?"

Salvus grinned at the young man and complimented, "Nothing gets by you, does it?"

Dan offered no response as he inspected the armor.

"The shield," informed the satyr, "was found by a group of Pedwhips in a centaur's cave, less than a mile from the castle. After they paraded their newfound treasure back to the fortress, unaware the object was now feared by the Reclaimers, they were baffled when Spiritus Malus ordered the armor banished from the castle and into the bottom of the forest's Great Chasm. Knowing they'd be risking their lives traveling the great distance to the gorge, the Pedwhips discarded the shield to a place in the castle where it would never be discovered by the Reclaimers—here in the dungeon." Glancing from face to face, he asked, "So, why have you sought out the castle?"

As the self-designated leader of the group, Sam replied, "We're here on a mission."

"What kind of mission?" inquired Salvus.

"Well," stated Sam, "Dan believes his older brother was taken captive by the Reclaimers some years ago."

Looking down at the seated teenager, the satyr asked, "Is this true?"

"Yeah," he affirmed. "I know my brother, William, is being held here. We even discovered his soccer jersey in the kitchen when we sneaked into the castle."

Before he could continue, Salvus pushed his hair back from his face and reminded, "Dan, just because your brother went missing doesn't necessarily mean he's here; he could be anywhere."

Dan refused to be dissuaded and recounted, "Back when my brother was seven and I was five, we were playing on the outskirts of the forest when he vanished suddenly. My parents have since told me that the police searched everywhere for him, but discovered nothing, except his stuffed animal near the majestic oak—the portal to this world."

"I've heard stories about this portal on the other side of the forest," exclaimed an excited Salvus. "So, it really exists?"

"Oh yeah," assured Cindy.

"You mean the four of you traveled from another world and then through the depths of the forbidden forest in my world?" asked a doubtful satyr.

"Yeah," replied Sam. "Never underestimate what you can accomplish as a team."

"The only thing," continued Dan, "which will activate the portal are the beams of a full moon; and there was a full moon the night my brother disappeared. I'm sure William didn't end up in Lawton in your world, near the edge of the forest, or our friend Doctor O'Brien would have told us. So, I have to presume he's being held upstairs on the sixth floor."

Anticipating Dan's next question, Salvus explained, "I very seldom have contact with the guests. Only on very rare occasions have I seen them when I happened to be near the rear staircase, as they were entering the courtyard for their exercise. But even then, I'm thankful the Reclaimers didn't see me; for if they had, I would have been disciplined. However, the couple times when I have seen the guests, they were in a trancelike state and never spoke. From what I can gather, their lives consist of eating, sleeping, and walking about the courtyard. But I'll bet I haven't seen them more than a couple times during the last hundred years."

Wanting more answers, Dan persisted, "Will you take us to the sixth floor?"

Realizing the infraction, if detected, would not go unpunished, Salvus admitted, "I'd like to help you, really I would, but if I'm seen aiding trespassers, especially ones with the intention of snatching a guest, we'd all be tortured, or even worse, banished to the forest."

Dan lowered his head in discouragement, as if hitting a dead end, but then raised his sights and implored, "Please, Salvus, we've come such a long way."

The satyr thought for a moment and then compromised, "When the time is right, I'll show you the room through a secret passageway."

"Why can't you show us now?" blurted Jimmy.

"Even though it's seldom safe visiting the sixth floor," explained Salvus, "there are times when it's not as dangerous. Trust me, you don't want to enter the guests' room when all the Reclaimers, or at least the majority of them, are in the castle. I'll let you know when the time is right." The satyr concluded his remarks by offering his guests a tour of the dungeon.

Sam, who was intrigued with the tunnel network, accepted the offer. With Salvus at the lead, he immediately trailed, with his lance in hand, followed by Jimmy, with his weapon at the ready, and Cindy, who assisted Dan.

Standing near the first tunnel, Salvus—in a whisper, since he was directly in front of the opening—explained, "Obviously, these tunnels were here long before my arrival, but I was initially told by the Pedwhips they stretch from one end of the castle to the other. Over the years, to relieve my boredom, I've proven the Pedwhips right by exploring every inch of every tunnel. During my excursions, I discovered small holes at the top of the passageways. I presume these openings transmit my music to the upper levels of the castle."

Salvus paused to await Cindy and Dan's slow arrival to the tunnel. He then continued, "Many years ago, I spotted a rat in my quarters scurrying across the dirt floor and vanishing behind the far corner wall. Upon a closer inspection, I felt a draft behind the wall. Once I removed a dilapidated wooden covering, I stumbled upon a stone staircase that led to the castle roof. It was only a matter of time before I found three more staircases at the remaining corners of the castle. So technically, you can reach any level in the fortress from the dungeon virtually undetected."

Gazing into the first tunnel, the travelers noticed it was constructed of irregular stones and was roughly four feet in diameter. Obviously, any trip through the tunnels would be grueling at best, since the passageways weren't large enough for the average-size person to stand upright.

As the party of five advanced to the next tunnel, Dan struggled to outpace his co-travelers and eventually caught up with the satyr. Walking alongside Salvus, and fully intent on learning the whereabouts of his brother, he asked, "Have the Pedwhips ever seen the guests?"

Salvus slowed his pace, so as not to overburden the limping teenager, and responded, "I would imagine; but like me, I would guess only rarely. What you need to understand, Dan, is the Reclaimers will do anything to persuade the guests to trust in them alone and no one else...not me, not even the Pedwhips. This way, the guests place their lives in the hands of the Reclaimers...until, of course, it's too late for them. Even when the Pedwhips deliver meals to the guests, for example, they merely scrape their pincers upon the door and then back away immediately. They're not permitted to see the guests, nor are the guests permitted to glimpse them. That's precisely why the rear staircase is off limits to the Pedwhips and me. And as far as the courtyard...well, you probably haven't seen it. But if you had, you would have noticed the castle walls facing the quad have no openings. Trust me, that's not by accident. This way, the guests can't see the castle workers…only the Reclaimers, who remain at their sides. As far as the garden and orchard are concerned, the Reclaimers clear the courtyard of the Pedwhips before the guests arrive for their exercise. But getting back to your question, Dan, I'd imagine over the years and on very rare occasions, some of the Pedwhips have seen a few guests."

After peering into the second passageway, Salvus sensed his tour group was becoming disinterested. *And why not,* he thought, *once you've seen one tunnel, you've seen them all.* Raising his voice, but not too loudly, so he wouldn't be overheard by the Reclaimers, he suggested, "Why don't we head back to my living quarters?"

None of the travelers responded, although their immediate turnabout suggested they were ready.

Retracing their steps, Dan prodded, "So, Salvus, has anyone ever seen the inside of the room where the guests live?"

"Dan," rebuked Sam, "must you be such a nuisance to Salvus?"

Defending the young man, the satyr replied, "That's quite alright. It's been a long time since I've entertained guests; I'm enjoying our conversation."

Taking advantage of Salvus' receptivity, Dan restated, "Has anyone seen the room?"

"Actually," disclosed Salvus, "I heard that about ten years ago, when a Pedwhip was delivering a meal to the guests' room, he scratched the door and had just turned to walk away when he heard, or should I say he didn't hear, the door close behind him. With the door slightly ajar, the Pedwhip quietly backtracked and peered into the room. He counted five guests, though he couldn't see the wall directly behind the door; so there may have been more residents. From his stolen glance, he noticed it was a long, narrow room that was poorly lit; two small openings let in fresh air, but only minimal sunlight. I would imagine the openings in the wall are purposely undersized to deter forest creatures that have acquired an appreciation for human flesh from entering the guests' room. Despite the fact that the Reclaimers aren't fond of light, they've learned from past experiences that if their guests are denied adequate sunlight and exercise they quickly develop rickets."

Back in the central part of the dungeon, Jimmy revisited the wall with the torturous instruments and asked, "Salvus, have these ever been used?"

The satyr's silence and his immediate withdrawal to his sleeping area suggested to the travelers that perhaps they had been used on him in the not too distant past. The satyr disregarded the question.

On witnessing Salvus' reaction to the crude devices, Sam and Jimmy leaned their weapons against the dungeon wall.

Perhaps, thought Sam, *Salvus had felt the end of the chains and that the rusty implements had been permanently mounted on the wall, near his living quarters, as a constant reminder from the Reclaimers of what would happen to him, should he be accused of insubordination.*

Noticing the men had abandoned their weapons, the satyr whispered, "Thank you."

Stepping from his sleeping area, he approached and informed his four guests, "Since you won't be leaving the dungeon for a day or so—"

"A day or so!" blurted Dan.

"Sh," warned Salvus, "they'll hear you."

Knowing Dan was becoming irritable, Salvus, against his better judgment—and while staring at the unforgivable instruments on the wall—explained that the most opportune time to visit the sixth floor would be in a day or so when most of the Reclaimers would be away on a hunting expedition.

Observing the satyr's reaction to the torture wall and his unusually low voice, the travelers knew he had put his life on the line for them.

After a period of silence to confirm the absence of noise or movement on the floorboards overhead, Salvus advised, "I think all of you should spend your time here and away from the upper regions of the castle." Looking around the dungeon's living area, he added, "It's not much, but at least it's safe."

With her gaze fixed on a towering mound of garbage in a distant corner, Cindy asked, "So, how long has this trash been piling up?"

"Quite awhile, I'm afraid," admitted Salvus. "I try to burn it once a year in the fireplace, but…well…I don't remember burning it last year."

Within seconds of knocking a wooden crate to its side, Cindy bent over to close the lid. She spotted a decaying rat inside the carton and shrieked.

"Sh," warned Sam.

To pass the time until their invasion of the sixth floor, the travelers and Salvus directed their attention to cleaning the living area, making it as presentable and livable as the conditions and surroundings would permit. After an area was cleared of trash, Jimmy grabbed a discarded broom, presumably from the early 1800's, and began sweeping the dirt floor.

"Jimmy," whispered an annoyed Sam, "enough already. Put the broom down; you're stirring up a dust cloud."

Jimmy, who finally was intent on cleaning, rolled his eyes in disgust.

Against a nearby wall, Dan unfolded his sleeping bag and positioned it alongside a lice-infested drop cloth that served as the satyr's sleeping gear. "So, Salvus," he asked, "why are there probably only a handful of guests, but fifty Reclaimers?"

After nearing his sleeping area and plopping to his bedding alongside Dan, the satyr began, "I understand that centuries ago, when diseases were rampant and medications were scarce, each of the fifty Reclaimers had as many as three guests assigned to him, whom he'd tend, feed, and protect until their deaths. Then, the assigned Reclaimer would incorporate their entire nonphysical being: knowledge, thoughts, memories, and ultimately their souls."

With their sleeping gear arranged, the remaining travelers headed to Dan and Salvus' area where they sat upon the floor and listened to the satyr recount the Reclaimers' history.

"But nowadays," admitted Salvus, "no one knows the exact number of guests. However, if the Pedwhip's story is true about there being just a handful of visitors upstairs ten years ago, then I'd presume only several Reclaimers have an assigned guest. Granted, I've seen the visitors descend the rear staircase a couple times in the past hundred years or so, but who's to say that what I witnessed were all the guests. Unfortunately, the last time I glimpsed the visitors was nearly fifty years ago. There could be ten, twenty, or even forty guests on the sixth floor right now. I just don't know. But I do know that in recent years, I've seen a number of Reclaimers leave the castle to hunt exotic pets in the forest and to lure ailing wayfarers and stray hunters into becoming permanent castle residents. Obviously, the Reclaimers' woodland excursions confirm that at least some of the snake-men are guest-free, which means there can't possibly be fifty guests upstairs at this very moment."

Disbelieving of Salvus' comment, Cindy exclaimed, "Hunters? You mean people freely enter the forest to stalk savage beasts for sport?"

The satyr extended his legs, propped his hoofs three feet up the rock wall, and recalled, "About twenty-five years ago, an expedition of the Reclaimers in the woods proved most rewarding. Apparently, three middle-aged hunters, consumed by their desire for a kill, were drawn deeper and deeper into the dismal forest until they were lost and relied on the nonexistent mercy of the forest and its inhabitants. Approaching the huntsmen, three Reclaimers unleashed their mind-controlling powers over the disoriented men and convinced them to become permanent residents of the fortress."

Salvus paused to clear his throat. Not accustomed to conversations, especially of such length, he was parched. Lowering his hoofs from the wall, he rose from his drop cloth, grabbed a grimy wooden bowl from a trash heap, and submerged it into a barrel that was strategically positioned to collect droplets from the rafters. After several noisy gulps, he asked, "Can I get anyone something to—"

"No!" shouted the four travelers.

As Salvus retraced his steps to his bedding, Dan asked why his leg and back were still sore from his trip across the moat, since he was in the castle known for its healing powers.

"Trust me," assured Salvus, "your pain has eased considerably, even though you may not think so, simply because you're within these cursed castle walls. But for complete recovery and no pain, you must be under the personal and watchful care of a Reclaimer."

Cindy grabbed Dan's camping pillow, rested on her stomach, and said, "Salvus, when we were near the castle's clearing, we experienced bizarre thoughts…thoughts like we'd never endured in our lives. Thinking it might be an odor in the air, we protected ourselves with these." She lifted her bandanna from around her neck.

"I, too, remember those mental sufferings," admitted Salvus, "when I first approached the castle seeking asylum many years ago. And like you, once I was inside the castle, the feelings of doubt, evil, and anxiety faded quickly. When I asked a Pedwhip the reason for the anguish, I was told these thoughts of despair are caused by the Shrivel-Toed Lizards that emerge from the soil, shortly before sunset, to feed on the sweet-tasting zini blossoms that thrive at the base of the castle walls and in the rock joints throughout the structure. During their feast, the droppings from literally thousands of lizards cover the castle walls. The by-product of the droppings is a powerful, odorless gas that fills the air outside the castle walls for an extended length of time. Apparently, the noxious gas causes a chemical imbalance in the brain which, in turn, produces unimaginable thoughts. On days when the air is still, if you look closely, you can actually see a fine haze. Many times, the areas outside the castle walls are plagued with this odor for days or until it rains. It's the nonporous castle walls that prevent the gas from overrunning the fortress or the grassy area in the courtyard. That's why the guests are able to exercise there unaffected. Anyway, after the sun falls below the horizon, the lizards burrow themselves in the soil until the following early evening."

Salvus reflected for a moment and then added, "Actually, these feelings of doubt that you and I experienced before entering the castle really don't surprise me."

"Why not?" asked Dan.

"Because," reasoned the satyr, "doubt is oftentimes the precursor to despair. And in this case, despair in the castle."

Referring to Salvus' earlier explanation on the habits of the Shrivel-Toed Lizards, Cindy speculated, "Then that's why the ground was broken up between the moat and the castle."

"Yeah," replied Salvus, "that's right." Running his fingers through his hair, he elaborated, "When I asked the Pedwhips how their species escaped the harmful effects of the invisible toxin, they explained that when they're in the midst of the gas, they breathe through their gills. Apparently, this is less poisonous than inhaling the contaminated air through their noses."

The satyr fell silent at the sound of movement overhead.

Once the noise on the first level ceased and the travelers redirected their gaze from the ceiling to the satyr, he added, "Their gills enable the Pedwhips to leave the castle, in groups, to frolic at the edge of the forest virtually any time of the day." After another moment of silence and an upward glance to confirm lack of movement, he cautioned the travelers, "Although the dreadful thoughts have ended, since you're inside the castle, they will return the moment you leave this fortress, unless you take proper precautions. Don't lose your face coverings."

"Thanks," replied Sam, "we'll remember."

Despite the fact it was only about noon, Sam suggested he and his co-travelers nap, since they couldn't venture anywhere for a day or so.

Though it wasn't twilight, Salvus quietly enchanted his long-awaited visitors with the lyre.

Within minutes, the travelers nodded off; except Dan, who couldn't sleep, knowing his brother may be only six floors above.

CHAPTER TWO

The Hidden Staircase

AFTER THE MUSIC STOPPED AND SALVUS ASCENDED THE unsteady steps, Dan staggered to his feet, grabbed his flashlight, and limped to the far area of the dungeon to explore the acoustic tunnels. At each passageway, he stopped and placed his head inside, hoping to hear the faint voices of humans on the floors above. Hearing nothing at the sixth tunnel, other than Sam's and Jimmy's heavy snoring in the background, he debated on escaping for a few minutes into the inner recesses of the passageway. *After all,* he thought, *surely the others will sleep for hours, since they were up all last night and early morning assembling the wooden plank and crossing the moat. And as far as Salvus, he probably won't return until the others awake.* With his rationalization cemented, he stooped and entered the tunnel.

After a backbreaking five-minute walk in a bent-over position, he sat upon the ground and leaned against the tunnel wall to ease the growing pain in his leg. The respite provided him the perfect opportunity to visually examine the passageway. Salvus was right; directing the flashlight's beam, the tunnel seemed to go on forever.

With the absence of human voices echoing in the tunnel from the floors above, he abandoned his ill-timed exploration and decided to return to his sleeping area. With one mighty push against the wall, it collapsed, tumbling him backwards into a smaller enclosed passageway. The flashlight, which had fallen to the ground, revealed a stone step and several scampering rats. With the touch of a rodent dashing over his hand, he jumped to his feet. Within seconds of stomping his uninjured foot upon the ground, a lone rat that had taken an interest in the flashlight rushed to the safety of the darkness beyond the light's beam. He snatched the flashlight. Aiming its beam ahead, a stone staircase came into view. The steps, much like the acoustic tunnel he had just left, seemed to go on forever and in near total darkness.

Recalling Salvus' story that the castle boasted a stone staircase at each of its four corners, Dan presumed since this flight of stairs was far removed from a corner wall—plus the fact that he literally stumbled into its inner chamber—it was obviously undiscovered, which intrigued him even more. After sweeping his foot across the first step, two lingering rats dropped to the landing and raced through the newly-created opening and into the main acoustical tunnel. The same foot maneuver cleared the next few steps of the annoying rodents. On the fourth step and amid the dim light, he unknowingly rested his full weight on what he believed to be the stone staircase, when he heard a high-pitched squeal; the backbone of a rat was crushed. He continued his ascent.

Ten steps up, while resting upon another landing, he noticed bands of light between several vertical boards on the left-hand wall; the teenager had unknowingly discovered a secret passageway to the first floor. With one hand, he lightly touched the boarded area, hoping the small wooden door would slide or push in. Even though it wasn't the sixth floor and it wasn't the corner staircase that Salvus mentioned he had explored, he was curious what remained hidden behind. With the aid of the flashlight, he discovered several nail heads lodged deep within the boards; the passageway was tightly sealed. He ascended another step, but not before dashing three oversize rodents with his boot.

Throughout his ten-minute upward trek, Dan discovered that the secret passageways to floors two through five were also nailed shut. As he stepped upon the sixth floor landing, the light beam died.

"Oh, come on," he whispered, while shaking the flashlight.

After several taps of the flashlight against the hidden staircase wall, the beam was reborn. Squatting and then reaching for the boarded entryway, he hoped the opening would slide or at least was loosely nailed. As he pushed, he heard a faint noise.

"Come on, move," he implored, as he attempted to slide the plank to the left and then to the right.

Hearing the noise again, he sensed he was making headway. Setting the flashlight to the ground, he used both hands to jostle the wooden opening. The noise was heard again, but this time a bit louder, indicating progress. Removing his grip from the boards, and while rubbing his sweaty palms against his jeans, he heard the scraping sound again.

"What the—" he exclaimed.

With his hands resting at his sides, the noise reverberated up the hidden staircase. His eyes widened; the sound wasn't coming from the boarded entry, but from the steps below. Reaching for his flashlight, he felt a weak vibration upon the stone staircase.

The young traveler aimed his flashlight below at the unknown pursuer; the beam dimmed.

"Not again," whispered an alarmed Dan. "Why won't this work?"

His consistent tapping of the flashlight against the palm of his hand proved ineffective. With no alternative, he rose to his feet and scaled another fourteen steps.

As he feared, the steps ended at a flat stone landing. Unfortunately, he was now on his knees, since the ceiling was only feet above the landing. In a frenzied state, he searched the walls on either side for a means of escape. Nothing moved, though something moved in the darkness below. Reaching overhead, he discovered another plank, but not before cutting his finger on a rusty, projecting nail. Since the boarded exit was well within his reach, he pounded his fists against the slats; the noise below grew louder. With no luck, he dropped to his back and pushed against the opening with his feet. Even the agonizing pain didn't preclude him from pushing with all his strength, to the point blood dripped from his injured leg.

"Please, God, please," he whispered.

With one powerful kick, the wooden opening flew upward and landed on the castle roof. Dan snatched the flashlight and escaped.

Although the hour was about one in the afternoon, near total darkness enshrouded the castle roof. A fine mist had only recently begun to fall. Fully aware that simply resting the plank atop the opening would not deter whatever was pursuing him, he scanned the roof for a place to hide.

"Great," he said to himself, "now it works," as he aimed the flashlight's beam at his strange surroundings.

●

In the dungeon, the three travelers remained in a deep sleep, as Salvus lingered in the vacated kitchen preparing a feast. Normally, the satyr's meals were delivered through the dumbwaiter, but he often took advantage of the kitchen and its provisions whenever the Pedwhips were away. From around the corner, he heard the raspy voices of two Reclaimers. The satyr immediately took notice, since it was rare for the snake-men to descend to the main level, except when patrolling the Hall of Admittance.

"I've discovered something," disclosed the first Reclaimer from the nearby corridor, "which will ensure we have future guests at the castle. Despite the fact the number of residents continues to dwindle, very soon we'll have visitors…and in great numbers."

"We've been scheming to entrap travelers for centuries," admitted the second Reclaimer, "but with only minimal success. What makes you think your discovery will prove fruitful?"

"Just wait," promised the first Reclaimer, "you'll see; and then I'll replace Spiritus Malus as our new sovereign."

The Reclaimers entered another room, adjacent to the kitchen. Their conversation slowly faded. Salvus couldn't decipher another word. Though mildly interested in their discovery, he was more hungry than inquisitive. He resumed his meal preparations, while periodically listening for the Pedwhips, who would soon return from their labor in the castle garden and orchard. This would be his signal to escape the kitchen and revisit his quarters. But for now, the hallway was silent; Salvus dropped another slab of cheese on his tongue.

●

With the limited area the flashlight permitted him to view, Dan noticed the castle roof was relatively flat with a narrow trough running the length of the fortress near its outer edge. As he noticed earlier, during the group's initial view of the castle from the perimeter of the clearing, the roof's edge was adorned with many battlements—or squared notches—that were symmetrically placed every several feet along the roof.

He heard the scratching noise again, but this time it was louder than before. Suspecting a castle creature was nearing the entrance to the roof, he quickly resumed his search for somewhere to hide. With no success, he glanced back at the opening. Returning his gaze, he spotted a rope resting on the castle roof…less than ten feet from where he stood. After dashing to the rope, he returned the flashlight in his pocket, made a double slipknot, and secured the rope around the nearest squared notch. Just before lowering himself, he eyed the back side of a colossal wasp squeezing its head and abdomen through the tight roof opening. Noticing only one wing, he presumed its deformity forced it to crawl up the stone staircase. As the wasp forced itself through the opening, Dan released his grip and descended three feet.

From the side of the castle, he distinctly heard the scratching of the wasp's feet upon the stone roof, as the insect searched the area for its victim. Within minutes, the mist in the air and his waning strength caused Dan to slip another two feet; he quickly gripped the rope and averted a further descent.

Hearing shuffling from below, the wasp scurried to the edge of the roof.

In fright and fatigue, Dan looked to the right and then to the left for a place of shelter. To the left, he noticed a gargoyle. Although unusually situated more than a hundred feet from the nearest castle corner, he was too preoccupied to give its odd location a second thought. From his visual angle, he could detect only a pointed ear on the stone artwork. Unable to distinguish its complete facial features, he supposed the gargoyle was the representation of a demon.

Glancing upward into the falling mist, he was grateful the wasp was not overhead; he was also grateful the beast's scraping noise seemed fainter than before.

Maybe the wasp took cover from the mist and returned to the stairwell, he thought. As he maintained his upward gaze, his thoughts continued, *But, if it's heading down the hidden staircase, how will I return to the dungeon?*

Lowering his head to rest his aching neck, he glanced to the left again. The stone gargoyle was pointed directly at him.

That's odd, he thought. *I could have sworn it was facing directly ahead into the forest.*

In the midst of his thoughts, a crash of thunder was heard, a bolt of lightning was seen, and the gargoyle's eyes blinked. An unintentional outcry slipped from his lips; the wasp altered its destination from the roof's opening to its edge.

In the momentary flash of lightning, Dan noted that the gargoyle's eyes were sunk deeply into its head and were partially overshadowed by a large protruding brow that extended the length of its weather-beaten face. A fine-edged horn in the center of its forehead commanded the attention of any onlookers; a stony goatee dipped nearly two feet below its chin. The creature's jagged teeth and elongated granite tongue did not escape Dan's fixed gaze.

A scraping noise atop the castle roof directed his sights upward. Focused on the wasp peering over the roof's edge, Dan spotted something lash at him from the corner of his eye. The gargoyle had released its tongue in his direction. Fortunately, he was beyond its reach. An abrupt tug on the rope was felt; Dan slipped another two feet.

Unable to fly with one wing, the wasp struggled to reel in its meal.

Dan had just taken another tight grip on the rope, when he felt the castle wall vibrate. Since he was beyond the reach of the gargoyle's tongue, the stone creature was bashing its head against the castle wall, attempting to drop Dan to his death.

The mist had developed into a steady rain. Between the constant banging of the gargoyle against the castle wall and the wasp's attempt to raise its prey to the roof, not to mention the growing pain in his arms, Dan briefly entertained the idea of releasing his grip and plunging into the moat. *After all,* he thought, *even if I make it back to the roof, I'll still have to battle the ravenous wasp.* The eel in the moat, however, dispelled his notion of release.

As he remained deep in thought, his lifeline shook violently. Gazing upward, his heart dropped to his stomach. With no success in gripping the wet rope, the wasp was descending the cord to its victim.

A lash was felt against his left arm.

The wasp's turbulent descent had shifted the rope to the left, just within range of the gargoyle's tongue.

While lowering himself to escape the reach of the stone creature and the approaching wasp, Dan hatched an idea. Several feet further down the castle wall, he paused and watched the wasp descend, until it was positioned level with the gargoyle. Dan took a death grip on the rope, placed his feet firmly against the wall, and raced along the facade to the left. With the wasp focused on its next meal, it was oblivious to its imminent end. As the traveler had suspected and hoped, the gargoyle sank its granite teeth into the wasp's abdomen.

Dan darted to the right; the wasp was ripped from the cord by the gargoyle's powerful jaws. From several feet away, he watched a flutter of movement, as the wasp attempted unsuccessfully to free itself from the creature's grip. Unable to clutch its prey, since the spirited sculpture consisted of only a head and neck, the remains of the wasp dropped to the moat. Upon impact, the eel shot from below the water's surface, landed atop the remains of the floating one-winged insect, and pulled it below. The violent churning within the moat was heard six stories up.

As Dan ascended the rope, far to the right of the gargoyle, he kept a close eye on the stone demon, watching it grind the mouthful of abdomen. Once the flesh was swallowed, the head resumed its banging against the castle wall; Dan slipped two feet down the rope. With a tightened grip, he slowly pulled himself to the roof.

Aware no evidence of his secret visit to the roof should be left behind, he returned the rope to its original location. After picking up the plank and setting it partially atop the opening, he climbed in and pulled the wooden covering in place. Reaching for his flashlight, he switched it on. To his surprise, the beam lit up the landing and several steps below.

With the wasp in the belly of the eel and the gargoyle now motionless on the castle wall, Dan refocused his efforts on his return trip to the dungeon. As expected, the pain in his leg that he had disregarded when battling the beasts had returned. With growing discomfort, he limped down the hidden staircase, thankful no additional castle creatures or Reclaimers were encountered. With the exception of the plentiful rats that populated the stairwell, his trek to the dungeon was uneventful.

Upon his arrival at the entrance to the sixth acoustic tunnel, he paused and listened for voices. He knew if Sam discovered his sole adventure, he'd be furious…and rightfully so. To his delight, his co-travelers were still sleeping, as confirmed by Sam and Jimmy's persistent snoring. Peering around the corner of the tunnel to Salvus' sleeping area, he was also thankful the satyr was still absent. He crept to his sleeping area and rested atop his sleeping bag.

●

In the kitchen, Salvus heard the distant voices of Pedwhips in the hallway; the part crayfish, part human, and part fish creatures were returning from the garden and orchard.

"We'll finish staking the tomato plants, after the rain ends," suggested a Pedwhip.

Suspecting the Pedwhips were only feet around the corner of the kitchen entrance, Salvus dropped another slab of cheese on his tongue and escaped to the dungeon.

With one eye partially open, Dan watched Salvus poorly maneuver the wobbly steps. Before the satyr reached the bottom landing, Dan shut his discerning eye and was asleep within minutes. After all, his excursion to the castle roof proved exhausting.

CHAPTER THREE

The Rest-Upon

At three o'clock in the afternoon, Sam awoke to an unsettling noise. As he opened his eyes and rolled onto his side, he was pleased to see the teenagers sound asleep. Looking a few feet beyond his slumbering companions, he eyed Salvus squatting on his hoofs, with his back facing the group, and his hands inside Cindy's backpack. Quietly rising from his sleeping bag, he sneaked up behind the satyr and forcefully jerked his right shoulder; Salvus lost his balance and dropped to the floor.

"What are you doing in Cindy's bag?" demanded Sam.

Wanting his act to go unnoticed, the satyr replied, "The bag was sitting on the dirt floor and I was brushing it off."

Sam wasn't buying his story and asserted, "I knew there was something about you I shouldn't trust. Well, if you're looking for something valuable to steal, you've got the wrong group."

"I wasn't trying to steal anything," insisted Salvus.

Grabbing Cindy's bag from the satyr, Sam continued, "They're just kids; leave them alone."

The commotion awoke the teenagers, who quickly neared Sam and Salvus.

"What's going on?" asked Cindy.

"Why don't you ask Mr. Kleptomaniac?" said Sam, before handing Cindy her bag. "Look inside and see what's missing."

Cindy sat on the ground and unzipped her knapsack. To her astonishment, fresh peaches, cooked bacon, and four cheese sandwiches were concealed below the apples and tomatoes that she had dropped into her bag upon the group's entry into the castle's kitchen.

"While you were sleeping," explained Salvus, "and since the Pedwhips were gardening, I took advantage of the kitchen amenities to have a snack, cook some bacon, and make a few sandwiches; I thought you'd enjoy them on your return trip. I know you're not leaving right away, but since it's so seldom that I have free access to the kitchen, I had to take advantage of it. I know it's not much, but if I confiscated any more, the Pedwhips would surely notice."

In his entire life, Sam had never been more humiliated or ashamed than at that very moment. Emotionless, he glanced down at Salvus, who was now sitting beside Cindy, and mumbled, "I'm sorry," and then shamefacedly returned to his sleeping area.

"Salvus," exclaimed Cindy, "this is great! But you didn't have to."

"I know," replied the satyr, "but in just the few hours we've spent together…well…it's been the best time I've had in decades. I'm usually looked down upon, but not by you four. So, I wanted to repay you with a small act of kindness."

Before she realized what she was doing, Cindy reached over and gave him a hug, saying, "Thank you, Salvus. I'm sure it'll make the best meal we've had in a long time."

Glancing up at the teenage men, Cindy noticed Jimmy had already taken two bites from a cheese sandwich he snatched from her open backpack. "Jimmy," she blurted, "that's supposed to be for our trip back."

"I can't help it," he mumbled, with a mouthful, "it's bread!"

Dan extended his hand to Salvus to offer a friendly shake; the satyr gratefully accepted. Jimmy was equally thankful and displayed his feelings with a two-handed shake, while firmly clutching the half-eaten sandwich between his teeth.

Salvus suspected a hearty handshake was something Jimmy rarely offered.

Noticing Sam rearranging his sleeping gear, the satyr instructed the teenagers, "Wait here," and then trotted in Sam's direction.

"Sam," he said, "I know you were just looking out for the kids and I appreciate it…really. I'm happy to know they'll be in good hands on their trip back."

Sam, who was now resting on his knees atop his sleeping bag, lowered his head, stared at his camping pillow, and confessed, "I'm sorry. But why didn't you just tell me?"

"Oftentimes," reminded Salvus, "good deeds are better left unspoken and unnoticed."

Sam shook his head, conceding, "I just worry about the kids so much, as if they were my own."

"I suspect you do," said Salvus. Glancing at the teenagers, he continued, "You're a lucky man."

"Yeah," he admitted, "I know."

As Sam rocked off his knees to stand, Salvus gripped the traveler's elbow to steady him. Attempting to lighten the mood, the satyr remarked, "I think I'll make a few more sandwiches for Jimmy."

The men joined the teenagers.

The rest of the afternoon was spent in whisperlike conversations, mostly updating Salvus on the adventures they experienced during their journey to the castle. At 6:00 p.m., a loud bang startled everyone, except Salvus; dinner had arrived by way of the dumbwaiter. Rising to his goat frame, the satyr retrieved a large wooden plate overloaded with fruits, vegetables, and cheese. Without a moment's hesitation, he evenly divided the food into four groups.

"Um, Salvus," informed Cindy, "there are five of us here."

Looking up from slicing an apple with the knife that accompanied the platter, he replied, "I know; I'm not hungry."

"You've got to eat something," urged Dan.

Salvus handed Dan a piece of apple, stressing, "You four need to build up your strength. There'll be plenty of time for me to eat later."

Dan accepted the apple wedge, broke it in half, and handed a portion to Salvus, reminding, "You also need to build up your strength."

The satyr accepted the fruit.

During the meal, it crossed the minds of the travelers that Salvus, though half-man and half-goat, was the most human person they'd ever met. Thoroughly enjoying the meal and the company, the diners failed to notice nearly two hours had elapsed since they first reclined on the floor to eat. A deafening sound echoed throughout the dungeon. The four travelers jumped; Salvus remained calm. A Reclaimer had struck a pipe with a golden scepter, sending the high-pitched noise down six flights to the dungeon. The Reclaimer was demanding music.

Salvus crawled to his sleeping area, grabbed his lyre, and began plucking the strings. To alleviate the pain in his leg that had returned as a result of prolonged sitting, Dan leaned back on his elbows, stretched out his legs, and watched Salvus' long fingers enchant the four travelers and the guests six stories up. All watched attentively as the lyrist meticulously played music that was completely foreign to their ears. Cindy remained visibly awestruck with the satyr's impeccable talent.

At 9:00 p.m., the travelers headed to their sleeping areas; the music played on. As Cindy doused Dan's leg and back with whiskey, the patient remained captivated that such peaceful music graced the passageways of such a sinister castle.

Not to belittle Salvus' musical ability, thought Jimmy, *but after nearly two hundred years of practice, you should be fairly good.*

Within an hour, the group nodded off.

Early the next morning, before the travelers stirred, Salvus ascended the steps to the kitchen; a route he seldom took, but he was on a mission. Preparing a stew in the metal pot over the open flame of the fireplace, with his back facing Salvus, was Marcus, the Pedwhips' head cook.

"Good morning, Marcus," greeted Salvus.

Startled, Marcus turned around quickly.

On seeing the satyr, he let out a loud gasp, before admonishing, "Salvus, you scared me. What are you doing up so early?" Before the satyr could reply, the cook added, "My gosh, I haven't seen you in the kitchen for years. What brings you here this morning?"

Without skipping a beat, the satyr explained, "I woke up just a short time ago with horrible hunger pains; I thought I could get a little extra breakfast this morning."

"Are you feeling alright?" asked the Pedwhip.

"Oh, yeah," he answered, "just hungry."

Letting the ladle rest in the pot, Marcus stepped to a nearby cabinet, grabbed a wooden plate, and loaded it with fruits, vegetables, cheese, and bread. "It's a good thing the crops have done exceptionally well this year," he informed.

Accepting the platter from Marcus, Salvus acknowledged, "I appreciate it."

The satyr promptly set the plate on the center table and returned to Marcus' side, near the fireplace.

"What's wrong?" asked the Pedwhip.

"Nothing; I thought I'd help you stir the stew for a few minutes."

"Oh," replied Marcus, "that would be great."

In truth, Marcus was the only Pedwhip whom Salvus trusted and he wanted to repay his genuine kindness.

In the dungeon, Jimmy—as was most unusual—awoke before the rest of the group. Sitting up in his sleeping bag, he noticed his co-travelers were still asleep. On seeing Salvus' empty drop cloth, he wondered where he might be, until he heard his voice and that of another being at the top of the steps. Glancing to the corner of the dungeon, he knew that then would be the opportune time to explore one of the corner staircases that Salvus had mentioned earlier. Beset by a growing urge to investigate the unknown, he rose from his sleeping bag. *I'll be gone for only a few minutes,* he thought, before snatching Dan's flashlight.

The boards which covered the entrance to the corner staircase were not nailed to the wall; rather, they were simply leaning against the opening. All was quiet, as Jimmy removed each board and placed them gently against the neighboring wall; that is, until he accidentally slammed the fourth board against the third, producing a loud bang. He quickly pressed his hands against the boards to muffle the sound, before offering an over-the-shoulder glance at the sleepers. Cindy stirred slightly and rolled onto her side, facing the corner staircase. *Thank God,* thought Jimmy, *she didn't open her eyes.*

With the seventh and final board resting against the adjacent wall, Jimmy crawled through the opening. With his back turned, he failed to notice Cindy opening her eyes and—thanks to the light streaming down the steps from the kitchen—witnessing his departure. She closed her eyes, as if it were a dream. Minutes later, she sat up and glimpsed Jimmy's empty sleeping bag. Jumping to her feet, she dashed to Salvus' sleeping area, since the fireplace obstructed her view of the satyr's drop cloth. Seeing his bedding was also empty, her anxieties were eased, thinking Jimmy would be safe in the corner staircase with Salvus at his side. Then, she heard the satyr's voice echoing down the steps from the kitchen. Sam's snoring, however, prevented her from hearing what was being discussed at the top of the steps.

Knowing Sam would be irate, if he learned of Jimmy's latest clash with the rules, she darted to Dan's sleeping area and woke him. Once her co-traveler's eyes opened, she whispered, "Jimmy's gone."

"What?" muttered a drowsy teenager.

"Jimmy's gone," she whispered again, before pulling his sleeping bag off his shoulders and helping him to his feet.

"Gone where?" asked Dan, while pulling his sweatshirt over his head.

"Sh," demanded Cindy, "you'll wake Sam."

Standing only a few moments brought intense pain to Dan's leg. He stumbled slightly, before Cindy helped him regain his balance. After leaning him against the dungeon wall for support, she searched the area for the flashlight; it, too, like Jimmy and Salvus, was missing. She snatched the lantern from the ground near the dumbwaiter, retraced her steps to Dan, and helped him to the corner staircase.

Inside the opening, the glowing lantern revealed stone steps, nearly four feet wide, which were scarred with countless imperfections and concaved in the center, suggesting that at one point in its history the staircase was overused.

Dan guessed the steps in the corner staircase were a bit wider than the ones in the hidden staircase, which he climbed yesterday afternoon. But he knew that no one, not even Cindy, should learn of his previous sole adventure. *If we make it back to our world,* he thought, *maybe I'll tell them then.*

The travelers suspected the steps were hundreds of years old. Noticing the wretched filth and debris which covered them, they also presumed the steps hadn't been traveled upon in quite some time.

Now fully awake, Dan released himself from Cindy's supportive grip around his waist. "I'm fine," he lied, "thanks."

●

As Salvus stirred the stew, he and Marcus engaged in a number of topics; the most prominent being a fellow Pedwhip, Judas, whom all of his fellow species' members despised.

"He's always making life more difficult for us than it already is," explained Marcus, "and he's constantly trying to befriend the Reclaimers." As the head cook added a few more tomatoes to the stew, he further disclosed, "It's to the point now he works alone. None of the Pedwhips feel safe around him. I mean, Judas would betray any Pedwhip the first chance he got." Dropping his voice to a near whisper, he confessed, "As you've probably suspected, none of the Pedwhips—except Judas, of course—hold the Reclaimers or their actions in high regard. We simply endure what we must in exchange for the safety of the castle, much like you, Salvus, I presume. I guess what I'm trying to say is that you can trust any of the Pedwhips, but I wouldn't confide in Judas."

Taking the ladle from Salvus, Marcus tasted the stew and declared, "Yeah, I think it's done." The Pedwhip submerged the long-handled spoon into the pot, drew another ladleful of vegetable stew, and raised it to Salvus' lips for a taste.

After swallowing, the satyr confirmed, "Oh, yeah, it's done...and hot!"

Marcus returned the spoon to the pot, walked to a medieval cupboard, and grabbed several wooden bowls, acknowledging, "Thanks for your help, Salvus. We should do this more often."

"Yeah," replied the satyr, "I enjoyed our talk."

Salvus headed for the dungeon staircase, but stopped two feet short of the entryway; he had forgotten the plate of food which Marcus had given him minutes earlier. He turned and approached the center table. Noticing the head cook watching him, he grabbed the platter of produce, while also taking advantage of an excellent opportunity, and asked, "Marcus, is it true?"

"Is what true?" inquired the Pedwhip, after expanding his retractable fins and fanning himself to offset the oppressive heat from the kitchen fireplace.

Taking a bite of an apple from the plate, Salvus chewed, swallowed, and then continued, "Is it true the Reclaimers are going on another hunting expedition?"

Marcus returned to the fireplace, asking, "Now where did you hear that?"

The satyr took another bite. As he chewed, he mumbled, "I don't know; just around."

"Salvus," warned Marcus, "you know I can't tell you. Come on, you know how secretive the Reclaimers are about their forest trips. My gosh, you'd think they're fearful someone or something would usurp their power and rule the castle and its guests in their absence— like anyone could or would even want to."

Taking a third bite of the apple, Salvus neared the head cook and attempted another approach for an answer. "How'd you enjoy the music last night?"

Scattering the logs under the pot to extinguish the flame, the Pedwhip asked, "What kind of a question is that? You know I love your music, as do all the residents. But it's been ages since you've played the melody I like. You know, the one that goes like—" Marcus hummed his favorite tune.

With the head cook's back facing him, Salvus snatched another block of cheese from a nearby table and dropped it on the platter. "I'll make a deal with you, Marcus," he promised, "tell me about the expedition and I'll play your favorite melody on my lyre tonight."

Marcus turned, neared the center of the kitchen, and rested his two human hands upon the table. "I don't know, Salvus," answered an uneasy Pedwhip. He fanned himself again before reminding, "We could be punished severely if the Reclaimers learned I shared confidential information with you."

"Oh, come on, Marcus," prompted the satyr, "what's the big deal? It's not like the other Pedwhips won't know they're gone."

Tapping his pincers upon the hard floor, producing a clacking sound, Marcus eventually yielded, "It's my understanding they're leaving tonight at 8:00. Apparently, they're after something special this time, though I never heard what they're hunting."

"Are they all going?"

"I suppose," answered Marcus, "but I don't know for sure. It'll probably be like their last trip several months ago when all the Reclaimers went, except for those tending the guests upstairs and the one monitoring the Hall of Admittance…as if a visitor would apply for residence on the one night they're away."

Attempting to appear only partially interested, Salvus halfheartedly asked, "Hey, Marcus, just out of curiosity, since I've never visited the guests' room and I haven't seen the residents on their exercise route in decades, how many guests are living in the castle now?"

Marcus raised his eyes and bit his lower lip, trying to recall. "I'm really not sure since, as you know, we're never permitted inside the guests' room. But it's funny you should ask."

"Why's that?"

"Just last week," informed the head cook, "I was ordered to prepare eleven meals, instead of the usual twelve." After a momentary pause, the Pedwhip inquired, "Salvus, why all the questions?"

"No reason," he replied, "just curious how many are in my nightly audience. Speaking of which, I should practice your melody today, since I haven't played it in years."

After Salvus thanked his friend again for the plate of food and was heading to the dungeon stairs for a second time, Marcus blurted, "Remember, you heard nothing from me."

Salvus turned, displayed a grin, and asked, "Heard what?"

Retrieving all the information he needed, in addition to the large plate of food with an extra block of cheese for his recently-arrived guests, Salvus hobbled down the steps quite proud of his accomplishments. Just four steps down, he halted. *Tonight?* he thought. *But my friends just arrived.* As much as it pained him to think of their departure, he knew he must deliver the latest news for their own safety.

⚫

Jimmy had ascended to the third floor. Unlike the first two levels, he spotted light escaping between several vertical boards to the left.

This must be an opening to the third floor, he thought.

Setting the faulty flashlight upon the landing, he searched for a knob or handle. After receiving a splinter, he discovered a rusty latch.

Once the metal bar was lifted from its notch, he slid the wooden opening to the right and peered inside to confirm the absence of Reclaimers and Pedwhips. On detecting no creatures, he advanced on all fours. He was only halfway through the entry, when the boarded covering—since it was at an incline—closed on him. Reaching back, he slammed open the access panel. Rising to his feet, he beheld a fully furnished room with two walnut desks, row upon row of bookshelves lining the walls, and several unconventional reading chairs with free-standing arms. "What weird looking chairs," he whispered, and then dismissed the thought as quickly as it arrived. He had entered the Grand Library.

Looking overhead, he noticed three age-old chandeliers, complete with candleholders, but as he suspected, no candles. Two narrow openings, free of iron bars, graced the far right wall, welcoming the sparse early morning sunlight which struggled to overpower the darkness that enveloped the castle. On the distant wall hung an enormous tapestry that extended from the fifteen-foot ceiling. The floor itself was adorned with a red and dark blue Persian rug that stretched nearly the length of the library. Turning to the right, he neared a cobblestone fireplace, whose mantel displayed several antiquated reading glasses. Not escaping his attention was the small paneled door that only minutes earlier concealed the opening through which he crawled. The access panel was constructed in such a way that when wedged open, it came within inches of abutting the fireplace.

●

In the corner staircase, Cindy and Dan spotted dim light filtering down the dark corridor and illuminating their path.

Cindy switched off the lantern.

Reaching the third floor landing, they crawled through the secret access and entered the library.

"Jimmy, what are you doing?" demanded Cindy in a low voice. Before he could defend his actions, she warned, "Sam will be furious. We've got to get out of here now!"

After inspecting a cracked urn on the mantel, Jimmy yielded,

"Alright, I'm coming. I was just checking out the room; I didn't break anything and no one saw me." With one last sweeping look of the stately library, he exclaimed, "This place is awesome; I mean, look at it!"

Cindy took in the sights; she was instantly drawn to the tapestry on the far wall. Walking across the ornate rug for a closer inspection of the hanging artwork, she discovered the tapestry was a three-dimensional cloth. "How bizarre," she said, "it's 3-D. Nothing like this exists in our world."

Jimmy was pleased she found something of interest; something to deflect her attention from him and his sole expedition, if for only a few minutes.

Salvus resumed his awkward descent of the staircase to the dungeon. He had just set his hoofs on the dirt floor at the base of the steps, carrying a plate of digestible treasures, when he noticed Sam slumbering, three empty sleeping bags, and the wooden planks—which only recently covered the opening to the corner staircase—leaning against the adjoining wall.

Regrettably, the constant creaking of the kitchen floorboards above the travelers' sleeping area kept Sam awake throughout the early morning hours. Finally dozing off at 4:00 a.m., he was unaware of the teenagers' escape.

Salvus dropped the platter of food, darted to Sam's side, and violently shook the shoulder of the sleeping traveler. "Sam…Sam," he yelled, "they're gone! Get up, now!"

Sam opened his eyes and witnessed the satyr snatching two lances.

"Look," said Salvus, as he pointed the weapons in the direction of the empty sleeping areas.

"Oh, God!" exclaimed Sam, while jumping from his sleeping bag. Grabbing a weapon from his friend, the men darted to the corner of the dungeon. "I'll bet you anything that Jimmy's behind this," accused Sam.

"I just hope they're okay," warned Salvus, "and that none of the Reclaimers saw or heard them." The light streaming from above to the base of the corner staircase prompted him to speculate, "They must have entered one of the floors."

"Why do you say that?" asked Sam.

"Because," explained the satyr, "this stairwell is usually darker than death."

In the library, Cindy analyzed nearly twenty scenes which decorated the tapestry; each featured extraordinary detail. At the center of the cloth, she viewed a grotesque middle-aged man holding a raised sword with towering flames in the background. Much like the majestic oak which fed her curiosity a couple weeks earlier, she reached to touch the 3-D phenomenon. Before her hand made contact with the cloth, the man's sword, about two inches in length, penetrated its spatial boundary and grazed her index finger.

"Ouch," she exclaimed. "What the—"

"What's wrong?" asked Dan from a distance.

Cindy turned to her friend, who was supporting himself against the mantel, and explained, "This guy on the tapestry just cut my finger with his sword."

"What?" asked a doubtful Dan, who pushed away from the fireplace and limped across the rug.

Cindy returned her attention to the hanging cloth and examined a different scene. The next image depicted another middle-aged man with his arm resting on a centaur's back. As she drew closer to translate the Latin inscription that was embroidered below the man and his four-legged beast, she distinctly felt a drop of moisture run down her cheek; the man within the artwork spit at her.

Jumping back, she exclaimed, "This is just too weird."

Dan was nearly halfway across the library, before realizing she was not in mortal danger; he stopped and sat on the edge of a desk, easing the pain in his leg.

Cindy's unearthly predicament also coerced Jimmy, who only

moments earlier had discovered similar diminutive, three-dimensional figures within the fibers of the Persian rug. He neared the tapestry.

Suspecting something behind the hanging masterpiece was the source of the disturbing events, Cindy stepped to the edge of the tapestry and lifted it from the wall to examine its reverse side. She quickly jerked her head from behind when she felt a sharp pain. A bird, portrayed near the border of the tapestry, took a peck at her finger. She yanked her hand from the cloth and stepped back for a panoramic view.

Now standing alongside Jimmy, she viewed all the scenes. "Oh, my gosh," she exclaimed, "that's an Oswagi Bird," as she pointed to the tapestry's edge.

Jimmy had advanced only two steps for a closer look, when Cindy grabbed his shoulder and warned, "Not too close."

"You're right," he seconded, "it's an Oswagi Bird. And look," as he directed Cindy's attention to other scenes detailed in the artwork, "there's the eel, the oak, and a blinding light beside the tree."

Scratching her scalp, Cindy guessed, "If I didn't know any better, I'd say these are scenes of the Reclaimers' banishment from hell and their arrival into this world."

Overly intrigued with her theory, Dan stepped from the desk and was nearing his friends, when an unusually sharp pain shot down his leg; he limped to a nearby chair. Upon his collapse to the seat, he was trapped. The chair went spastic, crossing its two freestanding arms over each other and constricting around Dan's lower chest. He screamed, as he tried to escape the death grip; his efforts were useless.

At the sound of his cry, Salvus and Sam bolted the remaining steps; Cindy and Jimmy drew their fixed gaze from the enchanted tapestry to see Dan's blue face. Racing to his side, each teenager grabbed an arm of the chair and valiantly tried to release its hold on their friend.

"Pull!" yelled Jimmy.

"I am!" screamed Cindy.

The chair was unyielding; Dan was now wheezing.

Salvus darted through the opening in the wall. After dropping his lance to the rug, he gently caressed the back of the furniture. Within seconds, it released its grip, ever so slowly, until Jimmy pulled his friend free; Dan hadn't the strength to remove himself.

With Dan flat on his back, trying to catch his breath, Salvus asked, "What happened?"

"He just sat on the chair to rest his leg," presumed Cindy, "when the chair came alive and went berserk."

"When he sat on the what?" asked a puzzled satyr. Before Cindy could respond, he blurted, "That doesn't make any sense. Did he seek the rest-upon's permission?"

"The what?" asked Jimmy, who was now sitting on the floor and resting his hand on Dan's shoulder.

"You know," explained Salvus, "did he touch the rest-upon for permission?" Seeing the blank looks on the travelers' faces, he demonstrated. Taking his hand, he gently touched the right arm of the rest-upon. "If permission is granted," he explained, "the back of the rest-upon will lean forward slightly...like a bow. Then you know it's safe to rest upon it."

With all eyes fixed on the seat, the travelers were speechless when they witnessed the chair's back lean forward.

Salvus sat down.

"Then," continued the satyr, "when the rest-upon wants you to rise, it simply leans its back forward again."

Within thirty seconds, the chair gently nudged him forward.

Rising to his feet, Salvus questioned, "Honestly, don't you have rest-upons in your world?"

"Of course we do," snapped Cindy, "but they're called chairs. And they don't move and they don't squeeze the life out of you."

"Chairs?" repeated Salvus.

"Yes," replied Cindy, "chairs."

"And they're always asleep?" asked the satyr.

Not knowing how to respond, Cindy shook her head in complete disbelief.

"How weird," admitted Salvus.

A deep cough from Dan summoned the group's attention downward.

"How are you feeling?" asked Sam, who lowered himself to his knees beside his companion.

Dan nodded slightly; he hadn't the strength yet for a verbal response.

Knowing the travelers were not safe in the library, Salvus urged the group to return to the dungeon immediately, despite Dan's present condition.

As Sam and Jimmy helped the ailing teenager to his feet, Sam asked whose bright idea it was to explore the corner staircase.

"I didn't mean any harm," said Jimmy.

"Dan could have been killed," reprimanded Sam. "Honestly, Jimmy, you've got to be more careful and start following orders."

Jimmy lowered his head and admitted, "I know."

Salvus stepped forward, placed his hand on Jimmy's shoulder, and cautioned, "I hope the Reclaimers didn't hear Dan's scream."

"I thought they were on the sixth floor," said Jimmy.

"Yes, they usually are," replied Salvus. "But that doesn't mean they never visit the library or they couldn't hear Dan's scream three levels up."

While wrestling Salvus' lance from a clan of three-dimensional, miniature trolls within the threads of the rug, Cindy asked, "Hey, Salvus, have you ever inspected the tapestry on the wall?"

As she watched the trolls vanish within the rug's fibers, Salvus replied, "Of course, many times. It's a depiction of the Reclaimers' expulsion from hell to this castle. I've been told they keep it on permanent display, not only as a reminder of the disgrace they endured, but also as a reminder for revenge someday."

"You mean the Reclaimers visit this room?" asked an edgy Cindy.

"From time to time they do," informed Salvus, "when they want a book to read to their guests. By the way, I wouldn't go near the tapestry; it can be a little, shall I say, spirited?"

"Yeah," said Cindy, "I'm sure it can," as she wiped blood from her finger to her jeans.

Aware the Reclaimers visit the library on occasion, Jimmy backed Salvus' earlier comment that the group return to the dungeon.

All agreed.

Sam and Jimmy helped Dan through the secret opening; Cindy followed behind, lugging the flashlight, the lantern, and two lances.

Once the travelers were standing on the corner staircase, Salvus crawled through and locked the access panel behind him. Within minutes, the five arrived safely in the dungeon.

CHAPTER FOUR

The Trophy Room

As Sam and Jimmy lowered Dan atop his sleeping bag, Cindy took advantage of her friend's temporary immobility and reached for the whiskey bottle.

Salvus gathered the food from the floor that he dropped earlier when noticing the empty sleeping areas. With each piece of produce he gathered, he rubbed it against his grimy toga, which only smeared the filth.

Noticing his dilemma, but noble gesture, Sam pulled a clean shirt from his backpack and tossed it to the satyr, who recleaned the food.

After Cindy treated Dan's leg injury, she examined his back. Though the wounds below his shoulder blades were not nearly as severe as the gash down his leg, she, nonetheless, drenched his back with the liquid cure-all. Dan barely flinched. To prevent the onset of a deadly nervous condition from the world's atmosphere, she next distributed Doctor O'Brien's pills to her traveling companions.

Salvus left some of the produce near the dumbwaiter, before carrying the rest of the partially clean food to the travelers' sleeping area. "Why don't we have something to eat?" he suggested.

All gathered around.

Between bites, the satyr updated the group on the details he acquired during his conversation that morning with Marcus in the kitchen.

"So, we're leaving the castle tonight?" asked an excited Cindy.

"I'm afraid so," replied Salvus.

"What do you mean, you're afraid so?" she questioned.

"Oh…nothing," he responded. "I know you have to go, but…well…I've really enjoyed your company."

After snatching an apple wedge from Salvus' plate, Jimmy proposed, "Why don't you come with us?"

"Oh, no," he replied, "I couldn't."

"Why not?" asked Cindy.

Ashamed to admit his deep-rooted fear of the forest that stemmed from the unprovoked massacre of his species as a child, the satyr simply responded, "It's too complicated." Intent on changing the unpleasant subject, he whispered, "So, what's your plan for releasing William, presuming he's in the guests' room?"

With everything the group had endured since their arrival in the castle's kitchen, no one, not even Dan, had given any thought to their plan of escape, beyond climbing one of the corner staircases to the sixth floor.

Noticing the awkwardly long pause, Salvus challenged, "You don't have a plan, do you?"

After clearing his throat, stalling for time, Sam defended, "Well, it's not so much that we don't have a plan, as much as we haven't figured out how to put it into motion."

"Yeah," agreed Jimmy, "that's it."

"I see," said an unconvinced Salvus. To help his friends narrow in on an escape plan, the satyr reached for the shield and reminded, "Well, as I explained earlier, the Reclaimers are vulnerable to their reflections…like the boy from the 1600's who escaped the castle with this shield."

"Are you sure the Reclaimers aren't afraid of light?" asked a hopeful Jimmy.

"Quite sure," affirmed Salvus.

Taking the shield from the satyr, Sam jumped to his feet and proposed, "How about this?" In demonstration, he held the shield against his face. "Once our eyes are protected," he continued, "we enter the guests' room. Hopefully, the Reclaimers will tremble from their reflections, buying us enough time to grab William, if he's there, and escape to the forest."

"I know William's there," insisted Dan. "I just know it; he's got to be."

Cindy, who was now relaxing on her back and supported by her elbows, sarcastically asked, "That's our plan?"

"Well," replied Sam, "it's the best strategy I have for now."

"Wait a minute," mumbled Jimmy with a mouthful of cheese. After swallowing, he challenged, "If we're covering our faces with a shield or some other shiny object, how are we supposed to see where we're going?"

"Yeah," seconded Cindy.

Again, after stalling a few seconds for time, Sam suggested, "Maybe we could go like this." Holding the shield a few inches from his face, he focused on the ground beneath the protective armor and walked to a distant wall.

"I don't know," remarked a skeptical Salvus. "Who's to say the Reclaimers won't slither their heads between you and the shield; they're pretty flexible that way, you know. And besides, there may be as many as eleven Reclaimers in the room, compared to our army of five."

"Oh, no," blurted Sam, after lowering the armor to his side. "We appreciate your help, Salvus; but it's far too risky for you to join us."

"But there's got to be something I can do to help," he insisted.

"The information, food, and, of course, your friendship," related Sam, while retracing his steps to his dining companions, "have been a tremendous help."

En route to the dumbwaiter to gather the surplus food for the travelers' bags, Salvus spun and volunteered, "Hey, maybe I could distract the Reclaimer, who'll be stationed in the Hall of Admittance, while you make your escape over the drawbridge!"

Completely mortified he had overlooked the Reclaimer on duty, Sam reluctantly asked, "Are you sure you're up for it?"

"Absolutely," he replied.

"Okay, then," agreed Sam, "we'll rely on you to divert the Reclaimer's attention near the castle entrance."

Salvus turned, resumed his approach to the dumbwaiter, and placed the extra produce in the four backpacks. "You'll need these provisions for your return trip," he said. "I'll see if I can gather some more food before you leave."

"Thanks, Salvus," said Cindy, "you've been a big help."

As Dan rested his leg, the remaining travelers searched the trash heaps for any shimmering objects. The treasure hunt revealed a variety of castaways: old clothing, a partially decayed pincer of a former Ped-whip, rotten food, and ultimately, a silver serving platter that Jimmy unearthed. Granted, it was severely tarnished, but Sam got to work right away buffing it to its original reflective brilliance. During their extended search, Cindy located the silver platter's mate and a broken mirror.

With several hours remaining before their departure to the sixth floor, Sam insisted he and his co-travelers occupy their time practicing their maneuvers, while supporting the shiny objects in front of their faces.

Shortly before 2:00 in the afternoon, as Dan took a respite from his defensive exercises to rest his leg, he shoved his hands inside his sweatshirt pocket; William's stuffed animal was missing. *Oh, no,* he thought, *where could it be?* He searched his sleeping area and his backpack, but found nothing. *Did I lose it in the library?* his thoughts continued. He knew the stuffed animal would be crucial to William recalling his childhood memories, not to mention that if the toy was spotted by a Reclaimer, the travelers' unlawful entry into the castle would be exposed and their lives would be placed in serious danger. He waited for an appropriate time to slip away from the group and revisit the third floor.

What seemed an eternity to Dan was actually only fifteen minutes, before Salvus hobbled the stairs to gather extra produce and the remaining travelers rested at their sleeping areas. Within twenty minutes, Sam, Jimmy, and Cindy nodded off, thanks to their intense strategic training. Salvus was heard speaking with a being in the kitchen. Rising silently to his feet, Dan grabbed his flashlight and neared the corner staircase. After the boards were quietly removed from the entry, he was on his way.

Only a few steps beyond the first floor landing—and thinking he was far enough away from the group—he switched on the flashlight. Although this was his second trip up the particular staircase, he was still amazed with the debris on the steps and the foul smell. Within minutes, he was on his knees, facing the third floor secret passageway. Like Jimmy earlier, he unlatched the access panel and crawled into the library. Still on all fours, he glanced toward the chair that had captured him earlier and spotted William's stuffed animal resting behind the seat on the Persian rug. He rose to his feet, placed the flashlight in his sweatshirt pocket, and limped to the chair, being wary not to touch the furniture. While in a bent position retrieving the family heirloom, he heard voices in the hallway and witnessed the library door opening slowly.

A Reclaimer, with his back facing the room, was telling a fellow Reclaimer in the hallway that he'd just be a moment.

"I'll grab the *Epic of Gilgamesh* and be right there," informed the Reclaimer, Carmus, at the doorway.

With the stuffed animal in hand, Dan placed it alongside the flashlight in his pocket and quietly, but quickly, neared the hidden passageway—his safe refuge. Just three steps into his retreat, he froze; the wooden door had closed on itself. He, nevertheless, continued his brisk walk to the secret entry, hopeful that opening the access panel would go unnoticed and unheard. Sitting on his heels, he tried to slide the door; it wouldn't budge. With its latch located on the opposite side, he was trapped. He debated briefly on kicking in the boards, but immediately realized that doing so would leave not only himself open to discovery, but his friends in the dungeon.

"Tell Spiritus Malus I'll be just a second," ordered Carmus, who was still standing in the doorway, with his back facing the library and Dan.

Rising to his feet, Dan turned and scanned the room for a place to hide. With no luck, he stepped to the fireplace and climbed inside. Standing within the hearth, he noticed the sides of the flue were composed of jagged stones, protruding a few inches from the inside wall of the chimney. With the utmost care, he placed his feet upon two projecting stones and grasped two overhead rocks. Elevated from the chimney floor, his boots were hidden from the approaching library visitor.

Completely motionless, the teenager overheard, "Alright, just let me grab the book," demanded Carmus, who turned and slithered into the library. "Now where did I put it?" he mumbled to himself.

A second, but deeper, voice was heard within the room. "Do you really think he'll die tonight?" asked the second Reclaimer, Julius, who had followed Carmus into the library.

"I've seen the signs a thousand times," gloated Carmus. "Yes, I'm sure he'll die tonight."

Feeling an unexpected draft, Dan gazed up the flue. Though the intense rays of the afternoon sun failed to penetrate completely the castle's invisible barrier, a meager amount of daylight conquered the darkness and made its journey down the chimney, permitting Dan to glimpse movement at its peak, three stories up.

Oh, no, he thought, *now what?*

With his hands and feet firmly planted against the sides of the flue, he sensed a dull vibration; soot settled upon his glasses. The young traveler found himself in a quandary: remain in the chimney and confront whatever was descending or flee from the confines of the fireplace and into the hands of two Reclaimers. Eventually, the decision was made for him. Without warning, his injured leg succumbed to its mounting pain; it slipped and dangled in midair.

Seconds later, his other leg lost its footing on the jagged stone, but fortunately, after Carmus was heard declaring, "Here's the book."

"Let's go," pleaded Julius. "Spiritus Malus is waiting for us; you know how impatient he can be."

Baffled, yet equally grateful, the Reclaimers failed to hear his missteps, Dan remained suspended by his hands until he heard the library door slam. Taking a final upward glance, he saw a shape closing in on him. He dropped to the base of the fireplace and rolled into the library. After staggering to his feet and backing away from the hearth, he eyed an immense centipede emerge from the cobblestone fireplace. Instinctively, he continued his backward retreat toward the library door. Regretting he had left his lance in the dungeon, he was presented another dilemma: confront the creature or take his chances in the third floor main corridor.

Maybe the two Reclaimers are long gone, he thought, *and on their way to the sixth floor.*

As Dan stared at the approaching creature with its anterior biting appendages, he was amazed that, for a centipede, it traveled very quickly. Even more astonishing was the fact the creature was nearly three feet high and roughly halfway across the library floor before it cleared the hearth. Not wanting to make any unnecessary noise that would summon the Reclaimers into the room, he opted against throwing objects at the oncoming arthropod.

While he had been debating his plan of action, he had been unconsciously approaching the library's door, backwards. His back side brushed the doorknob. Reaching behind, he turned the knob, opened the door, and stepped into the hallway. Glancing to the right and then to the left, he was thankful no Reclaimers or Pedwhips were nearby. Engrossed in scanning the corridor, the centipede was drawing closer. The clacking sound of several pairs of legs stepping on the hard floor from the Persian rug redirected his sights from the hallway to the creature, which was now less than five feet away. Losing no time, he slammed the library door and foiled the centipede's meal.

He had just placed his hand inside his sweatshirt pocket to confirm the stuffed animal and flashlight were still secure when he heard voices around the corner. He darted five feet across the hallway and tapped on a door. On hearing no response from inside, he turned the doorknob. To his amazement, the door was locked. The voices around the corridor were now so loud, he trembled. In his justified excitability, he glanced to the right and spotted a skeleton key suspended by a rusty nail. He yanked the antiquated key from the wall and jammed it into the opening. Success was achieved; he unlocked the door, stepped inside the narrow room, and quietly shut the door behind him—moments before Spiritus Malus and Talus turned the hallway corner.

Within the safety of the room, the teenager stood alongside the closed door, paralyzed with fear to move a muscle. Spiritus Malus and Talus halted their side-to-side motions on the opposite side of the entry and reveled in their discussion about the dying guest, three flights above. Moments later, the voices faded; the Reclaimers slithered down the hall.

•

Salvus descended the dungeon steps, clutching another platter of food he had pilfered from behind Marcus' back. Stepping on the lower landing, he noticed that the boards, which usually covered the corner staircase, were resting against the adjoining wall. *Jimmy,* he thought. Glancing toward his guests, he saw Jimmy and Cindy sound asleep; Dan's area, however, was empty. He dropped the wooden dish of provisions to the ground and dashed toward Sam, who also was slumbering. Shaking his friend, he exclaimed, "Dan's gone!"

Since Sam had not yet fallen into a deep sleep, he awoke quickly and peered to Dan's sleeping area. "What's his problem?" he exclaimed. "He promised he wouldn't go in search of William on his own."

"You stay here and keep an eye on the other two," demanded Salvus, "while I search for him."

The conversation stirred Jimmy and Cindy.

"What's going on?" asked Jimmy.

"Nothing," answered Sam, "go back to sleep."

"Dan's missing," reported Salvus.

Staring at Dan's empty sleeping area, a puzzled Cindy asked, "Why would he leave the dungeon after experiencing what he did on the third floor?"

"I don't know," replied Salvus, "but let's hope he's got a logical explanation."

"I don't care what his purpose was for leaving," declared Sam. "No reason can justify his actions."

Salvus was now near the corner staircase with a lance in hand. Glancing back at the older traveler and then to the teenagers, he ordered, "Stay here and don't make a sound; I'll search the floors above. If the Reclaimers spot me, I may be disciplined, but not as severely as if you were discovered. If I have to, I'll search the entire castle; I'll find him. You stay here and out of sight."

"Alright," agreed Sam, "but do your best to remain inconspicuous."

"That's my plan," admitted Salvus, before bending over and crawling through the opening.

Sliding the paneled door to the first level, the satyr was grateful there was no sign of the young traveler in the furnished room; he latched the access entry shut and ascended the staircase. Resting on his hoofs on the second floor landing, he unlatched the access panel and had slid the door barely an inch, when he froze. Ultimately, he decided against throwing open the passageway door. Rather, he placed an ear to the boards and listened for possible commotion. On hearing nothing, he ascended to the third level where he half expected to find Dan, since the group had visited the library earlier.

After lifting the latch and sliding the paneled door barely several inches, Salvus jolted back and dropped his lance to the staircase; the oversize centipede had thrust its venomous appendages at the satyr. Grabbing his weapon from behind, he jammed it into the opening and grazed the creature; the centipede withdrew slightly. As he opened the access panel another six inches, the centipede made a second lunge. Sustaining a deeper gash, the arthropod made a further retreat into the library. Crawling through the opening, the door closed upon him. During the unfortunate setback, the creature made a third charge; Salvus, however, successfully repelled the centipede's latest attack, forcing it into the deeper recesses of the room. Before rising to his hoofs, however, Salvus reached behind and wedged open the paneled door. Once inside the library, several more attempts were made by the centipede to overpower its prey, but all were met with the lance. After suffering six brutal stabbings, the creature escaped up the chimney. With the centipede's exit, Salvus feared the worst; he scanned the room for Dan's remains.

Across the hallway, Dan pulled his flashlight from his pocket. Considering the large opening in the wall at the far end of the room, he was surprised only minimal light entered, even to the area below the bar-free opening. No sooner had he turned on the flashlight when, in his nervousness, he dropped it to the floor. Picking it up, he was horrified. Lining each of the two walls were piles of human bones. From the corner of his eye, just outside of the flashlight's beam, he witnessed several rats scampering to the safety of the skeletal mounds. He gagged at the vile smell of decaying flesh that clung to many of the bones. Covering his nose to impede the ungodly smell, he spun to the sound of voices beyond the door.

"That's strange," noted Carmus from the hallway, "the key is in the keyhole and the door is unlocked."

"Maybe during last week's deposit," suggested Julius, "Talus forgot to lock the door."

"Spiritus Malus must be made aware of this infraction," insisted Carmus. "If Ranthea is allowed access to the hallway—and potentially to the guests' room—our years of vigilant care and attention to our visitors would end in complete disaster."

The moment the squeaky doorknob turned, Dan switched off the flashlight. Still covering his nose, he dashed to the nearest pile of bones and hid between the wall and the skeletons.

The door creaked open; Carmus and Julius slithered in, dragging a human corpse.

"I told you this one would die tonight," boasted Carmus. "But I didn't suspect it would happen within the hour."

After the two creatures disrespectfully dropped the body to the floor, Julius asked, "Should we summon the Harpies?"

"No," answered Carmus, "they can smell dead flesh from miles away. Trust me, Ranthea, their lord, will be here within minutes."

Movement at a nearby wall drew the attention of the Reclaimers.

Dan's ailing leg developed a spasm, which knocked a human skull from the pile.

As the two Reclaimers neared the area, a rat darted across the floor.

Carmus and Julius slithered back to the open door, but not before commenting that the rats were becoming as much of a nuisance to the Reclaimers as the overcrowding trolls.

Dan exhaled sharply when he heard the door close behind Carmus and Julius; his heart sank to his stomach, however, when he heard the door lock. There was no way out.

What's a Harpy? he thought.

He abandoned his thoughts of Harpies and gazed upon the deceased, near the locked door. Approaching the lukewarm corpse, he repeated over and over, "Please, don't let it be William; don't let it be William."

Standing over the recently departed, he switched on the flashlight and discovered that the cadaver was an elderly man. Unfortunately, his relief was short-lived; a thud was heard from behind.

Ranthea had arrived for her meal.

Turning to the large vertical opening on the distant wall, Dan beheld a winged beast, perched on the opening's ledge, with the head, arms, and trunk of a woman, but the wings, tail, and legs of a bird of prey…complete with flesh-ripping talons. As a substitute for a human mouth, the creature bore the beak of a raptor. On seeing the physically repulsive and reeking beast, Dan instantly recalled from his mythology class last year that Harpies were female birds that lived off the flesh of humans—dead or alive.

Ranthea jumped from the opening to the floor and slowly approached the corpse and the young traveler, who were roughly forty feet distant. The bird-woman's talons made a spine-chilling sound, as they scraped the floor. Ranthea made a loud screech, before she picked up speed in Dan's direction and became airborne.

Dan dropped his flashlight, reached for two femur bones, and aggressively repelled the oncoming talons of Ranthea, who was now hovering above.

Lashing both sets of talons, Ranthea ruthlessly tried to pierce the young man, who had dropped to his back, putting as much distance between himself and the overhead claws. A quick and powerful upward thrust of the femur bones deflected one of Ranthea's legs. Unfortunately, the second set of claws slashed Dan's sweatshirt and inflicted a minor flesh wound to his side, as he rolled to avoid a direct assault. Seeing a plump rat racing from a nearby mound of bones, Ranthea swiftly gored the rodent with her right claws, as she plunged to the floor. The creature's talons raised the skewered rat to her awaiting hand, tossed it into her open beak, and devoured it whole. The few moments it took the bird-woman to capture and consume its morsel of food was enough time for Dan to rise to his knees and dive into a pile of bones. With the presumed pilferer surrendering his claim on the corpse, Ranthea lowered her beak and ripped the flesh from the elderly man. Between mouthfuls, the bird of prey shrieked with delight.

Fortunately, Ranthea's cries of pleasure did not go unheard; they reached the pointed ears of Salvus across the hallway. Fearing the worst, he bolted from the library to the locked door across the corridor. In a frenzied state, he unlocked the door and threw it open, drawing the attention of Ranthea, who raised her head and assumed a guarded position over the corpse.

With his lance raised and aimed at the Harpy, Salvus slowly closed the door behind him, but left it ajar. "Dan!" he yelled. "Are you here?"

The young man, who was trembling beneath a pile of human bones, feared to make the slightest sound…not even to respond to his friend.

With his eyes fixed on the bird-woman standing over her meal and maintaining her defensive posture, the satyr yelled again, "Dan!"

Amid heavy breathing, the teenager knew he had to respond. *If not,* he thought, *Salvus will leave the room and I'll be alone with the Harpy.* He mustered the courage and poked his head from a pile of bones.

At the sound of bones crashing to the floor, Salvus and Ranthea gazed in the young man's direction.

Salvus made a wide sweep around the bird to Dan; the Harpy screeched.

Once the satyr was a safe distance from the bird-woman, he helped his friend to his feet. Then, with added caution, the men circled the Harpy, en route to the door.

Ranthea thrust her lethal beak in the direction of the fleeing men, as Dan stooped to grab his flashlight. Fortunately, the territorial creature refused to step from the vicinity of her meal.

Salvus and Dan made a successful retreat to the door.

Suspecting the shrieks may have been overheard by the Reclaimers, Salvus quietly opened the door and peered up and down the hallway. Noting the corridor was free of the snake-men, he ordered, "Come on, let's get back to the library and down to the dungeon."

With a captivated stare at the feasting Harpy behind, Dan alerted, "We can't."

"Why not?"

"There's a giant centipede across the hall," informed the teenager.

"It's alright, Dan," assured Salvus, "it fled up the chimney."

"Are you sure?" asked Dan in a troubled voice.

"Yeah," promised Salvus, "I'm sure."

Dan removed his sights from the Harpy and was turning to exit the room, when he blurted, "The passageway in the library is locked; we can't reach the dungeon through the library."

"The passageway is open," said the satyr, "I made sure of that."

After taking one final look up and down the hallway, the men left the Harpy to her meal, locked the door, and entered the library. Dan was the first to crawl through the secret passageway and onto the corner staircase.

Descending the steps, Salvus asked, "Why'd you leave the dungeon? You know it's far too dangerous in the upper levels of the castle."

Midway between the third and second levels, the two halted their stride; Dan placed his hands inside his sweatshirt pocket. Amazingly, even throughout his ordeal with the bird-woman, the stuffed animal was still in his pocket. Removing the toy, he showed it to his friend and explained, "This fell out of my pocket earlier this morning when I was attacked by the rest-upon in the library. I knew I had to find it before a Reclaimer spotted it or our lives would be in danger."

Salvus bit his lower lip and eventually admitted, "I suppose I would have done the same thing." Taking the stuffed animal from the teenager, he asked, "But why did you enter the Trophy Room?"

"The Trophy Room?" asked Dan. "What's that?"

"After a guest dies and his or her non-corporal being is incorporated into the assigned Reclaimer," disclosed Salvus, "the corpse is then tossed into the long room, which we just left, for the Harpies' enjoyment. Over the centuries, thousands of bodies have been dumped in the room."

Salvus returned the toy animal to Dan, who returned it to his pocket.

"It's called the Trophy Room," explained the satyr, "because it displays the untold number of the Reclaimers' triumphs."

"That's disgusting," replied Dan. Applying pressure to his slightly bleeding side, he recounted, "After I ran into the centipede in the library—and since the access panel locked behind me and my lance was in the dungeon—I had no choice but to run to another room. I was in the Trophy Room for only a few minutes before two Reclaimers delivered the body."

"Did the Reclaimers see you?" demanded Salvus.

"No."

"Are you absolutely sure?"

"I'm positive," answered Dan, "not in the Trophy Room or in the library."

"They were in the library, too?" asked an alarmed Salvus.

"Yeah," answered Dan, "they were looking for a book. But I swear, Salvus, neither of the Reclaimers saw me; I hid in the fireplace."

"Well," replied the satyr, "I guess there's no harm done, since no one saw you and you're still in one piece; but let's get back to the group."

The young traveler and Salvus resumed their downward trek to the second level.

CHAPTER FIVE

Smoke and Mirrors

With Dan leading the way down the corner staircase, he occasionally glanced behind in the dim light to his friend, who was painstakingly descending the staircase upon his goat frame. For as often as Salvus had traveled the steps over the past two hundred years, his gait was still awkward, at best.

The men were barely several feet above the second floor landing when Dan heard shuffling from behind. The satyr had taken a misstep, dropped his lance, tumbled down three steps, and slammed into Dan. The teenager staggered and fell upon the second floor landing.

Seeing a beam of light alongside the paneled door that was partly open, Dan left his flashlight on the stone landing, where it had settled during the fall, and reached for the access door.

"No!" yelled Salvus from behind, who was laboring to his hoofs.

The satyr's command was too late; the wooden passageway was wedged open.

In reaction to Salvus' unexpected warning, Dan—who remained on all fours—turned to face his friend. Suddenly, he was heartlessly yanked through the opening and into the second floor room, where he was hurled across its wooden floor.

As he lay on his back, three young men immediately attacked him. While the first assailant secured a firm neck lock on him, the second aggressor delivered violent blows of his boot to Dan's ribs; the third attacker pounded his fist upon Dan's chest. Even more disturbing than the skirmish was the appearance of the men. As Dan raised his eyes, he was in disbelief; each assaulter was an exact replica of himself in every detail…down to the matching sweatshirt and jeans.

Drawing on reserved strengths to escape the choke hold, Dan racked his brain to uncover the origin of his duplicates and the reason for their unprovoked attack. As he struggled to free himself, he squirmed and saw Salvus leap from a mirror, near the center of the room, and dash several feet away. *What's happening?* he thought. As his gaze followed the satyr racing across the floor, he was mystified and visibly shaken to see Salvus, his gentle friend, pouncing on another satyr, who was pinned to the ground by two identical satyrs.

Another blow was delivered to Dan's ribs, but this time directly on the flesh wound inflicted by the Harpy minutes earlier on the floor above; he groaned.

"Stay on the floor!" yelled the restrained satyr.

As Dan's replica loosened its grip around his throat—only to inflict a deadlier grasp moments later—the teenager stole another passing glimpse at the satyrs. Presuming Salvus was the one restricted to the ground, he noticed that even though his friend was being kicked violently and stomped upon by three sets of goat hoofs, he made gradual progress in the direction of a floor lamp that held two lit candles…the obvious source of illumination in the room.

Dan was baffled that glowing candles graced the castle notorious for its darkness, not to mention the Reclaimers' preference to darkness over light. Even more astonishing was the trampled satyr's valiant efforts to reach the light fixture, as if their lives depended on it.

Dan's thoughts were abruptly abandoned, as he suffered the tightest grip yet around his neck. Gasping for air, he fearfully eyed his remaining look-alikes grab his legs and contort them into anatomically impossible positions. With his esophagus obstructed, he was unable to scream. Rather, a loud and pronounced moan was heard.

To ensure the young trespasser would never again step foot near the opening to the forbidden room, the two replicas were single-minded in breaking his legs.

Dan groaned again.

As another unforgivable leg distortion was inflicted, the room went dark; the assailants vanished with the light.

Salvus had been victorious in wrapping his tail around the vertical pole of the floor lamp, crashing it to the ground, and extinguishing the flames.

The men remained sprawled on the floor, panting.

Amid his acute pain from the recent scuffle, Salvus crawled in complete darkness to Dan's side and whispered, "Are you alright?"

After a few more labored breaths, while clutching his ribs, Dan self-diagnosed, "Yeah, I think so, but where—" He took a large gulp before continuing, "Where did the men and satyrs go?"

"They're gone; we're safe now," promised the satyr. "Give me a second and I'll explain." He collapsed from all fours to his back.

The two remained silent and motionless for nearly five minutes.

On hearing a poorly subdued moan, the satyr extended his hand to his friend's shoulder and asked a second time, "Are you sure you're alright?"

"Yeah," he replied, "just a few bruised ribs, I think."

Realizing Dan's side should be inspected, even before they resumed their journey down the corner staircase, Salvus knew he had to relight the candles, but not before rearranging a few items in the room.

On detecting movement in the darkness, Dan asked, "Salvus, where are you going?"

"Stay on the floor," he ordered, "and don't move. There's something I need to do before lighting the candles."

Salvus neared the center of the room, constantly waving his hand through the engulfing darkness, searching for three freestanding floor mirrors. Once the reflective pieces were located, he pushed them against the right wall, making sure their back sides were facing the room. "There," he remarked, as he repositioned the final mirror.

Dan, who remained motionless on the floor and clasping his ribs, was slowly regaining his strength. An annoying creak startled him. He struggled to his knees, asking, "What was that?"

"Nothing," answered Salvus. "Stay put; I'm trying to find some wooden matches in this cabinet." After opening the bottom drawer of an antique cupboard in total darkness, the satyr disclosed, "You may find this hard to believe, Dan, but the Reclaimers actually insist that matches be readily available in this room, but only this room."

"Why?"

"Here they are," declared Salvus, as he grabbed what felt to be wooden matches.

"Why," asked Dan again, "do the Reclaimers insist matches be kept in this room?"

With the strike of a match, the satyr's face was aglow above the newborn flame. "Let me light the candles," he insisted, "and I'll do more than explain; I'll show you."

As the satyr extended the burning match at arm's length in search of the downed floor lamp, Dan asked if it would be easier to grab his flashlight from the corner staircase.

Embarrassed he hadn't thought of it earlier, the satyr mumbled, "That's alright; I found the lamp."

After the floor lamp was raised to its four-legged base, Salvus lit the two candles.

With light cast upon the long, narrow room, Dan's focus was immediately drawn to aquariumlike compartments that were built into the right wall, near the illuminated floor lamp, but above the mirrors' range. He estimated nearly a hundred tanks aligned the wall, with each partition encaging an unearthly species. "What are all those?" he asked, as he rose from his knees to his feet and limped to the wall.

"These," answered the satyr, "are the Reclaimers' former pets."

"Pets?" questioned Dan.

"Yeah," replied Salvus. "I'm not sure how much you know about the Reclaimers' banishment from hell, but upon their exile, they were permitted to bring their pets." Stepping alongside Dan, he elaborated, "Since their appalling pets had no souls, they obviously couldn't live forever…not even within the cursed walls of this castle. To this day, the Reclaimers remain so emotionally attached to their pets that they occasionally visit this room, which is why they demand matches be stocked in the cabinet. Even though the snake-men prefer the darkness, they will endure the slight discomfort of light to view their beloved deceased." Drawing his face closer to a tank which housed a creature that resembled a lizard with the head of a vulture, the satyr revealed, "Only the souls of the guests upstairs are more prized to the Reclaimers than their pets—even if their pets are dead."

"But they're not dead," interjected Dan. "I just saw that raptor flap its wings in the tank."

"Actually, Dan," said Salvus, "they are dead. You see, the Reclaimers treasured their pets so much that they delved into the supernatural to concoct a liquid potion which stimulates the muscles of the creatures. Heck, even the eyelids of some of their beloved beasts flutter, giving them the appearance of life. But trust me, there's more life in a doorknob than in one of these creatures."

"Salvus," asked Dan, "is that why you, the Pedwhips, and the trolls aren't imprisoned in the guests' room by the Reclaimers?"

Uncomfortable with the direct question, the satyr ignored his comment and forewarned, "Dan, while the Reclaimers are probably occupied preparing for tonight's forest hunt, it's still not wise that we remain in this room much longer. Besides, your friends are probably worried about you."

"But, Salvus," reminded Dan, "there's nothing to do in the dungeon except rest until tonight."

Suspecting he and Dan were safe for a few moments, not to mention he wanted to spend as much time as possible with his new-found friend before the group's untimely departure, Salvus reluctantly answered Dan's prior question, "Yes, since neither I nor the Pedwhips nor the trolls have a soul, in the truest sense of the word, the Reclaimers don't attempt to mentally dominate us. As a result, we're not banished to the sixth floor." Taking another glance at an expired creature in a nearby tank, he maintained, "But even though I don't have a human soul, I do know the difference between right and wrong."

Dan rested his hand upon the satyr's shoulder and declared, "You're one of the most human persons I've ever met."

"Thanks," replied Salvus, who immediately added, "and as far as the trolls, there's not a human bone in their bodies. At least the Pedwhips are one-third human, though the way they constantly flare out their fins and flap their gills at the first sound or sight of danger, I oftentimes think they're more fish than crayfish or human."

Stepping to an oversize, fluid-filled compartment, Dan was intrigued with its inhabitant: a large wasp. *Hmm*, he thought, *I wonder if its offspring or mate is now in the belly of the eel.* Fascinated with the unnatural encasement, he reached to touch its outer boundary, when his hand was knocked away by his friend. "Salvus," he exclaimed, "I was just going to touch the glass."

"It's not glass," explained the satyr. "It's a wall of fluid, retained by the Reclaimers' sorcery. Any disturbance to its outer surface will release the liquid to the floor, along with the dead creatures. Needless to say, the Reclaimers would be enraged. They'd most likely suspect me as the culprit and immediately search the dungeon, where your friends are presently waiting."

Dan lowered his hand to his aching side, prompting Salvus to order him to lift his sweatshirt.

"I'm fine," lied Dan.

"Nevertheless," insisted Salvus, "I'll have a look."

Unwillingly, Dan raised his shirt and bared his side. He jerked at the satyr's light touch.

"Well," admitted Salvus, "the lighting's not the best in here, so I can't say for sure. But it doesn't feel like you have any broken ribs, though I'm sure you'll have a few nasty bruises in a few hours."

As Dan glanced at his waist, he was amazed that the recent attack by the Harpy in the Trophy Room had drawn only minimal blood. So little, in fact, it escaped Salvus' examination in the poor light. Perhaps even more astounding to Dan was the fact that William's stuffed animal was still in his sweatshirt pocket, even after the clash with his personal replicas.

"How are your legs?" asked the satyr.

"A little sore," admitted Dan, "but nothing's broken."

"Trust me," said Salvus, "you'd be in a lot more pain right now, if you were outside the hexed castle walls." He directed his gaze from Dan to the back side of a nearby mirror and continued, "We should count our blessings; we were lucky this time."

"What do you mean lucky?" asked Dan.

Touching the back of the mirror beside him, Salvus replied, "Where to begin?" He removed his hand from the mirror, tightened the rope around his waist, and updated his young guest. "About two hundred years ago, when I was first exploring the corner staircases of the castle, I heard an uproar inside this very room. Curious of the commotion, I unlatched the secret opening from the corner staircase. Within the lit room, I witnessed a dozen or more trolls desecrating the tanks in the wall and feasting upon the creatures' corpses. The paranormal fluid from dozens of vandalized tanks flooded nearly the entire room. Knowing I would be as guilty as the trolls if discovered, I closed the paneled door and resumed my explorations on the upper levels."

"But how did the trolls—" asked Dan.

"Anyway," interrupted Salvus, "over the next few weeks, my increasing interest in the pets encaged in the wall consumed me. I hobbled up the corner staircase to this floor again. However, unlike my initial journey, this time I was yanked into the room, just like you were earlier. After several minutes of fierce combat with three identical satyrs, a Reclaimer, who happened to be passing in the nearby hallway, threw open the door at the far entryway."

Dan pushed his glasses farther atop the bridge of his nose and peered to the opposite end of the room to the main entrance. "Where did the satyrs come from," he asked, "since you mentioned earlier your species was annihilated by a flock of Oswagi Birds?"

"That's why," explained Salvus, "I had to reposition the mirrors, just now, before lighting the candles."

"I don't understand," admitted the young traveler.

"Apparently," clarified Salvus, "within days of the initial desecration of many of their pets by the trolls, Spirituo Malus charged a team of Reclaimers to create guardians of the tanks to ensure their remaining lifeless pets were never consumed. In response, three snake-men devised a rather ingenious protection system."

"What's that?" asked Dan.

"They placed six mirrors in this room," explained Salvus, "one in the center, facing the access panel at the corner staircase, and two other mirrors positioned strategically a few feet away from the center mirror to capture the image projected from it. The same configuration of three mirrors was also arranged at the opposite end of this room, with the center mirror facing the main entry door. Once the six reflective pieces were craftily situated, the Reclaimers cursed them, so the moment an image was captured in either center mirror by anyone or anything entering the room, its reflection was instantaneously projected to the two neighboring side mirrors. Before the intruder could advance just a few feet into the room, the three identical images of the trespasser leaped from the mirrors and attacked the prowler." Recalling his stumble upon the corner staircase minutes earlier, he acknowledged, "It's a good thing I dropped the lance in the stairwell."

"Why's that?" asked Dan.

"Don't you see?" prompted Salvus. "If I had been carrying the lance when I bolted through the access panel to save you, the weapon's image would also have been captured in the mirrors and I would have had three armed satyrs attacking me and then assaulting you. Believe me, Dan, the images are intent on butchering any invader, even if it's their own species."

Dan redirected his fixed gaze from the back side of a mirror, which Salvus had recently pushed against the wall, to the set of mirrors at the far end of the room. "What about those?" he asked. "Shouldn't we move them?"

"They're intentionally positioned to foil the entrance of any trespasser, who may enter from that side of the room," explained the satyr. Noticing a look of uneasiness on his friend's face, he added, "Don't worry; we're safe from casting our images into those mirrors, as long as we remain on this side of the room."

"So," stated Dan, "the three satyrs and my look-alikes were the result of our images being transmitted to the mirrors, when I opened the access panel, after my stumble to the landing."

"Yes," confirmed the satyr.

Thinking back to Salvus' story of his initial encounter with the hostile satyrs, Dan asked, "What happened to the satyrs that attacked you, when you were first exploring the castle nearly two centuries ago?" Before Salvus could respond, he added, "And why wasn't the image of the Reclaimer, who opened the main door, cast into the center mirror that was facing him?"

Salvus stepped to another tank and explained, "You haven't met the Pedwhips, but when I questioned one of them about the mirrors, after my clash, he explained that since light is necessary for an image to be created, captured, and sustained, then when the room is darkened, the replica vanishes. After all, you can't see your reflection in a mirror in darkness, nor can you see your hand in front of your face without light. The deaths of the three satyrs were purely accidental. When the Reclaimer threw open the door, a strong breeze from the well-ventilated hallway extinguished the sole burning candle near the main entrance. Basically, the darkness vanquished the three murderous satyrs. That's how I knew our only chance of survival against the images, just a short time ago, was to quench the flames of the floor lamp." The satyr took another glance at the back sides of the distant mirrors and admitted the word 'image' was far from the truth.

"I keep calling them images," he remarked, "but don't be fooled. In reality, the replicas are as much alive as we are. They are three-dimensional with skin and bones, body temperatures, great strength, and a determination to safeguard the pets in the wall, as if the dead creatures were their own offspring."

"But if any being that enters this room is duplicated," asked Dan, "after the intruder is killed, can't its replicas descend to the dungeon?"

"That's a good question," complimented Salvus. "But don't worry; the dungeon's perfectly safe. You see, the lifelike images were created to protect the dead pets in this room. The guardians never journey beyond their boundaries, though as you've witnessed firsthand, they're capable of pulling someone or something into the room, if they believe the trespasser presents a danger to the Reclaimers' pets. In the end, species will slaughter their own kind—satyrs will fight satyrs, trolls will assault trolls, and humans will battle humans—all for the safety of the deceased pets. After all, who knows the frailties of an intruder better than one of its own kind?"

"I don't get it," admitted Dan. "The power of the cursed mirrors doesn't make any sense."

"What do you mean?"

"If the mirrors can replicate any being placed in front of them," he proposed, "then why don't the Reclaimers simply duplicate their dead pets?"

"I asked the same question of the Pedwhip," admitted Salvus, "who explained that although the physical attributes of the expired creatures can be created, their individual feelings and unique affections cannot. The Reclaimers were so devoted to their hellish pets that nothing short of their total rebirth would do." The satyr glanced to a mirror and disclosed, "The mirrors purposely fall below the range of the lowest tanks, so their pets are never inadvertently copied. To recreate their beloved beasts, without their treasured emotions, would be too painful for the Reclaimers."

After offering another glance to the main entrance, Dan turned to his friend and asked, "But what about the Reclaimers? If they visit this room on occasion, can't they or their replicas slither through the secret passageway and enter the dungeon?"

"Your friends are fine," reassured the satyr. "Any staircase is extremely cumbersome for the snake-men to master, which explains why they descend the Grand Staircase only when absolutely necessary, like hunting, grabbing a book from the library, monitoring the Hall of Admittance, or visiting their pets. And even then, the arduous task of traveling a staircase is poorly accomplished and with embarrassing difficulty. Trust me, they won't risk slinking down the steps to explore a grubby dungeon; heck, the Reclaimers are even more clumsy on steps than I am."

Confounded with such anomalies in the room, Dan shook his head before asking, "But why wasn't the image of the Reclaimer, who opened the main door on you many years ago, captured in the mirror?"

"Look closely at the far mirrors," commanded Salvus, who pointed to the end of the room.

The traveler had advanced only several steps closer to the back sides of the distant mirrors when he noticed that, unlike the ones which previously faced the secret access panel, none of the three mirrors extended to the floor.

"Even though the Reclaimers are savagely cruel beasts," explained Salvus, "they're not stupid. Knowing they also would cast images into the mirror—in addition to the pain they would suffer in viewing their reflections—the snake-men purposely installed mirrors that could steal images only two feet or higher above the floor. After countless trips to visit their dead pets over the decades, they've mastered their technique. Just like the Reclaimer, who entered the room and spotted me battling three satyrs years ago, the snake creatures unlatch the door from the hallway, drop to their serpent bellies, and slither to their pets at the wall. Below the liquid tanks, they are free of the mirrors' range."

"And they go to these great lengths," questioned Dan, "simply to visit their deceased pets?"

"I'm afraid so," answered Salvus. After positioning his toga that had slipped down one shoulder, he acknowledged, "Granted, the mirrors' images have slaughtered many invaders in the past, but the trolls are clever creatures also. Over the years, and after countless troll deaths at the hands of their barbaric replicas, the annoying little creatures have learned to enter through the main door, also on their stomachs. I suppose it's just a matter of time before the Reclaimers create a new potion to protect this room."

The satyr and Dan remained standing near the tanks, absorbed with the spastic movements of the dead pets, when Salvus jerked his sights from the liquid-filled compartments and blurted, "Oh, no; how could I have been so stupid? How could I have forgotten?"

Spinning around and expecting to spot more replicas charging them, Dan was pleased to discover he and his friend were alone in the room.

A detectable look of fear, however, settled upon the satyr's face.

"Salvus," demanded Dan, "what's wrong? What did you forget?"

The satyr wrinkled his nose and took a prolonged whiff.

"What's wrong?" yelled Dan.

"Oh, no," whispered the satyr. Before Dan could ask again, Salvus skittishly scanned the pet room and ultimately focused on the floor lamp several feet away. "Run for the lamp!"

"But, Salvus," pleaded Dan.

"Now!" screamed the satyr.

Dan followed his friend's lead, as he raced the few feet, jumped upon the lamp's base, and gripped the center pole.

Once the human and the satyr were atop the lamp's four-legged pedestal, Dan ordered, "Salvus, what's going on?"

"Can't you smell it?"

"Smell what?"

Salvus refused to answer; he kept his gaze fixed near the main door.

Dan's sights followed the satyr's hypnotic look. Within seconds, a wisp of dark smoke rose from beneath the floorboards and hovered near the room's main entry.

"What is it?" whispered Dan. With no response, he placed his hand on Salvus' arm to draw his attention.

The satyr jolted.

Now squeezing his friend's forearm, Dan demanded, "What's the danger of the smoke?"

Eventually directing his attention to his companion, Salvus said, "I can't believe I forgot about—" He shook his head in disbelief, confessing, "I'm sorry I put your life in danger."

"Alright, Salvus," urged Dan, "what's so dreadful about the smoke and why are we standing on the lamp's base?"

"That's not smoke," informed the satyr, "that's the Shamus Seeker."

"The what?" asked Dan.

"The Shamus Seeker," restated Salvus.

"So," questioned Dan, "if it's more than twenty feet away, why are we standing on the lamp?"

Noticing the smoke remained stationary, Salvus explained, "The Shamus Seeker lives directly below the floorboards on this level and drifts between rooms seeking out prey."

Suspecting Salvus was not easily frightened, Dan's anxiety was heightened, as he observed the satyr's mounting fears when speaking about the Shamus Seeker. "What does it prey upon?" he asked.

"Essentially," answered the satyr, "it draws every drop of life fluid through the pores of any breathing creature."

"What?" asked a skeptical teenager. "You can't be serious." Noticing the lingering look of terror on his friend's face, he added, "But how?"

"The Shamus Seeker," explained Salvus, "is composed of microscopic liquid particles that the creature must constantly resupply in order to survive and thrive."

"If that's the case and it's seeking us out," suggested Dan, "let's run for the corner staircase."

"We'd never make it," warned the satyr.

Glancing back at the smoke creature, Dan evaluated, "Salvus, we're closer to the corner staircase than the Shamus Seeker is to us; I'm sure we can outrun it."

"Trust me," revealed Salvus, "I've seen it move before; we'd be captured in a matter of seconds."

"When did you see it move?" he asked.

"Years ago," related Salvus, "I openly defied the Reclaimers' order never to venture beyond the main level of the castle. Obviously, as you know, I've explored every inch of this castle using the four corner staircases; but the Reclaimers remain unaware of my unseen excursions. The snake-men insist I never visit the other levels to ensure I never associate with their guests." The satyr paused to confirm visually that the dark smoke had not advanced; he then resumed, "I'm not sure what took possession of me that morning so long ago, but I was determined to climb the Grand Staircase and investigate the nearby rooms. Thankfully, my trespassing went unnoticed by the Reclaimers, though Marcus, the Pedwhips' head cook, spotted me and insisted I return to the dungeon for my own safety. While the snake-men are not overly annoyed with my presence in the kitchen and other rooms on the main level—though even there, they offer me cold-hearted glances—they'd be enraged if they found me wandering on an upper level. Needless to say, I would be severely punished."

"So," asked Dan, "how did you learn of the smoke?"

"Soon after Marcus discovered me on the second floor," explained Salvus, "I heeded his advice and was walking down the hall, en route to the dungeon, when I heard voices from around the corner. Unsure of what or who was approaching, I hid alongside the grandfather clock, near the Grand Staircase. My anxieties were calmed when I discovered the voices were those of four trolls and not Reclaimers. The moment the dwarfish creatures turned the corner and were shuffling up the corridor opposite me, I resumed my trek down the hallway. Something, however, compelled me to look back. It was then I noticed the trolls entering the alchemy lab, two rooms to our right. Suspecting the troublesome creatures were up to something mischievous, I postponed my trip to the dungeon and neared the lab."

The satyr offered a glance to the secret access panel and then to the Shamus Seeker, confirming Dan's earlier speculation they were closer to the corner staircase than the smoke creature was to them.

Dan took a tighter grip on the floor lamp.

Salvus eventually abandoned his visual survey and continued, "As

I opened the door to the lab, I was amazed at seeing the trolls in an exceptionally violent ruckus, smashing and tossing glass beakers and experimental potions to the floor. Knowing the noise would alert the nearest Reclaimer, I was just closing the door, intent on returning to the dungeon, when I spotted a column of dark smoke rising from beneath the floorboards, amid the spilled concoctions, and capturing the nearest troll."

Salvus shook his head and altered his voice to a regretful tone, admitting, "Though I can't stand those destructive and repulsive little creatures, I still couldn't help feeling sorry for the doomed troll." The satyr maintained his somber disposition and clarified, "Unfortunately for me, the troll was facing the doorway. Within a matter of seconds, all the troll's body fluids were extracted and absorbed into the Shamus Seeker; the troll barely had time to scream. There on the floor, amid the broken beakers, lay an emaciated troll with its skin cleaving tightly to its bones. The unbelievable speed of the dark smoke thwarted the escape of two other fleeing trolls, which also met the same fate. Only one troll was spared."

"But, Salvus," asked Dan, "why hasn't the smoke attacked us?"

Ignoring the question of his young friend, the satyr resumed his story, "Not knowing which, if any, rooms in the castle were safe from the Shamus Seeker, a few days later I met secretly with Marcus, who informed me the Reclaimers had only recently begun testing a new mist elixir in the lab which, when perfected and released into the forest, would track humans, whose body temperature and heat pattern are distinct from all forest creatures. Once humans were captured in the mist, the elements of the paranormal fog would overpower and control their senses, place them in a spellbound state, and lure them to the castle. However, Marcus also told me that when the Reclaimers discovered the shattered glass in the alchemy lab, within minutes of the trolls' demise, they also realized their experimental mist potion, consisting of rare ingredients, was lost forever."

A thrashing tentacle of an expired pygmy kraken strangler in a nearby tank distracted the satyr. He continued, "In time, it was learned the trolls had smashed dozens of toxic chemicals to the lab floor, along with the trial mist potion. The various ingredients mixed, creating a hybrid of the Reclaimers' original intended mixture. The new elixir now seeks out the body heat of anything—trolls, humans, Pedwhips, satyrs, even rodents." Salvus took a death grip of the floor lamp's pole and informed, "The Reclaimer supervising the experimental research was Shamus; hence the smoke creature's name."

"So," said Dan, "the Shamus Seeker has control of the castle."

"Not exactly," replied Salvus. "After months of observing the behavioral patterns of the smoke creature, the Reclaimers noticed the creature couldn't penetrate rock. And since the castle is constructed almost entirely of stone, the movements of the smoke creature are greatly restricted."

"Let me guess," remarked Dan in a sarcastic tone, "but not in this room."

"Sorry," admitted the satyr. "Immediately below this wood floor," he explained, "is a stone foundation, just like the level above us. So, the Shamus Seeker can float only on this level."

"But I thought you said the smoke creature can travel between rooms," stated Dan.

"Yes," replied Salvus, "but just in the rooms to our right and left, since the walls between the rooms are composed of only wood." Noticing Dan gaze toward the secret access panel with a concerned look, Salvus eased his anxieties by explaining, "The thresholds at the corner staircase and at the main entry to this room are also constructed of stone. So, the smoke creature can't breach the corner staircase or the hallway; nor can it penetrate any other area of the main corridor through the adjoining rooms, since the entire wall at the main entrance of this room, from one end of the castle to the other, is a stone load-bearing wall. This, by the way, is what protects the Pedwhips when climbing the Grand Staircase to deliver the guests' meals."

"Are you sure the Shamus Seeker can't drift through the access panel and into the corner staircase?' asked an unconvinced teenager.

"Quite sure," reassured Salvus. "As Marcus later explained to me, even though the Shamus Seeker can rise between the joints in the floorboards, the lowest fringes of the creature must remain rooted in the narrow subfloor, between the wood and the stone, where it was created." Noticing his companion retained a bewildered look, he summarized, "Trust me, Dan, the Shamus Seeker can hunt only in this room and in the rooms next to us."

"So basically," reiterated Dan, to alleviate his fears for his friends in the dungeon, "the smoke creature's prowling is restricted to the second level, and just in the rooms between the corner staircase and the main hallway."

"Yes," replied Salvus, "which is why I never explore this level…at least not on this side of the main corridor."

"And the Reclaimers," asked Dan, "risk encountering the dark smoke every time they visit their pets?"

"Not at all," replied the satyr.

"Salvus," snapped Dan, "you're not making any sense."

After repositioning his hoofs on the floor lamp's base, the satyr emphasized, "What you need to understand, Dan, is that the Shamus Seeker can't locate its prey by sound, which is why we can speak in our normal tone. I ordered you on the lamp's legs because the creature detects its potential victims purely by heat. Above the floor, even only a few inches, our body heat is undetectable to the creature. But since the Reclaimers are already dead, they have no body heat or warmth. Believe me, there's not a single warm feeling among the fifty snake-men. With no heat emitting from their lifeless bodies, the Reclaimers are free to slither anywhere on this level, including their pet room and the alchemy lab."

Harboring doubts of his friend's explanation, Dan challenged, "Are you certain the Reclaimers aren't tormented by the dark smoke?"

"Positive," affirmed Salvus. "Twice in the past, from the safety of the main corridor, I secretly watched a Reclaimer enter the smoke in the alchemy lab and exit the dark cloud completely unscathed."

"Your tail!" screamed Dan.

In his lengthy narrative of the Shamus Seeker's birth and boundary restrictions, the satyr unknowingly had lowered his tail within an inch of the wood floor. Grabbing his tail and securing it between a hand and the lamp's pole, he remarked, "Thanks; that could have been unsightly for you and deadly for me."

Dan took another glance at the far end of the room and asked, "So, how long before it floats to another room?"

"It's hard to say," answered the satyr. "But Marcus told me the Shamus Seeker can remain suspended above the floor for hours—even days—before attacking or retreating."

"Days!" exclaimed Dan. "I don't have days; I'm leaving the castle tonight."

Engrossed in monitoring the minute drifts of the Shamus Seeker, Salvus had unintentionally overlooked the group's nearing departure.

"Salvus," demanded Dan, "think! There's got to be a way of out-smarting the smoke creature; we have to get back to the dungeon before nightfall."

"Short of yelling to our friends two levels down," said Salvus, "which would certainly attract the Reclaimers and put all our lives in danger, there's nothing we can do. I've never heard of anyone or any-thing escaping the Shamus Seeker; the creature lives to kill."

"But, Salvus," pleaded Dan, "there's got to be something." The traveler scrutinized the narrow room from his four-inch perch for a covert exit. Focusing on the fluid-filled tanks beside him, he asked, "What about the liquid in the tanks?"

"What about it?"

"If we spilled fluid on the floor," suggested Dan, "would it prevent the smoke creature from detecting our body heat, if we were standing in it?"

Salvus looked at the tanks and admitted, "I don't know; but I'm sure I don't want to try it, only to find out it doesn't."

"What about—" asked Dan.

"Sh," whispered the satyr.

"I thought you said the Shamus Seeker can't hear sounds," said Dan.

"Sh," demanded the satyr again, as he listened intently.

With his back facing the room's main door, Dan took a firm grip on the floor lamp and turned his head in the direction of Salvus' stare. He heard it too: voices in the hallway.

Trapped on the four-legged lamp base, Dan and the satyr were at the mercy of the Reclaimers. Both knew if the door opened, they—and ultimately their friends in the dungeon—would be dis-covered and their journey to rescue William would end with mortal consequences.

Dan held his breath, nervously awaiting the door's opening.

The voices in the hallway faded unexpectedly.

After several moments of deadly silence, Salvus whispered, "That was too close; I suppose they headed to the alchemy lab."

"Salvus," insisted Dan, in a low voice, "we need to think of a get-away plan now, before one of the Reclaimers pays a last-minute visit to his dead pet, prior to the hunting trip tonight." A sharp pain in his previously contorted legs compelled Dan to slip one foot nearly two inches down the lamp's base. In a panic state, he quickly raised it alongside the other.

Observing the momentary misstep, Salvus and the teenager remained motionless, staring at the Shamus Seeker for any forward movement. To their satisfaction, Dan's body heat, barely two inches above the floorboards, remained undetected.

"Come on, Salvus," implored Dan, "there must have been stories over the years about something or someone outwitting the smoke creature."

"No, nothing," replied the satyr. "The only thing—" He paused, eyed the back side of a mirror behind him, and remarked, "I wonder."

"Wonder what?" asked an impatient Dan, who stared at the mirror's back side.

"I wonder," continued Salvus, "if we could use this mirror to our advantage."

"How so?" inquired the teenager.

Salvus turned to his friend and asked, "Remember when I told you about the three trolls being drained of their body fluids in the alchemy lab?"

"Yeah."

"As the Shamus Seeker was killing the first troll," reminded Salvus, "the other three, at least for a few moments, were safe from the creature."

"What do you mean?" asked Dan.

"I mean," explained the satyr, "that while the Shamus Seeker was busy taking the life from one creature, the other three had an opportunity to flee." Salvus lowered his sights near the floor lamp's base and asked, "How are your legs?"

"A little sore from the bending and twisting," replied Dan. "Why?"

With his tail still firmly grasped between one hand and the lamp's pole, the satyr raised his other hand to his face, scratched his cheek, and asked, "Are you well enough to run…to run as if your life depended on it?"

"Sure," insisted Dan. "But I thought you said we couldn't outrun it."

Ignoring Dan's comment, Salvus admitted, "It's probably a long shot, but it's the best idea I've got." Noting the Shamus Seeker remained motionless at the far end of the room, he restated, "Maybe we can use this mirror beside me to aid in our escape."

"I'm listening," urged Dan.

"If we create a diversion, we may buy ourselves enough time to break free from this room."

"Go on," prodded the teenager.

"I suggest we jump from the floor lamp at the same time," suggested Salvus. "You run along the back side of the mirror; I'll dart between its front side and the wall. The mirror will capture my image, which will leap from the reflective glass, and chase after me."

"But," reminded Dan, "you said we couldn't outrun the Shamus Seeker."

"Technically, we can't," agreed Salvus. "However, if another warm being is trailing us, the smoke creature will most likely halt its pursuit of us for a few moments to absorb the body fluids of my double."

"Most likely?" questioned Dan.

"Sorry," answered the satyr, "I can't say for sure. I'm basing my theory solely on what I witnessed in the alchemy lab between the trolls and the Shamus Seeker."

Knowing his brother's rescue and the safety of his friends depended on his safe departure from the pet room, Dan attempted to reassure himself by asking, "Do you really think we can run faster than your look-alike? I mean, what if he catches up to us—then what?"

"That thought crossed my mind, too," said Salvus, "but I'll bet that even in your present condition, you'd reach the access panel before my replica catches you. As much as I hate to admit it, we satyrs aren't the most agile, especially when running. I'm sure you can beat him to the corner staircase. And as far as outpacing my own species, I think my two or three second head start will leave him in my tracks."

Realizing the satyr was putting his life on the line again for the travelers, Dan proposed, "Salvus, why don't you wait here until the smoke creature drifts to another room? I'll step in front of the mirror and race my double to the secret access panel. I don't want you risking your life for me and my friends."

"Nonsense," snapped Salvus, "I'm going with you. Besides, you'll need my help tonight when fleeing the castle."

Knowing a covert exodus from the fortress would be next to impossible without Salvus' distraction in the Hall of Admittance, Dan reluctantly agreed to the satyr's offer.

"Are you sure your legs are alright?" asked Salvus again.

After taking a few seconds to stretch his lower limbs upon the floor lamp's base, Dan replied, "Yeah, I'll be fine."

The satyr closely inspected the mirror, which stood two feet from the wall, and then analyzed the escape path. "Okay," he ordered, "on the count of three, I'll run between the mirror's front side and the wall; you race along the back side."

The two escapees took a deep breath before Salvus slowly and clearly pronounced, "One, two, three."

Dan jumped from the lamp's base and landed four feet closer to the secret access panel; Salvus leaped and bolted to the corner staircase.

As the men were racing, nearly side by side, Dan offered an over-the-shoulder glance and spotted Salvus' replica, a few feet behind the sprinters, in hot pursuit. The Shamus Seeker, however, was rapidly reducing the distance between itself and the Salvus look-alike.

A loud and shrill scream was heard, as Dan lunged headfirst upon the wood floor and slid through the access opening. Within two seconds of his ungraceful entry, Salvus collided into him. Quickly spinning around, within the safety of the corner staircase, the men watched in complete horror as the Shamus Seeker inhumanely robbed Salvus' double of its life-giving fluid.

"Oh my God," exclaimed Dan, while eyeing the tragic outcome of the struggle. "The satyr's gaunt; you can see every bone in his body. What a horrible way to go."

Salvus closed his eyes and turned his head. Although the expired satyr, four feet in front of him, was only a look-alike, it greatly disturbed him. Deep inside, he secretly longed that by some freakish accident, the recently deceased satyr would have conquered its evil inclinations and become his companion. Sadly, since the curse upon the mirrors was all-controlling and irreversible, his hopes were rooted in unreality.

On seeing his companion shun the nightmare before him—and suspecting his friend's thoughts—Dan consoled, "Salvus, that wasn't a true satyr; it was simply a replica. You deserve better."

As the satyr was closing the access panel, Dan gripped his friend's wrist and shoved the miniature door wide open.

"What are you doing?" blurted Salvus.

"We need to remove the evidence," warned Dan.

"The evidence?" asked Salvus. "Why?"

Staring at the smoke creature directly ahead, Dan remarked, "When a Reclaimer enters this room to visit his pet, he'll see the skeletal version of you and know you were exploring above the main level." He removed his sights from the Shamus Seeker, looked at Salvus, and reminded, "And as you said, you'll be severely punished."

"I appreciate your concern," replied the satyr, "but right now, the group's escape is more important." Running his hands along the landing of the darkened corner staircase for the lance he dropped during his earlier stumble, he suggested, "Who knows, maybe the Reclaimers will suspect the trolls were trespassing in the room again."

"But not with your dead look-alike on the floor, they won't," reminded Dan.

"Here it is," announced Salvus, as he snatched the weapon.

Dan was not distracted by Salvus' find; he resumed his visual search of the room for a means to remove the corpse, without stepping upon the floorboards. With the nearby mirrors facing the wall, he was free to analyze the room's interior with no threat of creating deadly images.

His attention was drawn to a tank, directly above the two glowing candles of the floor lamp. The thrashing of a piranha's unusual spindly tail fin—adorned with countless suction cups to prevent its victim from plunging to lower depths with only a mouthful of ripped flesh—gave Dan an idea. "Hey," he shouted, "didn't you say any disturbance to a tank's outer surface would release the creature and the fluids?"

"Yeah," replied Salvus. "Why?"

After snatching his flashlight, three steps down, Dan searched the corner staircase for several rocks.

"What are you looking for?" asked Salvus.

Returning to the satyr's side, Dan dropped all but one of the stones upon the landing. Rolling the largest rock in his hand, he remarked, "Let's see how good my aim is."

"Careful," cautioned Salvus, as he grabbed his friend's extended arm. "It's probably safe to breach the entry with your hand, but why take needless chances if you don't have to, especially with the Shamus Seeker floating nearby."

Within seconds of its release, the stone fell short of its target by several feet and crashed upon the floor.

The smoke creature remained motionless.

An underarm toss of the fifth rock achieved success; the piranha and its encasing fluid cascaded beyond their spatial boundaries and fell to the floor, quenching the burning flames in the process.

With the room darkened, Dan switched on the flashlight and aimed its beam to the area where the deceased satyr once rested. Though not surprised, the men were grateful Salvus' double had vanished.

"Granted," informed Dan, "the three mirrors are still pushed against the wall and there's a dead piranha twitching in a pool of liquid on the floor, but since the dead satyr has dematerialized, there's no evidence which points directly to you. Now the Reclaimers may think the trolls invaded the room again to devour a few of their dearly departed pets."

"Thanks," said Salvus, "you may have saved my skin—literally."

"Don't mention it," remarked Dan, "you just saved my life."

Within seconds of the secret access panel being closed and locked, Dan blurted, "Hey, wait a minute."

"What?" asked Salvus, as he reached for the rock wall for balance and rose to his hoofs.

"How come I didn't notice any light alongside the access panel when I climbed the steps to the third floor in search of the stuffed animal?" Before Salvus could respond, the teenager shoved his hand inside his sweatshirt pocket. "I can't believe it," he declared, "it's still here." He pulled the toy from his pocket. "Maybe things are finally going our way."

"I'm afraid," admitted Salvus, "it was my fault."

"Your fault?" asked Dan, after returning the stuffed animal to his pocket. "What was your fault?"

"When I left the dungeon to look for you," he explained, "I opened the access panel on the first level and then shut it and locked it, since you weren't in the room. After I unlatched the paneled door on the second level, I had only begun to slide the door when I remembered the mirrors. Rather than throwing open the access panel, I pressed my ear against the boards to listen for any disturbance. When I didn't hear anything, I climbed to the third level."

As the men resumed their descent upon the corner staircase, Salvus admitted, "I guess I forgot to latch the access panel on the second floor before venturing to the third."

"But why," asked Dan, "weren't you pulled into the pet room?"

"I opened the paneled door just a crack," answered Salvus, "and even then, I was sure to keep my body away from the lit gap, so my image couldn't be captured."

As the satyr and the teenager stepped upon the first floor landing, Salvus paused; Dan maintained his downward stride to the dungeon.

Sensing his friend was straggling behind, Dan turned, aimed the light's beam at the satyr, and asked, "What's wrong?"

"I'm sorry I put your life in danger," confessed Salvus. "I feel horrible."

"Salvus," remarked Dan, after ascending two steps closer to the satyr, "don't worry; it was an accident. Besides, I never would have survived the Harpy or my replicas or the Shamus Seeker if it wasn't for you."

Uncomfortable with compliments, the satyr simply replied, "Come on, let's get to the dungeon."

Walking alongside the satyr, Dan jokingly admitted that the pet room gave a whole new meaning to the term, "smoke and mirrors."

"What are smoke and mirrors?" asked Salvus.

Before Dan could answer, the men were crawling through the opening at the corner of the dungeon.

Sam ran to the passageway, demanding, "Dan, where on earth

have you been? I strictly forbade any of you to leave this dungeon alone!"

After explaining the reason for his sole journey and detailing his adventures on the third and second levels, Sam abandoned his rehearsed chastisement. *After all,* he thought, *he was looking out only for the safety of his co-travelers.*

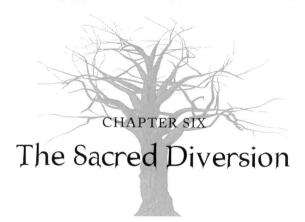

CHAPTER SIX
The Sacred Diversion

A FEW MINUTES AFTER 5:00 IN THE EVENING, THE DUMBWAITER made a crash landing to the dungeon level. Lifting its rusty handle, Salvus removed another wooden platter, brimming with produce, cheese, bread, and cooked bacon. In the corner of the dumbwaiter rested an oversize bowl of vegetable stew. As Salvus carried the food to the center of his living area, the four travelers, who had resumed rehearsing their defensive exercises upon Dan's rescue from the above floors, gathered around. Before the first morsel of food was swallowed, however, each traveler set aside a significant portion of their meal for storage in their backpacks. Even though the group was famished from their intense afternoon training exercises and wanted nothing more than to consume every scrap of food before them, they knew the provisions would be a lifesaver, when they were in the heart of the shadowy forest.

Since there was just one bowl of stew, Salvus passed the vessel to Cindy, who slurped a mouthful, and then handed it to Jimmy.

While the bowl was in transit, Dan asked Salvus to thank Marcus for the extra food, after the group fled the castle.

Moments after assuring his friend he would convey the group's appreciation, the satyr recalled he had promised the head cook he'd play his favorite melody that night. Salvus made a mental note, before accepting the bowl from Sam.

"Wouldn't it be easier," asked Cindy, "to rescue William when the guests are coming down the rear staircase for their exercise?"

"Good point," seconded Sam, after swallowing an apple wedge.

"Wouldn't it be easier to snatch a guest from the group, when they're on the main level?"

"Of course it would be easier," agreed the satyr, "but not safer."

"What do you mean," asked Jimmy.

"Well," informed Salvus, "when the guests come down the rear staircase for their exercise, their assigned Reclaimers are at their sides."

"But the assigned Reclaimers are also at their sides in the guests' room," reminded Jimmy.

"Yes," replied Salvus, "but if you try to rescue the residents as they're descending the staircase or within the guests' room, then you also have to battle another forty or so Reclaimers who are in the castle. But if we wait until tonight, when the majority of the Reclaimers are hunting in the forest, we'll have to deal with only the ten or so Reclaimers upstairs and the one monitoring the Hall of Admittance."

Salvus accepted the boiling stew again from Sam.

"You're probably right," agreed Cindy, "tonight won't be easy, but it will be safer—relatively speaking."

Once all had eaten, though not necessarily their fill, Cindy gathered the surplus food, which she and her friends had set aside, neared the dumbwaiter, and equally stored the provisions among the four backpacks.

"I'll see if I can gather more food," volunteered Salvus.

"Thanks," replied Sam.

Jimmy, who had resumed his meticulous inspection of the torture wall, turned to the satyr and asked, "Salvus, do the Pedwhips ever come down to the dungeon? I mean, should we worry they might spot us and alert the Reclaimers?"

"No," replied Salvus, "you're perfectly safe down here. It's only with great difficulty the Pedwhips carry food to the sixth floor with their front pincers, eight legs, and fins. And this they endure so as not to suffer the consequences of an irate Reclaimer. Trust me, they won't risk coming down these unsteady steps to inspect a foul dungeon. Besides, the Reclaimers overwork them so much in the garden and orchard they wouldn't have the time or energy to visit the lowest region of the castle."

With Jimmy's mind eased, Salvus rose to his hoofs in search of more food.

As the satyr climbed the steps, Sam quietly ordered his friends to gather their personal belongings and do the best they could to cram them into their backpacks, along with the food. "We must be ready," he warned, "at a moment's notice."

At Sam's suggestion, the travelers rolled up their sleeping gear, gathered what few possessions rested on the dirt floor, and packed them away. Dan purposely kept William's stuffed animal and holy water atop his belongings, in the event the situation called for either one.

Nearly thirty minutes later, the satyr returned lugging two wooden platters.

Looking at the amount of food, Sam confessed, "Salvus, I don't think we have extra room in our bags for all that."

Stepping across the floor to an old crate, Salvus kicked open the box and grabbed a weather-beaten canvas bag that still had a little life left. After dumping the extra food into the bag, he handed it to Sam by its frayed straps.

"Thanks, Salvus," replied Sam.

Knowing their departure was nearly upon them, Sam confessed, "Salvus, I wish there was something we could do to repay your hospitality."

"You already have," replied the satyr, "your company."

Dan stepped forward and pleaded, "Salvus, are you sure you won't come with us?"

As much as the satyr longed to travel with his friends, the fear of the forest and the possible annihilation of his species prevented him from accepting the invitation. "I'm sorry," he replied, "it's a long story, but...no, I can't."

Placing his hand upon Salvus' shoulder, Sam reminded, "Okay, when we come down the main stairs leading to the Grand Foyer, hopefully with William, you'll be sure to keep the Reclaimer who's on duty out of sight."

"Absolutely," promised Salvus. "You just be sure to get these youngsters out safely."

"Don't worry," replied Sam, "I will."

"And one more thing," insisted Salvus, "don't leave this dungeon until I visit the main level, to make sure the Reclaimers have left, and return to guide you to the guests' room."

"But, Salvus," remarked Sam, "you've been enough help already; we can find our way to the sixth floor."

"Absolutely not," warned the satyr. "There are too many disguised dangers along the way. For your own safety, wait for my return."

Realizing Salvus knew the castle and its deadly enticements better than anyone, Sam agreed to his demand.

At precisely 8:00 p.m., Salvus climbed the dungeon steps and dawdled around the kitchen area. He occupied most of his time talking with Marcus in the kitchen and in the adjoining rooms, but always maintaining a watchful eye and an attentive ear for any movement or sound in the Grand Foyer. As the satyr feared, the first Reclaimer down the Grand Staircase was Talus, who would be monitoring the Hall of Admittance that night and early morning.

Watching Talus cling to the banister with his human hands, while his snakelike lower body slid from step to step, was comical to Salvus. *It's no wonder they stay upstairs as much as they do,* he thought.

A noisy uproar was heard from the Grand Staircase, as well as around the corner. Without delay, thirty to forty Reclaimers descended upon the Grand Foyer, each equipped with a bow and arrow. Although the snake-men had embarked upon many similar expeditions over the centuries, Salvus never once witnessed a convergence of such magnitude. It was a horrible sight to behold.

As the satyr stood in the doorway, between the Grand Foyer and the hallway leading to the kitchen, the Reclaimers slithered by, though not a single one acknowledged his presence.

Marcus, who had recently exited the kitchen to witness the Reclaimers' gathering, stood behind Salvus, watching the tail end of the hunters depart the castle. "What a ghastly sight," he whispered.

"Yeah," agreed Salvus, "what a sight."

Marcus suspected Salvus was up to something. After all, the head cook couldn't remember the last time the satyr visited him twice in the same day and never had he witnessed Salvus' presence during the Reclaimers' mass exit to the forest. "Are you alright?" he asked.

"Sure," answered Salvus. "Why?"

"Well," replied Marcus, "it's just that I haven't seen you—never mind." As the two advanced down the narrow hallway, he asked, "Salvus, would you mind giving me a hand in the kitchen?"

"If it's all the same," suggested Salvus, "maybe I could help you later tonight. I've got a melody to rehearse."

"Oh, that's right," recalled Marcus, as the two entered the kitchen. "I nearly forgot. Go ahead and practice; I'll see you after the recital."

Salvus quickly exited the kitchen and descended the dungeon staircase, where his friends were anxiously waiting.

"They've just left the castle—all thirty or more," updated Salvus. "They must be after something of great importance, since all the unassigned Reclaimers were geared with bows and arrows."

"What about the drawbridge?" asked Sam.

"What do you mean?" inquired Salvus.

"When we arrived at the castle the other morning," explained Sam, "it was closed."

Lifting Cindy's bag and handing it to her, Salvus replied, "Yeah, it's closed on nights when the trolls are abnormally unruly, but never when the Reclaimers are on a hunt. This way, the bridge is always open, since no one knows for sure when they'll return. Trust me, it'll remain open tonight."

"But on nights when the drawbridge is closed," asked Dan, "what happens if an ailing person is seeking relief in the castle?"

"On those rare evenings," related Salvus, "several Reclaimers patrol from the heights of the castle, searching for future guests."

"But why," asked Jimmy, "weren't we discovered?"

"I'd presume," interrupted Sam, "because we were crawling on our stomachs."

"Probably," said Salvus, "but more than likely, you were just lucky. Very little movement escapes the attention of the Reclaimers."

By now, everyone had their bags strapped to their shoulders and their reflective pieces in hand. Since the travelers had never visited the sixth floor, Salvus grabbed the lantern to guide the group.

"Salvus," said Dan, while standing at the entrance to the corner staircase, "the last time—" He was prepared to forewarn that the last time he attempted to visit the sixth floor, the access panel was nailed shut. In a split second, however, he recalled that the hidden staircase within the acoustical tunnel—and not the corner staircase before the group—led him to the sixth floor…and beyond. He opted against mentioning the undiscovered hidden staircase and his sole journey to the castle roof.

"The last time what?" asked Salvus.

Without skipping a beat, Dan successfully covered his tracks, "Is this the last time we'll see you?"

"I'm afraid so," replied the satyr. "When you leave the guests' room, you must flee immediately to the forest. Only the shadowy woodlands will conceal you from the Reclaimers."

After removing the final board from the corner staircase at 8:15 p.m., the five began their ascent with great trepidation. En route, Salvus whispered to his friends that the moment they enter the room through the secret access panel, strict silence must be observed, since that particular room was directly across the hallway from the guests' room. Finally, he made the travelers promise they would not step foot inside the guests' room until they heard his music echoing from the dungeon. That would be the signal Talus, the Reclaimer on duty, was distracted.

Squatting upon the sixth floor landing, the satyr quietly wedged open the passageway door, revealing a small bedroom that was partially furnished with a bed and tall dresser.

In complete silence, the travelers removed their backpacks and set them in the middle of the floor beside the lantern.

Since the Reclaimers were already dead, Salvus reminded his friends their lances would be useless and suggested they leave their weapons in the bedroom with their bags. "You'll need complete concentration and the use of both hands on your reflective pieces," he warned, "to outsmart the snake-men."

Before his departure, the travelers shook Salvus' hand, except Cindy, who gave him a hug and quietly thanked him. Seconds after crawling through the passageway, the satyr poked his head into the bedroom and whispered, "Remember, listen for the music."

Only now admitting to himself the travelers' reflective pieces might prove ineffective against the Reclaimers, Salvus purposely left the access panel wedged open in the unfortunate event the group needed to flee the guests' room to the limited safety of the corner staircase.

With the satyr's departure, the travelers remained fixated on the bedroom's doorknob, while maintaining a firm grasp on their defensive armor.

Salvus descended the stone steps to the dungeon, covered the entrance to the corner staircase, scaled the steps to the kitchen, and entered the Grand Foyer. He stopped immediately before the door to the Hall of Admittance, took a deep breath, and then rapped the door with his knuckles.

From inside came an austere voice, "Have you come seeking relief?"

"It's Salvus," replied the satyr, from the opposite side of the door.

"Salvus, eh," remarked Talus. "What do you want?"

After another deep breath, he asked, "May I enter?"

"You may proceed," granted Talus.

As Salvus turned the lopsided snake-head doorknob, he trembled; he and Talus had met privately many years ago, which rekindled his extreme loathing of the Reclaimer and fueled his mounting apprehension.

Inside the Hall of Admittance sat Talus, coiled on a red carpet with his upper body supported vertically.

Salvus advanced and bowed.

"What do you want?" demanded the Reclaimer.

Mindful that the safety of his friends, five floors above, depended on his successful distraction of Talus, the satyr collected the courage to calm his voice, conquer his shakes, and boldly offer, "Sir Talus, since you're alone on duty tonight, I thought I'd honor you with some music."

Aware the Reclaimers valued his music and the Pedwhips' food preparations, both castle-working species knew the snake-men would never purposely inflict physical harm or mental persuasion upon them, unless of course, they did something unforgivable which merited such actions. In the not too distant past, a Pedwhip attempted to speak to a guest. Although the elderly woman was unable or unwilling to respond, the Pedwhip's action was deemed worthy of severe physical punishment.

"Why would you play music just for me?" questioned a suspicious Reclaimer.

"Sir Talus," schemed Salvus, "I thought you, of all the Reclaimers, deserved to be treated better than the rest. After all, you should have the sovereign honors which were wrongfully bestowed upon Spiritus Malus."

Engaging his mighty posterior muscles, Talus lifted himself higher above the carpet, glared at the satyr, and declared, "You speak the truth. And because of this, I will permit you to entertain me."

"Thank you, Sir Talus," replied Salvus, before a slight bow. He knew, however, for the travelers to hear his music, he had to play in the dungeon near the acoustic tunnels. But in order to lure Talus to the lower level, he had to fabricate a believable story. "One last thing," he requested, "if I may."

"You may speak," permitted the Reclaimer.

"Perhaps I can entertain you in the dungeon," he suggested, "which is where my lyre is now."

"Why should I go to the foul dungeon?" demanded Talus. "Bring the music to me!"

Fully aware of certain torture, should his plot be unearthed, Salvus, nevertheless, continued, "If you'll pardon me, Sir Talus, there's something you must see in the dungeon; something no other Reclaimer has been privileged to view."

Mildly curious, Talus ordered, "Bring it to me!"

"Sir Talus," replied Salvus, "forgive me, but it's something no one else should see, not even the castle workers—only you."

Talus suspected deception, but agreed, nonetheless, stating, "Very well; you may follow me to the dungeon."

The satyr bowed and remained in a stooped position, until the creature slithered beyond him. He knew that with nothing to present Talus in the dungeon, he was engaging in a treacherous act that in Talus' eyes would be unpardonable and therefore punishable. Trailing the Reclaimer to the kitchen, Salvus calmed his fears by thinking of the travelers' eventual safe retreat to the forest. Upon exiting the kitchen, he was grateful Marcus was nowhere around.

During the Reclaimer's awkward descent of the dungeon steps, Salvus implored, "Sir Talus, please pardon my humble quarters, but

I cleaned it as best I could for your audience." Thankfully, he had replaced the boards over the corner staircase entrance upon his return from the sixth floor.

Glancing around the area, Talus stated insultingly, "What a wretched place!"

•

On the sixth floor, the travelers were restless with the sound of no music.

"What's keeping Salvus?" asked Cindy.

"I don't know," replied Sam, "but we must be patient. I'm sure he'll start playing soon." Glancing to the middle of the room, he wondered how on earth they'd carry their bags that were bulging with food, not to mention an ailing person—presuming William was across the hallway.

With his back facing his friends, Dan secretly transferred the stuffed animal from his backpack to his sweatshirt pocket. Pleased with his covert accomplishment, he stepped alongside the closed bedroom door.

First in line for the five-foot odyssey across the hall was Dan, wielding the silver shield, followed by Jimmy and Sam, both brandishing a reflective silver platter, and finally Cindy, holding a large piece of broken mirror.

"Come on, Salvus," whispered Dan, "play."

•

In the lowest region of the castle, Talus demanded, "Show me what's unworthy of anyone else's sight."

"If you please, Sir Talus," implored Salvus, in an effort to delay the Reclaimer's request, "I'd like to play a melody first, one which I composed for your future ceremony, naming you as sovereign of the Reclaimers."

"Very well," replied an arrogant Talus, "you may regale me."

"Thank you, Sir Talus," replied a grateful satyr, before grabbing his lyre from the ground and playing Marcus' favorite tune.

●

The door on the sixth floor bedroom opened, producing a soft squeak. With Dan in the lead, the group crossed the poorly lit hallway; Dan rested his hand upon the doorknob of the guests' room. Within seconds of glancing back to confirm his friends had their protective shields raised, he turned the knob. Throwing open the door, the travelers invaded the sacrosanct quarters, screening their faces.

Immediately, shrieks were heard, as the assigned Reclaimers turned to face the disruption at the doorway and inadvertently glimpsed their sordid souls and their countless missed opportunities to inflict evil upon humanity. Viewing their inner reflections, the snake-men suffered a temporary loss of their physical strength and supernatural powers. They dropped and helplessly squirmed upon the cold floor.

With their eyes protected behind their glistening shields, the trespassers spread out and stepped among the immobilized Reclaimers on their advance toward the cots. Glancing occasionally below their protective armor, the intruders poorly maneuvered the room. Since Dan and Jimmy were the only two who most likely could recognize William, they maintained the lead, between the two rows of cots that lined the walls.

The first guest Dan eyed from beneath his shield, as he leaned in and over the individual, was a middle-aged woman, who remained silent, not even stirring when he lowered his face alongside hers.

Cindy and Sam, who lingered a few feet behind the young men, cautiously placed one foot in front of the other, sidestepping the incapacitated Reclaimers.

Dan soon realized the incessant wailing of the snake-men had stopped. *Perhaps they're slowly adjusting their eyes to the shields,* he thought. Darting to the third cot, before the Reclaimers fully recovered their mind-controlling strengths, he leaned in and placed his face beside a guest, whom he discovered was an elderly man, probably in his late seventies.

A scream was heard near the open door, followed by a loud crash; Cindy had dropped her mirror and collapsed to the floor. A Reclaimer had regained his former powers and had invaded the area between her and the protective mirror.

"Cindy!" yelled Sam, with his face hidden behind the reflective platter.

There was no response.

Trembling beyond belief, Dan froze, but only for a moment. A risky, though potentially promising, idea came to mind. "Jimmy," he yelled, "follow me back to the door."

With one eye shut for added defense, Jimmy yelled, "What?"

Pulling his shield even closer to his body, after noticing a snake's tail directly below, Dan ordered, "Walk with me to the door!"

"Why?"

"Just do it!"

The men retraced their steps to the doorway.

With his face protected behind a silver platter, Sam failed to notice his companions nearing the open door, though he did overhear a hushed conversation between the two. His attention shifted immediately from deciphering their comments to a Reclaimer's tail grazing his calf; he closed his eyes as tightly as he could.

The snake-men, nearly restored to their previous strengths, slithered amid the trespassers, hoping to entrap them, but careful never to raise their sights above the floor.

Once the touch left his leg, Sam opened one eye and inched to the right, carefully scanning the ground below his protective platter for Cindy's body. "There she is," he whispered. Unfortunately, before sliding his foot one step closer, he spotted a serpent's tail and saw Cindy's body lifted from the floor.

A revived Reclaimer had taken possession of the young traveler.

"Jimmy," divulged Dan, as he stood near the room's entrance, "I've got an idea, but I need to go across the hallway for something; wait here." Spotting a serpent's tail directly below his shield, he closed his eyes and bashed his armor against the head of an advancing Reclaimer.

After regaining his composure, he ordered, "Stay here, Jimmy; but get Sam's lighter, while I'm across the hall. Do you understand?"

"Yeah," replied a trembling Jimmy, "stay here."

Taking advantage of his friend's close proximity, Dan kicked him in the shin and yelled, "Get Sam's lighter, now!"

"Okay," acknowledged Jimmy, "get Sam's lighter."

Grasping the doorknob, Dan walked backwards through the room's entrance and pulled the door closed behind him, without his protective shield ever dropping below his eyes. In the safety of the hallway, he was surprised a Reclaimer hadn't followed him. *Maybe,* he thought, *by staying behind, the Reclaimers think they'll increase their odds with one less invader.* He quickly cleared his mind; he had a more important issue at hand. Closing the door of the bedroom, which he had just entered, he dropped to his knees and ripped open his backpack, with his shield close at hand, in the event a Reclaimer bolted into the room intent on one-on-one combat. After removing the votive candle that Father James Roberts had blessed before the travelers' transworld journey, he thought, *So, the Reclaimers aren't afraid of light, but what about holy light? It's a chance I have to take.*

Across the hall, Jimmy met up with Sam, who at first mistook him for the enemy and jumped.

"They've got Cindy," informed Sam.

"I figured that," he replied.

"How's Dan?"

"He's fine," answered Jimmy, "he's across the hall."

"He's where?"

Ignoring Sam's question, Jimmy ordered, "Give me your lighter."

After kicking a tail that was slithering between his legs, Sam demanded, "What for?"

Becoming annoyed with Sam's questions, Jimmy yelled, "Give me your lighter, now!"

Clutching the silver platter with one hand, Sam lowered the other into his pants pocket and pulled out the lighter. Handing it to Jimmy, he asked, "What are you two up to?"

Jimmy offered no response, partly because he thought the conversation had gone on too long, but primarily because he didn't know what Dan was plotting.

In the bedroom across the hall, Dan rose to his feet, put the blessed candle in his sweatshirt pocket—alongside the stuffed animal—raised his shield, and walked to the door. With his free hand resting on the doorknob, but before turning it, he quickly implored, "Saint Michael, watch over us."

With the brief, but sincere, prayer uttered, the bedroom door flew open and he was approaching the closed door of the guests' room. With his shield barely two inches from his face, he opened the door and entered. Behind his protective armor, he yelled, "Jimmy!" No response was heard. A second time, "Jimmy!"

"Over here," yelled his friend.

"Keep talking until I reach you," ordered Dan.

Not knowing what to yell, partly due to his escalating fears, Jimmy kept repeating, "Dan, Dan, Dan!"

Walking cautiously in the direction of the oncoming voice, Dan soon found himself standing beside Jimmy and Sam. Beneath their protective shields, the men counted five tails.

"Do you have the lighter?" asked Dan.

"Yeah," replied Jimmy.

Dan grabbed the lighter. With one hand supporting his shield and the other holding the lighter, he needed a third to remove the candle from his pocket. "Jimmy," he ordered, "take the lighter back."

"What?"

"Take the lighter back!" yelled Dan.

Jimmy snatched the lighter; Dan removed the votive candle.

"Jimmy," he continued, while holding the candle near his friend's side, "light it, now!"

With his protective platter firmly grasped in one hand, Jimmy lit the candle.

Without delay, deafening shrieks—louder than the previous screams of agony—forced Sam and Jimmy to drop their protective armor, close their eyes, and cover their ears. Dan nearly dropped the candle, but miraculously maintained a grasp on it and endured the cries of torment. His shield, however, fell to the floor, as he also closed his eyes.

On hearing the piercing screams in the dungeon through the acoustic tunnels, Talus strongly suspected Salvus was behind this latest insurrection.

As the satyr raised his head from his lyre and displayed a noticeable grin, Talus, who was only feet away, whipped his powerful tail at Salvus, knocking him against the fireplace. During the collision, he struck his head against the hearth and fell unconscious.

Furious he had been duped, Talus took hold of the motionless satyr, dragged his prisoner across the dirt floor, and chained him to the torture wall.

With the candle's flame illuminating the guests' room, the men eyed the Reclaimers slithering between the cots to the farthest wall from the candle and coiling themselves atop one another. They used their human hands and snake tails to shield their eyes from the afflictive blaze. For the first time since their banishment from hell, they were enduring unbearable and prolonged anguish.

Spotting Cindy on the first cot, the men dashed to her side. She, too, like the guests, was in a trance state. Hoping she would snap out of it, since she only recently had slipped into her hypnotic state, Sam and Jimmy dropped to their knees, one on either side of the cot, and attempted to elicit a response from her. With no reaction, Sam tapped her cheeks.

With Sam and Jimmy at Cindy's side, Dan set the candle to the floor and searched the remaining cots for William. In his haste, he slipped on a piece of glass from Cindy's broken mirror that had scattered nearly halfway up the guests' room. Using a nearby cot to lift himself, he glanced at the guest on the canvas bed. "William?" he whispered. Seeing the guest's distinctive birthmark on his neck, which he now remembered seeing as a child, he raised his voice and asserted, "William, it's me—Dan."

In his hypnotic state, the young man offered no response, regard-less of Dan's pleading.

Removing the stuffed animal from his pocket, Dan held it in front of his older brother.

Again, William offered no reaction.

Dan returned the heirloom to his sweatshirt.

Seven cots behind, Cindy jerked uncontrollably, before gradually escaping her trance.

"Cindy," whispered Jimmy, "are you alright?"

She remained silent.

"Cindy," pleaded Sam, "say something."

She blinked; with great difficulty, she mumbled, "Eyes…his eyes—"

"Yes," prodded Sam, "what about his eyes?"

"The blue flames of hell," she revealed, "in his eyes; the fires of—" She turned her head on the pillow in complete horror.

Resting his hand on her head, Sam consoled, "You're safe now. The Reclaimers won't spellbind you anymore; I promise."

"The blue flames of hell?" questioned Jimmy.

Directing his gaze across the cot, Sam explained, "As with any fire, the blue flames are the hottest. And since the Reclaimers were once confined to the pit of hell, I'm sure they suffered the most intense heat, which is what I presume Cindy looked upon."

A squeak captured the attention of Sam, who looked over Jimmy's shoulder and saw Dan lifting a young man from a cot. "Is that—"

Sam hadn't finished his question, when Jimmy turned and blurted, "Oh, my gosh, it's William." He jumped to his feet and darted to the Clay brothers. "William," he exclaimed, "it's me, Jimmy—you know, the kid next door."

William remained motionless and silent.

Dan jerked his head, when he detected movement at the back of the room.

A Reclaimer was slithering backwards, very erratically, and wildly whipping his tail. The snake-man was determined to reach the candle at the far end of the room and snuff out the flame.

Even though the Reclaimer was far removed from the candle,

Dan wasn't taking any chances. "Here, Jimmy," he ordered, "hold William for a minute." Nearing Sam, he asked, "How is she?"

"I think she'll be fine," predicted Sam, "but it will take a little time. She's been through a hellish ordeal."

Placing his face next to her ear, Dan whispered, "We'll be right back; Sam and I need to do something."

To the surprise of her co-travelers, Cindy nodded slightly.

The men knew she'd be fine.

After grabbing the blessed candle from the floor, Dan insisted, "We need to raise this, so the Reclaimers can't extinguish the blaze with their tails."

"Good idea," said Sam, as he followed Dan's visual search overhead. No additional words were spoken. Sam squatted to the floor; Dan sat atop his shoulders. Bracing himself against a cot, Sam lifted his friend.

Positioning the glowing candle within the chandelier took a few moments longer than expected, since Dan wanted to be certain it was anchored securely.

Back on the ground, Sam slapped Dan on the back and praised, "Your candle idea…that was brilliant…absolutely brilliant."

"Yeah, Dan," seconded Jimmy from across the room, "that was awesome."

As Dan expected, William made no response or gesture. Glancing at Cindy, he noticed her raise a thumb, as her approval of a job well done, though no words were spoken.

"Dan," asked Sam, "how long will this candle burn?"

After glancing above to confirm the candle was still stable, he answered, "It's a two-hour votive candle, which means we have to move fast. Let's get these guests downstairs."

"Guests?" questioned Jimmy.

"Yes," replied Dan, "we're taking all of them."

"But, Dan," challenged Sam, "we can't attend to all their needs during our return trip; besides, we don't have a surplus of Doctor O'Brien's pills."

This was one dispute Dan was determined to win. With steadfast conviction, he promised, "We'll manage somehow; they all have families, too—just like William." He returned to Jimmy's side and took his brother into his arms; it had been a long time. Sadly, there was no return of affection. William's arms dangled at his sides, as Dan supported him. *But for now,* Dan thought, *this will have to do.* He was happy to have him alive.

"If we're taking all the guests," reminded Sam, "we better move."

Releasing his embrace, Dan rested William against his side and helped him out of the room and down the Grand Staircase. Sam lifted Cindy from the cot and carried her down the steps, as Jimmy helped the elderly man escape. Once in the Grand Foyer, William, Cindy, and the elderly man were placed on the floor and leaned against a wall. No one would be escorted outside the castle until all residents were freed from the sixth floor guests' room.

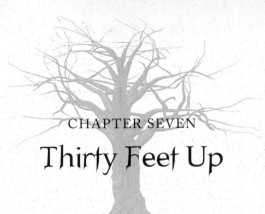

CHAPTER SEVEN

Thirty Feet Up

SALVUS WAS BRUTALLY AWAKENED BY A THRASH ON HIS BACK from a homemade leather whip.

Hearing he was conscious, Talus released a second lash and accused, "That's for deceiving me."

Salvus let out a slight moan.

With a third scourge, the Reclaimer charged, "And that's for being a satyr."

Slithering to the torture wall, Talus placed his head alongside Salvus', yanked the satyr's head back by his lengthy hair, and recalled, "Ah, this brings back such fond memories. Why it seems like only yesterday you were chained to this very wall and I was whipping you for helping an elderly guest to her feet after a stumble."

Talus slithered back to the fireplace and unleashed a fourth powerful blow, denouncing, "And that's for your repulsive kindness." He took a momentary break, leaned against the hearth and declared, "I know the screeches of the Reclaimers upstairs are your doing and they probably need rescuing. But I'm having far too much fun down here torturing you. After all, if the guests are escaping, the moment they step beyond the castle walls, their ailments will return and they, in turn, will return to their cots. Let my miserable co-Reclaimers suffer for all I care."

With a fifth thrash of the whip, Salvus screamed; he couldn't endure the pain any longer, much to the pleasure of Talus.

With William resting comfortably in the Grand Foyer, Dan was prepared to race back to the sixth floor when Sam intercepted him and insisted, "Stay here with your brother. You've waited a long time for this reunion. Jimmy and I will help the remaining guests from the room."

"Thanks, Sam, but we don't have a lot of time." Darting up the staircase two steps at a time, enduring the pain in his leg, he reached the guests' room in record time. Glancing down the narrow room, he estimated there were nearly a hundred cots, evenly divided along two walls. To the left of the distant wall, next to the coiling Reclaimers, he spotted a small inner room. After snatching his shield from the floor, he verified the Reclaimers were still powerless by kicking the tail of a snake-man; the creature remained motionless. Assured it was safe, he stepped into the secret room, where he discovered a miniature library, complete with ancient manuscripts and hardbacks resting flat on several warped bookshelves. He approached a small desk in the corner of the room. Resting on the furniture was an oversize, leather-bound book which was open, but positioned upside down, with its pages facing the desktop. Before lifting it, he read its title, *Healing Elixirs and Practical Potions*. The curious traveler raised the book from the desk and turned it over to reveal the marked page.

"God, no," he whispered.

Knowing he couldn't lug the large volume through the forest, he ripped the page from the book, hopeful there were no other copies in the main library and that the Reclaimers hadn't memorized the particular spell.

"Dan, are you here?" was heard from the main room.

Pushing himself from the desk, the teenager poked his head through the entry of the small library and yelled, "Yeah, Sam, I'm coming."

On seeing his head emerge from the inner room, Sam motioned for him to come along and then exited the guests' room.

Dan folded the ancient parchment entitled "Relocating Portals" and shoved it in his pocket. Though unsure whether or not the

Reclaimers had begun concocting the dreadful potion, he was convinced, now more than ever, he and his companions had to reach the
enchanted oak as quickly as possible. He grabbed his shield and darted
from the secret room. After taking one final look at the Reclaimers—
who remained coiled, but now shivering—he bolted to the opposite
end of the room and slammed the door behind him, making the holy
light as intense as possible.

Sam was three flights down, as Dan reached the top of the Grand
Staircase. Descending the steps, he was intercepted on the fifth floor
by a Pedwhip. With his shield firmly clenched, but with no weapon,
he was startled and defenseless.

"Excuse me," greeted the Pedwhip, "I mean you no harm. My
name is Marcus, one of the kitchen cooks."

"What do you want?" asked an uneasy Dan.

"I know you're Salvus' friend," replied the Pedwhip. "I suspected
he was hiding and feeding you and your companions in the dungeon,
but I said nothing to the Reclaimers or other members of my species
because Salvus' friends are also my friends."

"What do you want?" asked Dan a second time.

"Salvus is a good friend of mine," admitted Marcus. "The
Reclaimer, Talus, has him chained to a wall in the dungeon and is
torturing him."

Before another word was spoken, Dan was racing down the Grand
Staircase, gripping his shield. He stopped abruptly on the third floor
landing; a semi-human scream echoed through the castle. Scheming
a rescue plan, he raced back to Marcus' side and demanded, "Get me
a candle, now!"

"I'm sorry," he remarked, "the Reclaimers don't allow candles in
the castle."

"What about the candles in the pet room?" inquired Dan.

A bewildered look draped the Pedwhip's face before asking, "How
do you know about—"

"Marcus," interrupted Dan, "what about the candles in the pet
room on the second floor?"

"The Shamus Seeker," reminded Marcus, "would drain the life
from us within seconds, which wouldn't help Salvus' situation."

"Think, Marcus," ordered Dan. "Salvus' life may very well depend on it."

The Pedwhip raised a pincer to scratch the back of his neck, while trying to recall where a candle may be hidden in the castle. "Wait a minute," he blurted, "follow me."

The human and the Pedwhip dashed down the fifth floor hallway to an overcrowded closet, where castle supplies and guests' possessions were stored.

Once inside the room, Marcus disclosed, "I remember seeing a candle here when I was looking for an apple picker, but my gosh, that was so many years ago."

"Where are the surplus candles for the pet room stored?" asked Dan.

"I don't know," confessed Marcus. "The Reclaimers are the only ones who know their whereabouts."

Dan joined in the search by wildly throwing lids off boxes and bursting open containers, until finally, "Here it is!" announced an excited Pedwhip.

Dan grabbed the half-spent candle. In a flash, he was rushing up the hallway to the Grand Staircase, bearing the candle and shield. He took an immediate right and scaled the final flight of stairs, where he darted into the bedroom that concealed the secret passageway and dragged its dresser into the guests' room across the hall. While positioning the chest of drawers beneath the chandelier, he thought, *I hope this works. Can the qualities of a holy flame be transferred to another candle, making it also a holy flame?* He wasn't sure, but he was sure he had to try. Climbing atop the dresser, he touched the unlit candle to the burning flame of the votive candle. Using a hand to protect the newborn blaze from the breeze in the well-ventilated room, he jumped from the dresser and was closing the door behind him when he hatched another idea. *What about a surprise attack?* he thought.

The traveler entered the small bedroom, crawled through the open access panel, and descended to the lowest region of the castle. Within minutes, he was standing behind the boarded entry to the dungeon with the candle brilliantly aglow. Between the slats, he witnessed Talus raising a whip against Salvus.

If the candle doesn't work, he thought, *at least I have my shield.*

With a powerful kick, the passageway boards flew across the dungeon; two planks smashed into several pieces upon impact with the fireplace. The candle's glow invaded the dungeon. Before Talus could turn to see what had disturbed his enjoyment, he, like his co-Reclaimers earlier, let out a high-pitched shriek and fell to the floor.

After scrambling through the opening and securing the candle on an overhead beam, well out of reach of Talus' tail, Dan raced to Salvus. Enraged at seeing his friend's arms and goat legs chained to the wall, he yanked the key from a nail on the fireplace and freed him.

The satyr fell backwards into his arms.

With great pains, Dan assisted the satyr in his climb up the dungeon steps and through the kitchen. From the hallway adjoining the kitchen, he peered into the Grand Foyer and was comforted at seeing Cindy wide-awake and coherent. *Thankfully,* he thought, *she wasn't under the Reclaimers' power very long.*

While Dan was rescuing Salvus in the dungeon, Jimmy had grabbed two bags—Cindy's and Dan's—from the upstairs bedroom for the clothing inside. Since the number of guests and travelers exceeded the number of bandannas that were fashioned before the group's entry into the castle, Cindy, Jimmy, and Sam were ripping old clothing and converting them into makeshift facial coverings for the guests to deter the mental effects of the poisonous atmosphere, once they passed beyond the castle walls.

Stepping into the Grand Foyer, with his arm secured around Salvus' waist, Dan eyed Cindy securing a bandanna over William's face.

On spotting Dan and the injured satyr, the travelers rushed to his aid.

"What happened to him?" demanded an irate Cindy.

"One of the Reclaimers," replied Dan, "was having a field day with him on the dungeon's torture wall." Redirecting his stare from Salvus to Cindy, he asked, "How are you feeling?"

"Much better," she replied. "Jimmy told me what you did up there; thanks."

"Don't mention it," said Dan, who quickly added, "is the whiskey in one of those bags?"

"Yeah," answered Cindy, "for Salvus?"

"Yes," he replied. "He should be treated before we leave; he's going with us."

With difficulty, Salvus raised his head from Dan's shoulder and mumbled, "No, please; I can't."

"Salvus," warned Dan, "it's too dangerous now for you to remain in the castle."

For the satyr's own safety, Cindy also attempted to persuade him to leave with the group by admitting, "Besides, we could benefit from your knowledge of this world's oddities on our journey back."

Salvus was too weak to argue.

After helping the satyr to a wall in the Grand Foyer, Dan gently placed him on his stomach; Cindy lowered the upper portion of his toga and then opened the whiskey bottle. Detecting movement from the corner of his eye, Dan turned and spotted Marcus approaching from the Grand Staircase.

"Thank you," expressed the Pedwhip, "for saving Salvus."

"Um…listen, Marcus," explained Dan, "Salvus isn't safe anymore in the castle."

"Yes," he agreed, "I know."

"Anyway," continued Dan, "it would be better for him if he went with us. Do you understand?"

"Of course," answered Marcus, "I agree, though he will be sorely missed."

Dan looked down at Salvus, then back to the head cook and asked with genuine interest, "Marcus, will you and the other Pedwhips be safe in the castle, when the rest of the Reclaimers return from their hunt?"

"Oh, yeah," replied a confident Marcus, "we'll be fine; especially since none of the assigned Reclaimers saw us aiding the guests in their escape. But I appreciate your concern." With his sights now fixed beyond the open drawbridge, he wished, "Good luck with your return journey."

"Thanks," voiced Dan, before directing his attention to his brother. "William," he prodded, to draw a response. Ultimately, he wasn't surprised with his brother's silence. *After all*, he thought, *William's probably been in a trance state for years and likely hasn't spoken a word since his abduction.* Reaching for his bag that was resting on the floor beside Cindy, he blurted, "Oh, my gosh, I almost forgot."

"Forgot what?" asked Cindy.

After pulling a medication bottle from his bag, Dan reminded, "William's asthma pills from Doctor O'Brien."

"Oh, that's right," recalled Cindy, before lowering William's frayed bandanna.

Dan extended the pill to his brother's lips and gently, but firmly, commanded, "Okay, William, open up."

Even though Cindy and Dan were not expecting a verbal response, they were surprised when he opened his mouth.

Dan dropped the pill on his brother's tongue and instructed, "Swallow." He heard a gulp. Looking at Cindy, he admitted, "Well, that went a lot easier than I thought it would." Resting his hand on his brother's shoulder, he congratulated, "Good job."

Cindy raised her eyes and looked to the left; Dan did likewise. All the guests, Salvus, and the travelers were present and accounted for. Estimating the Reclaimers would descend the Grand Staircase in less than ninety minutes, Dan directed the travelers to help the guests over the drawbridge and into the clearing.

Taking the lead, Dan raised William to his feet, replaced the bandanna over his nose and mouth, and helped him beyond the castle entry and over the drawbridge to the grassy area. Five paces behind, Sam was assisting Salvus, Jimmy was escorting an elderly man, and Cindy was guiding a middle-aged woman to freedom.

The men returned to free another round of guests; Cindy remained in the clearing, keeping a watchful eye on the first shipment of evacuees. As the second group of residents stepped off the drawbridge, the middle-aged woman and the elderly man, from the first delivery, had become restless. Before the third round of castle dwellers cleared the entry of the fortress, the middle-aged woman and the elderly man staggered to their feet and retreated over the drawbridge; a man from the second group of deserters, who suffered from leprosy, immediately followed. On seeing members of the first and second groups withdrawing, Dan grabbed the arm of the castle-bound woman from the first round of evacuations, while supporting a man from the third group. To his astonishment, the woman exhibited forceful resistance, leading him to fear her volatile behavior might land her in the moat and in the jaws of the eel. With regret, he allowed the woman and her two male companions re-entry into the castle.

Dan resumed delivering the guest on his arm to the clearing, where he witnessed Cindy's unsuccessful efforts at persuading the depleting number of guests to remain seated on the ground.

Once the three returning residents were sitting inside the Grand Foyer entry, the travelers noticed a marked improvement in their physical conditions. Granted, their relief was only partial; but the moment their assigned Reclaimers returned to their sides, they would experience complete recovery. Within minutes, all the residents had either returned to the Grand Foyer or were en route. Sam, Dan, and Jimmy stationed themselves in the middle of the drawbridge, attempting to direct the returning guests back to Cindy. Considering the feeble state of the residents, the men were amazed with their tenacious opposition; it was a losing battle for the liberators.

"Dan," reminded Sam, "we can't force them to come with us, no matter how much we'd like them to."

Sensing defeat, Dan unwillingly yielded, until he saw William approaching the center of the drawbridge. He neared his sibling to foil his retreat to the castle.

Like the residents before, William resisted violently.

It was obvious to Dan the asthma medication had not yet eased his symptoms.

Although beset with labored breathing, William battled his younger brother, until Sam stepped forward and delivered a flawless uppercut, knocking the older sibling out cold.

"Sam!" yelled Dan. "What'd you do that for?"

Bending over to help Dan lift his brother, he explained, "Look, we've come too far to go home empty-handed."

Jimmy, who remained standing above his co-travelers, seconded Sam's explanation.

Of course he's right, thought Dan, *but he didn't have to knock him senseless.*

Dan and Sam dragged William from the drawbridge to the grassy area.

In the end, the four original travelers, Salvus, and William remained in the clearing, as the guests sat upon the floor near the Grand Foyer entrance, awaiting the return of their assigned Reclaimers from the sixth floor when the votive candle exhausted its fuel.

The travelers took one final look at the residents inside the castle walls, before focusing their attention and energies on their hike through the ominous forest.

"Wait a minute," blurted Cindy. "The rest of our bags and weapons are upstairs."

Hoping to persuade at least one guest to join them, Dan volunteered, "I'll grab the gear."

Sam stepped forward and offered, "I'll give you a hand."

"That's alright," remarked Dan, "I can manage. You lead the group through the clearing; I'll catch up."

"Are you sure?" asked Sam.

"Sam, hurry," he demanded. "We don't have much time." Dan grabbed his shield from the clearing and darted to the drawbridge. As he approached the guests in the Grand Foyer, he slowed his pace to study their facial features; unfortunately, all eyes were directed at the floor.

On the sixth level, he opened the guests' room door. To his delight, the Reclaimers remained coiled against the far wall, venting an occasional screech. Offering an overhead glance, he inhaled sharply; the votive candle was nearly half consumed. Slamming the door behind him, he raced to the bedroom across the hall and snatched the remaining bags, the lances, and the lantern. Overloaded with baggage, he clumsily descended the steps to the Grand Foyer. After dropping the supplies to the floor, he scrutinized the guests again. Though their sights remained downcast, he extended a hand in the direction of the huddled group, hoping someone would accept his invitation to freedom.

No one stirred.

Disheartened, he bent over, gathered the gear, and stepped beyond the castle entry, while maintaining a backward look at the guests, in the unlikely event someone, at the last minute, changed his or her mind. Sadly, no one accepted the path to independence.

With his sights focused on the residents, the young traveler failed to detect a presence at the opposite end of the drawbridge. A clacking sound startled Dan. He looked ahead and spotted Judas, the traitorous Pedwhip, fearlessly nearing the middle of the wooden bridge. Despite the fact the creature stood only a few inches higher than Dan, he had been forewarned of the Pedwhip's powerful pincers and venomous stinger.

Raising his claws in a show of force, Judas threatened, "I don't think you'll be as lucky as your friends, who left the castle in one piece," before he opened and slammmed his flesh-ripping pincers.

Dan dropped the bags, the lantern, and all the lances—except one. With a spear in one hand and his shield in the other, he slowly, but cautiously, advanced to the center of the drawbridge, declaring, "I don't want to fight you; I don't want any trouble."

"Your death will be no trouble," promised a haughty Judas.

"Look," remarked Dan, through his bandanna, "all the guests are in the Grand Foyer, so no harm done."

After stealing a backward glance to the travelers, who were escaping through the clearing, Judas returned his gaze to Dan and asked provokingly, "They're not *all* in the Grand Foyer, are they?"

Securing a death grip on his weapon, Dan yelled, "My brother was stolen from me and my family thirteen years ago, I'm taking back what is rightfully ours!"

As the conversation heated, the two parties drew closer to one another. Once within range, and quite suddenly, Judas shot his left claw upward and to the right, directly at Dan's head; the teenager valiantly redirected the oncoming pincer with his shield.

The adversaries, now within feet of one another, traveled in a circle—lance, shield, and pincers raised—as if each was attempting to slip behind the other's back, trying to detect a flaw in the other's defensive tactics.

Dan knew he was at a disadvantage, since Judas' pincers were nearly three feet longer than his arms. Aware of his anatomical shortcoming, he had to rely on his mental superiority to create a scenario that would reverse the odds in his favor. *But what?* he thought.

Judas' lengthy tail whipped forward.

Even though Dan's quick footing prevented a direct contact with the deadly stinger, the tail collided with the armor, throwing him several feet away. Upon impact with the drawbridge, the shield flew from his hand and came to rest, just beyond his reach, near the edge of the drawbridge…thirty feet above the moat.

Seizing the opportunity, Judas charged Dan, who leaped for the shield, rolled onto his back, and wielded his lance with such speed, strength, and accuracy that he pierced the creature's left pincer, as it descended upon him. The approaching right claw was successfully deflected with his shield.

The creature wailed in agony.

As Dan maintained a firm grip on his spear, the Pedwhip yanked its injured pincer away; the lance was heartlessly dislodged from the predator's claw and remained in the traveler's possession. With Judas retreating a few steps in anguish, Dan jumped to his feet and assumed a defensive posture; he knew the battle had just begun.

A loud scream was heard from the clearing; Sam was running to his friend's defense.

As Dan glanced, he also witnessed the other travelers nearing the castle. Unfortunately, during his momentary distraction, he failed to see Judas thrust his tail, once more, in his direction. By the time he eyed the stinger's approach, it was too late to swerve from its path. Again, whereas his shield prevented a direct contact with the deadly stinger, he was hurled a few feet back, crashing upon the drawbridge, but managed to grasp firmly his shield and lance.

Within seconds, both pincers were overhead.

With power and precision, Dan pierced the creature's right claw, as it swooped upon him for the kill.

Another roar was heard from the creature.

Overly engrossed with piercing the creature, Dan inadvertently lowered his shield. In that brief moment, the Pedwhip tightened its previously injured left claw around Dan's arm. Luckily, with the creature's loss of blood, its grip was weak and the traveler escaped its clutch with only a minor injury. As the Pedwhip withdrew a few steps, Dan accidentally released his grip on the lance, leaving it embedded in the creature's right claw.

Distracted by a loud thud from behind, Judas turned and saw Sam standing on the drawbridge. The creature's dilemma of fighting both men quickly vanished, when two trolls crawled from beneath the drawbridge and confronted Sam.

With the Pedwhip visually preoccupied with the new arrivals, Dan bolted to his feet and yanked his lance from the creature.

Judas howled; the battle resumed.

Wielding two large sticks from the clearing, since the supply of lances rested within the castle entry, Sam prevented the trolls' immediate onslaught. One creature charged, but was instantly repelled by the end of the branch. Coordinating their efforts, one troll crept around its prey, while the other remained facing its victim.

Waving one stick in front and poking the other behind, Sam temporarily foiled the trolls' advance.

The miniature beast from behind screeched; Sam turned to confront it. With his back vulnerable, the second troll sprang upon him and sank its claws into his backpack. He rocked spastically to drop the predator, while maintaining a defensive posture against the troll's mate that was waiting for its opportunity to strike.

Several feet nearer the castle, the clash intensified. Dan became more aggressive, trying to inflict a mortal wound on Judas, whose strength was waning, due to his recent injuries. Focused on slashing the Pedwhip's throat, he was oblivious to the creature's tail, which swung around and crashed into his waist. Thankfully, the stinger never made contact. Again, he was thrown several feet away, losing his lance, but still clenching his shield.

Even with his bloodstained claws, Judas stood proudly near the edge of the drawbridge and declared, "This was far too easy." As he lowered his tail below the drawbridge, for maximum velocity when thrusting it overhead and forward, he yelled, "Get a taste of this!"

With the shield in hand, Dan pitched it into the moat, creating a loud splash.

Upon its impact with the water, the eel shot from the depths of the moat and sank its teeth into Judas' dangling tail, severing it.

The Pedwhip's scream captured the attention of the savage trolls who—upon noticing the blood and the diminishing strength of Judas—abandoned Sam and leaped upon the Pedwhip.

Judas' two rearmost feet hopelessly struggled to regain a footing on the edge of the drawbridge.

Dan staggered to his feet, as Sam raced to his side. Together, they witnessed Judas lose his balance and plunge into the moat, taking the trolls with him. The dark waters churned with such intensity that within moments, the drawbridge was drenched.

The travelers bent over and rested their hands atop their knees, catching their breaths.

"Thanks," said Dan.

"Don't mention it," replied Sam, after a loud gulp. Tapping his companion's shoulder, he motioned him to look behind, toward the castle entry.

The teenager turned and saw Marcus. After an extended exhale, he approached the head cook. "I'm sorry, Marcus," he remarked. "I didn't want to fight him, but he insisted."

As he inspected Dan's bleeding arm, Marcus disclosed, "I witnessed the entire conflict. You did what you had to do; I understand."

Walking up behind Dan, Sam discreetly grabbed the bags, lances, and lantern and waited beyond earshot.

Dan apologized again, to which Marcus remarked, "Given Judas' vindictive and deceitful actions over so many years, it was only a matter of time before tragedy struck." Noticing the remaining travelers and Salvus at the foot of the drawbridge, he warned, "You better leave, before the Reclaimers descend the staircase."

The two exchanged farewells.

With the shield submerged in the moat, Dan joined his co-travelers and fled across the clearing at a fast pace.

CHAPTER EIGHT

Three Dots in the Backward Sky

RACING THROUGH THE CLEARING, AS FAST AS THE TWO AILING travelers would permit the group, Dan was pleased William had recovered from Sam's jab and Salvus was maintaining a fast clip, though still in a great deal of pain. Realizing the limited evening moonlight that graced the clearing would be more than they'd enjoy in the forest, Dan slowed his pace and asked Cindy for Doctor O'Brien's pills.

"We took one this morning," reminded Cindy, after she and her co-travelers came to a standstill.

"I know," he acknowledged, "but for William. I don't want him getting jittery during the night."

As Dan waited for the pill, Sam reminded everyone to keep their bandannas secured over their faces for at least the next hour, since they were still susceptible to the gaseous fumes of the lizards' droppings.

After accepting the tablet from Cindy, Dan lowered his brother's facial covering and dropped the pill in his mouth.

William immediately choked.

Dan slapped him between the shoulder blades and watched closely for him to swallow. When he did, he congratulated, "Good job," before replacing his brother's bandanna.

The six resumed their sprint and within minutes had reached the edge of the clearing and the entrance to the woodlands. Before stepping into the forest, however, Sam spotted a wide parcel of flattened underbrush and presumed it was the area where the Reclaimers slithered into the forest earlier that evening. "I think it will be safer," he advised, "if we enter at another point."

"But, Sam," reminded Cindy, "we need the supplies we hid a short distance inside the forest, just before we crawled to the castle."

"Cindy," whispered Sam, "it's not worth risking our lives. For all we know, the Reclaimers may be just a short distance from where we stand."

"You may be right," said Cindy, "but we need the plastic containers for water." After glancing at her companions, she reluctantly added, "And as much as I hate to admit it, we will probably need the extra clothing for homemade bandages in the days ahead."

Although Sam had hoped the return trek would be uneventful, he knew the chances of someone sustaining additional injuries were high. "Alright," he yielded, "I'll slip into the forest and gather our belongings. But in the meantime, I want all of you to remain in this spot, without breathing a word, until I return."

The travelers accepted the terms.

With lance in hand, he ventured into the woods.

Staring beyond the clearing to the castle, Cindy whispered, "What a gloomy place; I couldn't imagine being held a prisoner within those cold walls for years or perhaps decades."

"I just wish the other guests would have accepted our ticket to freedom," replied a troubled Dan.

"You did the best you could," affirmed Cindy. "You can't let their reluctance in leaving the castle to eat away at you."

"I know," he admitted. "But if only—" His comment was cut short by the sound of crushing plants.

Sam emerged from the woods, lugging the spare supplies.

"Did you see any Reclaimers?" blurted Dan.

"Thankfully, no," whispered Sam. Glancing back to the forest, he speculated, "Maybe they're deeper in the woods."

Restless to begin the second half of their journey, the group geared up and entered the forest, a great distance to the left of the Reclaimers' tracks, to avoid a potential face-to-face conflict with the armed snake-men.

The group maintained a fast pace, hoping to escape deeper into the forest before the Reclaimers in the castle regained their former powers and inevitably trailed them. Each traveler knew eventually they'd have to hike to the right to intersect the path that would ultimately lead them to the oak. But they also knew they had well over a week to readjust their heading.

Nearly an hour into their hike, the group tired, especially the men who were assisting the injured party members: Sam and Jimmy supported Salvus; Dan aided William. Agreeing to stop for a few minutes, Cindy helped Dan lower his brother to the ground; Jimmy and Sam did likewise with Salvus. Removing their bandannas, the travelers took a deep breath. To their relief, no one experienced evil or doubtful thoughts.

"Dan," suggested Cindy, "I should treat your arm."

"Not now," insisted Dan. "Besides, Judas barely broke the skin."

Knowing she would tend his wound before they retired that night, she dropped the issue.

"Well," said Sam, "we completed half our journey. But the last half, I'm afraid, will be a bit more difficult."

"What do you mean?" asked Cindy.

"For the remainder of the trip," ordered Sam, "we can't light any campfires, since I'm sure the Reclaimers would spot the blaze."

"So," remarked Jimmy, "I guess that means cold meals and cold nights, without the—"

Jimmy fell silent; clanging sounds echoed through the forest.

"What the heck is that?" asked Dan, in a raised voice to overpower the annoying clamor.

Salvus—who was resting on his stomach, since his injuries prevented him from reclining on his back—raised himself to his elbows and announced, "The candle's out."

"How do you know?" asked Dan.

"The noise you're hearing," explained the satyr, "is the Bell of Summons which hangs in the Great Tower. It usually rings only once a month, and even then, only one time."

"Why only once a month?" continued Dan.

"That's the signal to the chief Oswagi Bird," clarified Salvus, "it's time for Spiritus Malus' monthly flight to the enchanted oak. The savage bird lands on the castle roof and carries the sovereign Reclaimer over the forest to the tree."

Looking to his co-travelers, Sam interjected, "There's your answer on how Spiritus Malus reaches the tree so quickly."

"But tonight," continued Salvus, "even though there's no full moon, the bell continues to ring."

Fearful of the answer, Cindy, nonetheless, asked, "What does that mean?"

Lowering his head to the ground, as if already admitting defeat, the satyr explained, "A flock of Oswagis will soon descend upon the castle roof. I can promise you at this very moment the Reclaimers, who were hunting tonight, are racing back to the castle. In a short time, a vast number of Oswagis and Reclaimers will be searching for us. Since there are just a handful of guests in the castle—and presuming one Reclaimer will be assigned to the Hall of Admittance—I'd guess nearly forty snake-men soon will be hunting us."

"But since the birds can't land in the dense forest," remarked Jimmy, "aren't we safe?"

"I'm afraid not," replied Salvus. "The Reclaimers will scout from above; and they'll scout until we're found. After all, they have an eternity at their disposal." Laboring to his hoofs, and detecting fear on the travelers' faces, he attempted to ease their worries by suggesting, "We'd be better off hiking beneath the largest trees; maybe we'll get lucky."

Trying to imagine the birds and snake-men in flight, Jimmy interjected, "Wait a minute. How do the Reclaimers ride the birds, if their lower bodies are nothing but disgusting snake tails?"

"Granted, I've witnessed it only a couple times," informed Salvus, "but it's actually quite amusing. The bird drops its belly to the ground, allowing a Reclaimer to slither aboard. Once atop the winged beast, the bird raises itself. Then for security, the Reclaimer wraps its lengthy tail around the torso of the bird and constricts."

Though it was too early for the Oswagis to be soaring overhead, the travelers, nevertheless, gazed upward.

"The canopy is so thick," observed Dan. "There's no way they could possibly spot us."

"Let's hope not," answered Salvus. "But remember, even though the forest is dense and dark, I've been told there are areas that have fewer trees and occasional clearings—like the lakeshores, the vast treeless area near the Great Chasm, and a dozen or more grasslands, where the centaurs live and hunt. We'd be wise to keep our eyes and ears open."

Only then the bell fell silent.

Knowing each toll beckoned one Oswagi and one Reclaimer, Sam insisted the group advance deeper into the forest, being careful to avoid the perilous areas of which Salvus had warned.

Cindy snatched two bags, the lantern, and the lances; Dan grabbed the remaining bags and lifted his brother. Jimmy and Sam raised Salvus between their shoulders and followed the three young travelers. The party hiked another two hours until all were exhausted.

Finding a flat plot of ground, overshadowed with massive tree limbs, the travelers set up a fireless campsite. With everything the group had endured that night, no one, not even Jimmy, felt like eating. At Sam's insistence, however, each traveler enjoyed an apple, which Salvus had supplied before the group escaped the castle. During their light meal, hardly a word was spoken, though the towering limbs were constantly scanned. One issue, however, which was discussed was night patrol. Since the four original travelers were fit to assume watch, Sam insisted Salvus and William get a full night's rest. Cindy volunteered for the first patrol, followed by Dan, Jimmy, and finally Sam.

After the meal—and as the travelers were heading to their sleeping areas—Cindy demanded, "Dan, let me take a look at your arm."

"I'm fine," he snapped, "it's just a scratch."

On overhearing his comment, Sam approached his bickering companions and ordered, "Dan, let's have a look."

After raising his jersey shirtsleeve, the onlookers were surprised Dan was telling the truth; his injury was nothing like he'd sustained in the past. However, uncertain what microorganisms infested Judas' claw, Cindy grabbed the whiskey bottle. Everyone strongly suspected they would not be so lucky with their next patient.

Walking several paces from the fallen tree, upon which the group had relaxed and enjoyed their apples, the three travelers dropped to their knees beside Salvus, who was relaxing on his stomach.

"Salvus," said Cindy, "I hate to do this, but if I don't, your wounds will probably get infected."

The satyr offered no response; Sam lowered his friend's toga.

Salvus stretched out his arms, squeezed Dan's hand, and then Sam's, while Cindy poured the disinfectant. During the application, his facial features—what little Dan and Sam could detect in the dim light— revealed intense agony, though not a sound was heard.

"Salvus, are you alright?" demanded Dan, as the satyr delivered a death grip on his hand.

The satyr remained silent.

Glancing behind, Dan spotted William sitting alone against a tree. In their flight from the castle and in his much-needed assistance restraining Salvus, Dan felt he had unknowingly neglected his brother. *But then again,* he thought, *during our hike through the forest, I made countless efforts to communicate with him, but met silence with every attempt.* Staring at his brother, his thoughts rambled, *My gosh, I want to hear your voice. I want to tell you that mom and dad never gave up hope you would return; I want to tell you—*

William rose from the ground, returning Dan's fixed gaze.

The younger brother jumped to his feet and neared his sibling. Once within arm's reach, he whispered, "William, it's me; Dan, your brother." This time he expected he would speak; again, he remained silent.

Just when Dan's hopes were fading, William reached into his brother's sweatshirt pocket and grabbed the stuffed animal.

Even though no words were exchanged, Dan knew William was slowly recalling his childhood memories and gradually emerging from his spellbound state.

Before retiring—and knowing the group was short of sleeping gear—Dan unzipped his sleeping bag and spread it on the ground to accommodate two people.

The damp night air had quickly settled upon the fireless campsite.

After watching Dan and William crawl atop their sleeping bag, Cindy stepped to the brothers and tossed her blanket.

Salvus, on the other hand, preferred sleeping without covers, as he had done for decades in the dungeon, though he eventually accepted Jimmy's blanket.

Within minutes of Cindy's watch, the remaining travelers were slumbering beneath the protection of the impenetrable canopy.

Falling asleep, shortly upon his return from night patrol, Dan was unexpectedly awakened by heavy breathing. Rolling onto his side, he saw William sitting up, gasping for air. Dan jumped to his feet and darted to Cindy's area. Violently shaking her, he yelled, "Cindy! Cindy!"

"What time is it?" she mumbled.

"Where's William's asthma medicine?" he shouted. "He's having an attack."

Cindy sprang from her sleeping bag and dived to her backpack. Ripping open the knapsack, she grabbed the canister of pills. In her reckless state, she dropped the open bottle.

Dan snatched a pill from the ground and raced to his sleeping area, where William had collapsed to his back and was barely conscious. Placing his hand behind his brother's neck, he raised his head, dropped the pill into his mouth, and demanded he swallow. William did as he was told.

Cindy dashed to the brothers' sleeping area, carrying a cup of water, but spilled half of it en route.

Dan pressed the cup against William's lips. "Drink it all," he ordered.

Again, William did as he was asked.

Witnessing the events unfold, Cindy realized William was beginning to trust Dan, probably like he once erroneously trusted the Reclaimers. But Dan's insistence was out of love and not selfishly motivated like the Reclaimers' commands.

The commotion drew Jimmy from his patrol station and Sam and Salvus from their sleeping areas.

"What's wrong?" demanded Sam.

"He just had an asthma attack," answered Dan.

"Will he be alright?" asked Jimmy.

"Yeah," replied Dan, "I think so."

Within minutes, William's breathing slowly returned to normal.

Returning the empty cup to Cindy, Dan commended, "Thanks; I don't know what we'd do without you."

In exchange for the cup, Cindy handed Dan the medication bottle, stressing, "You better keep this near you, in case he has another episode."

Dan accepted the bottle of pills and placed it alongside his sleeping bag.

Jimmy returned to the lookout post, as Sam and Salvus headed to their slumber areas. Barely halfway to her sleeping bag, Cindy retraced her steps to Dan's side and asked, "Has he said anything yet?"

"Not yet," he replied, "but I'm sure he will soon."

"I'm sure he will, too," assured Cindy, who quickly added, "Good night," and neared her sleeping bag, where she dozed within minutes.

At 6:00 the next morning, the travelers were stirring. One by one, they approached the fallen tree, where they had enjoyed an apple, just hours earlier. William arrived, assisted by Dan, while Sam, returning from his patrol post, aided Salvus to the breakfast site. Cindy and Jimmy soon followed.

Just before ending the blessing, Sam interjected a petition for a safe journey that day, to which all seconded with a resounding, "Amen." In addition to Sam leading the prayer, which was most unusual, Dan was equally shocked at seeing William making the sign of the cross. Having witnessed this solemn gesture, he presumed his sibling had been praying during his captivity in the castle—in secret, of course—for the past thirteen years.

Dan's thoughts were interrupted by Sam's remark, "We'll continue our hike today, but end the moment Salvus and William tire. I don't expect to cover a great distance, but whatever we accomplish will be that much more than if we didn't travel at all." After grabbing a stale marshmallow from the bag, he asked, "Did anyone notice anything out of the ordinary during their watch?"

In turn, the three remaining patrollers reported nothing newsworthy.

"Nonetheless," continued Sam, "I'm sure the Reclaimers are still hunting us, since I doubt they'd give up after only a few hours. So, we'll march today, but all of us should scan the sky for our pursuers, whenever the canopy separates."

"I'd also suggest," warned Salvus, "that during our hike, we keep our conversations to a minimum; the Oswagis have a keen sense of hearing."

"Good advice," said Sam. Looking directly at Jimmy, he repeated the urgency for silence.

Jimmy rolled his eyes, before cramming an entire marshmallow in his mouth.

"Sam," said Cindy, in an apologetic tone, "before I went on patrol, I never asked about your back."

"What about my back?" he asked.

Dan leaned forward on the toppled tree, glared at Sam, and reminded, "Your back that the troll was riding last night on the drawbridge."

"Oh, that," laughed Sam. "The troll's claws hardly broke my skin."

"Then you won't mind us taking a look," challenged Dan, "like you insisted inspecting my arm last night."

A hesitant Sam rose from the grounded tree, turned his back toward Cindy, and lowered his shirt.

To her surprise, only two scratches were barely noticeable.

After pulling up his shirt, he explained, "The disgusting troll sank its claws into the backpack; I guess I was lucky."

"I guess so," remarked Dan.

"Speaking of which," recalled Cindy, "Dan, I'll need to treat your arm and Salvus' back before we begin our hike."

The satyr reacted to Cindy's suggestion by choking on an apple wedge.

"Salvus," explained Cindy, "you'll experience less pain each time your wounds are treated. Don't you trust me?"

The satyr shook his head.

"Smart man," replied Dan.

In less than an hour, the patients were treated, the travelers had taken Doctor O'Brien's medication, and an extra asthma pill was prescribed for William to prevent a relapse during the day's hike. Once the campsite was cleaned and the sleeping gear was packed away, the group set out to diminish the distance between themselves and the enchanted oak.

As expected, Sam took the lead, followed by the Clay brothers, Cindy, and finally, Salvus, who was assisted by Jimmy.

A short distance into their trek, Sam glanced behind and was pleased that William was walking on his own without Dan's help. *I think the medication is finally taking hold,* he thought, *and I'm sure the hike in the open air is doing him some good.*

The group pressed on.

By midmorning, it became painfully obvious to the four original travelers they were more exhausted than they expected, though no one mentioned it. The path that they had embarked upon to the left of the Reclaimers' tracks at the castle was nothing like the trail they stepped upon from the oak to the castle weeks ago. The new path was covered with entangling weeds and undergrowth; its slight, but steady, uphill climb challenged the group. However, despite the difficult terrain and their fatigue, the group trudged forward. Throughout the four-mile trek, each member constantly scanned the canopy and the blue sky, whenever a strong wind swayed the towering limbs.

Finding a barren plot of ground, the travelers dropped their bags and sat for a meal of fruits, vegetables, and cheese—all courtesy of the castle workers. During lunch, very few words were exchanged; the group had adapted to the silence during their hike.

Eventually, Sam spoke up, "Dan, do you think William can walk a little more today?"

Recalling his brother had no trouble keeping pace with him during the morning hike, he speculated, "Yeah, I think so."

"And you, Salvus?" asked Sam.

"I'll be fine," assured the satyr.

Within an hour, the meal was devoured and the group resumed their march up the path, approaching an immense clearing.

As Sam neared the grassland, he halted and looked overhead for possible predators. To his satisfaction, the cloudless sky was free of Oswagis. However, he was ultimately presented a dilemma: cross through the clearing in the open sunshine and enjoy a respite from the towering limbs, but placing the group in potential danger, or avoid the meadow and hike around the perimeter of the field, just inside the darkened forest. *Granted, the second option would be safer,* he thought, *but the open air would be good for the group. But what if—*

Suspecting Sam was debating their route, Dan blurted, "If we run through the clearing, we'll reach the other side faster than if we walked along the fringes of the forest."

"I know," replied Sam, "but what if something is waiting in the field for an ambush or lurking in the nearby treetops for an easy swoop in the clearing?"

The six took a vote. After another overhead inspection, the travelers hiked at a fast pace through the open field, which was nearly a mile across.

The gentle breeze and the warm sunlight proved invigorating to the group, until Jimmy looked over his shoulder and spotted three dots in the backward sky.

"Oswagis!" he yelled.

The sprinters instinctively glanced back, while maintaining their forward dash.

Knowing the entrance to the forest at the opposite end of the clearing was farther away than the border of the woods to the right, Sam altered his course to the nearby trees. The remaining travelers followed.

Under the protection of the limbs, the group rested on their knees, eyeing whether the Oswagis and their Reclaimer passengers would descend to the field or fly beyond. Within minutes, three Oswagis made a bumpy landing in the adjoining field.

"Do you think they spotted us?" whispered Cindy, with her sights never leaving the birds of prey.

"I don't think so," replied Sam in a soft voice, "since they landed deep in the field."

As the group remained motionless, the four original travelers recalled their initial encounter with the unsightly Oswagi species.

Noticing the three Reclaimers slithering in various directions in the grassland, Sam guessed they were tracking something...perhaps evidence of a recent passage in the field.

A lone Reclaimer was just several yards from the travelers' trail to the safety of the forest when William began panting.

Is it his asthma or his memories of the oppressive Reclaimers? thought Dan. Whatever the cause, he quietly, but quickly, reached for the medication bottle and dropped a pill in William's mouth. With his brother's face pressed against his chest to muffle his wheezing, William's breathing gradually returned to normal.

As the snake-man drew nearer to the crushed undergrowth of the travelers' escape, the Oswagis uttered a shrill cry, capturing the attention of the Reclaimers.

"Do you think the birds smelled us?" whispered Cindy.

"Sh," warned Sam, "remain perfectly still…and don't look into the Reclaimers' eyes."

Without warning, a centaur sprang to his feet in the waist-high prairie grass, directly ahead of the birds of prey, and bolted up the meadow in the opposite direction of the Oswagis and the Reclaimers.

Slithering to the birds, the snake-men secured themselves atop the Oswagis, which immediately took flight for the four-legged half-man, half-horse creature. From their vantage point, the travelers couldn't see what happened next, since the grassland sloped down into a hollow. Moments later, the centaur was seen galloping up a small mound in the clearing with the Oswagis in hot pursuit.

"If it wasn't for that centaur," explained Sam, "I'm sure the Reclaimers would have discovered our tracks." Rising to his feet, he advised the group to resume their hike, but within the safety of the forest.

Everyone unconditionally agreed.

After another four hours of difficult hiking—and upon detecting exhaustion on the faces of his companions—Sam recommended the group end their day's journey and rest for the night.

"But, Sam," urged Dan, "we still have a couple more hours of daylight; I think we should keep moving, especially since we're making better time than we thought."

Removing his backpack, Sam glared at Dan and asked, "Why are you in such a hurry? William may be doing alright but—" He paused to verify the satyr was out of earshot and then continued, "But Salvus is still in considerable pain." Before Dan could defend his remark, Sam recalled his earlier convincing comment and challenged, "Wait a minute; you were also the first to persuade the group into taking the shortcut through the clearing."

Dan was overly preoccupied with the Reclaimers' interest in relocating the portal and would stop at virtually nothing to reach the oak, before its transworld powers vanished. Though part of him wanted to tell Sam about the potion recipe in his pocket that he ripped from the Reclaimers' book in the library, he also knew Sam would be livid that he wasn't informed earlier. Squeezing the ancient parchment in his pocket, he explained, "I just want to make sure we reach the oak before the next full moon, that's all."

"That's an honorable gesture," praised Sam, "but not at the expense of a friend's health or life." Resting his hand on his companion's shoulder, he urged, "Now come on, let's get a meal started."

If Dan had his way, he'd travel all day and all night; but at the same time, he knew Sam was right. After all, the group never would have escaped the castle without Salvus' quick wit and sacrifice. Noticing Sam had outpaced him, he slowed his stride and pulled the parchment from his pocket to reread the alarming potion. Taking a closer look, he counted thirty-two ingredients; all were marked off, except two: a centaur's tail and a Bozeman's quill. *What's a Bozeman's quill?* he thought. Baffled with the unknown ingredient, he refolded the document and returned it to his pocket.

Sensing his companion was lagging behind, Sam turned and ordered, "Come on, Dan, let's get a meal started."

Nearing his co-travelers, Dan first approached William, who was clearly becoming more acclimated with the group, since he was sitting on a log near Cindy and Salvus and not alone against a tree. But he remained silent. "Are you hungry, William?" he asked.

The older sibling simply nodded, while clutching the stuffed animal.

Initially, Jimmy thought a man William's age holding a toy was most peculiar, but then correctly assumed that merely holding it reawakened his childhood memories. Taking a few steps closer to the dinner area, Jimmy opted for the forest floor over the fallen tree.

Again, tomatoes, apples, and cheese were served. Realizing a hunt for meat was definitely out of the question, for fear of being spotted by the Oswagis and Reclaimers, no one complained about the menu, though Jimmy did alert Sam to the scarcity of drinking water.

"Remind me tomorrow," remarked Sam, "and I'll see if I can find a pond or a lake somewhere close by."

Although the lantern was resting beside the toppled tree, no one dared to switch it on, lest it attract their pursuers. However, since the group was eating earlier than normal, minimal fading sunlight miraculously reached the forest floor.

During the meal, Sam asked Cindy if she'd been keeping her daily log.

"Yeah...well...kind of," she replied.

With a slice of tomato between his jaws, Sam muttered, "What do you mean kind of?"

After counting the vertical marks on the inside back cover of her novel that she ripped from her book, she updated, "I think we've been gone seventeen days."

"How sure are you?" asked Sam.

"Well, I may have missed a day or two," admitted Cindy, "but no more than two."

Reaching for his cup, Dan clarified, "If there are thirty days between each full moon, then we've already spent more than half our allotted time in this world. And if two days are missing, we have only eleven days left to reach the oak."

Sensing the group was becoming overly concerned, Sam reassured, "We'll be fine, as long as we keep to the path and avoid any further encounters with the inhabitants of this wretched forest."

"Yeah," agreed Jimmy, "and remember, on our way to the castle there were a couple days we couldn't hike because of injuries, not to mention the fact we spent considerable time in the castle, which we obviously won't be doing on our return trip."

Now was Dan's opportunity to gain some backing for his covert scheme. "Why don't we sleep two hours less each morning," he proposed, "and use the extra time hiking? After all, the forest isn't that much brighter during the day than in the early morning hours."

Taking a vote, Sam was the only one who objected to the idea, reasoning everyone needed as much sleep as possible, especially considering the rough terrain. In the end, he accepted the majority's ruling.

When the meal was finished and the immediate area cleaned, Dan volunteered, "I'll take the first shift."

"And I'll sit the second," offered Cindy.

After a prolonged glare from his young co-travelers, a weary Jimmy grudgingly agreed to the third shift.

"Sam," directed Dan, "you're relieved of duty tonight."

"Well then," he replied, "if that's the case, I'd suggest all of you retire early; 4:00 a.m. will be here before you know it."

As the group rose and prepared to leave the immediate area, Cindy cleared her throat, drawing the attention of the men. As her companions turned, she shook the whiskey bottle and asked, "Salvus, Dan…aren't you forgetting something?"

"Cindy," snapped Dan, "my arm's fine."

"And what about your leg and back," she challenged, "from your clash with the troll over the moat just days ago? I'm sure they haven't healed that quickly." Before he could counter her suspicions, she added, "I'm sorry I forgot to treat them earlier."

"My back and leg are fine," insisted Dan.

"And what about your back, Salvus?" she asked.

"My back?" stalled the satyr. "It hasn't felt better in years."

"No way are you two getting off that easily," vowed Cindy. Noticing her friends' looks of disgust, she demanded, "Do you think I enjoy this?"

"Yes!" blurted both patients.

Knowing it was against Cindy's nature to yield, Dan lowered his shirt and raised his pant leg. To Cindy's astonishment, his injuries were nearly healed, though large scabs were clearly forming.

Salvus turned and lowered his toga, unveiling several deep thrash marks. Observing his look of discomfort when simply dropping his garment, Sam stepped beside his friend and gripped his upper arm; Dan clasped his opposite forearm. Upon application, Salvus jerked, but just slightly. Sam, Dan, and Cindy, however, were not fooled; they knew it was more painful than he was letting on.

As the two treated men neared their individual sleeping areas, Dan overheard Salvus mumbling, "I think I'd be safer in the castle with the Reclaimers."

Even though it was only 10:00 in the evening, the travelers readied their sleeping bags and blankets. Sam was right; they knew 4:00 would come soon. After arranging the sleeping area for William and himself, but before leaving for his post, Dan gave his brother an asthma pill and instructed, "I'll be sitting over there," as he pointed to the right, "so if you need anything, just come get me, okay?"

William offered no audible response; simply a nod.

Because the travelers retired earlier than normal, Dan's two-hour shift would end at midnight, whereas Cindy and Jimmy would sit the 12:00 and 2:00 a.m. shifts, respectively. The evening air was unusually warm, making it difficult for Dan to remain alert. He had just begun to nod, when he spotted a familiar flicker in the trees.

"Ceremonia," he exclaimed, in a voice loud enough to be heard by her, but not by his sleeping companions.

The illumination twirled about the canopy.

"Ceremonia!" he yelled again.

The light drew closer. Since his leg still bothered him, though he'd never admit it to Cindy or Sam, he slowly rose from the patrol log. Like before, he witnessed an intense beam of light emanating from her and encircling her six-inch body. The brilliance gradually enlarged, as her body size increased—matching the expanding glow—until the tree nymph was five-and-a-half feet tall and standing several paces in front of him.

The teenager nodded slightly and greeted, "It's great to see you."

"It's good to see you, too," acknowledged Ceremonia, as she stepped a bit closer.

The awkwardness of the situation resulted in a moment of silence. Eventually, Dan swallowed his pride and admitted, "Look, Ceremonia, I'm sorry I wasn't entirely honest with you when we were hiking to the castle. I shouldn't have tried to trick you into slipping me information you didn't want to share."

Taking another step nearer the repentant man, the tree nymph remarked, "Thank you, Dan. I've been told it's not easy for humans to admit their wrongdoings."

Glancing to the campsite in the distance, Dan blurted, "Oh, I almost forgot; we found my brother in the castle!"

"You did?" asked an excited tree nymph.

"Yeah, he's right over there," as he pointed to the double sleeping area.

"That's wonderful," exclaimed Ceremonia, who quickly added, "how are the others?"

"They're fine," answered Dan, "except for Salvus."

"Salvus?" questioned the tree nymph. "Who's Salvus?"

After slapping an unearthly-size gnat on his arm, he explained, "He's the satyr from the castle that the Reclaimers were mistreating. Anyway, knowing his life was in danger if he stayed in the castle, we asked him—well, I guess we pressured him—to join us."

"What happened to him?" inquired Ceremonia, as she stared at the campsite.

"His back is pretty beat-up from the whippings he suffered the night we left the castle," he informed. The teenager followed the tree nymph's gaze to the fireless campground, before adding, "But he seems a little better."

Lowering herself to the patrol log, Ceremonia revealed, "I'm not surprised."

"What do you mean?" asked Dan, who remained standing beside the tree nymph.

"There's something in this world's atmosphere that's both a blessing and a curse," she explained. "On the one hand, the air causes humans to endure anxiety attacks; but on the other hand, it has a favorable effect on the body's healing system."

After seating himself upon the patrol log beside his friend, Dan recalled, "Salvus said the castle walls are cursed to ease the afflictions of the guests within the fortress."

"That doesn't surprise me either," responded Ceremonia. "It seems the Reclaimers grow more powerful, cunning, and ingenious with each passing century…if that's possible." The tree nymph abruptly jumped from the log.

Thinking he may have upset her, Dan apologized, "I'm sorry, Ceremonia; did I say something that offended you?"

The tree nymph offered no response; she scanned the darkened canopy.

"Ceremonia," implored Dan, "what's wrong?"

Eventually lowering her sights to the forest floor, she whispered, "It's Gloria."

"Gloria?" he asked. "Who's Gloria?"

"She is…I mean…she was my cousin."

"What happened?"

Ceremonia returned to the log and admitted, "I didn't want to burden you with my problems, since you have enough on your mind already. But I needed to talk with someone."

Resting his hand upon Ceremonia's, he repeated, "What happened to your cousin?"

"Two nights ago, during an evening drizzle," detailed the tree nymph, "Gloria was sleeping in the canopy, when she slipped from a jungatin leaf and floated toward the forest floor. I was half asleep and didn't notice her drifting downward." Ceremonia lowered her head; she was visibly upset.

Clutching her hand, Dan urged, "Go on."

"When I eventually spotted her floating to the ground," she explained, "I sprang from the tree fork that I had dozed upon and dived to her rescue. But I was too late. The mouth of Bacchus, the centaur, swallowed her."

"Ceremonia," consoled Dan, "I'm sorry; I'm really sorry. Is there anything I can do?"

Wiping her nose on a sleeve of her garment, she responded, "No—I mean, yes! Be on your guard, since it has been only forty-eight hours since Gloria's death."

Curious how the tragic turn of events could affect the travelers, Dan confessed, "I don't understand."

"During one of our earlier conversations," reminded Ceremonia, "I explained that when a centaur consumes a tree nymph, the horse creature has the ability to alter his appearance for three days and three nights. Bacchus still has another twenty-four hours to change his disguise and lure any member of your group into danger."

"We'll be careful," promised Dan, before removing a handkerchief from his pocket and giving it to his grieving friend.

Observing his kindhearted response and genuine interest in her welfare, Ceremonia realized her initial judgment of him was made in error. Beyond a doubt, she knew he was a decent man, unlike the centaurs, who were virtually the only other male species she had ever known.

She rose from the log, walked a few paces from her friend, and was immediately enveloped by a glow of light. Within seconds, the brilliance condensed around her, until she was reduced to six inches in height. She shot to the darkness of the canopy.

Dan's upward gaze was diverted by movement in the distance. Lowering his eyes from the towering limbs, he spun and glimpsed Cindy approaching for her tour of duty.

"You're awfully jumpy," she teased.

"Ceremonia was just here," blurted Dan.

"Ceremonia?" questioned a doubtful Cindy. "Really?"

"Yeah."

"How is she?"

"Not too good, I'm afraid," answered Dan.

"What do you mean?"

"During our trip to the castle," recalled Dan, "do you remember her telling us that her species is constantly hunted by the centaurs, and if a tree nymph is consumed by one, the horse creature can change his appearance for three days and three nights?"

"Yeah," she replied, "vaguely."

"Well," he continued, "Ceremonia lost her cousin, Gloria, to a centaur, just two nights ago."

"Oh, no," voiced a worried Cindy. "How is she taking it?"

"Not great," replied Dan, "but there's nothing we can do at this point." He advanced several feet closer to the campsite, turned, and warned, "Be extra watchful during your patrol, in case the centaur, or whatever he's changed himself into, is nearby."

"I'll be alright," assured Cindy. "Get some sleep."

As Dan slipped into the darkness, Cindy admitted to herself she was terrified of the stalking savage man. Disclosing her fear to Dan, however, would unintentionally compel him to sit another shift, which he didn't need, especially considering the strenuous hike he and the others would endure in a few hours. Though his injuries were healing nicely, she suspected he was still in pain and needed the rest. She glanced to the canopy, hoping to spot the familiar light, but nothing glimmered. Lost in her heavenward stare, she heard a rustling noise. Peering into the darkness, she spotted Dan approaching, carrying the blanket she loaned to him and William.

"Dan," questioned a startled Cindy, "what are you doing?"

"Don't worry," he remarked. "I rolled my end of the sleeping bag over William, who's already asleep; he'll be warm enough."

"I mean," clarified Cindy, "what are you doing here?"

"I thought I'd rest with you for a couple hours," he replied, "and keep you company."

Cindy knew he was denying himself sleep for her safety, not her company. However, suspecting he would leave if she insisted, she accepted his offer.

After spreading the blanket across Cindy and himself, he jokingly asked, "So, how long before Jimmy gets sick of tomatoes?"

Cindy chuckled before admitting, "I'm surprised he hasn't grumbled already."

The travelers enjoyed one another's company for the remainder of Cindy's shift, until Jimmy shambled to the patrol site at 2:10...ten minutes late.

After relating Ceremonia's loss and cautioning Jimmy to be especially vigilant during his watch, Cindy and Dan walked to their sleeping areas.

Cindy nestled into her sleeping bag, as Dan rearranged his sleeping gear to accommodate William and himself.

From the darkness was heard, "Thanks, Dan; good night."

Turning his head in the direction of the voice, he reminded, "See you at 4:00."

CHAPTER NINE

Metamorphosis

At the end of his patrol, Jimmy woke his co-travelers at 4:00 a.m. for an early start.

Gathering around the fallen tree, the band of six finished the few cereal grains that were discovered at the bottom of Dan's bag and completed their meal with an apple.

"Sam," reminded Jimmy, "we need to find some water today, remember?"

"Yeah," confirmed Sam. "While we're keeping an eye on the canopy and the sky beyond for Oswagis and Reclaimers, let's also be on the lookout for signs of water; and we can't be picky. I don't care if it's a lake, a pond, or even a puddle; we're running dangerously low."

Refusing to interrupt their chewing rhythms, the hungry travelers simply nodded. After their meal and medication, the group collected their camping gear, gripped their weapons, and hit the path for another grueling hike.

Today's the first time, in a long time, thought Sam, *all members of the team are able to walk without the aid of another; although I suspect Dan's leg is still bothering him. And William... well, as long as he takes his medication, he'll have no trouble keeping up with the group. Even Salvus seems to be walking at a good clip all by himself.*

For a change in their routine, Dan proposed that he and William take the lead, suspecting it would be therapeutic for his brother. For the first time in his life, William was directing others, instead of following orders. Observing his facial expression, as he walked alongside, Dan was convinced William was enjoying his newfound role.

The travelers hiked several hours that morning, while constantly scanning the upper limbs and the sides of the footpath. Fortunately, there was no sign of the Oswagis or the Reclaimers; unfortunately, there also was no sign of water.

After reclining on a level plot of ground, concealed beneath the thick foliage, Cindy and Dan opened their knapsacks and removed a few apples and tomatoes from their depleting surplus for the noon meal. Taking note of the rations, Sam trembled at the thought of embarking upon another hunting expedition in the uncharted forest. Though he suspected the Reclaimers were still in pursuit, he knew he had no choice, if he wanted to replenish the dwindling food supply.

Sam's horrid hunting thoughts were distracted by Dan's visual preoccupation with something beyond the makeshift campsite.

"Dan," asked an observant Sam, "what's wrong?"

Without disrupting his forward gaze over Sam's shoulder, the teenager whispered, "What's that?"

"What's what?" asked Sam, as he spun and stared into the relative darkness.

"That," replied Dan, before directing Sam's attention beyond an inconspicuous path in the woods. "It's glimmering." He rose to his feet, speculating, "Maybe it's a stream or something."

Now standing alongside his young companion, Sam peered up the side trail and also noticed a sparkle. "You may be right," he replied. "Maybe the path was formed by forest creatures plodding their way to a water source."

On hearing Sam's theory, Dan grabbed three lances from the forest floor. "Come on, William," he urged.

As expected, his brother offered no verbal response, but joined his sibling and Sam on their approach to the obscure path.

Glancing back at Cindy, Jimmy, and Salvus, Sam ordered, "You three stay here; we'll check it out. If it's water, we'll call for you."

"But, Sam," implored Cindy, "what if—"

"No buts," interrupted Sam, "wait here with the others."

Reluctantly, she returned to her log and restlessly watched her three co-travelers step upon the unexplored path.

The water searchers had advanced just several feet up the trail, when Cindy asked Jimmy and Salvus, "Should we join them?"

"Sam ordered us to stay put," answered Jimmy. "Besides, if it's water, he said he'll let us know."

After rising unsteadily to his goat hoofs, Salvus gazed upon the footpath and the areas on either side. Cindy suspected her satyr friend was gifted with a sixth sense.

Within seconds, the precise moment Cindy was determined to defy Sam's order and trespass upon the side path, the yell of water was heard from beyond the trail. "Bring the plastic containers!"

Grabbing a lance and the plastic containers, Cindy bolted to the path, accompanied by Salvus, who also was bearing a weapon. Noticing Jimmy resting on a log, she ended her dash, glanced back, and demanded, "Aren't you coming?"

"How many people does it take to gather water?" replied a worn-out Jimmy. "Besides, there are only three containers."

"Fine, Jimmy," snapped Cindy, in a sarcastic tone. "Stay here by yourself; but if something enters the campsite, remember to scream loudly."

With Cindy's dose of reality, Jimmy jumped to his feet and was soon taking the lead up the side path.

When the three caught up with the others, they were greatly disappointed; it wasn't a lake at all, but rather a small stagnant pond with a repulsive odor.

Just beyond the pool of water lay an open field, which prompted Sam to warn, "Let's be quick about this; I want someone scanning the sky for Oswagis and Reclaimers, while everyone else helps fill the containers."

Cindy dropped the plastic tubs, pinched her nose to ward off the offensive smell, and asked, "Sam, are you sure this water's safe to drink?"

Sam knelt on the ground. With no water collection bucket, since the rope rested at the bottom of the castle moat, he cautiously dipped his index finger into the standing water and replied, "No, Cindy, I'm not sure; but I'm sure it'll be fine after it's boiled. Besides, it'll have to do for now, until we find another water supply."

Jimmy snatched a container from the ground and handed it to Sam; William accepted the second tub. Grabbing the last container, Cindy crossed to the opposite side of the pond.

William plunged his container into the cloudy water, alarming his co-travelers.

"Any movement in the sky?" asked a tense Sam, as he closely eyed William's immersed hands.

"No, nothing," replied Jimmy.

With no ill-fated effects from William's impulsive act, and since the water hole was shallow, Sam felt reassured submerging his fore-arms. Cindy also sensed it was safe dunking her hands in the pool, confident a water source that size couldn't possibly harbor a predatory creature. Once the containers were brimming, the group returned to the safety of the campsite.

"I guess we don't have a choice," yielded Sam, after setting a water container on the ground.

"A choice about what?" asked Dan.

"I mean," explained Sam, "we don't have any choice but to light a fire to boil the water, so it'll be sterilized. But let's do it quickly and pray nothing spots the fire from above the canopy."

After gathering a few dead branches and dried leaves from the footpath, Sam lit the kindling, but not before stressing, "This is the only time we start a fire."

Within minutes, a healthy flame was burning beneath a cooking pan. The group waited patiently for the water to boil, as they anxiously scanned the limbs overhead and the woods beyond.

Only then, Cindy realized she had left her lance at the pond. Knowing Sam would be upset—and rightfully so—if he learned her lance was left behind, since the loss of a single weapon could conceivably result in the loss of a life, she waited until the men had their backs turned and were busying themselves watching the water boil, before she slipped out of sight and hiked to the pond.

During her sole trek, she calmed her escalating fears by telling herself, repeatedly, the water hole was free of creatures and it was just a short distance from the campsite. Reaching the pool safely, she traced its perimeter until she came to her lance. After rising from grabbing the weapon, she turned and spotted a white stallion sipping from the pond's opposite side. As she crept in its direction, the startled horse retreated a few feet. Thinking it may be frightened by the lance, she gently lowered herself and set the weapon on the moist soil. Rising ever so slowly, she paused briefly, before placing one foot in front of the other and inching her way to the stallion that remained motionless, but staring at the approaching intruder. At arm's reach, she gradually extended her hand to the steed's neck. In an attempt to gain its trust, she petted it for a few minutes. Assured it was appeased, she placed her hands on its back and pulled herself up.

The stallion remained motionless and seemed unalarmed.

Cindy was treated to a slow trot around the pond.

This horse will really come in handy, she thought, *for the remainder of our trip.*

She enjoyed another lap around the water hole.

At the campground, Dan, without turning from the fire, teased, "Hey, Cindy, want to taste the boiling water? Cindy?" He turned to the spot where she had been sitting, just minutes earlier, and saw only her backpack.

Within seconds, five sets of eyes were scanning the temporary campsite.

"Where'd she go?" asked Dan.

"Cindy!" yelled Jimmy.

There was no response.

Suspecting she may have returned to the pond—and knowing the water source was creature-free—Sam felt comfortable asking the Clay brothers to check it out.

"Sure," replied Dan; William nodded.

"While you're getting her," he continued, "we'll pour the sanitary water into the bottles; it's still hot, but it'll cool in the containers."

The two brothers grabbed their lances and headed up the side path. On nearing the pool, they spotted Cindy riding the wild stallion.

"Wow!" exclaimed Dan. "Look at that."

The brothers' arrival caught the attention of the spirited horse, which immediately turned and dashed toward the clearing—away from the men and the pond. The siblings ran in pursuit; Cindy enjoyed the ride. The stallion came to a sudden halt, turned to face the approaching brothers, and instantly transformed itself into a centaur.

Staring at the half-man, half-horse beast, Dan's heart sank to his stomach; the centaur was missing his tail.

Witnessing the transformation from a beautiful steed into a gruesome creature, Cindy screamed, but she was beyond the earshot of Sam, Jimmy, and Salvus at the campsite. At a great personal risk, she leaped from the brute, hit the ground, and raced to the brothers. Unfortunately, she had advanced only several feet, when the centaur resumed his swift gallop and effortlessly swept her off her feet and into his brawny human arms.

With his hostage fixed in his grip, the creature reversed his course and bolted deeper into the clearing, leaving the young rescuers in the distance.

"Cindy!" yelled Dan.

"Cindy!" screamed William.

Dan looked at his brother in complete amazement. Realizing it was not the time, nor the place, for jubilation, he grabbed William's arm and ordered, "Come on; let's get the others."

After discovering and recovering Cindy's deserted weapon, the siblings dashed to the campsite, where they found Jimmy introducing Salvus to Ceremonia, who had recently appeared.

"Sam," yelled Dan, who was nearly breathless, "it's got Cindy!"

Sam dropped the last filled water bottle into a backpack, spun on his heels, and shouted, "What's got Cindy?"

"A horse," informed Dan, "that turned itself into a centaur."

With a weapon in hand, Sam jumped to his feet and was racing to the side path, when Dan restrained him by his shoulder and explained, "It's too late; she's already out of sight. We tried to run after her, but the centaur was too fast."

"How can a horse change into a centaur?" yelled a raging Sam. "And who would do such a thing?"

"Bacchus," blurted Ceremonia.

Stepping alongside the centuries-old forest native, Sam demanded, "Who's Bacchus?"

"He's that murderous creature who devoured my cousin," she related. "Turning himself into a horse doesn't surprise me. That's about all the species can visualize transforming themselves into; they're so empty-headed."

"Alright…alright," interjected Sam. "Will you help us find Cindy?"

Ceremonia ignored Sam's request and stepped toward the unfamiliar traveler. "You must be William."

The young man nodded.

"I'm Ceremonia," introduced the woodland dweller, "one of the tree nymphs; it's nice to meet you—finally."

Walking a few feet to the winged lady, Sam pleaded, "Ceremonia, will you help us? You must know where Bacchus has taken Cindy."

With her eyes lowered, the tree nymph shamefully admitted, "I'm sorry; I can't. As much as I'd—"

"What do you mean you can't?" snapped Dan.

"I'd really like to," replied Ceremonia, "but considering the declining number of my kind, the risk is far too great."

"What about Cindy?" challenged Dan in a harsh tone. "Don't you care about her safety?"

"Of course I do," admitted Ceremonia, "but—"

"Then help us," demanded Dan, "if not for Cindy, at least for revenge against Bacchus. Don't you owe it to your cousin?"

Dan's retaliatory remark cut Ceremonia to the core. Nonetheless, she cowered, "I'm really sorry; I'd like to, but I just can't."

"Fine," replied a furious Dan, while tightening the grip on his lance, "then we'll find her and free her ourselves."

The remaining men grabbed their weaponry and followed Dan up the side path, leaving Ceremonia alone near the fading fire, where she wrestled with her conflicting emotions between the tree nymphs' primary task of tending the woodlands and what the centaurs had reduced her race to become—fearful and neglectful of the forest areas where the half-man and half-horse creatures roam.

How dare Bacchus kill my cousin, thought Ceremonia, *and then have the audacity to instill fear in me!*

At the pond, the men meticulously tracked the hoof prints of the centaur across the clearing; Salvus was especially gifted in trailing the drunken beast.

Spotting a flicker of light in the corner of his eye, Dan focused on the miniature Ceremonia, hovering a few inches overhead, yelling, "I've seen Bacchus entering and leaving his cave many times."

"Thanks, Ceremonia," praised Dan, with his eyes fixed on the illumination.

Extending her small arm to the left, she ordered, "Follow me!" In a flash, she was twenty yards ahead of the posse, which pressed forward, as quickly as the tall hindering grass would permit.

Nearing a cave—just a stone's throw inside the forest, on the opposite side of the clearing—Ceremonia pointed and said, "That's it."

Sam raised his lance to shoulder height.

Knowing he was preparing to storm the cave, Ceremonia flew in front, motioned him to stop, and commanded, "No, wait here; I'll lure him out."

"No, Ceremonia," whispered Dan, "it's too dangerous. You've done more than enough already."

"You were right, Dan," she admitted. "Bacchus has reduced my species to idle spectators. Thanks for reminding me of what we've become. I need to…no…I have to do this." She gestured the men to hide near the side of the cave's entrance.

Once the covert rescuers were out of view, Ceremonia blazed brightly in front of the cave, hoping to capture Bacchus' attention. Floating a short distance into the hollow rock was all it took to send the centaur racing out of his dwelling and in her direction. Even the tree nymph was surprised at his speed, considering his intoxicated state. She soared into the clearing; Bacchus followed. Throughout the chase, she kept inciting, "You're nothing but a drunken beast," which drew the centaur deeper into the grassland.

The moment Bacchus was a remote figure in the clearing, the five men invaded his rocky abode and found Cindy locked in a cage—the sides and back of which were the cave wall—with several iron bars covering the opening of the natural niche.

"Are you alright?" exclaimed Sam, after dashing to the recess in the wall.

"Yeah," replied Cindy, "just a little edgy; but I'm okay."

Noticing a wooden bowl of wine and a key resting on a lopsided table, directly opposite the cage, Sam stepped to the lone furnishing. As he reached for the key, two bats plunged from the inner heights of the darkened cave and sank their fangs into his wrists.

Cindy screamed; William rushed to his rescue.

The older brother grabbed the bats and applied precise and targeted pressure to the sides of the flying mammals' heads, dislodging their bloody grasp. Once released, and still in his grip, he smashed the nocturnal animals against the rock wall; the bats were no more.

Speechless at first, Sam eventually complimented, "Thanks, William. Where'd you learn to do that?"

The young man lowered his head, as if fearful to respond, but ultimately raised his sights to Sam and mumbled, "Bats in the castle."

Cindy wedged her face between two iron bars and exclaimed, "He spoke."

The remaining travelers—except Dan, who heard him blurt Cindy's name at the pond—expressed like wonderment.

With the corroded key in hand, Sam handed it to William who, by every right, deserved the honor of releasing the captive.

After Cindy was freed, the travelers rushed to the cave's entrance, with their weapons raised. Salvus stepped ahead of the group, took a prolonged whiff, and peered around the corner, confirming the coast was clear. As the satyr stepped beyond the den's border, the group followed. Dan and William brought up the rear of the evacuation line.

"You learned that at the castle?" whispered Dan.

"Yeah," whispered William, "there were a lot of bats in the Great Tower."

Resting his hand on his sibling's shoulder, Dan cautioned, "Don't let mom catch you doing that; she'd freak out."

●

Alluring Bacchus deeper into the meadow, Ceremonia glanced backward and glimpsed the rapid approach of a lone Oswagi Bird, without a Reclaimer aboard. Bacchus, still intoxicated, was oblivious to the looming danger, since the bird's shadow had not yet crossed his forward path. The bird of prey remained perfectly silent, keeping its wings at rest, as it glided. Suspecting the Oswagi would favor the moist meat of a large centaur to her, Ceremonia resumed her crafty flight maneuvers to entrap Bacchus.

The moment the Oswagi was directly overhead, the tree nymph plunged several feet and flew between the centaur's legs. With Ceremonia out of the Oswagi's path of destruction, the bird swooped twenty feet, sank its talons into Bacchus, effortlessly plucked him from the ground, and raised him higher and higher into the atmosphere.

Ceremonia redirected her flight destination to the fleeing travelers.

The men and Cindy were barely halfway across the clearing when Ceremonia flickered overhead, warning, "Hurry, before Bacchus turns himself into something else."

Instinctively, all eyes focused heavenward and witnessed Bacchus transform himself into an Oswagi Bird. The captured Bacchus Oswagi positioned himself to graze his tail, with its rare venom strain, against the underside of his captor.

Detecting an abrupt surge in its prey's weight, the natural Oswagi glanced below and quickly released its bulky victim, before the Bacchus Oswagi could deliver his poison.

With the two birds now flying by their own powers, a merciless battle ensued in the sky, as the Bacchus Oswagi outsoared the natural Oswagi and then nose-dived, gashing the right side of the natural Oswagi with his talons. In the midst of its anguish, the natural Oswagi bashed its deadly tail against the head of the Bacchus Oswagi, delivering a whiplash.

Taking advantage of the Bacchus Oswagi's temporary disorientation, the natural Oswagi tightened its tail around its victim's neck and applied as much pressure as its diminishing strength would allow. Unfortunately, the natural Oswagi hadn't ensnared the Bacchus bird long enough for the venom to flow. Within seconds, the natural Oswagi screeched, as its adversary freed himself from the stranglehold and gored his tusks into the natural Oswagi's torso.

As the travelers continued sprinting—and Ceremonia soaring—across the grassland and nearing the forest, they periodically glanced aloft to witness the mortal aerial combat. Once beyond the pond and inside the refuge of the woods, the travelers eyed the Bacchus Oswagi riding atop the natural Oswagi with his talons stabbing the enemy. The Bacchus Oswagi's enormous weight overpowered the wounded natural Oswagi, forcing it to lose considerable altitude.

In the blink of an eye, the Bacchus Oswagi transformed himself into a two-thousand-pound boulder. The natural Oswagi plummeted at an incredible speed and was crushed by the massive rock upon its impact with the open field. There was no hope for the natural Oswagi; it closed its eyes forever.

Ceremonia and the travelers knew they had to remain undetected in the forest, for Bacchus still had until midnight to alter his appearance from a massive stone into something more threatening.

Reaching the campsite, the travelers silently, but quickly, gathered their gear and opted against hiking on the path which they had traveled upon since their escape from the castle. Instead, the group decided they'd venture to the right, until they crossed the original footpath that led them to the castle during the first leg of their month-long journey. This tactical deviation, they also hoped, would put a greater distance between themselves and the enchanting centaur.

Since Bacchus had the ability to transform himself for several more hours, they also agreed they would hike until the midnight hour—until they were sure his powers had expired. The group trudged through the dense brush and entangling vegetation for nearly an hour, before reaching what they presumed was the original path. Before stepping upon the new trail, however, each member scanned the area, making certain it was free of predators, not to mention Oswagis and Reclaimers that may have landed in the clearing and slithered to the deeper recesses of the forest. Seeing nothing, the weary travelers stepped on the path and resumed their homeward trek.

Since the group had no choice but to march until midnight, Sam was grateful his friends were relatively injury-free and were determined to get as far away from Bacchus as possible.

Picking up her pace, Cindy stepped alongside Sam and asked, "How are your wrists?"

During the recent aerial combat and the exodus from the campsite, Sam had ignored his injuries. Holding up his hands for a closer inspection, he was surprised that even though his wrists were bleeding, he was not in a great deal of pain and no arteries had been punctured. "Actually, the cuts aren't that deep," he replied.

"Nevertheless," insisted Cindy, "they still should be treated. For all we know, those bats may have been rabid."

"Not now, Cindy," admonished Sam, "we need to keep moving."

Refusing to heed his warning, Cindy swung her knapsack from her back and removed the whiskey bottle, without losing a step. "Hold out your wrists," she demanded.

Sam reluctantly submitted.

As the cure-all was poured, Sam clenched his teeth, to which she responded, "Deep enough to sting though, huh."

Again, without disrupting the rhythm of her walk, she returned the bottle to her bag and ripped two shreds of cloth from an old shirt. After swinging the bag to her back, she wrapped Sam's wounds with ease.

"You're becoming pretty good at this," said Sam, after examining her bandaging.

"Yeah," replied Cindy. "You guys have given me a lot of practice over the last couple weeks."

Looking ahead, then to the canopy, and finally to the sides of the new footpath, Sam remarked, "I wonder where Ceremonia went."

"I don't know," replied Cindy, following his gaze, "but I'm glad she appeared when she did."

"Yeah," agreed Sam, "so am I."

Dan, William, and Jimmy, who lagged several feet behind Cindy and Sam, struck up a conversation, which helped pass the time and divert their thoughts from their exhaustion.

"So, William," asked Jimmy, "what was it like in the castle?"

William, who was still having moderate difficulty verbalizing his thoughts, eventually responded, "It was mostly uneventful."

"Did you hear that, Dan?" chuckled Jimmy. "His time in the castle was uneventful."

Dan remained silent. Though he was thankful the group's extended daily hikes would place them at the oak's base sooner, his conscience troubled him for not alerting Sam to the manuscript in his pocket. After all, he promised Sam he wouldn't keep anything from him.

"Dan," snapped Jimmy, "are you even listening?"

"Sorry," he remarked, "I was just thinking."

After offering a backward glance to Salvus, who was trailing the three men, Jimmy returned his sights to Dan and restated, "Your brother claims that life in the castle was dull."

"What was it like, William?" asked Dan.

"Well," replied the older sibling, "I don't remember much, since most of the time I was under the hypnotic state of my personal Reclaimer, Daedalus."

A sudden gale split the canopy, exposing the sky; the travelers took notice.

With no sign of Oswagis, William continued, "I know it sounds strange that I knew I was in a trance, but I do remember it and I also remember wanting nothing more than to break free from the mental powers of Daedalus, so I could think and act on my own. But his superior faculties overpowered my determination to flee."

"You mentioned the Great Tower," reminded Dan.

"Yeah," replied William. "I escaped Daedalus a few times over the years, usually during one of the group's many marches to the court-yard, when he was distracted by some commotion in the castle. You see, when Daedalus was distant from me, his persuasive powers were slightly diminished, which permitted me to slip away from the group for a brief time. I remember one time, in particular, walking down the rear staircase, when there was a loud crash in the Hall of Admittance. Daedalus left my side to investigate the disruption. I imagine he inspected the hall, and not another Reclaimer, since he was one of the senior officers, after Spiritus Malus. Anyway, because I was the last person in the group, none of the other Reclaimers saw me escape, since they were focused entirely on their assigned guests. I never learned the cause of the ruckus in the hall, though I suspect it had something to do with the trolls; they were always a nuisance to the Reclaimers. When Daedalus was distant, despite the fact that my asthma slowly returned, I could actually remember people and things I wanted to think about. For a brief time, there were no restrictions on my thoughts."

"What'd you think about when you were free?" questioned Dan.

"It was during those rare occasions," explained William, "when I thought about mom and dad—and you, Dan. Anyway, after Daedalus left to survey the hall, I remained motionless until the other guests and their assigned Reclaimers turned the corner. Then, I raced down the corridor and climbed the steps to the Great Tower. Knowing I couldn't leave the castle permanently—since I attempted to flee a few years earlier, but found my breathing problems returned the moment I stepped outside the fortress—I stayed in the Great Tower for a short time, enjoying my solitude and my freedom of thought, until my panting became unbearable. Ultimately, I had no choice but to return to the guests' room, where Daedalus' sorcery eased my labored breathing. Like I said, leaving the castle wasn't an option."

"Yeah, we've been told," recounted Jimmy, "the castle walls are cursed by the Reclaimers to relieve the sufferings of its inhabitants; but complete recovery demands a Reclaimer close at hand."

"Did Daedalus punish you for wandering to the Great Tower?" asked Dan, with a worried look.

"No," replied William, "though he did eye me closely from then on. After all, he figured he had an investment in me."

Opening a backpack, which originally held an abundance of fruits and vegetables, William pushed his medication bottle aside, removed the stuffed animal, and revealed, "I remember this toy as if it were another life."

"Yeah," remarked Dan, "the police found it near the base of the oak the night you vanished. Ever since then, mom's kept it on your bed in our room."

Squeezing the toy, William asked with great hesitancy, "Are mom and dad alright?"

"Oh, sure," answered Dan, "though they're a bit older. Mom took your disappearance pretty hard. I remember dad telling me, not too long ago, that for years she'd leave the house only for emergencies and church. Her social life was nonexistent and she'd spend most of the day, when I was in school, sitting in our bedroom holding that stuffed animal."

William dropped the ragged toy into the backpack and admitted,

"I'd love to see them again, but…I don't know…it's been so long, it may be too difficult for them."

"Difficult?" blurted Dan. "Are you serious? I can't even begin to imagine how excited they'd be, especially mom." Halting his stride, he vowed, "William, I'll make sure you get home; I promise. You have to return; mom's suffered too much."

Jimmy, who had slipped back alongside the satyr minutes earlier, when the brothers' conversation shifted to family matters, asked, "Salvus, how are you holding up?"

"I'm fine," replied a poorly convincing satyr.

As he scanned the sides of the footpath, Jimmy continued, "So, do the woods look familiar to you?"

"No," replied Salvus, "it's been too many years, even though many of the forest sounds that haunted me as a child still do. I guess some memories always trouble a person."

CHAPTER TEN

Intangible Killers

FROM THE REAR OF THE LINE, JIMMY AND SALVUS NOTICED Dan and William had picked up their pace. Looking beyond the Clays, they saw Sam and Cindy stepping nearer the brothers; Jimmy and the satyr advanced.

"I think," proposed Sam, "we'll stop here for a few minutes to rest and enjoy an apple. But don't get too used to it, since we'll be hiking again in fifteen minutes."

The travelers agreed, before Cindy reached into her bag and removed six apples. The group sat upon the ground, three leaning against the backs of the others, so a panoramic view for predators, Reclaimers, and Bacchus was maintained at all times. To Jimmy, it seemed he had just sat down, when Sam ordered the group to gear up. Grabbing their lances from the forest floor, the explorers headed up the path.

Though the forest was unusually dark during the day, Sam suspected—after a lengthy hike—the sun beyond the canopy had set, since the forest insects had begun their nocturnal recital hours earlier. His wrist injuries required he carry his wristwatch in his pocket. Removing the treasured heirloom, he informed his friends it was 10:45 p.m.

Without warning, a familiar flash of light appeared in the treetops.

"It's Ceremonia!" shouted Cindy.

"Sh," warned Sam. "We don't want to announce our whereabouts to the Reclaimers or Bacchus."

Lowering herself to the group, but refusing to enlarge herself, for fear Bacchus would spot the radiance required for her growth to full size, she updated, "I've scouted a wide area of the neighboring woods and I haven't seen Bacchus or anything that's cursed with the characteristics of a newly-transformed centaur. But remember, he still has another hour or so."

"Yeah," said Sam, "we plan on hiking until midnight."

"Ceremonia," asked Cindy, "would it be safe to light a fire after midnight?"

Glancing at Sam before responding, the tree nymph eventually warned, "Probably not; although Bacchus' powers will have expired by then, you still have the Reclaimers to contend with. Granted, I haven't seen any in my travels tonight, but that doesn't necessarily mean they've returned to the castle."

After taking a noisy gulp from his water bottle, Dan asked, "Ceremonia, do you know how much farther to the oak tree?"

Again, after looking at Sam, as if seeking permission to reply, she answered, "I believe it's still quite a ways ahead, probably several days' hike by foot."

Sensing Ceremonia's estimation was disheartening to the group, Sam urged, "Come on, let's move; we're losing precious travel time."

The travelers resumed their march, but this time, under the watchful eye of Ceremonia.

Sam looked at his watch three more times before announcing it was 12:05 a.m.

After bidding her farewells, the tree nymph darted to the canopy.

"Now can we rest?" pleaded Cindy, whose stare was lost in the treetops with Ceremonia's swift departure.

"Yes," answered Sam, "now we can rest; Bacchus is no longer a threat to us." On observing the physical appearances of his friends and easily detecting fatigue, he volunteered, "I'll take the first watch." Looking at Dan, he asked, "Are you up for patrol?"

"Sure," replied the weary teenager. *After all,* he thought, *I'm the one who proposed the extended daily hikes.*

"Alright," informed Sam to his friends, "Dan will take the second watch. But remember, we rise at 4:00 a.m."

Jimmy, who was already unrolling his sleeping bag, turned in Sam's direction and snapped, "Four! Are you crazy? It's already after midnight."

Approaching the young man, so as not to be overheard and alarm the others, Sam admonished, "Do you want to reach the tree in time or not?"

Jimmy remained close-mouthed.

"Then," advised Sam, "we need to cover as much ground as possible in a day. We're all tired, I know, but either we press forward or we delay our departure from this world for another month."

"I'm not just tired," admitted Jimmy, "but I'm so sick of this forest."

"So am I," said Sam, "but we must endure it a little longer." With Jimmy now nestled in his sleeping bag, Sam ordered, "Get some shut-eye and I'll see you in a few hours." He left his friend's side and neared the patrol spot.

William and Dan, likewise, prepared their sleeping area and were just settling in when William offered, "Dan, why don't you sleep until 4:00? I'll take the second watch."

"Thanks, but I'm really not tired," lied the younger sibling.

Noticing William had already dropped to his back, Dan reminded, "Don't forget your pill."

After sitting up and reaching for his bag, William opened the medicine bottle and swallowed a coated tablet. Before leaning back, however, he looked to Cindy's sleeping area and commented to Dan she was already asleep. Realizing she had overlooked her nightly ritual, William approached her area, grabbed the whiskey bottle, and walked to Salvus.

"Oh, no," complained the satyr, "not you, too. I thought I'd get a break tonight."

Dan's faint laughter was heard a short distance away.

"Sorry, Salvus," reasoned William, "but later you'll be happy I did this."

"Maybe," he yielded, "but not until much, much later."

After treating the satyr, William moved to his next patient, Sam, who was on duty. He freely offered his wrists. The watchman presumed having his wounds disinfected was greater mental therapy for William than physical therapy for himself.

Next, he approached Dan with the open bottle.

"What's that for?" asked the younger sibling.

"Your leg," replied William.

"What about my leg?"

"Cindy told me of your bad luck when crossing the drawbridge at the castle."

"Did she also tell you it's healing fine," replied Dan, "and a scab is forming?"

"Then you won't mind me taking a look," challenged the doubtful sibling.

After motioning him to raise his pant leg, William was surprised Dan was telling the truth. His gash was healing nicely and a hardy scab was clearly visible, even in the near total darkness. William, however, drenched the wound for good measure. "Now your back," he ordered.

Knowing he couldn't dissuade his brother, Dan removed his shirt and rested on his stomach. During his treatment, he was grateful William had become a useful member of the party and that his co-travelers had accepted him, though they and he didn't look too kindly on him bearing the whiskey bottle.

"How's that?" asked William, before replacing the cap to the bottle.

"It was fine before you started," joked Dan.

William retraced his steps to Cindy's area, replaced the bottle in her bag, and returned to his brother's side. Before reclining, he vaguely detected Sam pacing several yards in the distance. Without a campfire or the glowing lantern, he was amazed how dark and menacing the forest had become in the stillness of the midnight hour.

Unlike his brother, Dan suffered from a guilty conscience, which kept him awake. Rising from his bedding a few minutes before 2:00 a.m., he announced his approach, so as not to startle Sam, and neared the patrol log.

"Is it time already?" asked Sam, followed by a prolonged yawn.

"Just about," answered Dan, who lowered his head, trying to think of an opening for the unpleasant conversation.

On witnessing his companion standing motionless and silent, Sam prompted, "What's on your mind?"

Dan cleared his throat and began, "Sam, I meant to show you something earlier," as he slipped his hand into his jean pocket.

"Show me what?" asked a curious Sam.

Before removing his hand from his pocket, the teenager continued, "Remember at the castle when you called to me from the doorway of the guests' room to the distant inner room?"

"Yeah," recalled Sam. "But what's that got to do with—"

"The room," interrupted Dan, "was a small library."

Knowing it was out of character for Dan to discuss frivolous matters, Sam ordered, "Spill it, Dan. Tell me what you found."

Dan pulled the ancient parchment from his pocket and handed it to Sam, explaining, "Since I wasn't sure if the Reclaimers had an identical book in the main library or if they had memorized the potion, I ripped that page from the book."

Sam unfolded the document and read its contents quietly to himself, as he rested upon the log that he had occupied for nearly two hours. After reading the dire potion, "Relocating Portals," he looked up at the teenager and admitted, "We don't seem to get any breaks, do we?" He scanned the ingredients, once again, before commenting, "Everything's marked off, except two."

Dan was shocked Sam didn't engage in another lecture about keeping him informed on all developments. He suspected his lack of sleep precluded him from another verbal reprimand or perhaps he was engrossed with the new predicament at hand. Squatting at Sam's feet to make eye contact, he confessed, "I'm sorry I didn't show you earlier. That's why I suggested we cross the clearing instead of hiking along the fringes of the forest and why I've been so adamant about covering as much ground as possible in a day." Extending his finger, he pointed to one of the last two remaining ingredients and alerted, "I don't know if you noticed it, but Bacchus was missing his tail."

As he folded the ancient manuscript along its creased lines, Sam replied, "No, I didn't notice. I was focused on rescuing Cindy." After a deep exhale, he tried to put the teenager's mind—and his—at ease by speculating, "But Bacchus could have lost his tail in a bizarre accident or something. Just because he's missing it, doesn't necessarily mean the Reclaimers are to blame."

"Sam," replied Dan, "I appreciate your trying to ease my worries, but what are the odds? I've got an awful hunch the Reclaimers have Bacchus' tail in their possession."

Sam rose from the log and was returning the parchment to Dan, when he jerked his hand back, reread the unmarked ingredients, and asked, "What the heck is a Bozeman's quill?"

"I haven't the foggiest," admitted Dan. Accepting the manuscript, he asked, "Should we tell the others?"

Sam returned to the log, rested his head in his hands, and mumbled, "No, not now; I'll know when the time is right."

Clasping his companion's forearm, Dan insisted, "Get some rest; I'll take over."

"Alright," yielded Sam, as he stepped from the log and neared the inner campsite.

As Dan suspected, Sam remained wide-awake, worrying about the alarming omen and the decreasing likelihood of reaching the enchanted oak in time.

●

Dan woke his co-travelers at precisely 4:00 a.m. As expected, Jimmy was the last to stumble from his sleeping bag. After the bedding was crammed into their bags, the six gathered for breakfast, at which time Sam updated, "The food rations are running extremely low. So, I suggest we each have an apple; we'll save the tomatoes for lunch and dinner. Hopefully, I'll hunt soon."

"Do you think you'll hunt today?" asked Cindy.

Sam was presented with a serious dilemma. Hunting would exhaust precious travel time, especially since he wasn't sure how many more hiking days were needed to reach the oak before the next full moon. But with little or no food, his friends' strength would wane, making it virtually impossible to sustain their long daily treks. In response to her question, he compromised, "Maybe I'll do a little hunting today, while you're eating lunch."

Dan sized up the group's plight and Sam's potential solution quickly and accurately. "I'll join you on the hunt today," offered Dan, who sacrificed his apple by returning it to Cindy's bag.

However, his act of kindness did not go unnoticed.

"Dan," pressured Sam, "if you expect to hunt with me today, you'll need your strength; eat up."

The teenager grabbed the apple from the bag and took a bite.

"Sam," proposed Jimmy, "if we can't light a campfire, how are we going to cook whatever you catch?"

Another dilemma arose.

"Well," replied Sam, in a frustrated tone, "maybe I'll have to break my rule again. Who knows, maybe the Reclaimers have given up and have returned to the castle. But since we can't say for sure, we'll extinguish the flame as soon as the meal is cooked, presuming I'm lucky in the hunt."

Within an hour, the travelers had finished their meager breakfast, strapped on their gear, and were marching up the trail. The morning hike proved to be one without incident; no Oswagis, Reclaimers, or predators crossed the group's path. As the six broke for lunch, Sam and Dan abstained from their meal and were preparing to slip into the nearby woods, when William asked to join in the hunt.

"Sure," teased Sam, "maybe you can kill our dinner with your bare hands, like the bats." Sam rejected Salvus' offer to join the hunting party, suggesting he patrol the campsite with Jimmy and Cindy. After all, he wasn't totally convinced the Reclaimers had abandoned their search.

Throughout their one-hour hunt, the travelers managed to stir a few rabbits from the undergrowth, but the prey dodged their weapons.

Pulling his wristwatch from his pocket, Sam announced it was 1:10. Knowing they had to retrace their steps to the campsite, he advised the brothers, "We'll try our luck tomorrow; let's head back to camp."

The men were barely several minutes into their retreat when William asked the question that tormented everyone, "Sam, how many more days of hiking before we reach the tree?"

Sam repositioned his bow that had slipped from his shoulder and shook his head, admitting, "There's no way of knowing for sure. So, I suggest we travel as long and as hard as we can each day. Heck, I'd rather arrive too early than too late."

William pulled Dan and Sam by their shoulders and whispered, "Sh." Looking ahead, between two large trees, the older brother caught sight of another gathering of rabbits. Before Sam grasped the bow from his shoulder, William had a hand on the weapon and was slowly removing it, so as not to startle the cottontails.

Handing William an arrow, Sam cautioned, in the lowest of voices, "Don't release until I say. I'll try to get a second with my revolver."

William pulled the string taut; Sam closed one eye and aimed the pistol.

"On the count of three," whispered Sam. "One, two, three."

Within seconds, the hares scrambled to the safety of the under-growth—all but two. The men let out a light cheer, as Sam and William gave one another a firm slap on the back.

"That ought to keep us going for a couple meals," estimated Sam. As the three walked to claim their prizes, he complimented, "William, between your bare hands and the bow, I'd say you're a natural huntsman."

●

At the temporary campsite, the dawdling travelers cleaned the area, which took only a few minutes, and then stretched upon the ground to rest their aching limbs, before their afternoon hike.

When the hunters arrived, proudly displaying their trophies, the three jumped to their feet to inspect their next meal.

Both rabbits were fairly large; one would probably feed the six, though nowhere near the point of gluttony.

Lowering her face to the long-eared mammals, Cindy was surprised neither had fangs, as she presumed most of the forest creatures were disfigured with. Knowing the group would be eating meat that night raised their spirits and infused a surge of energy, as they took to the path.

During the afternoon trek, a vote was taken on whether to break and eat dinner at 6:00 and then continue hiking until midnight or march until 11:00 and then enjoy their rabbit meal. The votes were cast; dinner would be served at 11:00. The remainder of the day's journey was not nearly as tiresome for the group, in part, because everyone knew they'd be feasting later that night. Each step brought them closer to the cooked rabbit.

Sam pulled his wristwatch from his pocket and notified his friends it was 10:15 p.m.

Cindy, however, failed to hear Sam's announcement; she was engrossed with an oddity up the footpath. "Sam," she directed, "look at the area ahead."

Sam looked up the trail and also noticed the peculiarity.

Along both sides of the uphill path, about a hundred feet from the travelers, stood a cluster of trees. For June, it was most unusual they didn't support any leaves. Even more strange was the surrounding terrain.

Ending their conversation, the men noticed their lead companions standing motionless, but pointing at something in the distance. Immediately, they stepped alongside Sam and Cindy to eye the anomaly.

"Salvus," questioned Sam, "do you recognize those trees?"

"No."

Throughout their journey, the party had grown accustomed to seeing tree after tree in the vast forest with hardly any open space between them, while supporting so many leaves the sky was hidden. But these trees were completely stripped of foliage and no undergrowth flourished below. Equally curious were the trees, which were separated from each other by twenty feet or more. It appeared as though someone or something had deliberately cleared the brush and smaller trees from around the larger ones. In near total darkness— for fear the lit lantern would attract unwanted visitors—the group advanced cautiously up the steep path, between the unearthly trees. Thankfully, as quickly as the trees and the uncommon terrain came into view, the abnormalities ended and the familiar undergrowth and dense trees appeared.

"Well," said Sam, "whatever weird trees they were, they're behind us now."

Cindy breathed a hushed sigh of relief.

Since the expanse of land atop the sloped path was reasonably flat, Sam suggested they pitch camp for the night. The thought of a rabbit dinner soon relegated the strange trees to the pages of ancient history.

"Why don't you set up your sleeping gear," suggested Sam to his co-travelers. "I'll gather some fallen limbs."

After unrolling the shared sleeping bag, Dan stared down the trail to the peculiar area and asked, "William, have you ever seen trees like those before?"

William dropped an asthma pill into his mouth, swallowed, and replied, "No, but remember, I haven't been in the woods for years. And the last time I was, it was near the castle and only for several minutes, before my asthma kicked in."

Without disrupting his gaze at the trees, Dan remarked, "They're just too creepy."

"It's probably just your imagination," downplayed William. After dropping the medication bottle in his backpack, he suggested, "Let's see if Sam needs help gathering branches."

In the darkness, the brothers spotted movement ahead and guessed it was the wood gatherer. "Hey, Sam," offered William, when he and Dan were within hearing distance, "do you need any help?"

Sam spun and responded, "Yeah, why don't you two find some rocks to border the campfire."

"Consider it done," replied the older sibling.

The young men had just begun to step away, when Dan turned and questioned, "Sam, if we're having a fire for just a short time tonight, do we really need the rocks?"

"Better safe than sorry," reminded Sam.

As the brothers left their older companion rummaging for dead branches in the dark, Dan headed to his sleeping area.

William trailed, asking, "Where are you going?"

"To get the lantern."

"Are you sure that's wise?"

"I'll have it on for just a few minutes," promised Dan. "Besides, look how dark it is. How are we going to find stones in the dark?"

With growing reservations, William reluctantly agreed.

After snatching the lantern from atop his sleeping bag, Dan suggested, "William, empty your canvas bag; we'll put the stones in it."

The older sibling dumped the bag's contents; within minutes, the brothers were on the footpath, searching for large stones.

Dan wandered aimlessly down the trail in the direction of the bizarre trees, prompting William to follow and ask, "What's wrong?"

Without interrupting his wide-eyed gaze at the oddity, Dan maintained, "I'm telling you, there's something weird about those trees; I can feel it. I could swear we're being watched."

Grabbing his brother's arm, William warned, "That's all the more reason to avoid the area."

Dan broke free of the grasp; he was determined to investigate the phenomenon.

●

Sam returned to the campsite, carrying an armful of fallen branches. "Where are Dan and William?" he asked.

"I saw them walking down the hill a few minutes ago," answered Cindy, who was taking a breather on a nearby log. "Why?"

Before dropping the limbs to the ground, he informed, "I asked them to find stones to border the fire." With an impatient look, he continued, "But I can't wait all night." Certain Cindy was cold and hungry, he suggested, "I guess I could start the fire now and set the rocks around it later, once they return."

Cindy remained silent, staring at the darkened path below.

After methodically arranging the wood, so the fire could breathe when ignited, Sam lit the dried leaves under the limbs. The flame rose quickly to the branches. Though the fire was barely seconds old, the dry wood progressively raised the blaze in intensity until the campsite was aglow.

●

Aware he and his sibling were still in view of Sam and the others, Dan kept the lantern switched off. As the brothers neared the strange trees and barren ground, they did their best—with the modest light streaming from the nearby campfire—to search for rocks, while also investigating the area. They separated, but maintained a constant conversation to ensure the other was not in any danger. As the fire atop the slope grew to a roaring blaze, the light steadily invaded the desolate area.

Dan screamed; then, complete silence.

The younger sibling was knocked to the ground; his glasses flew from his face and the unlit lantern rolled near the footpath. He labored to breathe, while trying to grasp something coiled around his neck. Sadly, each time he placed his hands to his throat to release the strangler, nothing was felt—only his bare neck.

He rolled onto his side. Looking across the wasteland for anything to aid in his escape, he eyed a branch's shadow inching its way to his ankle. The dark image secured its hold and pulled him in the opposite direction of the elusive shadow choking him. The merciless yanks of the intangible killers knocked him on his back. In a frenzied state to escape their grip, he glimpsed above and was stunned. The overhead limbs were completely motionless; not even the slightest breeze stirred them.

The shadows, created by the campfire atop the hill, had assumed lives of their own and were slowly squeezing the life from Dan. His efforts to remove them were useless.

William restlessly searched the terrain, until he spotted his brother in the distance. Focused on the tree ahead and Dan beneath it, he was unaware of a dark killer encroaching from above. It struck quickly, wrapping itself around its victim's dangling arms and waist and lifting him into the air; a neighboring shadow positioned itself to penetrate his mouth. William clenched his teeth and pressed his lips together to block its oral invasion. Seeing Dan in the campfire's glow—and knowing he needed immediate help from their friends atop the hill—he put his life on the line and screamed. The shadow entered his mouth and descended his esophagus.

At the campfire, Cindy, rose from the log and whispered, "Sam, did you hear that?"

"Hear what?"

She stared down the hill to the trees and claimed, "I could have sworn I heard a scream and then—"

"Then what?" prodded Sam, before throwing another dead branch on the fire.

"Then—nothing." She advanced several feet down the hill, peering at a reflection upon the ground.

Sam, who was still tending the flame, rose from his knees, turned, and also sensed something was wrong; the air was too still.

Taking a few steps farther, Cindy yelled, "It's Dan's lantern on the ground!"

Without delay, the two were racing down the slope.

From their sleeping area, Jimmy and Salvus saw their friends darting down the hill; they joined in the pursuit.

Once Cindy and Sam reached the bleak area, she stooped to grab the lantern, when she was thrown to the ground by a creeping shadow that grasped her ankle; a second dark image tightened its grip around her throat.

In the split second before he dropped to the ground to free her, Sam spotted William suspended in midair, behind the tree, with a shadowy figure protruding from his mouth.

The older Clay was unresponsive.

With no success releasing Cindy, Sam scanned the area for a clue to his friends' release. In his visual search, he saw Dan, also behind the tree, being slammed against the ground by two shadows that were savagely tugging the teenager against each other. Unable to grasp the dark assailants, Sam was baffled with the deadly situation. His persistent attempts to dislodge the dark images from Cindy's neck and ankle were ineffective.

Jimmy and Salvus, who had just arrived at the ghastly scene, froze in complete disbelief.

"What to do? What to do?" Sam kept asking himself. Catching sight of the blaze atop the hill, he suspected the campfire not only created the shadows, but was also sustaining them. *How can I overpower the light of the fire?* he thought. *By the time I race up the slope and put out the flame, the three will be dead.* His focus was drawn to the reflection at the edge of the footpath. *But what about*—his thoughts continued. He sprang to his feet, raced to the trail, and snatched the lantern from the ground. While turning, he jumped backwards; a dark image was approaching. As he had hoped, the shadow at his feet vanished the instant he switched on the lantern; its intense beam obliterated the dark image.

Suspecting William had endured the worst suffering, since he was already unconscious, Sam darted to the back side of the tree with the lantern aglow. As the artificial light met the shadows around his waist and in his mouth, they also expired; William fell to the ground.

"Jimmy, Salvus," yelled Sam, "drag William to the path; but stay clear of the roving shadows."

With Dan only feet away from his brother's limp body, Sam approached his shadows; they disappeared under the lantern's high beam. Finally, Cindy was released from the death grip of the mysterious predators; both she and Dan were carried to the safety of the footpath.

Keeping the lantern aglow, Sam ordered Jimmy and Salvus to keep a watchful eye on the shadows near the edge of the trail, before he fell to his knees and performed mouth-to-mouth resuscitation on William.

"Come on," yelled Sam, between breaths.

William remained motionless.

"Come on," he pleaded again.

Despite his complete exhaustion and shortness of breath, Dan struggled to a seated position. Watching Sam attempt to revive his brother, he crawled to William's side. "Breathe!" he yelled.

To the relief of the group, William eventually coughed and then struggled to catch his breath.

Before waiting for his condition to improve, Dan blurted, "Are you alright?"

"Yeah, I think so," responded William, followed by several more deep coughs.

Looking to the other recent victims, Sam asked, "How are you two?"

"I'll be okay," replied Cindy.

"I'm fine," assured Dan.

After raising his sights to the leafless limbs and then lowering his gaze to the lifeless ground, Sam admitted, "So, there was something odd about this area after all. It seems these trees have their own method of clearing the ground, so no saplings soar above their reach and overshadow them from the sun."

As he listened to Sam speculate, Dan realized his vision was blurry. "My glasses," he exclaimed, "they're somewhere near the tree."

"Rest, Dan," ordered Sam, who grabbed the glowing lantern and cautiously approached the barren area in search of the spectacles.

Near the base of the tree rested the glasses; surprisingly, they were intact. Several feet distant lay William's canvas bag. Sam recovered the items and returned to the refuge of the path without incident.

Dan placed his glasses on the bridge of his nose and gazed about. The stark trees permitted an unobstructed view of the night sky. Staring into the heavens, Dan shouted, "Look, it's the first quarter moon!"

"What does that mean?" asked Cindy, who glimpsed beyond the limbs.

"It means," explained Dan, "the next full moon will rise in seven days."

"Are you sure?" asked a hopeful Jimmy.

"Positive," assured Dan.

"Well," declared Sam, "now we know we have a week left in this dismal world."

"Seven days couldn't come soon enough," admitted Cindy.

"I agree," said Sam. "But we mustn't let our guards down; we're still in a world of danger—literally." Seeing Cindy shiver, he suggested, "Come on, let's get back to the warmth of the fire."

Jimmy, Salvus, and Sam helped their recovering co-travelers up the hill, where they would dine on rabbit.

Cindy, William, and Dan rested on the forest floor near the fire; Jimmy returned the lantern and bag to the Clay's sleeping area.

From the distance, Jimmy heard, "Bring an asthma pill."

After snatching a tablet from the medication bottle, Jimmy returned to the fire at the exact moment Sam was placing a rabbit in a pan over the open flame.

"I know you took a pill earlier," recalled Dan to his brother, "but you better take another one, just in case."

As the group enjoyed the warmth of the fire and the smell of the sizzling rabbit, Sam interjected an item of unpleasant news, reminding, "Let's enjoy the meal, but then it's off to bed. We have another early rise."

Massaging her throat, Cindy pleaded, "Sam, just this once, can we sleep in?"

"I wish we could," he replied, "but the oak tree awaits us and we have just seven days to complete our journey."

Sam's eyes met Dan's; both knew what the other was thinking.

"In the future, I'll deny ever saying this," admitted Cindy, "but if we're late reaching the oak, maybe we could stay at the O'Brien's house until the next full moon."

Sam flipped the meat in the pan, set the cooking utensil aside, turned to the group, and revealed, "Look, there's something I kept from you, since I didn't want to cause any undue alarm."

"How could we possibly be any more alarmed," remarked Jimmy, "after what we've suffered the last three weeks?"

Not knowing how or even if he should respond, Sam chose not to reply.

Arranging the mess kits, Salvus asked, "Does it have something to do with the oak tree?"

Hiding his face in the direction of the fire, Sam answered, "I'm afraid so."

"What is it?" asked William.

Dan neared Sam's side and confessed, "Actually, I discovered something in the castle and only recently shared it with Sam. It was I, not Sam, who kept something from you."

Rising from a log, William neared his brother and warned, "Dan, after living amid hatred and deceit for thirteen years at the fortress, there's one thing I learned: a person must be honest with himself and with others or it eats away at him until there's nothing left but a foul-smelling core."

Clearing his throat, Dan began, "After we rescued the guests from the sixth floor, I discovered a smaller chamber at the back of the guests' room. When I entered, I realized it was a library with volumes of books on healing elixirs and potions."

"So, the Reclaimers don't have the natural ability to cure diseases," interjected Jimmy, "they use secret potions."

"Maybe," added William, "but believe me, I know for a fact they possess unmatched spellbinding powers. I endured it for years."

After turning the rabbit in the pan again, Sam urged, "Please, let Dan continue."

"Anyway," explained Dan, "there was an open potion book resting on a desk." He reached into his pocket and removed the parchment, clarifying, "I ripped a page from the volume." Before handing the manuscript to Jimmy, he concluded, "This is what I found."

After reading the potion's title, Jimmy whispered, "No, this can't be happening."

"What?" asked a fearful Cindy.

"According to that piece of paper," declared Dan, as he pointed to the document, "the Reclaimers are delving into a potion that relocates portals. I can only presume it's the portal in the oak tree."

Jimmy handed the manuscript to Cindy, who reviewed its contents in disbelief, before asking, "What's a Bozeman's quill?"

"I haven't a clue," replied Dan.

After everyone had the opportunity to analyze the document, Salvus returned it to Dan, who shoved it in his pocket. As expected, the travelers lost their appetites, including Jimmy.

"I'm afraid there's more," divulged Dan. All eyes focused on the teenager, as he reminded, "Bacchus is missing his tail—one of the last two remaining ingredients of the potion." As difficult as it was for him, he had to update his friends on their present situation. Looking directly at Cindy, he corrected, "So you see, we can't wait at the O'Brien's house, since the full moon, exactly seven days from now, will probably be our last chance to escape this world, presuming the Reclaimers haven't relocated the portal already."

On seeing a look of despair emerge on her face, Sam tried to instill hope by explaining since Dan ripped the page from the book, there was a chance the Reclaimers hadn't moved the portal yet.

"But how do we know for sure?" asked Cindy.

"Unfortunately," answered Sam, "there's no way of knowing, until we touch the oak during the next full moon. Anyway, that's why we're covering as much ground as possible in a day. We must reach the tree on time."

There was a moment of silence, as the travelers looked at one another. Turning to the fire again, Sam remarked, "I think the rabbit's done; hand me your plates."

"I'm not hungry," informed Cindy.

"Nor am I," said Jimmy.

Setting the tongs to the ground, Sam admitted, "Look, I know it's tough to hear; I couldn't believe it myself, when I first saw the parchment. But we need to eat to maintain our strength. We've got a lot of traveling ahead of us, but we'll make it in time. So, eat up."

With his optimistic prediction, Cindy handed her plate to Sam, who dropped a piece of rabbit on it and passed it to Salvus for a tomato slice. Within minutes, William led the blessing, imploring God's help for a speedy and safe trip to the tree.

All responded, "Amen."

To Sam, the rabbit was delicious, though no one voiced their approval. It was obvious the five were wondering if they'd complete their journey. Striving to redirect their thoughts, he volunteered, "I'll sit the first watch; if Salvus is up for it, he'll take the second."

After ripping a mouthful of rabbit flesh from the bone with his jagged teeth, the satyr nodded.

The rest of the meal was eaten in complete silence. One by one, the travelers set their empty plates on the ground and headed to their sleeping areas, except Dan, who stayed behind to help Sam clean the mess kits.

Pushing her anxieties aside, Cindy reached into her bag, removed the whiskey bottle, and walked to Salvus' area, where she treated his back injuries. Returning to Sam and Dan at the campfire, she alerted them that the second bottle of whiskey was empty.

"That's okay," said Sam, "there's another bottle; it should easily last seven more days."

Cindy offered no response, before turning and approaching her sleeping bag.

Knowing Sam was troubled, Dan asserted, "What we did, we had to do; we had no choice but to tell them the truth." With his gaze fixed on the darkened sleep areas, he confessed, "I should have told them earlier."

"I know we had to tell them the truth," remarked Sam, "but I wish it wasn't dreadful news about the portal." In frustration, he kicked a smoldering limb and stomped to the patrol post.

Dan extinguished the dying flames and walked to his sleeping area.

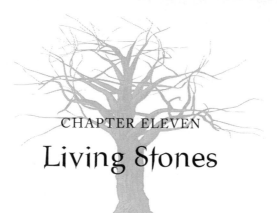

CHAPTER ELEVEN
Living Stones

IN THE WORLD THROUGH THE OAK TREE, NANCY CLAY KEPT her promise to Father James Roberts. Every morning, she and her husband—together with Sara Somer and the Parkers—attended Mass at Saint Augustine of Canterbury Church and then joined Father James in prayer, below the statue of Saint Michael the Archangel. With less than a week until the next full moon, Nancy and Jeff felt compelled to offer additional prayers and decided to leave for church earlier than normal. Fortunately, they met Father James, who was out for his morning jog.

The priest promptly unlocked the church doors, informing, "I'll join you in a few minutes."

The parents of the missing teenagers had endured unbearable mental anguish during the past three weeks. However, with Dan's supposed return just six days out, Nancy—in an effort to ease her agonizing mind—prayed constantly and busied herself with preparations for his arrival on June 30. Upon leaving the church, she thanked her parish priest for his continued prayers, before crossing the street to purchase several items at the market. At the top of her shopping list was a bottle of aspirin for her neck and ankle that had caused her intense pain since the previous night, as if she had been ruthlessly twisted. The pain had only moderately subsided.

Turning the corner of the produce aisle, she accidentally bumped her shopping cart into another customer's—Sara's. "I'm so sorry, Sara," apologized Nancy.

"That's quite alright," she replied, as she stabilized a wobbling carton of juice. Raising her sights from her groceries, she asked, "Nancy, do you always shop on Thursday mornings?"

"Not usually," she answered, "but I want to prepare a few meals before Dan's return and freeze them. This way, Jeff and I can spend more time with him."

Sara lowered her eyes to the contents in her cart and asked with great hesitancy, "Do you think Cindy, Jimmy, and Sam will also return next Wednesday?"

"I can't say for sure," answered Nancy, "but that's what I'm praying for. We need to believe they will return; we must keep our faith alive."

Sara pulled a tissue from her purse, dabbed the corners of her eyes, and admitted, "I want to believe; I really do. But many times, doubt creeps in."

"I'd suspect that's normal," consoled Nancy, "but we can't get discouraged." Grasping her friend's hand, she politely insisted, "I want you to spend next Wednesday at my house; together, we'll support one another, whether all, none, or only one returns. We must comfort one another."

Sara gently squeezed Nancy's hand and vowed, "You're right; we need to help each other through this. I'll be there next Wednesday; I promise."

After exchanging farewells, until they would meet again the following morning in church, the two parted.

In the parallel world, Salvus woke his friends at precisely 4:00 a.m. After rising from their sleeping bags, the travelers neared the area, where just a few hours earlier they received the alarming news of the Reclaimers' potion for relocating portals.

Removing three apples from a bag, Dan split them in half and handed the fruit to his traveling companions. They bowed their heads, as Sam led the group in prayer, asking for His guidance on their day's journey.

Shortly into their meal, Dan broke the annoying silence by asking, "Cindy, how are you feeling this morning?"

Without disrupting her downward gaze, she muttered, "Okay, I guess."

Dan rose to his feet, shoved his hands into his jeans pockets, and confessed, "I'm really sorry, guys. If you don't make it home, then it's my fault. My gosh, I entered this world simply to rescue William. I never thought it would end like this."

Sam sprang to his feet and rebuked, "That's enough, Dan. No one forced us to take this trip. We freely entered this world. As a matter of fact, I clearly recall you ordering us back through the oak the night we crossed over. You don't owe us an apology."

In their heart of hearts, Cindy and Jimmy knew Sam was right.

Only now raising her sights to her friend, Cindy admitted, "Dan, I don't blame you—honestly. Sam's right; I chose to take this journey and I also decided against staying at the O'Brien's house. It's my own fault I'm here."

Jimmy echoed the same sentiments.

"But if I didn't enter the tree," explained Dan, "then—"

"Dan," snapped Sam, "quit blaming yourself! It's not your fault we're here."

All were amazed at Sam's admonishing tone, which was followed by complete silence.

Moments later, Sam added, in a confident voice, "Besides, I'm sure we'll make it home. Remember, we endured worse conditions during our hike to the castle."

Like the previous night, the majority of the meal was consumed in silence. Afterward, the explorers gathered their gear and—with lances in hand—marched up the path. From 5:00 a.m. until noon, when they broke for lunch, Dan experienced an unquestionable feeling someone or something was watching over them. After all, no predator crossed their path during their seven-hour hike through the shadowy forest, known for its savage creatures.

When lunch was finished, but before embarking on the second leg of their daily journey, William stepped off the footpath to go to the bathroom. Barely several yards from the trail, though still within eyesight of his co-travelers, he leaped over several waist-high boulders to conceal himself; he placed his back to his friends. While relieving himself, he surveyed the nearby area. Within proximity of the larger boulders, which were now resting behind him, he took note of countless other rocks of smaller sizes and various shapes; all appeared notched. He attributed the moist soil to a recent rain and the horrible stench to a carcass.

Once finished, he turned and was stepping in the direction of the footpath, when he tripped over a fibrous cord that was drawn tightly between two of the larger boulders. As he lay on the warm ground, he spotted a row of smaller jagged rocks—cleverly disguised—just below the forest floor. Within seconds of jumping to his feet, the row of toothlike rocks sprang from the soil; numerous cords, which were previously buried in the earth, contracted instantly and joined the many rocks by their notches. William was trapped in the mouth of a Silex Dragon.

Legends of old spoke of the Silex Dragon, a 150-foot long reptile encased in stone, which had the unnatural ability of separating its body to capture its prey. When a creature stepped within its scattered rocky body parts, the dragon would reattach itself and entrap its victim. Perhaps the most abnormal characteristic of the dragon was its birth process. A newborn was regurgitated from its mother's stomach and remained only several feet distant, growing in size over decades, until it acquired mobility. Unfortunately, since the competition for prey among the forest creatures was so fierce, many infant Silex Dragons succumbed to starvation.

From the campsite, Cindy witnessed the unthinkable—boulders interlocking and forming a stone beast—and then saw William disappear within its jaws. She screamed, drawing the attention of her co-travelers, who also beheld the anomaly, moments before spotting a pair of eyes unveiling themselves from beneath protective layers of scaly skin.

As William darted to the entrance of the rapidly closing mouth—though cautiously, to avoid the deadly teeth—the beast's forked tongue toppled him backwards; its mouth slammed shut. Before he could rise to his feet, the dragon raised its head and smashed it against the forest floor; it was determined to toss its victim to the back of its throat and swallow him whole. William gripped the folds of skin inside the dragon's mouth to thwart its gulp.

Suspecting the dragon was trying to swallow its prey, Jimmy, without thinking of his own safety, dashed to the beast. The creature immediately suspended its raging head movements, opened its mouth, unraveled its ten-foot tongue, and effortlessly snatched its second victim.

Before Jimmy rose to his knees inside the oral cavity, William yelled, "Grab the side of its mouth!"

No sooner had the new arrival buried his hands into the dragon's skin, when the creature closed its mouth and resumed its violent upward and downward jerks.

With the beast's mouth shut, darkness surrounded the men. Although unable to see their hands in front of them, which were still clinging to the creature's skin, Jimmy screamed, "What do we do now?"

"I don't know," yelled William, "but there's got to be a way out; there has to be."

Outside the dragon, Salvus, Sam, Cindy, and Dan had grabbed their lances and were creeping at a safe distance along the side of the creature, ascending a hillside near the beast's head. The group had advanced barely twenty feet up the incline, when Dan hatched a rescue scheme.

With the Silex Dragon preoccupied thrashing its head and oblivious to the potential deliverers, Dan bolted from his cohorts and neared a small boulder that was resting on the forest floor, only feet from the dragon.

Seeing Dan approach the rock, Salvus yelled to halt.

The teenager, however, continued his advance.

Even though the satyr correctly identified the four-foot high rock before the Silex Dragon as its offspring, the distance prevented him from detecting that the young dragon had perished in the recent past.

With his heart beating, like it had never pounded since entering the forest, Dan glanced from behind the rock to capture the dragon's attention.

With the creature's eyes closed and engrossed in attempting to throw its two-course meal down its throat, it was unaware another morsel was within reach.

Dan yelled.

The dragon ceased its head twitches, opened its eyes, and extended its tongue in his direction. Since Dan remained protected behind the flat-base boulder, the creature wrapped its tongue around him and its dead offspring.

Dan was terrified, but remained convinced his plan would work.

Since the expired stone creature had a level bottom and was incapable of rolling, it and Dan were dragged to the beast.

The Silex Dragon opened its mouth and pulled in the young man and its deceased young. The moment the tongue was unraveled from the teenager and the rock, Dan ordered his co-captives, "Push the boulder back, before it jolts its head again!" Fortunately, since the floor of the mouth was moist, the rock slid rather easily.

Within moments, the boulder was wedged firmly in the dragon's air passageway. The creature swung its head from side to side and up and down in a lifesaving effort to dislodge the rock. With no success, it lashed its tongue inside its mouth to remove the large stone. In the midst of whipping its tongue, the men were thrown against the boulder and then to the side of the creature's mouth, where they quickly secured another firm grip. Regrettably, the men suffered numerous abrasions, as they were hurled about.

Since the remaining travelers were unaware of the condition of their friends inside the beast, Salvus, Sam, and Cindy continued their ascent of the hill, alongside the dragon's head. With precision, Salvus thrust his lance into the creature's left eye.

With its rapidly-diminishing air supply and a pierced eye, the dragon was experiencing extreme pain. The stony reptile, however, was determined to survive; it continued striking its tongue against its jammed offspring.

Although the men inside were receiving mounting injuries, they knew their lives depended upon their firm grasp.

After an intense struggle, the dragon expired and crashed its colossal head to the forest floor.

Cindy lost her footing at the tremor and stumbled from the slope to the ground. Luckily, she sustained no injuries or sprains.

Salvus and Sam raced to her aid. Though offering only a passing glance at the lifeless dragon, the two rescuers realized that upon its untimely death, in addition to closing its eyes forever, it had closed its mouth.

Salvus helped Cindy to her feet; Sam raced to the dragon's teeth-clenched mouth and shouted, "William, Dan, Jimmy!"

On hearing no response, Cindy and Salvus neared the creature's mouth and began yelling.

In reaction to the dragon's head crashing to the ground, only moments earlier, the men lost their grip and were pitched violently within the cavity one final time.

"William! Jimmy!" yelled Dan.

There was no answer.

Since the mouth of the beast was closed tightly, no light entered. In complete darkness, he yelled again.

Rising from the moist floor, William yelled, "Dan?"

"Are you alright?" asked the younger brother.

"Yeah, I think so," he replied. "Where's Jimmy?"

From four feet to his right, Dan heard, "I'm over here."

Walking in the direction of Dan and Jimmy's voices, William was soon at their sides, plotting an escape.

However, before devoting serious thought to a breakout, Jimmy warned, "William, next time you go to the bathroom, do it like everyone else and use the side of the footpath."

"Trust me," he promised, "I'll never make that mistake again."

Still hearing no response from inside, Cindy yelled even louder.

From within the creature's closed mouth, Dan faintly heard her. "We're okay," he yelled.

Salvus and Sam lifted the leatherlike skin which hung over the dragon's teeth. Since they had no means of extracting the teeth, Sam suggested he, Salvus, and Cindy gather large stones and pile them alongside the mouth. He knew they had to act quickly, since the men inside would soon run dangerously low on air.

Once a pile of stones was collected, Sam and Salvus again separated the skin; Cindy wedged the rocks between the upper and lower folds. The intolerable stench forced the rescuers to breathe through their mouths.

With the teeth exposed, Salvus and Sam pried the jaws with a sturdy tree limb. With the rows of teeth slightly divided, Cindy quickly, but cautiously, stacked the largest rocks between the jaws. With no less than fifty stones amassed between the rows of teeth, a substantial gap was created that would permit the prisoners to escape. However, before squeezing through, Sam cautioned his trapped friends against making any sudden movements, since the slightest jarring motion could displace the stones to the forest floor, slamming the razor-sharp teeth on anything or anyone in their path.

Because William had endured the creature's rancid breath longer than the other captives, Dan and Jimmy insisted he flee first. The older Clay stretched his arms through the gap and gently rested upon the lower jawbone, between two mounds of rocks. Salvus and Sam lifted him to freedom.

Throughout the two-minute ordeal, Cindy kept a watchful eye on the stones, making sure none were dislodged or shuffled.

Jimmy was the next man through the creature's mouth. Much like William, his valor was rewarded with a successful landing on the forest floor.

A postmortem spasm wildly shook the Silex Dragon. Nearly half the stones between the jawbones fell to the soil. The gap between the rows of teeth diminished considerably; Dan was unable to escape.

Aware his air supply would dwindle with the constrictive passage, Sam ordered everyone to gather the stones from the forest floor and force open the creature's jaws again.

As the group wedged the rocks, they clearly heard, "What the—" from inside the dragon's mouth.

With no blood flowing through the arteries at the roof of the expired beast's mouth, bloodsucking hookworms—which were affixed to the creature and stealing vital blood and nutrients—detached themselves and fell to the floor of the dragon's mouth; several landed within inches of the captive. In their frantic search for a warm blood source, the parasites anchored their posterior suction cups to the floor of the creature's mouth and sank their heads—with their miniature hooklike teeth—into Dan's ankles. With each puncture, he let out a moan; he pounded his feet upon the moist surface to rid himself of the worms.

"Hurry!" he yelled. "Something's biting my ankles; I can't shake 'em."

With the desperate cry, Sam positioned the last large stone and ordered Dan to extend his arms through the opening. As his upper body emerged, he set his waist atop the lower jawbone, being careful not to shift any of the strategically-placed stones.

With care and precision, Sam and William lifted him to safety.

Wielding his lance, Salvus removed the seven hookworms that had made Dan's ankles their new host.

As Cindy treated Dan's newest injuries, Sam peered inside the beast's mouth and focused on its elongated tongue. With extreme caution, he reached inside the oral cavity, pulled out two feet of the tongue, and dropped it to the forest floor.

"Dan," ordered Sam, "give me your machete."

"Why?" asked the teenager, who remained seated on the forest floor, receiving a whiskey treatment.

"Must you always be so inquisitive?" reproved Sam.

After a shrug of the shoulders, Dan handed him the weapon.

"We'll feast like kings tonight," predicted Sam, while slicing the tongue into several appetizing chunks.

"Gross," said Cindy. "There's no way I'm eating tongue for dinner, especially a dragon's tongue!"

After the men's abrasions were treated and the lance was retrieved from the Silex Dragon's eye, it was decided that—even though Dan probably couldn't travel at his normal pace—the hike would resume. After all, the deadline was rapidly approaching.

Before leaving the area, however, Salvus turned to the Silex Dragon and commented, "How ironic."

"What's that?" asked Sam.

After relating to his co-travelers what he had heard for decades concerning the rare species, the satyr concluded, "It's ironic the creature's death came at the hands of its dead offspring."

"So, you think the small boulder I hid behind," asked Dan, "was a young Silex Dragon?"

"Yeah," stated Salvus, "I'm pretty sure."

"But why," questioned Jimmy, "didn't the mother dragon unhinge its body when it was choking on its offspring or after it died?"

Only now removing his sights from the rock creature, Salvus admitted, "That, I can't answer for certain. But I'd imagine the wedged offspring in its throat somehow prevented it from disconnecting itself."

Unknown to the travelers and all forest inhabitants was the dragon's astonishing ability to compress its throat muscles, permitting the tendons throughout the length of its body to fall limp; the predator would then separate. Once disjoined, it buried its internal organs and muscles below the forest soil and camouflaged its outer stone body parts against the terrain. Even its eyes remained closed at ground level. The cunning creature left nothing to chance. Any woodland dweller could step amid the boulders unsuspectingly. However, the young Silex Dragon blocked its mother's air passageway, making it impossible to constrict her throat muscles; death was unavoidable.

"Speaking of the offspring, Dan," interjected Sam, "your act of heroism could have got someone killed."

"But, Sam," reminded Dan, "someone had to act fast."

Sam shook his head before admitting, "I suppose; but in the days ahead, let's remember to work as a team."

Dan remained silent; he suspected a future situation might call for a similar and immediate reaction.

With lance in hand, Salvus interrupted the conversation, reminding the group of the time factor, and then stepped to the footpath for another extended hike.

After several hours trudging through the forest, five travelers collapsed to a level plot of ground. Sam started a fire, reasoning that since the Reclaimers hadn't found them yet, they had likely returned to the castle. When the blaze was roaring, he dropped several pieces of dragon tongue into the pan.

"Sam," informed Cindy, staring at the sizzling tongue, "I'm really not hungry; I'll just have an apple."

"Cindy," suggested Sam, "would you just taste it? It's considered a delicacy."

"If it's a delicacy," she remarked, "then I offer mine to someone else."

Shortly after 11:00 p.m., the travelers were warming themselves by the campfire and handing their plates to Sam for a slab of tongue.

To everyone's surprise, including Cindy's, the tongue wasn't that bad; it wasn't that good either.

By midnight, Salvus was on patrol as his friends slept; Sam relieved him at 2:00 a.m.

CHAPTER TWELVE
Swordplay

THE NEXT MORNING OVER BREAKFAST, JIMMY ALERTED THE group there was nothing for dinner that night, except for a few soft apples and leftover tongue.

The rabbits from the previous hunt were devoured in record time, due to the extended hikes of the famished travelers.

Cindy curled her lips at the thought of a tongue meal again.

Sensing his friends didn't enjoy the choice food last night as much as he thought, Sam yielded, "Alright, even though plenty of tongue remains, I suppose I'll set out on another hunt this afternoon, while you're eating lunch."

Oddly enough, no one volunteered to join him on the proposed hunting expedition. Presuming their unwillingness was the result of complete exhaustion, Sam didn't question the issue and continued with his meal.

By 5:00 a.m., the group was on the move.

Shortly before noon, Dan stepped to the side of the footpath to go to the bathroom, when he heard a persistent low murmuring sound echoing amid the trees. Offering a backward glance to the group, and noticing they were absorbed in a conversation, he neared the noise. A short five-minute walk through the rough terrain lay a body of water. *I wonder if it's the same lake where we fought the octopus on our trip to the castle,* he thought. Racing back to the group, he cried out, "Sam, there's a huge lake on the other side of those trees."

Taking inventory of the water supply, Sam discovered that although there was some left, it was running low. The two additional travelers, understandably, placed an added drain on their reserve. "Since this may be the last time we see a lake," guessed Sam, "I suggest we take advantage of it."

Sam returned the backpacks to the forest floor and walked to the edge of the trail, where he rummaged for dead branches. Cindy unpacked the pan; Jimmy and Salvus joined Sam in collecting wood. Dan and William grabbed the three plastic containers.

Once the fire was ignited and burning on its own, Sam proposed, "Cindy, why don't you and Jimmy wait here and take a breather; the rest of us will gather some water."

Admitting to herself she may have been curt with Sam and Dan for their reluctance in telling the group about the relocation potion discovered at the castle, she decided to make amends for her actions by offering, "If it's alright, I'd rather help at the lake."

Noticing a faint smile emerge on her face, Sam asked, "Are you sure?"

"Yeah," replied a confident Cindy.

"Well, Jimmy," said Sam, "I guess you're here on your own."

Watching his companions secure their lances and step off the trail, Jimmy bolted to his feet, grabbed his weapon, and followed.

Dan was right; the lake was enormous.

Upon closer inspection, Cindy asked, "Isn't this the same lake with the sea creature?"

"I wondered that, too," replied Dan, "but something looks different about this one."

"Yeah," joked Cindy, "it doesn't have an octopus head floating on the surface."

As the six stepped nearer the shoreline, Sam was the first to squat. William and Dan dropped the plastic containers and raised their weapons directly over Sam's shoulders, in the event something made an unexpected appearance.

"I think this is a different lake," remarked Sam.

"How do you know?" asked Cindy.

"The water's crystal clear," he explained. "I can see the bottom; I don't remember the other lake being this transparent."

Since the lake was pristine, enabling the travelers to see the approach of any creature with plenty of time to react, Sam remarked it was probably safe to submerge the tubs by hand.

With their anxieties eased, William and Dan lowered their lances.

Sam grabbed the first container and plunged it into the icy water. Lifting it from the lake, he handed the precious liquid cargo to Salvus, who carried it to the campsite and poured it into the pan that was warming over the fire. The second tub was handled the same way, with Jimmy making the delivery to camp.

Sinking the third container, Sam spotted a school of small fish approaching from the farther depths of the lake. Without warning, several larger fish shot from the water, nearly striking the human trespassers. The five travelers and Jimmy, who was returning from the campsite, were amazed with the marksmanship and agility of the fish.

Sam had unknowingly disturbed a group of young flying swordfish and provoked their adult guardians.

In reality, though the fish were unable to fly, they were equipped with oversize pectoral fins that allowed them to glide through the air and target the shore, after a successful launch from the lake by their powerful tail fin.

Rising too quickly from his heels, Sam stumbled.

Before the travelers could counter the first air strike, eight more swordfish burst from the water, targeting the group.

"The swordfish think we're after their young!" yelled Sam.

As the fish hit the lakeshore, they squirmed back to the water, ensuring additional aerial assaults.

Watching remnants of the first raid re-enter the water, Sam ordered, "Kill as many as you can; they must not return to the lake."

In the midst of dodging another onslaught of six-inch aquatic spikes that were streaming ashore, the group amazingly speared many of the beached swordfish. Once stabbed, the fish were tossed near the tree line. In all, the travelers were the target of six attacks.

Rising carelessly from a stooped position, with his unprotected back facing the water, Jimmy received a spike between his shoulder blades. He dropped his lance and screamed.

William raced to his side and yanked the lake aggressor from his back. The hardened spike had penetrated nearly two inches. While keeping a watchful eye on the airborne swordfish, William dropped his lance and helped his friend through the woods to the campsite.

The men had advanced only a short distance into the forest, when they spotted a griffin, fifty feet ahead, en route to the lake to quench its thirst. Standing nearly five feet high at its shoulders, the beast had the wings and head of an eagle, complete with a deadly beak. From its neck back, it resembled a lion. Its front paws bore lengthy talons, whereas its hind feet supported smaller-size claws.

Attempting not to make any sudden movements that might startle the beast, the men remained completely motionless.

Dan, meanwhile, on noticing the absence of his brother and Jimmy at the lakeshore, left the water's edge for the campsite.

Having discarded their weapons at the lake, William and Jimmy were at the mercy of the griffin. Glancing to the left and then to the right, moving only his eyes, William spotted a large fallen tree that had been hollowed out by a forest creature. He decided to take his chances, thinking whatever lived in the excavated tree would be easier to battle than the griffin.

The lion creature advanced its front right paw in the men's direction.

"Jimmy," said William, through his clenched teeth, "on the count of three, we're running for that fallen tree to the right."

From the corner of his eye, William detected Jimmy nod slightly.

In a soft voice, William counted, "One, two—"

Before 'three' was whispered, the men were racing, as fast as Jimmy's injury would allow, to the grounded oak; the griffin trailed at an alarming speed. Fortunately, the thick wooded area prevented the creature from taking flight.

With the men nearly upon the tree, they dived to their stomachs. While nervously watching his friend advance frustratingly slowly into the oak—and upon hearing the crushing sounds of undergrowth behind growing louder and louder—William pushed him into the tree's cavity and then dashed in himself; the griffin was a mere five feet distant. The men crawled to safety in the inner recesses of the tree.

Although the imposing wings of the griffin hindered it from

entering the downed oak, its craving for warm flesh didn't prevent it from trying. Fortunately, the only success it achieved was sinking its front talons into the tree's hollow shell and drawing blood from William's calf.

Dan was now at the spot in the woods where his sibling and friend had veered only minutes earlier. Hearing a mighty roar, he instinctively tightened the grip on his lance and scanned the forest. In the woodland's dim light, he glimpsed a creature towering atop a fallen tree, driving its talons into its rotten trunk. He stepped in the direction of the battle with extreme caution and increasing fears.

Another talon entered the tree, narrowly missing Jimmy's neck. Sadly, a third piercing nicked William's ear; he let out a soft moan.

Cloaked in darkness, the trapped men couldn't see anything, though Jimmy felt something crawl into his shirt and bite his shoulder. He, too, let out a near-silent groan. Within seconds, another tree dweller dropped down his shirt.

With greater force than before, another talon invaded the tree's interior and grazed William's shoulder.

Dan had made an undetected arrival at the scene and was positioned several feet behind the engrossed griffin with his lance raised. On hearing a loud cry within the tree, he took careful aim, released his weapon, and pierced a rear leg of the creature.

The griffin howled, drawing the attention of Sam, Salvus, and Cindy, who were racing through the wooded area, en route to camp.

The injured beast jerked its head and beak toward its attacker, jumped from the toppled tree, and hobbled to the teenager.

With no weapon, Dan was bending over, snatching a fallen limb to drive back the limping beast, when he heard two shots.

Sam, only yards behind, had squeezed the trigger of his revolver.

The griffin collapsed to the forest floor and closed its eyes.

Dan spun and witnessed his friends bearing their lances and several swordfish. He quickly turned again and darted to the tree, poked his head inside, and yelled, "Are you guys alright?"

"Yeah," replied William.

"Something's biting me!" exclaimed Jimmy.

Dan reached in and pulled out William, who groaned, as Dan inadvertently grabbed his injured calf.

With the rest of the travelers standing near the fallen tree, Sam dropped to his knees, crawled a few feet inside the oak, and pulled out Jimmy.

Free of the tree, Sam couldn't help but notice Jimmy twitching. Wasting no time, he ripped off Jimmy's shirt; dozens of African Toe-Biters fell to the forest floor.

A rare species of water bugs, although prevalent along the lakeshores of Eldritch Forest, the African Toe-Biter measured nearly four inches in length and was equipped with three pairs of legs, of which the forelegs were elongated to grasp and secure its prey. Once restrained, the African Toe-Biter thrust its pinlike antennae into its victim and released a naturally-produced chemical to numb its meal before slowly feasting upon it. Even though the injection was not lethal or fast-acting on creatures the size of humans, the insect delivered a nasty sting to barefoot waders, thus its name.

Cindy gagged at the sight of the revolting bugs scrambling to the fallen tree.

After stepping over the griffin carcass, the six resumed their hike to the campsite. Dan assisted his brother, Sam helped Jimmy, and Cindy and Salvus gathered the lances and dead swordfish.

At camp, Cindy dropped the weapons and reached for the last bottle of whiskey. With Jimmy's shirt still removed, she poured a healthy dose on the insect bites and then to his swordfish injury, between his shoulder blades. William's calf, shoulder, and ear were treated in like manner. Ransacking through her bag, she removed the cleanest cloths she could find and wrapped Jimmy's upper back and then William's wounds. Though the injuries were nothing like the group had sustained in the past, they still placed the afternoon's hike in question.

Approaching Dan, Sam asked, "How are you holding up?"

"Fine," he replied, "still just a little jittery, I guess."

Suspecting he was still troubled with the recent griffin encounter, Sam praised, "You were brave to do what you did." After glimpsing the latest injured party members, he added, "We did the right thing. It was either killing the creature or it killing William and Jimmy."

With the fire still ablaze and the water now boiling, from their trip to the lakeshore an hour earlier, Sam grabbed a rag, carefully removed the scalding pan from the flame, and set it on the ground to cool, before transferring the contents to the water bottles. Against his better judgment, he decided to keep the fire burning and proposed fried fish for their late lunch. Within an hour, the meal was served. All were amazed that even after Jimmy's traumatic experiences with the swordfish, the griffin, and the African Toe-Biters, he had a substantial appetite.

During the meal, Sam admitted, "Aside from Jimmy's and William's injuries, I'd say the day, so far, has been better than most."

"What do you mean?" asked Cindy.

After swallowing a mouthful of fish, he explained, "Well, we refilled our water bottles and found food without venturing into the deep forest."

The travelers were too hungry to deny or agree with Sam's observation.

At the conclusion of the meal, Sam remained silent, debating internally what to do the remainder of the day.

The travelers sensed his predicament.

As much as Sam knew the group should continue their hike, he was genuinely concerned for Jimmy's and William's well-being.

Sensing his dilemma, Jimmy remarked, "I think we should move out."

"Yeah," seconded William, "there's still plenty of daylight left."

Taking the bait, Sam asked, "Are you sure you two are up for it?"

"Yeah, Sam," replied Jimmy, "I'm sure."

Before Sam could respond, William reminded him of the time factor and urged they resume their hike to the enchanted oak.

"Alright," agreed Sam, "but if your injuries start bothering you, we call it a day."

Jimmy and William agreed to the terms.

With the promise made, the travelers geared up, snatched their weapons, and were on the path heading home. So as not to overburden the recently wounded men, Dan carried his brother's bag; Salvus lugged Jimmy's.

Recalling that a short time ago they had set foot upon the path that would lead them to the oak, the four original travelers scanned the trees and nearby terrain for any recognizable features. Sadly, nothing looked familiar.

Too bad, thought Dan, *spray painting the trees didn't work.*

Nearly three hours into their afternoon journey, Sam pulled his wristwatch from his pocket; it was 5:00. He raised his hand, signaling the travelers behind to halt. Approaching Jimmy and William, he asked, "Do you want to take a break or continue on?"

The men glimpsed their co-travelers. Knowing their determination to reach the oak with time to spare, Jimmy and William insisted the march continue.

Over the next six hours, countless conversations developed between the Clay brothers and Jimmy about their childhood years.

"Remember," said Jimmy, "all the afternoons we'd play in your driveway and how your mom and dad worried needlessly that one of you might hurt me? Imagine that—one of you two hurting me."

"Yeah," recalled William. "It seems like another lifetime."

"But you'll have that life back," promised Jimmy, "in less than a week."

As much as Dan wanted to assure his brother they'd be home soon, he remained noticeably quiet. He suspected he and his friends would inevitably confront the Reclaimers again.

Jimmy spent the majority of the remaining hours relating his alleged sporting triumphs to William.

A few minutes before 11:00, Sam found a suitable plot of forest ground and proposed, "We'll camp here tonight."

The backpacks were dropped to the ground. Knowing the drill, the explorers prepared their sleeping areas; Sam prepared the meal.

Again, before igniting the fire, Sam briefly questioned his actions. On the one hand, he had recurring fears that the Reclaimers or Oswagis would spot the blaze; but on the other hand, he knew the group's extended hike demanded a hot meal. *I suppose if the Reclaimers haven't found us by now,* he thought, *they'll probably wait until the next full moon.*

Even though dinner was a repeat of lunch, the fish smelled just as good and tasted even better; their demanding hike had created strong appetites.

Halfway through the meal, Cindy agreed to the first watch; Salvus accepted the 2:00 to 4:00 shift.

CHAPTER THIRTEEN
The Seedling

EVERYONE WAS AT THE DINING AREA BY 4:15 A.M. SINCE THE temperature was already nearly seventy degrees, Cindy and Jimmy wore shorts. Suspecting fish or dragon's tongue wasn't the best choice for breakfast, Dan reached into his bag, pulled out three overripe apples, and broke them in half. The meal was served.

After William led the prayer, Cindy taunted, "Jimmy, you sure put up a fight last night with the whiskey."

Chewing a slice of apple, Jimmy inarticulately replied, "My back was fine; you just—"

Cindy looked at Dan for a translation of Jimmy's comment; he shrugged his shoulders and continued chewing.

"Alright, everybody," reminded Sam, "Cindy's just looking after us to make sure our wounds mend. You know, our injuries wouldn't have healed as quickly as they have if it wasn't for her."

"Thanks, Sam," replied Cindy, as she unscrewed the whiskey bottle and ordered, "let me see your wrists."

Sam, who was seated on the forest floor, made a poor attempt sliding backwards, asserting, "Thanks, Cindy; but I'm fine. The cave bats barely broke the skin."

Gulping his apple wedge, Jimmy teased, "Come on, Sam; she's just looking after us to make sure our wounds heal."

As she disinfected Sam's wrists, Dan placed his head alongside his brother's and bantered, "I'm glad the shadows only tried to strangle us or she'd be having a field day."

William, who remained engrossed biting a hardened marshmallow in half, simply nodded.

Returning the cap to the bottle, Cindy glared at Dan and sarcastically remarked, "Who knows, maybe you'll get lucky before our trip ends and need another treatment."

Sam rose to his feet, waved his wrists in the air to dry the alcohol, and reminded, "Our trip will never end if we don't get a move on. Let's clean the area and grab our gear."

Ninety minutes into their hike, Dan pointed to an area off the footpath and asked, "Cindy, does that look familiar to you?"

After scrutinizing a tree for a few moments, she eventually replied, "I don't know, Dan; all the trees look alike to me."

"No, not the tree," corrected Dan, "the red shrub. Isn't that the spot where the purple frog lashed its tongue at Sam, when he was gathering kindling wood on our way to the castle?"

Still uncertain, Cindy called for Sam, who was at the head of the line. Once alongside the young travelers, she had just begun to speak, when Dan interrupted, "Sam, isn't that the red shrub where the frog licked you, when you were gathering firewood during the rainstorm?"

Sam looked closely at the bush, cupped his chin between his thumb and index finger, and ultimately admitted, "It may be, but I can't say for certain. I'm sure there's more than one red shrub in these miserable woods."

Noticing Dan's fixed gaze at the plant for a few moments longer, Sam suspected he was trying to find something to reassure the group they were on the right path.

Dan was searching for anything familiar to put his mind at ease.

Shortly before noon, Cindy was the first to spot the friendly sparkle in the canopy, which was clearly visible in the darkened forest—even at midday. Within moments of touching ground, Ceremonia altered her appearance to her full-size stature. Since they had a guest, the group broke early for lunch.

After the fire was prepared and three swordfish were sizzling, Dan rested his hand on Ceremonia's and asked, "How are you doing since Gloria's…um…Gloria's mishap?"

There was a lengthy pause and a distant look in the tree nymph's eyes, as she reminisced about her cousin. Eventually, she spoke up, "I guess I'm doing okay. Actually, I've discovered that putting others' interests ahead of my own helps me deal with my grief. I admit it sounds strange, but it seems like the more selfless I become, the happier I am." With her sights now directed at the group, she asked, "Does that make any sense?"

Sam, the former philosophy professor, quickly affirmed, "Actually, it makes perfect sense. Unfortunately, many people don't realize it until late in their lives, making their earlier years often unhappy and unfulfilled."

Stepping nearer the flame to inspect what humans eat, the tree nymph acknowledged, "And I have Dan to thank for this fortunate lesson."

"Me?" questioned Dan.

"Of course," answered Ceremonia. "You were the one who insisted and ultimately convinced me to help the group find Cindy in the centaur's cave and reminded me of what my species had become." Looking at William, she added, "You've got a pretty smart younger brother."

"Yeah," replied William, before slapping Dan on the back, "I guess I do."

Catching sight of a billow of smoke rising from the pan, Sam jumped from his log and declared, "Lunch is ready; hand me your plates."

Although Ceremonia typically ate vegetation and an occasional slug, she bravely agreed to sample a morsel of fish. All eyes gazed upon her, as she dropped a piece of fish on her tongue. Waving her hand in front of her open mouth, she exclaimed, "Hot…hot."

Immediately upon swallowing—and to the surprise of the travelers—she asked for another taste; Sam happily agreed.

After a lighthearted conversation, the travelers cleaned the area and were back on the trail, though a little later than expected. Clearly, no one liked losing hiking time, but all enjoyed visiting with the tree nymph, who decided to travel with her friends a short distance. Even though no one voiced it, all felt safer with Ceremonia nearby.

As the group of seven hiked, the tree nymph spent time talking with each of the travelers. She was overly curious about humans and their behaviors. "So, Dan," she asked, "when you started your journey to rescue your brother, did you know of the dangers in the forest?"

Tightening the straps on his backpack, he disclosed, "Well, I'd heard a few stories, but in all honesty, I never imagined it would be like it's been."

"If you knew all there was to know about the creatures of the forest and the Reclaimers in the castle," she continued, "would you still have made the trip?"

Dan paused, glanced to his sibling, and responded confidently, "Yes."

Puzzled with his reply, since she had a partial knowledge of the misfortunes he and his friends had suffered, she emphasized, "Why?"

"Wouldn't you have done anything within your power to save Gloria?" he asked.

"I see," replied Ceremonia. "Perhaps human family bonds are close, like the family bonds of tree nymphs." She glanced behind to Jimmy.

Dan sensed she was preparing to leave his side to learn what makes Jimmy tick. As she turned, he blurted, "What's a Bozeman's quill?"

Completely baffled with the young man's knowledge of the rare object, the woodland resident spun to face Dan and asked, "What do you know about the Bozeman's quill and how did you hear about it?"

On overhearing the question, Sam and Cindy—who were walking a short distance ahead of the group—came to a standstill, before turning and approaching the tree nymph and Dan.

"I don't know anything about the quill," answered Dan. "I was hoping you did."

"How'd you hear about it?" inquired Ceremonia.

Dan looked at Sam, seeking permission to divulge the story. Sam nodded.

"When we were rescuing William in the castle," explained Dan, "I discovered a small library in one of the castle rooms and found a book on elixirs and potions. Anyway, the book was open to a particular potion that listed a Bozeman's quill as an ingredient."

The travelers were now standing around the tree nymph, anticipating her response.

Clasping her wrists behind her back, she began, "The Bozeman is a distant cousin of the dwarfish porcupine in this world; each weighs easily a hundred pounds, if not more. They live on the lower rock formations of the Great Chasm, where they thrive on molten rock. To be honest, I've seen just two or three in my lifetime. You see, the Bozemen emerge from the darkness of the Great Chasm, once every hundred years or so, to deliver their young which, during the first week of their lives, feast on the vegetation at the fringes of the abyss. Then they descend with their mothers to the deepest regions of the Great Chasm."

"So, what's so special about their quills?" asked Dan.

"Yeah," prompted Cindy.

"Legends say," detailed the tree nymph, "if a person boils a Bozeman quill, grinds it into a fine powder, and consumes it, the individual has the ability to relocate anywhere in this world. Basically, the person disappears from one point in space and reappears at another, virtually instantaneously. And from what little my ancestors told me about the quills, their translocation power is permanent."

Noticing the long faces surrounding her, Ceremonia asked, "Alright, what's so significant about this potion you discovered in the castle?"

Dan and Sam started to respond simultaneously, but the teenager withdrew.

Sam informed his winged friend that the ingredient was found in a potion titled, "Relocating Portals."

"I see," said Ceremonia.

Dan removed the manuscript from his pocket and handed it to the woodland inhabitant, who removed her hands from her back side and accepted the document. Though unable to read, she analyzed carefully the sketches which bordered the parchment.

"Since so few mortals cross over between our worlds," speculated Dan, "the Reclaimers probably think they can lure more guests to the castle if they relocate the portal to a well-traveled area."

After reviewing the drawings, Ceremonia returned the manuscript to Dan, speculating, "And you're worried they'll move the portal before the next full moon."

Dan remained silent.

A hopeful Cindy stepped between Ceremonia and Dan, proposing, "Hey, maybe we can grind the quill and relocate ourselves back to our world—or at least to the oak tree."

"I'm sorry, Cindy," replied the tree nymph. "The quills will relocate a person only within this world. And as far as the oak tree, the quills probably would transport you, but there aren't any at our disposal. I'm afraid the only way back to your world is the way you entered my world."

There was an extended period of silence, as the disturbing news settled in.

Eventually, Dan redirected his sights to the tree nymph and blurted, "Do you know if the Reclaimers have the quill in their possession?"

"I don't know," replied Ceremonia.

Dan was persistent. "Do you know when the Bozemen will make their next exit from the Great Chasm?"

"Dan," reminded Ceremonia, "since they leave the chasm so infrequently, I don't know when their next surfacing will be; I'm sorry."

Knowing she was trying to be as helpful as she could, without prematurely raising their hopes, Sam stated, "Ceremonia, we appreciate what you've done for us. But since we don't know when the Bozemen will emerge or if the Reclaimers have a quill, I suggest we move on."

Realizing Sam was attempting to salvage a little hope for his co-travelers, the woodland resident agreed, "You're right; I think it's wise you continue your hike to the oak, as if you had never learned of the quill."

At the tree nymph's suggestion, the seven resumed their brisk pace up the darkened path.

Over the next two hours, Ceremonia hiked with the group. Although a large amount of ground was covered, hardly a word was spoken; Ceremonia and Sam were not surprised.

Walking alongside Cindy, the tree nymph tried to raise her spirits, but it was a wasted effort. As much as Ceremonia enjoyed the group's company, she had prior commitments to keep with her fellow tree nymphs. However, knowing she had unintentionally dashed the group's hope of an instantaneous translocation to their world or the oak by means of a Bozeman quill, she decided to remain with them a little longer. As she neared Sam, who had resumed the lead, she glanced to an area ahead, where plants bloomed on the right side and boulders dominated the left. She ordered the group to stop.

"What's wrong?" asked Dan, as he peered up the trail.

Completely focused on what flourished about seventy feet ahead, Ceremonia ignored Dan's question and whispered, "I've never seen any on this side of the forest; they must be new arrivals."

"Ceremonia," asked Cindy, "what are you talking about?"

"We must keep our voices low," she warned.

"Why?" asked Cindy, in a softer voice.

"Do you see those blue flowers ahead," asked Ceremonia, "on the right side of the path?"

"Yeah," replied Cindy. "We have those in our world, too; they're called bluebells, though the ones in our world usually droop."

"Those plants, just a short distance up the path, have a brutal disposition," informed the tree nymph, "which is why they're called Jezebels in this world."

"What possible harm can flowers wreak?" questioned Dan.

"Plenty; trust me," assured Ceremonia, "if a passerby makes the slightest sound."

"Why don't we circle around behind the Jezebels?" suggested Salvus.

Since the left side of the path was bordered by boulders and the patch of Jezebels extended about twenty feet or so along the trail, Ceremonia thought it might be possible to trespass in front of them without incident. Nonetheless, passing a great distance along the back side of the deadly flowers would be the better alternative.

"Wait here," ordered Ceremonia. "I'll inspect the area behind the Jezebels."

In a flash, the tree nymph transformed herself to her six-inch size and flew around the bed of plants.

With the woodland dweller out of sight, Dan admitted, "I don't get it; they're flowers. Do tree nymphs have an unfounded fear of flowering plants?"

Taking a few steps closer to the plot of Jezebels, William seconded, "Yeah, they look pretty harmless and—" He abruptly ended his comment, but remained staring.

"What's wrong?" asked Jimmy.

"I know this will sound crazy," admitted William, "but I swear one of the flowers, at the end closer to us, turned its blossom in our direction."

"Maybe the flower was already pointing this way," suggested Jimmy.

Sam raised a finger to motion for silence and whispered, "I think we should heed Ceremonia's warning and keep our voices down."

As the travelers awaited the tree nymph's return, they remained moderately quiet, keeping an attentive eye on the plot of Jezebels.

Without warning, Ceremonia was hovering overhead. After a brilliant glow, but in complete silence, she assumed her full-size height.

"What'd you find out?" asked Dan.

"It's not good, I'm afraid," replied the tree nymph.

"What do you mean?" asked Jimmy.

"A swarm of flying wheel bugs has landed in the area, behind the Jezebels" informed Ceremonia.

"Wheel bugs?" asked Dan. "And how is a harmless insect not good?"

"Harmless?" challenged the forest dweller. "Wheel bugs have a worse temperament than the Jezebels. Trust me, I've witnessed the demise, or seen the remains, of many forest creatures at the hands of wheel bugs."

"What's a wheel bug?" asked Cindy.

"Wheel bugs," explained Dan, "are insects with wheellike protrusions on their backs. They're fairly common in our world and completely harmless to prey larger than themselves."

"And their thorns?" questioned Ceremonia.

"Their thorns?" asked Dan.

"At the slightest sound or movement," informed the tree nymph, "the flying wheel bug will fire a thorn from its back projection which, upon impact, releases a fast-acting toxin that attacks its prey's nervous system. And if the thorn misses its target, the wheellike structure rotates and shoots again. The effects of the poison are so instantaneous that I've seen an adult boar collapse in its tracks. The powerless victim is soon covered with voracious wheel bugs that ingest fur, scales, even clothing, until they reach the innermost layer of warm tissue. The prey is slowly eaten alive, unable to move or brush away the insects."

"If the wheel bugs are sensitive to sound," asked Cindy, "won't they hear us?"

"All the more reason to keep our voices low," whispered Ceremonia. Taking another glance to the flowers, she continued, "A walk in front of the Jezebels would be the safer route, especially since it's just a short distance across." She motioned the group to step back and take cover behind a nearby boulder.

From the distant side of the rock, William whispered, "Ceremonia, I could have sworn I saw a Jezebel turn its blossom in my direction earlier."

"I'm not surprised," remarked the tree nymph.

Concealed behind the large stone, Ceremonia explained the history and the evolutionary behavior of the flowers. "Like I said earlier, I've never seen them on this side of the forest; I've noticed them in the woods, beyond the castle. Luckily, there are not that many at the spot ahead and they border just one side of the path. But on the far side of the castle, there exist acres and acres of Jezebels."

After peeking around the boulder to eye the flowers, Dan asked, "What's so terrible about the flowers?"

"Basically," cautioned Ceremonia, "you must be absolutely quiet when passing in front of them."

"Why?" asked Cindy.

"The story is told," clarified the woodland dweller, "that centuries ago, these flowers were hexed by the Reclaimers, who found their former beauty intolerable. They were cursed with such a nauseating appearance and foul odor that insects ceased visiting their blossoms and the forest beasts stopped nibbling their blooms. Before their catastrophic curse, however, the flowers relied on the forest creatures—which ate and eliminated their blossoms—and the forest insects for their proliferation."

After glancing at the flowers, William admitted, "They don't look that unsightly."

"I wouldn't recommend it," warned Ceremonia, "but if you got a closer look, you'd notice the area inside the petals is completely black, with treelike sap that continually oozes up through the dark membrane and drips to the forest floor. The outside of the flower is disfigured with oversize lower petals that hang far below the rest, giving it an outward appearance of a bearded, drooling man."

"So, what's the big deal if the insects or forest creatures don't visit the Jezebels?" asked Jimmy.

"With no insects pollinating," explained the tree nymph, "and no creatures eating their blossoms, the Jezebels became aggressive to revitalize their dwindling numbers. In retaliation, the flowers perfected the art of shooting their seeds at unbelievable speeds and with incredible accuracy at any insect that flew within their line of fire or any creature that crossed their path. Once a seed was embedded, it germinated—using the beast's or insect's body as a host—until ultimately, the complete anatomy of the intruder was transformed into a Jezebel...oftentimes at a great distance from the spot in the forest where the seed was implanted. And I must say that their scheme of retribution and strategy for survival have been enormously successful just over the last century. At one time, only a handful of Jezebels disgraced the forest. But today, beyond the castle, there are fields and fields of the blossoms."

"You'd think the Jezebels would retaliate against the Reclaimers," reasoned Dan, "since they cursed the flowers."

"But the Reclaimers are immune to the seeds," explained the tree nymph, "since the host must be a living being. Remember, the snakemen haven't a single living cell among them."

After another glimpse to the plot of flowers, William asked, "But, Ceremonia, if we walk near the Jezebels, how will we avoid an onslaught of seeds?"

"If we remain perfectly quiet," stressed Ceremonia, "the Jezebels are harmless."

"But what if they shoot and we're hit by seeds?" asked an uneasy Cindy.

"Don't worry," assured Ceremonia, "you'll be fine; just remain perfectly quiet. However, I'd suggest no one look directly at the blossoms when you creep by, since their offensive appearance will likely cause you to gasp. Even the slightest pant is more than enough noise to initiate a deluge of seeds. And second, everyone should take off their boots, so you make as little noise as possible. Obviously, the flowers have exceptional hearing."

At the tree nymph's suggestion, five of the explorers removed their boots and held them in a tight grip.

Noticing Salvus' hoofs, Ceremonia advised him to tread lightly and not to drag his tail.

Aware silence must be maintained, the satyr simply nodded.

"To show you how easy it can be," whispered Ceremonia, "I'll go first." The tree nymph retained her full-size stature and remained visible. Since she was always barefoot, she had nothing to carry. The woodland dweller advanced nearly seventy feet up the path, slowly and quietly, until she reached the first Jezebel. However, the last twenty feet—the area immediately in front of the flowers—proved more nerve-racking for her, as well as the protected onlookers. After silently passing the blossoms without incident, she took shelter behind a large rock on the distant side of the flowers.

Sensing the nervousness of his companions, Sam stepped forward to test his light-footedness and silence. He reduced the distance between himself and the plot of flowers by a mere ten feet, when he softly cleared his throat. Hundreds of Jezebels rotated their blooms in the direction of the noise and fired thousands of seeds. Fortunately, Sam was out of range.

From behind the far boulder's protection, Ceremonia yelled, "Go back!"

The blossoms immediately turned to the tree nymph's location and shot countless seeds, which smashed against her rocky shield and tumbled to the ground.

Luckily, Sam reached the safety of his boulder unscathed. "I just wanted to show you five," he remarked, "how dangerous the flowers can be."

"Yeah, right," said Jimmy.

Peering from the side of the rock, Dan noticed most of the blossoms were still pointed in Ceremonia's direction, while a few blooms were directed at the group's boulder, indicating it still wasn't safe to proceed.

After several minutes of deadly silence, the flowers resumed their former position, with their blossoms facing straight ahead.

Attempting it again, Sam stepped from the boulder—carrying his boots—with his lance secured to his backpack. Advancing with extreme caution and complete silence, he soon approached the near side of the flowers. Resisting deep breaths, he inched the remaining twenty feet, until he reached Ceremonia, without alerting the Jezebels. His success provided the encouragement his friends desperately needed.

As William embarked upon his trek, he dropped a boot just feet into his journey. To the surprise of Ceremonia and the rest of the travelers, his blunder went undetected by the flowers.

Even his brother, who observed his misstep from behind the rock, was smart enough and resourceful enough to cover his mouth when letting out a weak gasp.

With the utmost caution, William lowered himself to the ground. *Don't let my knee pop...don't let my knee pop,* kept running through his mind. After lifting his boot from the footpath, he continued his hushed pace. In front of the Jezebels, he—like Sam—resisted the growing urge to glimpse the blossoms and successfully made it into the waiting arms of Ceremonia.

To everyone's surprise, the next two adventurers, the hoofed Salvus and the lumbering Jimmy, made the journey without the slightest noise or provocation.

From behind the boulder, Cindy whispered, "Dan, you go next; I'm not ready yet."

At her insistence, the young man neared the Jezebels. He was making a successful crossing, until he was three feet distant from Ceremonia's boulder. He surrendered to his temptation and did what the tree nymph strictly forbade; he glimpsed the cursed flowers. For as hideous as they were, the teenager inhaled only slightly. In fact, the noise was so faint that his co-travelers, only feet ahead, failed to hear it.

But it was loud enough for the Jezebels.

In a split second, Dan leaped to the sheltering boulder, narrowly missing a saturation bombing of seeds.

For several minutes, the flowers faced the rock which protected the five travelers and Ceremonia, while Cindy anxiously awaited the blooms to assume their peaceful positions. Behind the rock, the tree nymph reminded the travelers, in a whisper, that not a word was to be spoken, until Cindy was safely behind the boulder with them.

After the blossoms resumed their forward positions, Cindy started her silent approach, also with her boots in hand and her lance strapped to her backpack. Like Salvus' and Jimmy's trek, all were amazed the blossoms failed to stir, even once. When her refuge and friends were only feet ahead—and just as she was tasting victory—her bare foot crushed a withered leaf.

A crackling sound was heard.

Cindy spun quickly and placed her backpack to the Jezebels. As feared, a bombardment of seeds ripped holes into her knapsack. In desperation and fear, she dived to the protective rock and safety. Unfortunately, as she lunged, her right leg rose slightly into the air and received a seed in the ankle. The assault was so instantaneous that virtually upon the seed's contact, she had cleared the barrage and had touched ground behind the boulder. But the damage was inflicted. Within moments, not one, but both feet became so heavy, as if they were made of lead. She couldn't lift herself from the ground.

Glancing at her injured leg, Sam witnessed hairlike roots sprouting from her ankle and burrowing into the forest floor. To her co-travelers, Cindy appeared in a dream state.

"Cindy!" yelled Sam, to prevent her from losing consciousness.

"I can't keep my ankles apart," mumbled a dazed Cindy. "I can't keep 'em apart."

Sam was in total disbelief as he eyed Cindy's ankles fuse and gradually transform into a hardened substance. The skin tissue around her ankles was altering at the cellular level into a coarse bark. The men wildly ripped the bark and roots, while trying to separate her ankles. With each tear of her bark, even though semiconscious, she let out a deep moan. Unfortunately, new bark appeared as fast as the old bark was ripped away.

"It's not working!" yelled Sam. "Ceremonia, what do we do?!"

"Get her off the ground!" shouted the tree nymph. "Her feet mustn't touch soil for twelve hours or she'll transform permanently into a Jezebel."

With a thrust of the machete, Sam severed the sprouting roots from her ankle.

Cindy screamed.

Sam lifted her from the forest floor and carried her to a flat boulder—far from the range of the Jezebels. As the men tore bark from her legs, which had now risen to her calves, Sam shouted, "What is it with roots and grasses in this world?"

"What do you mean?" asked Ceremonia.

Pulling away layer after layer of bark, but without removing his sights from his transforming friend, he exclaimed, "Jimmy was attacked by a flesh-burning weed."

"How'd you free him?" she asked, while snapping a fresh root from Cindy's ankle.

"We used Dan's holy water," he answered.

"What's holy water?" she asked.

Ignoring Ceremonia's question, Sam looked at Dan and demanded, "Is there any left?"

Dan burst open his backpack and handed the bottle to Sam.

Hoping against hope, Sam drenched Cindy's ankle that held the seed. Upon contact, the area foamed and then bubbled. Within seconds, the seed dislodged itself, fell upon the boulder, and rolled to the forest floor.

"Well, I'll be," remarked an astounded Sam.

With success on her ankle, Sam soaked Cindy's legs, from her calves down. The bark unraveled, fell from the sides of her feet, and onto the forest floor. The roots shriveled and dropped from her ankle.

"Remind me to get a bottle of this," joked Sam, before returning it to Dan.

Sam lifted Cindy from the uncomfortable rock.

"No, Sam!" shouted Ceremonia.

"What?" he questioned.

"Her feet still can't touch the ground for twelve hours," she explained, "or the transformation process will start over again."

"Even with the seed gone?" asked a doubtful Sam.

"Although the seed has been removed," explained Ceremonia,

"the mutation below her skin can and will resume the moment she steps foot upon soil."

Sam returned Cindy to the boulder.

Dan grabbed a camping pillow from his backpack, placed it under Cindy's head, and remarked, "I think she should sleep here tonight—far above the ground."

Fearing another root episode, Sam agreed.

With the Jezebels in the far distance, the travelers prepared for their evening stay, cutting their daily hike short by several hours.

Having recently experienced a newfound joy in serving others, Ceremonia decided to forgo her activities with her fellow tree nymphs and spend the time tending Cindy's needs.

After unpacking the sleeping bags, Dan opened Cindy's and covered her and Ceremonia; the late afternoon air was damp.

To prevent Cindy from falling off the boulder and taking root, Ceremonia maintained her full-size stature atop the rock alongside Cindy. Taking added precautions, she rolled Cindy onto her stomach and positioned her mouth over the boulder's edge.

As the remaining travelers gathered at the inner camp, Sam suggested two men sit each watch that night and early morning, in the event Ceremonia needed help with Cindy.

The patrolmen agreed.

Nearing the boulder, Sam asked, "How's she doing?"

"She's finally asleep," whispered the tree nymph.

Detecting a worried look on his face, Ceremonia promised she'd watch Cindy throughout the evening and early morning hours, making certain her feet didn't slip to the ground. "Sam," she continued, "I know how eager all of you are, including Cindy, to reach the tree in time. But I'm afraid you won't get off to an early start tomorrow. Even if Cindy survives through the night, she'll be sore and unable to walk, even after the twelve-hour period."

Sam rested his hand on Cindy's back and said, "I just wish I knew how far ahead the oak was, so I could plot our time accordingly."

Ceremonia sat up on the boulder. Trying to ease his mind, she predicted, "Cindy will probably be alright tonight. I know it's early, but why don't you get some rest and let someone else take the first watch."

Sam lifted his hand from Cindy's back and approached his sleeping area, thinking, *The troll that attacked Dan and Cindy on our trip to the castle was right; Cindy would be transformed into a*—he shook the disturbing thought from his mind.

Throughout their patrols, the watchmen periodically heard Cindy coughing. Though it sounded revolting and painful, at least they knew she was still human.

CHAPTER FOURTEEN
Web of Suspension

SINCE THE GROUP KNEW THEY WOULD NOT BE HIKING THE NEXT day, the men slept until 8:00. As the patrolmen gathered for breakfast, Ceremonia remained atop the boulder, munching on leaves that were within arm's reach, while also keeping a close eye on Cindy.

Nearing the rock and carrying a cup of water, Sam offered it to the tree nymph, who gladly accepted it to wash down a few stubborn stems. Glancing to the ground, he noticed a puddle of yellowish fluid. "What's that?" he asked.

"It's Cindy fighting off the transformation process," explained the tree nymph, before taking a gulp of water. "It's tree sap; she's been spitting up all night."

Sam turned and had walked only a few paces nearer the inner camp, when he spun, looked at Ceremonia, and remarked, "Thanks for watching her throughout the night and early morning."

"You're welcome," replied Ceremonia. "I was happy to do it."

By now, more than fifteen hours had elapsed since Cindy's exposure to the Jezebel seed and the patient was slowly stirring. One loud productive cough woke her completely. Seeing her sit up on the boulder, the men raced to her side.

"How are you feeling?" asked Ceremonia.

"Thirsty," replied Cindy.

Sam dashed to grab two cups of water and returned to the rocky sanctuary. Handing her the first cup, he asked, "Do you feel…um…you know…different in any way?"

After drinking the entire cup of water in a matter of seconds, she returned it and reached for the second. With the cup pressed against her lower lip, she replied, "I guess I feel alright; just exhausted."

Once the second cup was emptied, Sam glanced at Ceremonia, who nodded. The two helped Cindy swing around and dangle her feet from the rock.

"Let's see if you can stand," suggested the tree nymph.

Sam and Ceremonia gradually lowered her to the ground, fully prepared to throw her atop the boulder at the first sign of sprouting roots. All travelers watched closely, as Cindy's right foot touched the soil and then her left. Gratefully, nothing germinated, though her feet still felt like lead. Cindy leaned against the rock, but ultimately reclined upon its cold, hard surface. The simple act of standing proved tiring.

After checking her forehead for a fever and discovering there was no high temperature, Sam insisted, "You rest here as long as you want. We'll be just a few feet away if you need anything."

"Thanks, Sam," replied Cindy, who closed her eyes and entered her dreamland.

The men returned to the dying campfire.

Immediately upon swallowing Doctor O'Brien's pills, Dan asked, "Sam, I don't mean to sound heartless, but do you think we'll still make it to the oak in time if we lose another day?"

"I don't know," mumbled Sam, "but Cindy obviously can't walk in her condition."

Racking his brain, trying to think of a way to avoid losing precious travel time, but without further draining Cindy's strength, Dan eventually proposed, "Sam, would you mind if Jimmy, William, Salvus, and I built a wooden litter for Cindy, just in case she's not able to walk later today or even tomorrow?"

Knowing the men would be idle the rest of the day, Sam agreed, but warned, "Stay in the nearby forest and keep your voices low. I don't want you attracting wheel bugs."

Grabbing their lances and the machete, the young men and Salvus headed for the neighboring woods to gather limbs and vines for the construction of the stretcher. By noon, they had created a crude, but sturdy, litter composed of more than a dozen large branches roped together with forest vines. The two branches, which extended beyond the span of the stretcher, were intentionally designed as handles to pull it and the patient across the forest floor.

Jimmy jumped upon the contraption and suggested, "Let's try it out."

His companions unenthusiastically agreed.

To their surprise, the stretcher easily supported Jimmy's weight, without showing any signs of strain.

The cries of jubilation awoke Cindy, who asked for more water. Glancing at Sam's wristwatch, as he handed her a cup, she exclaimed, "Oh, my gosh, it's 12:15; we need to move on."

Pressing his hands against her shoulders, as she attempted to step from the boulder, Sam ordered, "Whoa, hold on there. We're not going anywhere today."

"But, Sam," pleaded Cindy, "we need to keep moving. Time is running out."

Knowing her determination to reach the tree in time, Ceremonia asked, "Cindy, are you sure you're up for a hike?"

"Yes," she blurted, "I'm sure," before quenching her thirst.

Taking the empty cup, Sam placed it on the ground. Then, to be absolutely certain, he and the tree nymph lowered her bare feet to the ground; nothing shot forth from her ankle.

Sam called the men, who dragged their latest invention with them.

"What's that?" asked Cindy, eyeing the primitive apparatus.

"It's a litter," replied a proud Jimmy. "When you get tired of walking, we'll carry you up the path on it."

"Thanks, guys," said Cindy, "but I'll be fine."

"Nevertheless," insisted Sam, "since they took the time to make it, we'll take it along as a safety measure. If you tire, you'll be glad we did."

Within fifteen minutes, the camp area was cleaned and the sleeping gear was packed away.

Before leaving the campsite, however, the tree nymph wished luck to the travelers.

"Will we see you again, Ceremonia?" asked Dan.

"I'm really not sure," she answered.

"You've got to see us off at the tree—please," implored Cindy.

Observing the somber expressions of her friends, the tree nymph

WEB OF SUSPENSION

couldn't say no. "Alright," she promised, "I'll meet you at the oak during the next full moon."

As the group marched off, Dan glanced over his shoulder and witnessed Ceremonia reduce in size and dart to the canopy.

Five minutes into their afternoon hike, with Sam and Cindy assuming a slow pace at the lead, he reminded, "The moment your legs tire, I want you on the litter, understand?"

"Yeah."

The three men and Salvus took turns, in groups of two, dragging the empty stretcher.

Cindy walked on her own as long as she could bear; by 3:00 p.m., however, she could hardly move her legs.

Noticing her difficulty, Sam lifted her into his arms and set her upon the litter.

The men relieved one another dragging the loaded stretcher until 8:00, at which time, Sam insisted they postpone their hike and eat a meal, especially since they skipped lunch that day.

Before preparing dinner, Sam recalled that since the nearly fatal incident yesterday with the Jezebels, he never gave a thought to hunting. Inspecting three fish, he supposed they might be good for another meal. After convincing himself they were still edible, he gathered wood and started a campfire, hoping no creature would detect the flames or smell the fish.

After William led the prayer, the hungry travelers sank their teeth into the fish, which had a peculiar taste, but was consumed nonetheless. Within an hour, the group was on the path again, with Cindy on the litter. The party hiked until 11:45 p.m.

During conversations around the midnight fire, Cindy learned that no one tended the wounds of the injured travelers the night before. Considering all she had endured the previous day, Salvus and the men offered no resistance, as she opened the whiskey bottle. To her amazement, Salvus' back lacerations were nearly healed. Dan's leg and back injuries were also mending nicely. William's wounds, inflicted by the griffin, were already forming scabs. In Cindy's estimation, Sam's wrists didn't require an application. Unfortunately, Jimmy's back injury, wreaked by the swordfish, needed a few more days of healing and more applications of the liquid cure-all.

Taking advantage of the huddled travelers, Sam suggested, "I think we'll be okay during the early morning hours with just one person on duty. Besides, we all need to get as much rest as possible. And since my wounds are healed, I'll take the first watch."

William volunteered for the second tour of duty.

The next morning the group was up at 4:00. Within minutes, they were eating rank apples and pinching their noses to block the offensive odor.

After a good night's sleep, Cindy maintained her legs felt like their normal weight; her mind was set on a full day's hike.

Considering her improvement and—at the same time—not wanting to slow the group's progress to the tree, Sam agreed to abandon the litter.

Once the meal was consumed and the area cleaned, the travelers undertook a seven-hour trek until noon, at which time Sam reached for his bow and arrow; Dan and William grabbed their lances. The men were geared to stalk their dinner.

We've got to catch something, thought Sam, *or there'll be nothing to eat tonight.*

Before leaving for the hunt, Sam insisted the remaining travelers guard the campsite, enjoy half an apple, and rest for a period.

Cindy agreed to his terms, provided Sam and the other hunters each took half an apple along. After a useless argument, Sam and the Clay brothers accepted the fruit.

Throughout most of the hunt, the men remained quiet, as they scanned the expanse for movement. Eventually breaking the silence, Dan asked, "Sam, what do you feel like eating tonight?"

"Honestly," replied Sam, "I feel like sinking my teeth into a juicy hamburger or a hot dog, like we used to."

Pausing to observe undergrowth movement to the right, Dan soon returned his gaze to Sam and replied, "I don't think that'll be happening anytime soon."

Considering the thicket which blanketed the forest floor, the hunters were surprised rabbits, squirrels, and other small game remained scarce. Nonetheless, they persisted; their perseverance paid off, when roughly fifty feet ahead, they spotted several rabbits feasting on a bed of clover. With the rabbits facing away and upwind of the motionless hunters, the men felt confident in slaying at least one. Sam quietly swung his bow from his shoulder and pulled the string taut. William leaned his lance against his thigh and reached for Sam's revolver, which was lodged in his friend's belt. Dan raised his spear to shoulder height and aimed.

"One, two, three," whispered Sam.

In an instant, the arrow, the bullet, and the lance were released. The rabbits scampered into the thick underbrush—all except three, which lay lifeless atop the clover. To his astonishment, Dan lanced a rabbit from nearly fifty feet.

The brothers had just begun to approach the game, when Sam ordered them to halt. He surveyed the area for potential game stealers, like the Titan Spider, which snatched their kill in the not too distant past. Detecting nothing, the men advanced and secured their meal.

Upon their arrival at camp, Sam suggested that if everyone ate sensibly, the three rabbits would probably last until the thirtieth—the day they hoped to arrive at the oak.

The festive mood, however, was dampened with Jimmy's comment they were nearly out of water.

Sam was surprised, since he thought their recent trip to the lake would have been their last. "Well," he replied, "we'll just have to be on the lookout this afternoon for a water source."

Though the travelers were still famished after their insufficient lunch, they wanted nothing more than to cover as much ground that day as humanly possible. After a vote, the rabbit meal was delayed until later that night. The afternoon hike, although successful in the number of miles covered, was unsuccessful in spotting water.

Since each traveler had only half an apple for lunch, Sam thought it was best to eat dinner earlier than the usual 11:00 hour and then resume their hike after the meal. As was typical, Sam gathered kindling; the rest of the group prepared the camp area and organized the cooking supplies. By 6:30 p.m., all were relaxing alongside a warm fire, inhaling the smell of the cooked rabbit. Sam led the group in a prayer of thanks. Before concluding, he implored God for a safe and speedy trip to the tree and that the oak's portal was still active.

"Amen," replied the group, followed by Dan, who blurted a second, "Amen."

Despite the fact the water supply was extremely low, it was enough for the meal. The dinner conversation was practically nonexistent, since all knew the less they talked, the sooner they'd finish their meal and the earlier they'd be back on the trail, hoping to set a new record in the number of daily miles logged. By 7:30 p.m., the group was trudging up the path toward home.

Nearly an hour into the final leg of their daily hike, Dan thought it was strange—though he wasn't complaining—that the group never encountered a predatory creature the entire day, not even during the hunt. Thinking they might stir one from the brush if he thought about it long enough, he shook the superstitious idea from his head and struck up a conversation with William. "So, are you excited to see the old town again?" he asked.

"I suppose," replied William, "but a little worried at the same time."

"Worried?" asked Dan. "Why?"

"I don't know," he replied, after kicking a rock to the side of the trail. "I guess I'm a little concerned how, or if, the townspeople will accept me and all the questions they'll have about where I've been. I mean, it's been thirteen years."

"You've got nothing to worry about," assured Dan. "Remember, it's Lawton."

The brothers' conversation was interrupted by Cindy, who spotted water trickling over a slope at the forest's edge and down the footpath.

After bringing her discovery to Sam's attention, he speculated, "I think you're right. I'll check it out."

Dan and William grabbed the three plastic containers and, with their lances in hand, followed Sam a short distance into the forest.

Between two large trees was a small depression in the forest floor that had gathered sufficient rainwater to fill the sunken ground to overflowing. Even though the puddle was barely three feet across, Sam suspected it held enough water to fill their water bottles. It was also convenient, since it was just several feet off the trail.

Debating on whether to boil the water then and delay their march or carry it on their hike and sterilize it after they retired, Sam proposed the options to his friends. It was unanimous. Jimmy, Dan, and

William snapped the lids on the plastic containers and lugged the contaminated water in their backpacks for nearly three hours.

At 11:30 p.m., the group ended their trek and set up camp. Cindy arranged Sam's sleeping area, while he gathered wood.

As he was positioning the last few branches to start the blaze, Cindy pleaded, "Sam, since you're already building the fire, just this one time, can we keep it burning until morning?"

Knowing there hadn't been any sightings of the Reclaimers or Oswagis for days, Sam reluctantly agreed.

Cindy bolted to her sleeping area and dragged her gear nearer the newborn flame. The young men followed her lead.

By 12:20 a.m., the campsite was in order and the purified water had been poured into the water bottles. Since most of the wounds were healing nicely—and attempting to conserve the little remaining whiskey—Cindy treated only Jimmy's back.

The group retired by 12:30, except for Jimmy, who accepted the first watch, followed by Salvus.

With the dry cereal consumed days ago and the marshmallows recently exhausted, the travelers were left with stomach-churning apples and tomatoes for breakfast which they painfully swallowed. Thankfully, they had a sizeable meal the previous evening.

At 5:15 a.m., the group was back on the path, determined to put in another full day's hike. What bothered Sam, and he suspected the others as well, was that nothing familiar had been seen along the trail. Then again, he knew all the trees looked virtually identical, especially in the dim light. He remained hopeful, however, that someone would eventually spot something they remembered seeing upon their entry into the forest, nearly thirty days ago.

Throughout the morning, the travelers continually scanned the area for unwelcome predators. Dan, however, was looking for a singular object he distinctly recalled seeing weeks ago—the oddly-shaped sycamore tree. The march went on.

Rabbit was served for lunch; the group indulged.

Barely an hour into their afternoon hike, the travelers' pace slowly waned. The many miles traveled during recent days, the insufficient sleep, and the occasional meager meals were beginning to take their toll. Sam was troubled more than anyone since, being the oldest human in the group, he felt responsible for the safety and well-being of his co-travelers.

Attempting to ease his troubled mind, he asked, "Cindy, how are your legs?"

"They're fine."

"Are you tired?"

"Not really; I'll rest when I'm home."

Sensing his undue concern, Cindy declared, "Sam, we're all fine. You've done a great job in hunting and keeping us fed, not to mention your amazing ability collecting water from the most wretched places. We're fine."

Sam's worries were partially alleviated.

Stepping alongside Sam and Cindy, Salvus asked if, for a change, he could take the lead.

"By all means," offered Sam, "be my guest."

Glancing behind, Sam was pleased the young men were keeping up, including Jimmy, who had the tendency to straggle behind. They were engaged in a lively discussion about which of the three Ceremonia liked the best.

"You've got to be kidding," exclaimed Cindy to Sam, on overhearing their conversation. "Can you believe it? How typical."

Sam and Cindy turned and stopped in their tracks, allowing the men to catch up.

With her co-travelers at her side, Cindy criticized, "I can't believe it. We're in the middle of this godforsaken forest, trying to find our way home, and all you three can talk about is Ceremonia?"

"What else is there to talk about?" asked Jimmy.

Sam rolled his eyes in disbelief; he eventually remarked, "Speaking of which, I wonder where she is."

"She promised to meet us at the oak during the next full moon," reminded Cindy.

A disturbing thought crossed Dan's mind. "If Ceremonia promised to meet us at the oak during the next full moon," he explained, "and we haven't seen a sign of her, then maybe we're nowhere near the tree."

A strong wind separated the canopy.

Once the attention of the group was drawn from the treetops,

Sam stressed, "We can't worry about that now. If we remain focused and alert, I'm sure we'll reach the tree in time. Besides, we've got more important things to worry about…like keeping an eye out for the Reclaimers and the Oswagis. I'm sure they'll be visiting the oak on the thirtieth."

As the group resumed their walk, William eyed Salvus ahead and yelled, "Wait up!"

The satyr was far ahead of the group, since he failed to notice the travelers stop and discuss their latest dilemma. He turned to face his companions and—while switching to a reverse trot—shouted, "Hurry up; the oak tree awaits us!" He stepped backwards and was trapped in a thick spider web, spun between two elm trees, one on either side of the footpath.

Due to the considerable darkness, the web was undetectable to the five travelers, twenty feet away.

Salvus screamed; a Titan Spider descended its sticky web toward its next meal.

Hearing his shouts, the party raced to his rescue. Standing alongside the spun mesh, Sam grabbed his revolver and aimed for the approaching eight-legged predator. From his estimation, the creature was easily four feet long. He waited until the arachnid was closer to Salvus, giving him an unobstructed shot.

"Shoot!" yelled the satyr, as he struggled to free himself. "What are you waiting for?"

The remaining travelers brandished their lances to cut the web. But the snare was too gummy; their spears stuck to the thick fibers, making little progress in freeing their friend.

"Hold still!" ordered Sam. "You're shaking the web too much; I can't get a clear shot."

"Why don't you hop on the web and hold still!" shouted Salvus.

Sam never removed his stare from the spider, which was now just ten feet above the satyr.

Eyeing the potential rescuers on the ground, the creature slowed its approach, as if hoping to snatch its prey unnoticed.

Just a few more feet, thought Sam, *to clear the last limb.*

As he slowly squeezed the trigger, two green appendages lunged from the back side of a tree and grabbed the spider. A fearsome struggle ensued, causing the web to shake wildly. With the spider distracted, Sam put away his revolver and helped his co-travelers slice the web. Even with five members slashing, the network of fibers was only slightly damaged; Salvus remained a prisoner.

A loud thud was heard and felt. The two-hundred-pound spider fell to the ground, followed by an unearthly-size praying mantis, which spread its wings and glided to the forest floor, landing just feet from the arachnid. With the creatures engaged in mortal combat, hardly a passing glance was paid to the six trespassers.

The spider charged the praying mantis, but was instantly repelled, when the mantis extended its daunting front legs from its 'praying' position and knocked the arachnid onto its back. Unfortunately for the praying mantis, the spider landed near a slope. With a powerful rock, the spider rolled down the incline and landed on its eight legs; the battle resumed.

The five rescuers, never pausing from their slashing, periodically glanced behind to witness the skirmish.

For a brief moment, the spider had the advantage, as it shot a strand of its clinging fiber at the face of its adversary, forcing it to retreat several feet in the direction of the web and the rescuers. It frantically wiped the transparent substance from its face with its front legs.

Passing dangerously close to the travelers, the razor-sharp spines along the praying mantis' hind legs grazed William, ripping his pants and instantly drawing blood. In his pain, he dropped his lance and fell to the forest floor.

With Jimmy, Cindy, and Sam working on freeing Salvus, Dan dropped to his knees and applied pressure to his brother's exposed wound, while keeping a watchful eye on the creatures that were still engaged in a deadly clash just feet away. Tearing his own shirtsleeve, Dan wrapped it around his brother's leg as a temporary tourniquet. *This,* he thought, *will have to do, until a better time.*

"Let's go!" was heard from behind.

Looking back, Dan saw the satyr step from the web.

Sam knelt on the ground and helped Dan raise William to his feet. The group raced around the trees that supported the web and stepped on the footpath.

Glancing back, the travelers witnessed the praying mantis knock the spider onto its back with its powerful forelimbs. But this time, the praying mantis showed no mercy. It flapped its transparent wings in an offensive maneuver to confuse its prey and then sprang upon the Titan Spider, sinking one of its six-foot front legs—with its rows of sharp spines—into the spider's abdomen. The fatal wound was delivered.

The group turned and darted up the path.

Seconds later, Cindy offered a backward glimpse and eyed the praying mantis rotate its head 180 degrees toward the fleeing group. She gasped when she saw its compound yellow eyes atop its horrid triangular-shaped head, but maintained her fast pace.

The praying mantis dragged its victim into the darkness of the woods—in the opposite direction of the travelers—and devoured its warm meal.

Though the winged victor was feasting on the spider in the distance, the travelers took no chances and continued their sprint up the path for nearly twenty minutes.

William eventually moaned in agony.

Lowering him to the ground, Dan tore what remained of his brother's pant leg, as his friends gathered clothing from their bags for an improved tourniquet and bandages. Once William's leg was exposed, the full extent of his injury was revealed; he had sustained a severe gash from his knee to his ankle.

"Hang on, William," ordered Dan. "You'll be fine; I promise."

Looking down at Dan, who was now resting his brother's head on his lap, Cindy placed her hand on his shoulder and apologized, "Sorry; I have to do it."

Dan raised his sights to Cindy unscrewing the cap of the whiskey bottle. Recalling the excruciating pain he endured when his injuries were doused, he refused to permit his brother to experience the same agony. "No!" he yelled. "He'll be fine."

At the outcry, Sam seized Dan's arm and insisted, "We have no choice." Placing his face next to Dan's ear, he whispered, "If we don't apply it now, he probably won't make it through the night. His wound is deep—really deep—and he's already lost a lot of blood."

There was no response from Dan.

Taking charge of the delicate situation, Sam ordered, "Dan, find a thick piece of wood to place in your brother's mouth."

Dan lifted William's head from his lap, placed it gently on the ground, and scanned the nearby footpath for a sturdy limb. Walking several feet distant, he grabbed a suitable branch, snapped it in half, and returned to his brother's side.

After the wood was inserted, Sam further instructed, "Hold his hand; I'll grab the other."

With both hands, Dan clutched his brother's left hand.

As Cindy tilted the bottle, Dan squeezed hard and whispered, "I'm sorry."

The moment the first drop of alcohol touched the open wound, William sank his teeth into the branch, moaned loudly, and blacked out. It was now 4:00 in the afternoon.

The travelers set up camp where he lay.

Though not having an appetite himself, Sam knew he must warm a meal for the other travelers to keep up their strengths. After a trip to the forest's fringes, he returned with an armful of deadwood and started a fire.

In a dazed state, staring at the flames, Cindy said, "I'm not hungry."

"Not many of us are," speculated Sam, "but you need to eat or you'll never have the energy to reach the tree and ultimately home." Dropping a rabbit into the pan, he continued, "I want all of you to eat to regain your strength, since you'll most probably be making the trip tomorrow without me."

Cindy, who had reluctantly gathered the plates and utensils moments earlier, blurted, "What do you mean without you?"

Wrapping an old cloth around the pan's hot handle, Sam explained, "Tomorrow's the thirtieth. I don't want you four missing your cross-over. It may be the last chance you'll get. I'll stay here with William."

"No," snapped Dan. "William is going with us."

"Dan," reminded Sam, "we'd all like to return home; believe me. But we don't know how much farther ahead the tree is. If William awakes tomorrow, I can promise you he won't be able to walk. And if carrying him holds back the group and causes everyone to miss the portal, it's not fair, especially if it's the last chance to get home. All of you must return to your parents; William and I will stay behind, if need be."

"Sam," insisted Dan, "you go with the group. William's my brother; I'll stay behind with him. Besides, I was the one who initiated this journey."

"Absolutely not," replied Sam, in a commanding tone. "You've got a family waiting for you; I don't."

With neither man willing to compromise, Dan remarked, "There has to be another way—a way all of us can return home." Remembering the group had discarded the litter, he suggested, "If I build a new litter tonight, then can we all hike tomorrow?"

Sam was mortified he hadn't thought of the stretcher himself. After considering any possible negative consequences, he negotiated, "Alright, Dan, but these are the terms. First, you sit down here right now—all of you—and eat a warm meal. Afterwards, Dan and I will spend the night building another litter. Then tomorrow, Salvus, Jimmy, and Cindy will start on the path toward the oak; Dan and I will drag the litter. But you three—" he pointed to Salvus, Jimmy, and Cindy "—are not to wait for us, if we lag behind. If we slow down, you're to continue moving forward. Maybe, just maybe, you'll reach the tree in time. If William, Dan, and I also make it in time, that's great. But if we don't, at least you three will make it home."

Then it hit Sam, who thought, *What's to happen to Salvus? He can't go back to my world.*

His thoughts about his friend's welfare were interrupted by the satyr, who stepped forward and offered, "Sam, why don't I help Dan pull the litter tomorrow, while you join Cindy and Jimmy? After all, I have nowhere to go; my life is, and has always been, this world."

Bending on one knee to turn the rabbit in the pan, Sam politely refused his proposal, replying, "That's a noble gesture, Salvus; but I'll stay behind with Dan and William. They're my responsibility." He motioned his companions to sit.

All gathered closer to the fire and reclined on the damp forest floor. After Cindy handed each man a plate, Sam said grace, asking for a blessing on the food, upon the next day's travels, and that at least some, if not all, of the group would reach the oak, before the full moon rose.

Halfway through the meal, Dan left the warmth of the fire and walked to his brother, who was out cold atop his sleeping bag. "William," he whispered.

As he feared, there was no response or movement.

Upon his return to the campfire, Cindy asked if there was any change in his brother.

"No," he answered, "I'm afraid not."

When the meal was finished, but before the area was cleaned, Sam and Dan grabbed their weapons and the lantern and headed a short distance off the path to gather limbs and vines. As they combed the nearby forest, the remaining travelers sat at the campfire discussing their unthinkable predicament.

"I can't believe we've come all this way," acknowledged Jimmy, "and now there's a chance Sam, Dan, and William won't return home. I mean, the whole reason for this adventure was to rescue William." He tossed a twig into the blaze, admitting, "Talk about a plan backfiring."

"Yeah," replied Cindy, "but what can we do?"

Jimmy stared into the woods. By the light of the lantern, he eyed Dan climbing a tree and slashing a vine with his machete. He jumped to his feet, looked down at Salvus, and suggested, "You know, if we helped build the litter, it'll be completed sooner; then we'd have a few extra hours to hike, presuming we can convince Sam we should hit the path as soon as the project's done, instead of waiting until early morning."

Salvus rose to his hoofs and admitted, "You know I hate to see any of you leave. But if it helps you reach the oak in time—and ultimately your families—of course, I'll lend a hand."

Cindy reached to her side, grabbed two lances, and handed them to her friends, advising, "Tell Sam I'll keep an eye on William, so you four can work until the litter's constructed. In the meantime, I'll think of something to persuade Sam we should hike the moment it's built."

Jimmy and Salvus bolted to the nearby forest. Within moments, they were standing alongside Dan and Sam.

"What's going on?" asked Sam.

"We're here to help," answered Jimmy.

"Thanks, guys," said Sam, "but you need your sleep for tomorrow's hike."

"But, Sam," challenged Jimmy, "with two more workers, the litter will be finished in half the time. Besides, I'm too excited about tomorrow to sleep."

Sam squatted to lift a limb, rose to his feet, and unenthusiastically accepted the offer. "Alright," he yielded, "but under one condition. Starting at 9:00 tonight, we all take turns returning to the campfire for an hour's nap. This way, we'll all get at least a little sleep."

All agreed and the work resumed.

At 9:05, Sam ordered Jimmy to the campsite for a respite. Knowing the terms of their agreement, Jimmy willingly neared the fire, as the men continued their construction project, which was taking shape.

At 10:00, Dan was relieved of his duties and Jimmy returned to the worksite.

Beside the campfire, Dan knelt on the soil and tried to draw a response from his brother, who remained out cold atop his sleeping bag, but under Cindy's attentive eye. William failed to stir.

"He hasn't moved," informed Cindy, "not even when I dragged him nearer the fire."

Rising to his feet, Dan had just begun walking to his sleeping area, when Cindy asked, "Where are you going? Your sleeping bag's here under William."

Failing to create an immediate and convincing response, he simply replied, "I know; I'll stretch out on Jimmy's sleeping bag." The teenager faded into the darkness.

Though Cindy thought it was strange that he decided to sleep away from the campfire, instead of resting alongside his brother, she dismissed her concern and attributed his attitude to fatigue.

Nearly twenty feet behind Cindy and the glowing fire, Dan slowed his pace and turned to confirm her back was facing him. Seeing she was unmindful of his actions, he grabbed his flashlight and lance and darted across the footpath to the woods on the opposite side of the trail. He silently advanced ahead of the campfire and Cindy in complete darkness. Once beyond the campfire's glow and Cindy's vision, he stepped from the forest and onto the path. Switching on the flashlight, he was determined to find something familiar along the trail that would indicate how close they were to the oak. *After all,* he thought, *we've been hiking extra hours in the morning and evening for days to make up for lost time. The oak has to be nearby.*

While surveying the area for anything recognizable, it happened again; the invisible warm touch clutched his arm and led him into the woods to the right. The teenager attempted to engage the creature or person in a conversation, but like his brother, there was no reply.

The being guided him through the woods for nearly twenty minutes; they exited the forest and stepped upon another footpath. As the being turned Dan to the left, he somehow knew—beyond the shadow of a doubt—he and his co-travelers had been traveling upon the wrong path. *This has to be the one,* he thought. *Maybe when we crossed through the forest to escape Bacchus, we didn't travel far enough to the right. After all, the invisible being has never been anything but helpful.*

Dan waved his lance, hoping to make contact with the being, but there was nothing. Oddly enough, he sensed he was now alone. After exploring the area for a few minutes with the flashlight's beam, he retraced his steps through the unknown plot of forest.

●

At the campsite, his disappearance did not go unnoticed.

"Where could he have gone?" asked an irate Sam, after searching the neighboring woods and footpath.

"Dan!" yelled Jimmy a third time.

But there was no response—only the spine-chilling sounds echoing in the woods beyond.

"He said he was going to Jimmy's sleeping area," said Cindy.

After thrusting his spear into the ground, Sam yelled, "I swear, that boy better have a good explanation or I'll—"

"Sam! Cindy!" was heard in the darkness.

Dan was racing down the trail in the direction of the campfire, carrying his lance and lit flashlight. Slowing his sprint, he neared the fire, dropped his gear, and rested his hands on his knees, laboring to catch his breath.

Sam stepped closer, yelling, "Where the heck have you been?"

Still panting, Dan motioned his hand in front of his mouth; he was still breathless. After collapsing to his knees, he inhaled sharply and answered, "I went up the path a ways to see if there was something—anything—I'd recognize."

"You walked up the path alone?" reprimanded Sam. "Are you insane?"

"Please, Sam," replied Dan, "let me finish."

"I'm listening," said Sam, before crossing his arms over his chest.

"Anyway," he continued, "I walked about five hundred feet or so up the trail when the invisible warm touch returned. It grabbed my arm and guided me off the path to the woods at the right. I was led through the forest for about twenty minutes when I stepped foot on another trail; the being turned me to the left."

"So," replied an unconvinced Sam, "let me guess. Now you think this other path is the correct one."

"Yes," declared Dan. "Come on, Sam, you know this invisible being has never once misled us on our journey. Why would it do so now?"

"That's nonsense," blurted Sam. "This has to be the right path."

"Sam, if it's only a twenty-minute walk," proposed Cindy, "I think we should, at the very least, check it out."

After plopping himself on a log, Sam reminded, "But, Cindy, we may not have enough time as it is. Even a loss of twenty minutes could ruin your chance of returning home."

Gazing into the woods, where the men had been working, she asked, "How long before the litter is finished?"

Raising a hand to his brow, Sam closed one eye and estimated, "Maybe another couple hours or so."

"Then," said Cindy, "I suggest we hike the moment the litter is built, instead of sleeping. This way, if the other path isn't the right one, we wouldn't be any worse off for time than if we had slept."

Glancing at the determined faces of his companions, Sam knew he was about to lose the argument.

Noting his silence, Cindy implored, "Sam, please, we have to try."

Sam glared at his young friend and asked, "Dan, how sure are you this other path is the right one?"

Still on the ground, but now crawling to William, he answered, "I know this may sound strange, but when I was standing on the other path—even though the flashlight's beam barely broke through the darkness to reveal anything familiar—it just felt right. I can't put it into words; but, yes, I know it's the right path."

"Dan, it's not that I distrust your judgment," admitted Sam, "it's just we don't have the luxury of time on our side. But if you're that certain, I suppose we should explore the possibility. In the meantime, we have a project to finish."

Dan rested his hand on William's forehead, expecting he would rouse. With no reaction, he joined the men in the forest. Within an hour and a half, the litter was constructed and resting near the campfire.

Cindy placed a camping pillow and blanket upon the stretcher's hard surface, before the men lifted the unconscious patient aboard.

After the camping gear was packed away, Sam and Dan grabbed the extended handles of the litter and dragged it and William up the path to the point of entry into the forest where Dan had recently visited.

It was 1:00 a.m., June 30.

CHAPTER FIFTEEN
Instant Incineration

"ARE YOU SURE THIS IS THE SPOT WHERE YOU ENTERED THE forest?" questioned Sam.

"Positive," replied Dan.

The two ended their pace and set the litter on the footpath.

Watching Sam peer into the darkened forest, then back to the stretcher, Jimmy knew what he was debating. "Sam," he suggested, "I think we should pull William and the litter through the woods."

"But," replied Sam, "if the path through the forest isn't the right one, then we've wasted valuable time lugging the loaded litter for no reason. I think three should stay here with William and someone should hike with me to the path ahead."

As expected, the remaining travelers sided with Jimmy.

With Sam and Dan showing signs of exhaustion, Salvus and Jimmy lifted the stretcher handles and trudged through the forest. Cindy walked at the rear of the litter, periodically resting her hand on William's shoulder to prevent him from sliding off the transport. Sam, with lance in hand, led the group; Dan, also bearing a weapon, walked several paces behind the litter, protecting his friends from a possible rearward attack, while also keeping a close eye on his brother.

The travelers had hiked barely ten minutes through the unknown terrain, when Dan tripped on his dangling bootlace. Since the stretcher was only several feet ahead, he dropped his weapon to tie his lace.

From the nearby woods, he heard, "Help!"

With his bootlace still untied, he jumped to his feet and stepped off the flattened undergrowth to the sound of the feeble scream, leaving his lance behind.

"Help!" was heard again.

Advancing only two steps farther, he was strangled from behind. Several tendrils coiled around his neck and waist; he was yanked to the ground. His attempt to yell for backup was foiled, as leaves instantly invaded his mouth.

Glancing to his side, he eyed a band of nearly twenty forest Maskocites reveling in their latest capture.

Forest Maskocites, a grotesque woodland species, stood barely three feet high. Though small in stature, their perfectly disguised faces and bodies—shrouded in plant stems and leaves—allowed the creatures to roam the forest in safety.

On a closer examination, when their movements separated their body leaves, Dan noticed their repulsive physical features.

The creatures' faces were composed of bark, which housed a colony of miniature grubs that proved beneficial to the Maskocites. The wormlike larvae ingested crumbling bark, permitting a new layer to surface from the subfacial level. Their matching green eyes were crucial, since this perfect camouflage, set against their green leaves, protected them from larger predators and enabled them to stalk their prey undetected. In the absence of a traditional nose, the Maskocites sported two oversize nostrils. The apparent mouth of the species was unlike any Dan had ever seen. Four holes, each nearly an inch in diameter, disfigured the lower part of the face, directly above the leafy chin. The thick foliage, however, prevented the traveler from noticing any ears on the creature.

"Help!" was heard again.

The Maskocites had mastered the art of mimicry.

The teenager watched in horror, as a sole Maskocite spewed four more tendrils from its mouth holes at his ankles. Unable to scream with a mouthful of leaves or move with a body wrap of plant shoots, he was ruthlessly dragged atop the forest undergrowth. During the capture, moments earlier, his backpack fell to the ground; its contents were ransacked by two curious Maskocites.

Coming to a halt at the base of a towering tree, Dan eyed several Maskocites step closer. Each exposed three pairs of arms that were

previously concealed beneath their foliage. With six upper appendages, the creatures effortlessly climbed the tree, pulling Dan upward
by the tendrils that were coiled around his ankles, waist, and neck,
while still joined to the Maskocites' mouth holes.

●

On the footpath, Sam asked Salvus and Jimmy, who were pulling the
litter, how they were holding up.

"We're fine," spoke Jimmy, for both men.

"Will you be alright," he continued, "while I check on Cindy and
William?"

"Yeah," assured Salvus. "We'll keep an eye out."

"I'll be only a minute," promised Sam.

Standing beside the litter, he noticed Cindy had climbed aboard.
"Has he stirred?" he asked.

"He hasn't spoken a word," replied Cindy, "but he did move his
arm a few times."

"Well," remarked Sam, "hopefully he'll regain consciousness
soon."

"I hope so."

Eycing the whiskey on the stretcher—and optimistic the group
would reach the oak that day—Sam directed, "Hand me the bottle."

"I already treated William," she informed.

"I figured you probably did."

"Well," asked Cindy, "what do you need it for?" after handing him
the bottle.

"An early reward," he answered, before taking a swig.

Knowing he had been invaluable on their trip—and thinking if
they reached the tree that day, the need of the whiskey for medicinal
purposes would be virtually nonexistent—Cindy tolerated his brief
indulgence. However, by the third mouthful, she snatched the bottle,
replaced the cap, and set it beside her, reminding, "We need to save
some for William's leg."

"You're right," remarked Sam, who realized the alcohol failed to
satisfy him as it did in the recent past.

Before returning to Jimmy and Salvus, Sam peered behind the stretcher and asked, "Where's Dan?"

Cindy turned and scanned the sides of the footpath. With a puzzled look, she replied, "I don't know; he was just there a few minutes ago."

Tightening the grip on his weapon, he ordered, "You four continue moving. I'll backtrack and look for him. Maybe he's wandered off the path to go to the bathroom."

"Alright," replied Cindy, "but don't be long."

Both knew Dan's unannounced departure from the group was typically not the norm, although it did occur on occasion—like just a short time ago when the men were constructing the litter.

Cindy, however, had a gut feeling something was wrong. But being merely a suspicion, she didn't mention her concern to Sam, for fear it would needlessly alarm him.

Sam turned from Cindy and withdrew at a rapid pace into the relative darkness. As he approached the area where Cindy had last seen Dan, the Maskocites were still scaling the tree with their latest prize.

●

Thirty feet above the forest floor, the creatures slammed their victim on a sturdy limb.

Dan was relieved when the Maskocites severed their tendrils from their mouth holes—which eased the vines' grip around his body—but terrified, when the creatures unleashed another round of gripping tendrils, securing him to the branch. Still with a mouthful of leaves, he could only moan.

On several occasions during his abduction up the tree, the teenager chewed the leaves in his mouth and swallowed, hoping to scream for help. But as quickly as he gulped the leaves, more foliage sprouted in his mouth from the broken stems. It was a losing battle.

Countless vines entwined his ankles, calves, thighs, waist, and neck. The only areas free of the tendrils were his feet and chest. While wondering why his chest was left untouched, a Maskocite ripped open the teenager's shirt, lowered its face, and expelled mucus from its nostrils onto his chest. Dan immediately felt a burning sensation. He lowered his chin and eyed two green worms flipping in search of his heart. Once directly over the beating organ, they delivered an electric shock; Dan jolted his back off the limb and released a painful groan. A second round of shocks was delivered.

From generation to generation, the Maskocites conveyed the tale, in their incomprehensible grunts, that electrocuting its prey—especially a human—guaranteed prolonged and prolific lives to their tribal members. Upon the victim's death, the corpse was fed to the youngest members of the clan, ensuring fit and fearless future generations.

A third round of shocks jolted a restrained Dan on the branch.

After spotting Dan's abandoned weapon and backpack, with its contents scattered atop the forest floor, Sam noticed the breakage of plants and a compressed path upon the undergrowth, as if something of substantial weight had been recently dragged on it. He scanned the area before dashing up the path of the crushed weeds.

Amid electric shocks, the teenager heard, "Dan!" Sam was in proximity of the tree, where his friend was confined.

Unable to scream, Dan did the next best thing to capture Sam's attention. Spastically shaking his ankle, his untied boot crashed to the ground.

On hearing the thud, Sam darted the remaining feet to the tree. "Oh, no," he whispered, as he came upon his friend's boot. Staring into the canopy, he failed to spot the teenager, who remained perfectly concealed amid branches and leaves, thirty feet overhead. While absorbed in his upward gaze, eight tendrils wrapped around his waist and legs; Sam collided with the ground. He screamed, since he knew the remaining travelers were a considerable distance away and advancing farther out of earshot with each pull of the litter.

Cindy, who was tending William, since he had recently awakened, heard the distant cry. "Hey, guys," she demanded, "stop!"

The men came to a halt, set the litter to the ground, and neared Cindy and William.

"What's wrong?" asked Jimmy. Seeing a groggy William, he continued, "Hey, you've arisen!"

"Sh," ordered Cindy, "I think I heard a—"

"Help!" was heard in the darkness.

"That sounds like Sam," said Salvus.

Refusing to leave Cindy and William alone, Jimmy and the satyr spun the stretcher around and raced over the bumpy terrain to the cry for help.

●

The Maskocites had attempted, on several occasions, to overflow Sam's mouth with their leafy shoots. Unfortunately for the three-foot creatures, every time leaves were shoved into his mouth, they were immediately pulled out, only to wither and fall from their stems; the whiskey residue in Sam's mouth dehydrated the foliage. However, the remainder of his body was still vulnerable, which the creatures quickly ensnared with additional tendrils and lugged up a neighboring tree. The prisoner was fastened to a limb.

Within seconds, Sam heard the moans of Dan, who was strapped to another limb, only two trees over.

Jimmy and Salvus set the litter handles on a boulder, so the stretcher was on an incline, allowing the injured William an easy exit. Advancing a few yards, Jimmy and Salvus were soon standing over Dan's lance and backpack. Before venturing deeper into the woods, however, ten Maskocites, perfectly masked against their surroundings, targeted the men. Jimmy and Salvus struggled to free themselves from the constrictive vines, but made no headway.

Spotting two additional humans on the nearby litter, a creature climbed aboard.

Cindy raised a leg and released a powerful kick, knocking the Maskocite backwards to the ground. Upon hitting the forest floor, it was consumed in flames. The brilliant glow drew the attention of the remaining Maskocites, as well as Jimmy, Salvus, and William. Three of the creatures disconnected their tendril grip on the satyr and fled to the safety of the deeper forest.

With his arms free of the runners, Salvus grabbed a Maskocite and hurled it to the ground. Unfortunately, his throw didn't produce immediate combustion.

After landing on its six hands, the frightened creature jumped to its feet and scurried to the distant woods.

"What gives?" asked Salvus.

Too preoccupied with the five remaining Maskocites, Jimmy and Cindy failed to respond; William was gradually losing his struggle to remain conscious.

Snatching another Maskocite from behind that was dashing to the litter, Salvus lifted it by its stalky feet and dropped it headfirst to the ground.

It was consumed in a ball of fire.

Yelling to Jimmy, who had only recently freed his arms, Salvus ordered, "Drop them on their heads!"

Jimmy lifted a miniature creature by its feet, dropped it on its head, and created another fireball.

Glancing to the right, Cindy spotted more creatures emerging from the woods and charging the men.

Jimmy was hurled to the ground and received a mouthful of leaves.

From the overhead limbs was heard, "Douse them with whiskey!"

Recognizing Sam's voice, but baffled with his order and where-abouts, Cindy, nonetheless, opened the bottle that was resting beside her on the stretcher and filled her mouth. Crawling to the edge of the transport, she sprayed a mist at the Maskocites that were standing over Jimmy and binding him with tendrils. To her amazement, as well as Jimmy's and William's, the creatures immediately separated their vine attachments from their mouth holes. The stems shriveled from Jimmy's side and fell to the ground.

Opting against disgorging another series of shoots, the Maskoc-ites escaped to the refuge of the inner woods.

With the whiskey bottle in hand, Cindy jumped from the litter, neared Jimmy and an obstinate Maskocite—whose leafy appendages still filled her friend's mouth—and drenched Jimmy's face with alcohol. The leaves and shoots wilted; the creature released its hold.

Jimmy spit the leaves and stems from his mouth.

The Maskocite received an uppercut from Cindy, knocking it to the ground and bursting into flames.

Taking advantage of the species' newfound weakness, Jimmy sprang to his feet, raised a dwarfish beast by its legs, and threw it to the ground near three uneasy Maskocites. The hurled creature was torched. The latest setback sent the remaining Maskocites dashing out of sight.

With Sam's relentless yelling, the travelers soon spotted him secured to a limb, thirty feet up; seconds later, they discovered Dan. Recognizing the value of the whiskey, Cindy emptied two water bottles and filled them with alcohol. "Here," she said, before handing them to Jimmy and Salvus, "you'll need them to free Dan and Sam."

She returned the whiskey bottle to the litter.

The men filled their mouths with alcohol, crammed the water bottles in their pants pocket and toga, and neared the trees that held their friends captive.

"No," yelled Sam, as he eyed Jimmy approach his tree, "get Dan first!"

Jimmy turned and joined Salvus in climbing the tree that held their young friend. During their ascent, the men noticed a Maskocite overhead, attempting to hinder their rescue efforts. After all, to it, the prisoner was worth its suffering.

The satyr aimed and sprayed the contents of his mouth. As hoped, the creature's foliage dried up instantly; the Maskocite lost its coiling grip on the tree. In its panic and anguish, it failed to grasp a limb with any of its six arms. It fell to the forest floor and met its demise in a ball of flames.

Salvus refilled his oral ammunition.

Three more creatures were confronted while scaling the tree; all met the same fate. After the last Maskocite was misted by Jimmy and was plunging to the ground, it aimed a tendril that immediately wrapped around a horizontal limb. The creature remained suspended in midair.

Witnessing its apparent victory, Jimmy refilled his mouth and aimed below at the supporting vine. Immediately, the Maskocite resumed its free fall to the forest floor and was charred.

Jimmy took another mouthful of whiskey.

Below the canopy, four creatures stepped to the litter. With a lance in hand and whiskey in mouth, Cindy pierced a Maskocite's leg, behind its leafy covering. The intense pain forced it to stagger and ultimately fall backwards. The beast was no more. Two other Maskocites were sprayed with alcohol, sending them to the woods in torment.

Sadly, the last creature escaped Cindy's notice and silently mounted the transport from the rear. Before she felt or noticed its presence, a slimy vine choked her from behind. With waning strength, she tried to uncoil its grip, but to no avail. Tightening its stranglehold, the creature stepped to her side and eventually directly in front of its suffocating prey.

Just as she was losing the battle, William—whom she believed had fallen unconscious—reached for the whiskey bottle, soaked the beast's tendril, and booted it from the litter to its fiery grave. Regrettably, the kick triggered renewed pain in his injured leg.

"Thanks," said a short-winded Cindy. "What took you so long?" she teased, while massaging her neck.

William only grinned, after which the travelers gazed upward and saw Jimmy and Salvus perched on a limb, alongside Dan, spewing and then refilling their mouths. In all, William and Cindy counted six Maskocites tumble and suffer instant incineration upon contact with the ground.

While removing the tendrils from Dan, the liberators noticed the green worms flipping wildly upon his chest. With bottle in hand, the satyr poured a healthy amount of whiskey directly atop the tenacious invertebrates. Within seconds, one dislodged itself from Dan. The second worm, however, was ripped off his chest by Jimmy, who sustained an electric shock, causing him to lose his balance and nearly fall from the tree.

"What the heck was that?" he asked, after casting the worm below.

"I don't know," answered Salvus. "I've never seen anything like it."

The satyr kept a watchful eye among the branches, as Jimmy shook Dan to rouse him; Dan, like his brother, was slipping in and out of consciousness.

Seeing Sam two trees over, Salvus yelled, "We'll be there as fast as we can. It may take a few minutes."

On overhearing the satyr's comment—and on spotting foliage movement above Sam's head—Cindy took a mouthful of whiskey, placed the bottle in her pants pocket, and bolted off the litter to Sam's tree.

With the litter resting at an incline, William attempted to slide off. Unfortunately, his leg injury proved too painful for him to walk, not to mention climbing a tree.

Cindy scaled the tree with flawless agility. Once two feet below the branch that supported Sam, she targeted her mouthful of alcohol upward. After three refills and three more spurts, many of the vines—which had ensnared Sam—dehydrated. Two creatures released their grip and directed new shoots at a neighboring tree to escape with their lives. Within seconds of arriving safely on the branch, Cindy spotted one remaining creature, cleverly masked, that refused to surrender its latest prize. With a squirt and a kick, it also met a blazing end. Freed of the annoying vine creatures, Cindy raised Sam to a seated position on the limb. Fortunately, the Maskocites had not yet discharged the green worms upon his chest.

Two trees over, Jimmy was still shaking his friend. "Come on, Dan!" he yelled.

A thud was heard; an aggressive Maskocite had jumped from a limb above. Its abrupt appearance startled the men. The satyr countered by jerking his open water bottle at the intruder, drenching it with the Maskocite repellent. Like so many before, it fell to its death.

"How are we going to lower Dan?" asked Jimmy.

"I'm thinking," mumbled Salvus. "I guess we could—"

A prolonged moan was heard from Dan.

Shaking his shoulders, Jimmy ordered, "Come on, Dan, stay awake! We need to climb down."

As Jimmy attempted to raise his friend to an upright position, Dan groaned again. It was obvious he needed to rest.

Witnessing the ordeal from his lofty roost, Sam advised Cindy it was time to climb down.

"Are you sure you're up for it?" asked Cindy.

"No," he replied, "I'm not sure; but I'm sure Dan needs my help."

Cindy and Sam were grateful no Maskocites were encountered during their descent.

"Hopefully," remarked Sam, as he and Cindy touched ground, "the creatures have gone into hiding."

No sooner had he voiced his delight in the Maskocites' absence, when two beasts neared the litter. As the predators stepped upon the transport, William reached behind for anything to discourage their advance. Grasping something—though he wasn't sure what it was—he pulled his hand from behind and displayed Dan's flashlight. With no alarming reaction from the creatures, William was at their mercy. Taking a risk, he switched on the flashlight and aimed its beam into the green eyes of a Maskocite. Fearful of light, it jumped back two steps, tripped over the blanket, and tumbled to the ground. The intense flame forced the second creature to turn its head from the painful light to William. As he raised the beam again, the plant creature quickly covered its face with its six hands and dense foliage.

Seeing Sam and Cindy on the ground—and fearing the sole Maskocite before him might dart in their direction—William took advantage of the creature's protected face. He dropped the flashlight, lifted himself several inches off the litter, and slammed himself upon the roped branches. The unexpected and violent wobbling of the stretcher caught the creature off guard; it fell backwards to the forest floor. The warm glow was what William had hoped to see.

After accepting the whiskey bottle from Cindy, Sam resupplied his mouth, placed the bottle in his shirt pocket, and climbed Dan's tree.

Upon Sam's directive, Cindy headed back to the litter. With a mouthful of whiskey, she nearly gagged at the sight of two fading flames at the stretcher's base. Racing the remaining distance, she was calmed at seeing William resting on the litter and unharmed.

"What happened?" she demanded, before jumping upon the transport.

"A couple creatures paid me a visit," he said. Raising the flashlight, he continued, "Did you know they're afraid of light?"

Experiencing unwarranted guilt, Cindy confessed, "I'm sorry I left you and dashed to Sam's safety. I guess I wasn't thinking clearly."

"Don't be absurd," insisted William. "I was awake and not nearly in as much danger as Sam. You did the right thing."

Looking to the trees, the two witnessed Sam arrive safely alongside Salvus and Jimmy.

Dan was reasonably alert and speaking, but with great difficulty.

Knowing Dan needed to rest—but also aware it wasn't safe in the tree, not to mention William and Cindy alone below—Sam asked, "Dan, do you think you can climb down?"

"Yeah, I think so," he replied.

After removing his belt from his pants, Sam asked Jimmy to do likewise.

"What for?" he asked.

"We'll loop our belts around Dan's," explained Sam, "and then grip our belts, as we descend the tree. If he passes out or takes a misstep, we'll be there to support him." Resting his hand on Jimmy's shoulder, he stressed, "Can you handle this?"

Staring at the inflammation over Dan's heart, Jimmy declared, "Yeah; let's do it."

Since only a frayed rope encircled Salvus' waist, he volunteered to descend the tree first, with his whiskey close by.

In a matter of seconds, Sam gave the signal to proceed.

With added caution, the four descended the thirty feet. Although Dan remained conscious throughout the downward journey, he lost his footing on one occasion. Luckily, Sam and Jimmy anticipated the awkward step before it occurred and firmly clutched their supporting belts. As the teenager was suspended in midair from the stumble, Salvus reached up, grabbed Dan's legs, and secured them on another limb. After mustering their energies and rediscovering their courage, the vertical escape continued.

Watching their descent, William asked, "How's Dan?"

"I'm not sure," replied Cindy. "From what Sam and I could see from the other tree, it looked like Jimmy was trying to wake him."

William attempted to slide off the litter.

Cindy gripped his arm, foiling his escape, and warned, "William, you're in no condition to climb a tree. Salvus, Sam, and Jimmy are doing fine. There's nothing we can do."

William made another move to the edge of the stretcher, claiming, "There has to be something I can do."

"They'll be fine," promised Cindy, as she took a tighter grasp on his arm. After glancing to the tree, she continued, "Look, they're almost to the forest floor."

Upon touching soil, Jimmy snatched his neighbor's boot from the ground; Salvus and Sam supported Dan between their shoulders and raced to the litter.

Several feet from the stretcher, Jimmy recovered Dan's lance and backpack that had fallen to the ground during the initial attack.

After taking a few moments to gather the bag's scattered contents, Jimmy reached the litter in safety, but only after prodded by Sam yelling, "Come on, boy! We're not out of the woods yet!"

With Dan and William resting on the stretcher, under Cindy's watchful eye, Salvus and Sam grabbed the transport's handles and bolted up the rough terrain. Jimmy raced in front, bearing a lance in one hand and alcohol in the other.

Cindy opened the whiskey bottle and administered another treatment to William's leg. After learning of Dan's electrocution, she knew there was nothing she could do to ease his pain; time and sleep were the answers. As she cleansed William's gash, she realized the alcohol was nearly spent. *I hope no one sustains another major injury before we reach the oak,* she thought.

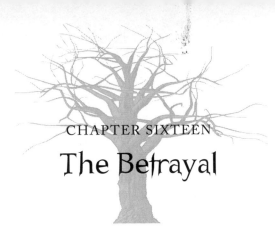

CHAPTER SIXTEEN

The Betrayal

THE RELATIVELY SHORT DISTANCE IN THE UNEXPLORED REGION of the forest that had previously taken Dan only twenty minutes to cross took the group nearly two hours, thanks to the loaded litter and the unexpected skirmish with the Maskocites. Eventually, the travelers stepped upon a new path.

"This is it," blurted Dan, who peered from the side of the stretcher.

Sam and Salvus lowered the transport to the ground.

Cindy jumped from the litter and stood alongside Sam.

After catching his breath, Sam directed the lantern's beam. Three of the original travelers, Sam, Cindy, and Jimmy, gazed about the partially lit footpath, hoping to spot an unusual object or an irregular-shaped boulder that they recalled seeing on their journey to the castle.

Dan slid from the stretcher.

"Get back on the litter," admonished Sam. "You shouldn't be putting unnecessary strain on your heart."

"Sam," replied Dan, "I'm just looking."

Knowing an extra set of eyes would be useful, Sam neared Dan, supported him around the waist, and helped him to the front of the stretcher.

Sam, Dan, Jimmy, and Cindy silently resumed their earthly and heavenward search.

Spotting nothing familiar, Sam confessed, "I don't know, Dan. This looks like any other path."

"It's that way," directed Dan, who pointed to the left. "I'm sure of it; come on. Let's walk a little ways; you'll see."

Restless to resume their trek, he freed himself from Sam's grip, stepped beyond Jimmy, and raced up the path.

Jimmy sprinted, until he was at his neighbor's side.

While keeping an eye on Dan and Jimmy dashing up the trail, Sam grabbed a handle of the litter before the satyr was ready; the stretcher tilted.

Salvus quickly reached for the opposite handle to prevent William from rolling off; Cindy jumped aboard.

The satyr, with a lance in hand, and Sam, bearing the lit lantern, raced up the path in pursuit of the young men, who were now so far ahead that complete darkness surrounded them. As Salvus and Sam increased their stride, the teenagers slowly came into the lantern's glow.

"Wait up, you two," yelled Sam.

Dan and Jimmy came to a halt, but only until the group was immediately behind them; the fast-paced hike resumed.

Amid the threatening sounds of the unknown creatures that lurked in the shadowy forest, the travelers scanned in all directions for anything familiar. No one mentioned what was weighing heavily on their minds: all sensed they were being watched. Salvus and Jimmy kept their lances ready for release.

After an hour's search, Sam dampened the spirits of his co-travelers by announcing, "I think we've traveled far enough. Let's head back to our original path."

Trusting in Dan's intuition and the invisible being, Cindy reminded, "Sam, we're really not losing any time, since both paths seem to run parallel to each other."

"You may be right," replied Sam, "but we don't know where this path will lead us."

"But," challenged Cindy, "we don't know where the other path would lead us either."

"To the tree, of course," snapped a weary Sam.

"But, Sam," she reminded, "we didn't see anything familiar along the other path either."

This was another argument Sam knew he'd lose. He unwillingly agreed to march farther up the unexplored path.

The group hiked another hour before Sam and Salvus set the litter to the ground. Looking at his wristwatch, Sam announced, "It's 5:00 in the morning, which means we've been off our original path for nearly four hours. I think we should cross through the forest and return to the other trail. We haven't recognized anything here."

Cindy and Jimmy found it difficult to admit that perhaps Sam was right; but not Dan. He knew they were heading in the right direction and that they were on the right path.

As Sam and Salvus were turning the stretcher to step into the woods to intersect their previous trail, Dan peered into the darkness and spotted the footpath converge with another trail to the left. "Look!" he yelled.

Sam and the satyr set the transport to the ground and stepped alongside Dan.

Pointing ahead, the teenager declared, "It's the two paths joining."

All remained skeptical, as they stared as far as the lantern's beam would permit.

"Don't you remember on our first day in the forest," recalled Dan, "we came across a path that split and we took the trail to the left? That's what we're on now. This is the path to the oak."

Stepping several feet in front of the group, Jimmy gazed ahead and vaguely noticed the convergence of the paths. "He may be right," he said.

"Well, come on," insisted Dan, as he rubbed his sore chest, "let's go."

Sam and Salvus turned the litter around again; the group advanced toward the merging paths.

Standing at the site, Sam glanced ahead and admitted, "Dan, I guess I owe you an apology."

"Why's that?" he asked, before following his companion's fixed look up the trail.

Sam pointed and exclaimed, "Look!"

The sycamore tree stood directly ahead.

With renewed vigor and excitement, the travelers lugged the litter and themselves up the path to the sycamore tree and beyond. Recalling they had another several hours of hiking before they reached the oak, a conversation developed concerning the paths.

"If the paths run parallel to each other, but ultimately converge," reasoned Sam, "then either way we would have ended up where we are."

There was no immediate response from his co-travelers.

After glancing back at his brother and Cindy, who remained resting on the litter, Dan eventually admitted, "I suppose, Sam, but then why did the being lead me to this path?"

"We'll probably never know," replied Sam, "but at least we know we're on the right path now."

The travelers jumped with the rustling of plants at the path's border.

Sam and Salvus dropped the litter; Jimmy and the satyr raised their lances.

Ceremonia darted from the darkness of the woods to the footpath in her full-size stature, alarming the group.

"Ceremonia!" yelled Cindy, who bolted off the stretcher and raced to the tree nymph.

"You nearly scared us half to death," said Sam.

"I know," teased the tree nymph, "I meant to." Looking at Cindy, she noted, "I see you've recovered from the Jezebels."

"Yeah," she replied, "thanks to you."

Throughout their bumpy journey on the newfound path, the throbbing pain in William's leg returned, causing him to slip out of consciousness, once again. For her part, Cindy administered a limited amount of the dwindling supply of whiskey at regular intervals.

Spotting William out cold on the stretcher, Ceremonia asked, "What happened to him?"

"He was attacked yesterday by a giant praying mantis," answered Cindy.

"He wasn't attacked," corrected Jimmy, "he was accidentally scraped by the mantis' thorny leg."

The mere touch of Ceremonia's hand upon the patient's forehead caused him to stir.

Dan leaped to the side of the litter and grasped his brother's arm. "William," he said, "can you hear me?"

The older brother slowly opened his eyes, but quickly closed them again.

"William," said Dan, squeezing his sibling's forearm even harder. "Come on, wake up."

After pushing his tongue through his closed lips to moisten them, William opened his eyes to the massive tree limbs suspended overhead.

"I understand you had quite an adventure yesterday," remarked Ceremonia.

"Yeah," he replied, with great effort, "though not as interesting as earlier this morning."

"What happened this morning?" asked the tree nymph.

"Disgusting plant people," explained Cindy, "that caught fire when their heads hit the ground."

"Oh," replied Ceremonia, "you met the Maskocites—or as we tree nymphs call them, the hotheaded species." With her eyes lowered, she shamefully admitted, "I'm sorry I forgot to warn you about them."

"That's alright," replied Jimmy. "In addition to their fiery inclinations, we also learned they abhor whiskey." Glancing at his neighbor, he disclosed, "And Dan got a few powerful shocks from some kind of bizarre worm."

Knowledgeable of the green worm's qualities, Ceremonia stepped alongside Dan and asked, "How are you feeling?"

"Not great," he admitted, "but not as bad as I was a couple hours ago."

"Nonetheless," advised Ceremonia, "you shouldn't exert yourself needlessly. It'll take a few days for you to recuperate."

"I told the boy to rest on the litter," informed Sam, "but I guess he's too excited about reaching the oak to heed my advice."

With his eyes completely open, William asked for water, to which Dan promptly supplied.

Once his thirst was quenched, Salvus and Sam grabbed the stretcher handles and marched up the path.

"I'm glad to see you've made it this far," praised the tree nymph.

"Yeah," replied Sam, "but around midnight, before we finished constructing the litter, Dan convinced us to switch paths to this one. I thought we were doing fine on the trail to the left of us, but I suppose either way we would have ended up here, since the paths seem to run parallel to each other and eventually meet."

"No, Sam, I'm afraid not," corrected Ceremonia.

Sam and Salvus stopped and lowered the litter.

"Why not?" asked Sam.

"How could I have been so neglectful," admitted Ceremonia.

"What do you mean?" continued Sam.

"When we crossed the woods to the right to escape Bacchus," explained Ceremonia, "I forgot to mention the path you landed on led directly into the Great Chasm."

"So," replied Cindy, "we'd just walk along the border of the chasm and continue our hike on the opposite side."

"I'm afraid it's not that simple," responded the tree nymph.

"What do you mean?" asked Cindy.

"Within the chasm," explained Ceremonia, "exists one of the few flesh-eating plants of this world. The voragonia vine grows on the inside walls of the chasm with feelers that extend from the deepest regions of the abyss to its surface and several hundred feet up the trail. The runners cleverly conceal themselves along the border of the forest—just on the edge of the footpath—waiting for prey. The feelers can sense the minute vibrations of a rodent crossing the path. When something's detected, the plant's runners quickly ensnare the victim from all sides, leaving an escape a virtual impossibility. Once grasped, the vines release a sticky substance which adheres the prey to the plant. Unable to free itself, the victim is pulled by the runners into the chasm, where it's devoured by the voragonia vine. And no creature is too large, since I've happily witnessed the plant capture and drag an adult centaur to the bottomless abyss. But since the plant's capture and discharge of the sticky substance takes place within seconds, I'm afraid that if you hadn't switched paths when you did, you'd be absorbed into the vine by now."

All eyes were fixated on Dan.

Nearing the young man, Ceremonia asked, "What prompted you to change paths when you did?"

"It wasn't me," he explained. "The invisible being led me to this path." As the tree nymph turned, he asked, "Who or what is this being?"

With her back facing him, she replied, "I can't say. Just know that someone wants to help you reach home."

"Then it's a person," concluded Dan.

Ceremonia refused to answer.

The awkward silence was broken by Sam suggesting, "Come on, several hours of hiking still await us."

The group advanced.

Throughout their march to the oak, William was fortunate to remain conscious more than unconscious, though it wasn't rare to see him unresponsive. He was slowly regaining his strength; but it would take a few more days before he could walk on his own...time the group lacked.

"Oh," blurted Ceremonia, "I almost forgot. Very early this morning, probably about the time you discovered this path, I saw the Bozemen emerge from the Great Chasm, which means it's highly unlikely the Reclaimers have concocted their potion. But even without the elixir, don't be surprised to see at least one of the Reclaimers at the tree's portal later tonight. After all, there will be a full moon and I'm sure they suspect you'll be nearby."

The travelers experienced mixed emotions. On the one hand, they breathed a sigh of relief, hopeful the portal had not been relocated. But on the other hand, they were fearful the Reclaimers were still trailing them.

Attempting to ease his co-travelers' worries, Sam changed the subject by asking, "Ceremonia, aren't the Bozemen in danger with the voragonia vine?"

The tree nymph grinned before replying, "No, not really. They're about the only species in this world the hostile vine won't entrap. Since the Bozemen live the vast majority of their lives in the chasm with the plant, they know its peculiarities. To protect their young, they exit the gorge on the sides that aren't cursed with the feelers. And if by chance a Bozeman encounters the feelers, its sharp quills prevent the vine from seizing it and releasing its gummy substance." Glancing up the path, she concluded, "The Bozemen will be fine."

After several more hours of toilsome hiking, the travelers let out a boisterous cheer when they beheld the majestic oak before them. The group dashed the remaining feet to the tree. It was 1:00 in the afternoon.

Embracing the solid tree, Cindy exclaimed, "We made it!"

"Yeah," seconded Sam, "but I'm afraid we still have a problem called Spiritus Malus."

The explorers knew their adventure wasn't over yet.

Staring into the distance, beyond the oak, Sam sadly noticed that darkness still shrouded the O'Brien's former residence and the outskirts of town.

Looking heavenward, the group glimpsed part of a blue sky, since the tree cover near the fringes of the woods was sparse. It was invigorating to see and feel a bit of sunshine peeking through the sporadic openings in the canopy.

Suspecting Spiritus Malus would make an appearance before nightfall, the travelers gathered near the base of the tree to review their survival strategies.

With William resting on the ground beneath the tree, the first thing the group decided was to put the unused litter to work for them. After digging a narrow trench several feet from the base of the oak—using their lances and hands—the travelers carried the transport to the furrow, wedged it in place, and covered its base with soil. In a matter of minutes, the litter was converted into a shield against the Reclaimers' bewitching eyes.

"Ceremonia," questioned Cindy, "are you sure you won't need the protection of the litter?"

"Quite sure," replied Ceremonia. "I'll patrol from the treetop."

Jimmy, who was testing the stability of the barrier, asked, "Ceremonia, other than their eyes, do the Reclaimers have any natural powers or is it just potions they use?"

"They do delve into potions," confirmed the tree nymph, "but don't be fooled for a second. Over the centuries, they've gained awesome powers, though their most invincible weapon is their ability to master another's willpower with their fixed gaze. To answer your question, Jimmy, they experiment with potions, but they also take full advantage of their enchanting strengths."

This is precisely what the group didn't want to hear, though it was the truth.

Detecting fear in the eyes around him, Sam urged everyone to join Jimmy on the ground. Behind the roped barricade, he instructed, "Now remember, keep your eyes closed at all times. But if for some reason you have to open them, make sure you glimpse only between the slats of the litter—and even then, look just at the foreground and not into Spiritus Malus' eyes."

On overhearing their strategy, the tree nymph debated whether or not to tell her friends the shield probably would be useless against the head Reclaimer's power. She ultimately decided that dashing their hopes would make them overly alarmed, thus making them more vulnerable. Patrolling from the treetop was the best assistance she could offer her friends.

The extended wait proved excruciating to the group. With hours until sunset, the travelers repacked their diminishing supplies and took turns napping, while at least three remained awake and vigilant—waiting for either the full moon to rise or Spiritus Malus to arrive.

As they waited, Ceremonia transformed to her small-size stature and perched herself on an oak limb with an unobstructed view.

Sam looked at his wristwatch nearly a hundred times before remarking, "Dan, it's 8:00; when do you think the portal will open?"

Crawling to the tree behind, Dan discovered it was still impenetrable. "I'm not sure," he replied, "but, hopefully, it will open before Spiritus Malus arrives."

Without warning, the group heard movement from behind the oak.

"Close your eyes," ordered Sam, "and keep them shut!"

The noise grew louder, until all sensed a being was standing behind them.

The primitive barrier was pushed over, producing a loud bang.

Sam was the first to defy his own order; he opened his eyes. Glancing up, his eyes met those of his evil twin in that world. Sam rose from his knees to confront his identical adversary; the other travelers jumped to their feet to resecure the barricade.

"Leave us alone," demanded Sam.

"Let me guess," replied the sinister look-alike, while watching the explorers raise the barrier, "you think this worthless piece of wood is going to protect you from Spiritus Malus?"

Knowing his friends overheard his comment, Sam replied in a confident and domineering tone, "Yes; it'll protect us for as long as we need."

Yanking Cindy's bag from her back, the evil twin asked, "What's this?"

With Cindy visibly shaken, Sam lunged at his opponent and knocked him to the ground. In the commotion, the leg of the malicious double struck the wooden barricade, sending it to the forest floor a second time.

William, even in his discomfort, struggled to his feet and helped his friends anchor the defense wall.

Glimpsing the brawl, the travelers witnessed the corrupt twin rise to his feet and deliver a blow to Sam's shoulder, dropping him to the ground and ushering in renewed pain to his previous injury that he sustained from the saber-toothed tiger thirty days ago.

Noticing his suffering, the look-alike jumped on him and pounded his shoulder.

Though in intense pain, Sam eventually threw off his opponent and held him in a neck lock, thanks to Cindy's scream moments earlier that caught the depraved double by surprise. Sam tightened his grip, until he felt a jab at his ribs; he loosened the stranglehold on his enemy.

The evil twin maneuvered atop Sam again. After delivering four additional punches to his shoulder, the look-alike reached to his belt and grabbed a dagger. After raising the blade into the air, but before sinking it into Sam's chest, the weapon was shot from his hand by an arrow. Looking several feet distant, the wicked twin saw he was now the target of three lances, a revolver, and a bow and arrow. The travelers had secured the barrier and were now securing their right to the tree.

Ceremonia began yelling moments earlier, but due to her small stature—not to mention the uproar on the ground—her warning went unheard.

The cruel Sam glanced to the sky behind the group and laughed.

High-pitched shrieks were heard; the Oswagis and Reclaimers had arrived.

Risking a quick glance during their dash to the safety of the recently-raised barricade, Dan estimated between thirty and forty birds and snake-men had descended.

Sam's double grabbed his knife from the forest floor and remained standing at attention. He was obviously untroubled with the aerial arrivals.

From behind the safety of the roped wall, Sam whispered, "Why didn't Ceremonia warn us?"

"I don't know," replied Cindy, in a low voice, "but I hope she's alright."

"Keep your eyes closed," Sam reminded his friends, one last time.

Resting on their knees behind the barrier—with their heads lowered to the ground—were Salvus, at one end, then Sam, Cindy, Jimmy, Dan, and finally William, at the opposite end. The sharp pain in his leg forced William to lie on his stomach with his head pressed firmly against the forest floor. Knowing the severity of his crime in aiding the escape of a guest, Salvus kept his eyes shut, for fear of retaliation.

Spiritus Malus dismounted his Oswagi that had landed a short distance from the oak and raised himself upon his powerful posterior muscles. Slithering nearer the enchanted tree, he caught sight of the barrier and mumbled, "What a feeble attempt." With nothing more than a flick of his finger, the wooden barricade was uprooted and hurled against a neighboring tree.

Cindy screamed, but amazingly, the group kept their eyes closed and their heads lowered throughout the commotion.

"Oh, who have we here?" asked Spiritus Malus, in a cynical tone, as he advanced closer to the group. "Could it be our former guest, William?"

Dan rested his hand on his brother's back, ordering, "Keep your eyes closed."

Noticing a pair of hoofs, Spiritus Malus folded his human arms across his chest and added, "And my dear friend, Salvus. We need you back at the castle. Our guests are not sleeping well without your music."

From the throng of Reclaimers, Talus yelled, "You traitor, Salvus. Wait until I get you back in the dungeon!"

Without lifting his head from the ground—and with his eyes tightly sealed—Sam yelled, "Salvus, keep your eyes closed!"

As Sam was warning the satyr, a voice was heard from beside the oak. "My lord," said Sam's evil twin, "have I pleased you this month?"

After raising and then slamming his tail upon the forest floor, Spiritus Malus threatened, "I told you I wanted the rest of this pathetic town in my possession by tonight's full moon. You have failed me for the last time."

The cunning twin advanced on his knees a few feet closer to Spiritus Malus begging for another month. "Then," he promised, "you'll have many guests at your disposal, once the entire town is blanketed in darkness."

Spiritus Malus looked beyond Sam's look-alike to the town and replied, "I will let you know my decision."

"Pardon me, my lord," implored the sinister Sam, now with fear in his voice, "but how will I know your decision?"

"Quite easily," he replied. "If you're dead, my answer was no; if you live, my answer was yes."

"I see, my lord," said the scheming twin, "thank you." He retreated a few paces on his knees, before rising to his feet.

With the travelers' eyes still closed, but now flat on their stomachs with their heads pressed to the ground and their hands covering the sides of their faces for added defense, no one, not even Dan, noticed William had opened his eyes.

The eyes of Spiritus Malus met William's; no words were spoken, so as not to alert the travelers to William's deplorable act. In complete silence, he covertly advanced on his elbows.

Ceremonia plunged from an oak limb to halt his approach to the sovereign snake-man; she hovered in front of William, attempting to block his forward stare. But her efforts proved ineffective. She soared to a limb, hoping another opportunity would present itself.

Spiritus Malus ended the prolonged silence by commanding, "Come, William."

From his prone position, Dan ordered William to keep his eyes closed, before removing a hand from the side of his face to rest upon his brother's shoulder. Feeling only soil, he screamed, "No!" Opening his eyes—but fixing his gaze solely on the ground ahead—he watched his brother inch his way to Spiritus Malus. With his vision still lowered, he crawled at a remarkable speed to his sibling. As he neared William's feet, he grabbed an ankle and attempted to pull him back to the tree.

In a trancelike state—and unaware of his actions—William yanked his leg from Dan's grip and kicked him in the face, knocking his glasses to the ground.

Dan mustered his strength and secured both William's legs.

The spellbound sibling, however, was determined to reach Spiritus Malus.

"No!" yelled Dan, as his brother crept farther ahead, dragging him along.

Unknowingly, William was betraying his brother to the powers of hell.

With one last attempt, Dan sprang on his brother to thwart his eventual imprisonment in the demonic castle.

William tossed his brother off, landing him on his back.

Dan's eyes met the deadly stare of Spiritus Malus, who was standing over the men. He screamed, seconds before entering a dazed state.

CHAPTER SEVENTEEN
The Leap

NEAR THE BASE OF THE TREE, CINDY ALSO SCREAMED AT WHAT she witnessed. Though she never lifted her sights above the brothers, who were incapacitated before her, she immediately shut her eyes.

Sam, with his gaze focused solely on the foreground, crawled to the siblings. But his rescue attempt was futile. Spiritus Malus had already lifted William from the forest floor and secured him atop his awaiting Oswagi. Sam was too far away and too late to save his friends.

Spiritus Malus approached Dan. As he was lowering himself to raise his second prisoner from the ground, he was slammed against a tree, as a mighty earthquake—like no one had ever lived to tell about—shook the forest to its foundation, toppling countless trees around the majestic oak and causing a mass exodus of birds to the safety of the air. Even the Oswagi Birds shrieked and stomped their feet in response to their unknown terror and confusion. In his fear of the earth's trembling—and upon hearing the uproar of the Oswagis—Sam jumped to his feet, placed his back to the Reclaimers, and darted to the oak.

An intense Light materialized between the Reclaimers and the travelers; it hovered two feet above the forest floor. From the Light was heard, "Touch the boy, you shall not!"

Since the Reclaimers were already dead and there was no slaying them, Spiritus Malus, unharmed, rose from the ground beneath the tree he collided with and slithered nearer the oval-shaped radiance. Still twenty feet from the Light, he sarcastically greeted, "Michael, how good to see you. Have you come to banish us again?"

No response came forth from the Light.

Spiritus Malus placed his human hand behind his back and motioned his subordinates to abduct the remaining travelers at the tree. With justifiable fear of the Light, five Reclaimers reluctantly obeyed their superior. They had advanced only a few feet, when they were cast into the air; jagged boulders broke their free fall.

"Approach the travelers, you shall not!" came from the Light.

Removing his stare from the intense glow, Sam focused on William, who remained sitting atop an Oswagi. Taking advantage of the distraction between the Light and Spiritus Malus, he made a wide circle around the clashing parties and was nearing William, when two mounted Reclaimers attempted to hinder his rescue mission with their overpowering mental faculties.

Without warning, two beams of light burst from the oval being and impaled the two Reclaimers and their Oswagis. The snake-men were thrown from their flying beasts; the birds of prey were temporarily immobilized.

With no further opposition, Sam helped his companion to the ground and to the safety of the tree. William had escaped his trance-like state.

Beneath the oak, the travelers stared at Dan, who remained motionless on the forest floor between Spiritus Malus and the Light. Sam and his friends somehow knew he was safe.

Scanning the area, Sam observed that the tremors had ceased and—since a great number of trees had fallen—considerable sunlight filtered through the forest canopy, though not completely. Turning and looking behind the oak, he noticed, however, that the shadow of death still clung to the town. In his visual inspection, he also spotted his evil twin standing behind the oak, but now exhibiting signs of fear.

Gazing upon the peaceful Light, Cindy grabbed Sam's forearm and whispered, "What is it?"

"I thought Spiritus Malus called him Michael, before mentioning another banishment," replied Sam.

"Could it be…you know," asked Cindy, "the heavenly spirit…the one Dan keeps praying to…Saint Michael the Archangel? I've heard about angelic beings, but I never really believed in them."

"I don't know who or what it is," answered Sam, who remained captivated with the Light.

Dan—who also had escaped his hypnotic state when the earth's tremors silenced minutes earlier—reached for his glasses and looked intently upon the outer limits of the Light, but not directly at its brilliance.

"Boy, rise!" ordered the Light.

Dan rose to his feet at the Light's command. Standing between the power of evil and the power of good, he felt protected.

"Spiritus Malus," heralded the Light, "because of your wickedness inflicted upon countless people over the centuries and since you have defiled the castle of your confinement into a fortress of perdition to passersby, it has been ordained by the Almighty that you and your fellow Reclaimers—together with the flesh-eating beasts and predatory plant life of the woods—will, from this day forward, be exiled to the lowest realms of the forest, powerless to corrupt souls."

As Spiritus Malus slithered closer to Dan, the Light ordered, "Halt!"

For a change, against his own willpower, Spiritus Malus froze in his tracks and was paralyzed from the neck down.

The bright Light lowered itself to the ground and slowly faded, revealing a six-and-a-half foot man of matchless strength, adorned with a pair of eight-foot, semitransparent wings. The warrior was clothed in a leather tunic, with mid-calf length sandals, and brandished a golden shield and sword.

At the imposing sight, the herd of Oswagis—with their Reclaimers aboard—staggered several steps back.

To Dan, the Man of Light appeared no more than thirty years of age, though he suspected he was much older.

Still unable to move, but able to speak, Spiritus Malus foretold, "Try as you will, Michael, you and your fellow archangels' attempt to banish us again will fail."

Standing beside the Man of Light, Dan fearlessly predicted, "He won't fail."

"Yes, he will," declared Spiritus Malus, "and for your allegiance to him, your soul will be mine for all eternity."

Dan shuddered.

The Man of Light rested his hand on the young man's shoulder.

Can it be? thought Dan, as he felt the familiar warm touch upon him.

Glancing down at the teenager, Saint Michael directed, "It's time for you, your brother, and your friends to return to your world."

Dan trembled at the thought of leaving the security of the archangel.

"Go now," urged Saint Michael, "your parents are waiting."

Before leaving the heavenly being's side, Dan acknowledged, "Thank you for your help on the journey."

The archangel simply nodded and then ordered, "Now go. No living mortal can witness what has been decreed or they will surely die of fright. Even now, the clouds of judgment gather."

Looking heavenward, Dan and Spiritus Malus witnessed dark clouds converging from the four corners of the sky, which only moments earlier had been cloudless.

Redirecting his sights to Saint Michael, Dan remarked, "But I don't understand. During parts of our journey you helped me and at other times your healing presence was far from me. And my friends never experienced your touch."

The angelic being lowered his head to the young man and explained, "When the tail of the saber-toothed tiger ripped a chunk of flesh from your ankle, I healed you, so that you and your companions could resume your hike to the castle. Likewise, when you were dangling above the Great Chasm and stumbling on the rock face below the Oswagi's nest, I was there to support you. Even the day you sprained your ankle, while heroically diverting the snake at the lakeshore from your friends, as well as the day when you and Sam were attacked by the octopus at the lake, I was at your side. But I purposely didn't heal you or Sam because several miles up the path, a pride of saber-toothed tigers was stalking prey. Had I restored you to health, you and your friends would have ventured up the trail and inevitably encountered the beasts…none of you would have survived." The archangel directed his sights to Spiritus Malus and warned, "One must never question the timing or the purpose of the Almighty. He—and He alone—knows what is best for you. As for why I never visited your friends, they require a deeper faith and an active prayer life."

Dan stared at the ground, shameful of his doubts.

Saint Michael removed his hand from Dan's shoulder and placed it under the traveler's chin. Raising his head so their eyes met, he stressed, "Now go, calamity is to visit the forest."

Dan stepped away, but immediately turned and asked, "What will happen to the castle guests, the Pedwhips, Ceremonia, and—" He looked back at the oak and asked, "And Salvus?"

"The castle guests," answered Saint Michael, "are all residents of this world; they will be led to safety. The Pedwhips and the tree nymphs will also be spared the wrath of God. Salvus will be free to roam the woods, after all predators have been annihilated from the forest's surface, below its surface, in the air, and in the waters. Tragedy will befall only the savage beasts of the woods."

After glancing at Spiritus Malus, who remained motionless several feet distant, the heavenly being warned Dan of his and his friends' misfortune, should they fail to complete their journey by explaining, "After the barbaric creatures of the forest receive retribution for their actions, the darkness of the forest will lift and the shade of the town will recede. You must make it through the tree's portal before the town's shadow passes beyond the majestic oak. The moment the oak is bathed in sunlight, the portal will be no more; you and your friends will be stranded in this world. Do you understand?"

"Yes."

"Now go," ordered the archangel, "before it's too late. And remember, you must not look back!"

As Dan turned again to approach the tree, Saint Michael watched him near his friends. The travelers bowed their heads slightly to the angelic being, who issued one final command, "Salvus, soon this forest will be liberated from death's grip. The Almighty has charged you to steward the forest."

The satyr graciously lowered his head a second time as a sign of acceptance and respect.

"But first," continued the archangel, "you must flee this area and run deep into the forest. For you, too, are not permitted to witness the Almighty's judgment on the Reclaimers and the savage beasts of the land, once they are gathered before me."

Salvus bid a quick farewell to his friends and dashed to the darker regions of the forest.

The travelers watched him, until he was out of view.

Since the Light's arrival, the travelers had gradually advanced from the oak in an attempt to identify the being. As a result, the tree stood a considerable distance behind them.

Before turning to face the oak, Sam bowed his head and asked, "What about Doctor O'Brien and his wife?"

"They will be enlightened of your safe return, presuming such is so," announced the archangel. Raising his eyes, he summoned, "Ceremonia."

In a flash, the tree nymph was floating above the archangel's shoulder.

"You and your species must also flee this area," he instructed, "until after the wrath of God has transpired."

After lowering her head, Ceremonia bid good-bye to her departing friends and soared to the canopy.

Taking one last look at the group, the archangel directed, "Face the tree. And remember, regardless of what you hear from behind, keep your gaze fixed on your destination."

Dan and Sam lifted William between themselves and rested his arms across their shoulders; the travelers made their final homeward approach.

Within seconds, excessive gales—accompanied with horizontal rain pellets—barraged the forest and the travelers. The ground resumed its relentless quaking beneath their feet. Deafening shrieks from thousands of creatures forced the explorers to cover their ears, for fear of losing their hearing. Dan and Sam inadvertently dropped William to the ground, as they protected their ears; William did likewise.

As the screeches subsided to a tolerable level, the men raised William to their shoulders and resumed their trek to the tree.

Cindy and Jimmy, who were ahead of the men—though still several feet from the oak—attempted to move forward, but the buffeting winds and rain slowed their approach until, ultimately, they were crawling on their hands and knees.

Sam, Dan, and William eyed the evil twin braving the gales and drawing near from the side; he stood between them and their companions ahead.

Reaching into his pocket, Sam's double tossed a handful of seeds to the wet soil. Even though the sinister twin was facing the direction of the Almighty's justice upon the Reclaimers, he was safe, as long as the men blocked his view.

Dan and Sam looked at one another; each knew what the other was thinking.

"One, two, three," yelled Sam, to prevail over the roaring winds.

The men dropped to their knees, lowering William with them, and exposed Sam's look-alike to the afflictions of the creatures that now stood in clear view.

The evil twin screamed in pure horror. Countless boils erupted on his face and ultimately over his entire body. The swellings on his face grew larger, until his facial characteristics were erased. His body, inflating beyond recognition, soon exploded, sending minuscule remnants of his corpse into the air, which were quickly dispersed amid the driving wind and rain.

With the evil twin obliterated and no longer obstructing his view, Dan looked ahead and saw Cindy and Jimmy making little progress against the headwinds; he also noticed the town's shadow was rapidly withdrawing in his direction.

To everyone's surprise, another series of shrill screams came from behind.

William attempted to turn his head to the shrieks, but Dan butted his head against his brother's, preventing him from glimpsing what no one was permitted to witness.

"We've come too far," yelled Dan into his brother's ear, "to lose you now!"

Over the wind, a scream was heard nearer the tree.

From the seeds that the evil twin sowed before his untimely explosion, prickly vines sprouted. Although not predatory, they delayed the group's advance to the oak. One of the runners wrapped around Cindy's leg. In Jimmy's efforts to free her, he let his guard down and was ensnared by another encroaching shoot.

Supporting his brother amid the thrashing wind and rain—while trying to maintain his own balance upon the quaking earth—Dan trembled at the sight of the rapidly retreating town's shadow. He racked his brain for a way to eradicate the gripping vines from his friends. Without delay, he screamed, "Mi—!"

Before the last syllable left his mouth, a golden sword materialized in his hand.

Now armed, the three men stepped to the hindering vines.

Dan wielded the blade and severed many of the plants' offshoots. Standing over Cindy and Jimmy, he yelled, "Lean back!" before raising the sword and driving it to the ground, slashing the vines that had claimed possession of his friends.

Just two feet from the oak, Cindy touched it. Learning it was soft, she jumped to her feet and entered the tree.

Glancing to the side of the oak, Dan noticed the O'Brien's former residence was now engulfed in sunlight. Switching his attention to Jimmy, who was demanding William go next, he yelled, "Go—now!"

Within seconds, Jimmy was through the oak.

Since the tree was not wide enough to accommodate the three men at one time, Dan motioned Sam to leap.

The shadow, which had previously swallowed up Main Street, was now positioned only feet behind the oak.

Dan waved the sword in front of Sam, ordering, "Go!"

Sam rested William against Dan's side and jumped into the tree.

Dan was surprised that even now, the storm, the quaking, and the screams of torment had not diminished. With great care, he stepped in front of William, rested the sword against his thigh, pulled his brother's arms over his shoulders, and drew them to his chest. With his brother's wrists gripped in one hand, he reached for the sword. No more than three feet from the oak, he glanced to its side and noticed the town's shadow was now touching the tree's bark. "God, please," he implored.

The shadow rocked between touching the oak and bouncing off its surface.

With his brother pressed firmly against his back and his wrists locked in his hand, Dan turned his head slightly and yelled, "Let's go home!" Then, leading with his right foot, Dan and William made their leap into the enchanted oak.

CHAPTER EIGHTEEN

The Great Chastisement

THE ARRIVAL HOME WAS SIMILAR TO THEIR PASSAGE INTO THE parallel world thirty days earlier. The travelers, failing to move from their point of entry, landed on top of one another. Slowly, and with shortness of breath, they crawled off each other and claimed their own plot of ground.

After a few minutes remaining flat on his back, but still gasping for air, Sam labored to ask if everyone was okay.

"Yeah," responded each one in turn, except William. Sam struggled to sit up and looked for his companion in the dim woods.

On seeing Sam staring at his brother resting beside him, Dan replied, "He's fine; just short-winded."

Sam reclined again on the forest floor.

As the travelers recuperated on the ground, various thoughts of resolution filled their minds.

Cindy was overjoyed to be home and swore to herself she'd try to be more engaging with her former female classmates.

Jimmy was also glad to be back in Lawton and promised himself he'd be more respectful of his parents and more helpful around the house.

After two trips to the perilous world, Sam vowed he'd never return; he also pledged to practice the faith and resume his teaching career.

There were no words to describe how William felt, resting on the ground in his world of birth after a thirteen-year absence. Nonetheless, he made an oath he'd spend the rest of his life helping Dan and the other members of the team in any way he could for redeeming his life.

Staring at the overhead limbs that were gently swaying in the late June breeze, Dan knew he had shed his youth in the parallel world and was now an adult. Unknown to him, his co-travelers also realized he had outgrown his adolescence the day he assumed charge evacuating the castle guests. In addition to telling the truth from that day forward, he also promised himself he'd be the best man he could be, knowing full well that even adults make mistakes. But he'd learn from them.

After resting for nearly ten minutes, Sam staggered to his feet, urging, "Come on, guys, you need to get home."

As the four travelers raised themselves to a seated position, the stately oak shook violently. They jumped to their feet—William stumbled to his—and withdrew several paces, watching the oak transform into a dogwood tree.

Once the vibrations ceased, Dan stepped forward and cautiously touched it. To his amazement, the tree was solid…even under the glow of the full moon. "Well we made it," he said, after turning from the tree and facing his companions. His difficult breathing from the crossover forced him to pause. Several moments later, he continued, "I know all of you freely joined me, and I also remember how demanding I was that you return the first night. But deep down, I guess I wanted you to stay. It's just that I knew your lives would be in danger; that's why I insisted you leave. And I'm sorry for the injuries my quest caused you. I suppose it goes without saying there's no way I could have made it back without your help." With his sights directed at his brother, he concluded, "Thanks to you, William and I are home. I know my gratitude isn't enough, but it's all William and I have to offer."

Sensing Dan was uneasy with his confession, Cindy stepped forward and—after giving him a hug—acknowledged, "Thanks for saving my life on more than one occasion. And by the way, even though I was scared to death most of the time, deep down, I wouldn't trade the journey for anything…not anything." She approached William, embraced him, and remarked, "It's good to have you home."

Sam also stepped forward, held Dan close, and recognized,

"Thanks to you, I'm blessed to have true friends; something I haven't enjoyed in decades."

Finally, Jimmy approached the Clay brothers and gave each a firm handshake. Taking two steps back, he declared, "Don't apologize, Dan, I wanted to take the trip...that is, until the Oswagi nest. But I'm glad I went and...well...thanks for saving my life a few times, too."

"Alright," remarked Sam, "enough with the sentimentalities. You all need to get home; your families are waiting."

"Actually," interjected Dan, "you all go home; there's something I have to do first."

"What's that?" asked Cindy, after lifting her backpack from the ground.

Stooping to grab the golden sword, he answered, "I need to visit the church."

The pain in William's leg forced him to recline on the forest floor moments after Jimmy's handshake.

As Dan secured his free arm around his brother's waist, Sam dropped to his knees and helped him raise William to his feet.

Realizing it would be difficult, at best, supporting William by himself to the church, Dan asked, "Sam, would you mind coming along?"

"Not at all," he replied. "I should have made a visit years ago."

As the five exited the forest and stepped upon Main Street, exhilaration consumed them all; they were finally home.

Dan never thought he'd admit it, even to himself, but he was thrilled to be back in Lawton.

Sam, William, and Dan hobbled up the sidewalk to the left, as Cindy and Jimmy took the pavement to the right, but not before agreeing to meet the next day.

Four blocks beyond the diner, the three men turned the corner and before them towered the massive structure, Saint Augustine of Canterbury Catholic Church. As the travelers headed up the sidewalk, movement was heard from behind. Although not expecting an unearthly creature, they, nevertheless, turned quickly.

Cindy and Jimmy had changed their minds and decided to join them.

Growing weary supporting William, not to mention their lingering shortness of breath, Dan and Sam stepped off the sidewalk and crossed the church's manicured lawn, saving a few steps. Noticing their boots were coated with mud from the torrential rains during their departure from the parallel world—and not wanting to track the filth inside—the men lowered William to the ground.

Dan cleaned the muck from his boots with his bare hands. Ripping a twig that was enmeshed in the mud, he sustained a cut. He dropped the shoot to the church grounds and never gave it a second thought. Unfortunately, his scratch was deep enough to draw several drops of blood that fell to the soil, atop the discarded stem.

After their boots were reasonably clean, the travelers ascended the steps to the main doors.

Dan hoped the church was unlocked, despite the fact it was nearly 10:30 in the evening. To his surprise, not only was the church open, but no worshipers were inside. Though mildly disappointed no one took advantage of the open church, at the same time, he was pleased, since he and his friends would have it to themselves.

The travelers genuflected and neared the marble statue of Saint Michael the Archangel. All eyes were drawn to the sculpture's right hand that was triumphantly raised, but missing its sword.

Lifting the blade he carried from the parallel world, Dan looked at his co-travelers and whispered, "I had a hunch."

Since William's leg injury prevented him from kneeling below the marble statue, he sat upon its kneeler and gazed upward; Cindy and Jimmy knelt in prayer.

Sam rested on his heels and instructed Dan to climb on his shoulders, since the artwork rose several feet from the floor. He lifted Dan to the statue's arm.

Given Sam's weakened condition from the crossover, he tottered momentarily; Dan gripped the statue's forearm for stability. He immediately felt a sensation of warmth and not a cold marble touch, as he had expected.

After Sam regained his footing and was standing upright, Dan was at the height of the statue's face. He leaned forward and inserted the golden sword into the open grasp of the sculpture's hand. Upon the sword's contact with the hand, a beam of light appeared at the tip of the blade and gradually descended its length, altering the gold to white marble. The travelers watched the transformation in absolute awe, including Sam, who nearly lost his balance at the sight.

Even Father James, who had recently entered the worship area to offer his Evening Prayer, watched in reverence from a distance, but without the travelers' knowledge of his presence.

As the light met the palm of the statue, the hand slowly clenched the sword's handle. The hand's movement was so imperceptible, only Dan witnessed the unexplainable event.

"Are you ready to come down?" asked a tired Sam, once the sword was marbleized.

Yeah," replied Dan.

As Sam lowered himself, Dan yelled, "Wait!"

Sam raised his friend to his former position.

Within one of the statue's eyes, a flicker of light emerged and grew in size and intensity, until the entire socket was aglow. Dan stared in wonder, as he watched Saint Michael step to the Reclaimers and Oswagis.

The young man was permitted to view—indirectly—what he and his co-travelers were not allowed to glimpse—directly—in the parallel world.

Since the remaining travelers and Father James couldn't see the re-enactment of the Almighty's chastisement in the statue's eye, they presumed Dan was offering additional prayers of thanksgiving, near the image of his favorite heavenly spirit.

Gazing into the statue's eye, Dan noticed Spiritus Malus had been released from his paralysis and mounted his bird of prey. As the teenager viewed the sky in the artwork's eye, he observed the clouds of judgment converge from the four corners of the heavens and nose-dive at an unimaginable speed atop the Reclaimers and Oswagis, encapsulating the beasts. Without delay, countless offshoots of the cloud burst from the core judgment cloud and dispersed in all directions, until the entire forest was blanketed in a dark, deadly haze. Throughout the expanse of the forest, the branches of the cloud tracked blood-thirsty creatures and plant life of all shapes, sizes, and appetites. Upon detection, the cloud's arms seized its victims—snatching them from the forest floor, the trees, the air, the water, and from beneath the soil—and pulled them through its extensive network of branches and into the core judgment cloud that Saint Michael guarded.

Throughout the ordeal, Dan saw the earth shake with such force that another abyss was formed…twice the size of the Great Chasm. From the new gorge, lava gushed forth. Massive and many trees, which withstood the previous quakes, failed to endure the latest pressures from below the forest's surface. They swayed and buckled, crashing to the ground and creating a dust storm, which added to the murkiness of the forest.

The core of the cloud, which imprisoned the Reclaimers and the Oswagi Birds, grew in size, as the savage beasts and flesh-eating plants were hurled inside.

Peering into the judgment cloud, Dan trembled; the creatures were being pitched in all directions, smashing against each other.

Once the horrific harvesting of predatory beasts and plant life was complete, the offshoots of the cloud receded into its core.

Saint Michael raised his sword and directed it to the sun. In a flash, seven beams of dazzling light and fire descended from the sky, met his sword, and ricocheted into the cloud.

Anxiously looking into the depths of the judgment cloud, Dan couldn't perceive anything, until untold numbers of lightning bolts flashed within. With each blaze of illumination, he witnessed various creatures being tossed about with gaping jaws, obviously screaming in torment.

The beasts and plant life were being cremated with each bolt of fire, until all that remained were ashes and flickers of light being hurled within the dark cloud.

As he watched their obliteration, Dan was enlightened to understand the flickering lights were the souls of the undying Reclaimers and their guests, whom they had incorporated into their beings over the centuries.

With greater and greater intervals between the lightning strikes, the judgment cloud condensed, arched through the sky, and plunged into the depths of the newly-formed abyss.

Dan was awestruck, as Saint Michael inhaled sharply and then released a mighty gust to the forest floor. The topsoil in the foreground rose into the air and traveled in the direction of the newborn chasm. The archangel's intense gale forced the nearby soil, which was loosened during the recent quakes, to take flight toward the abyss. With each subsequent chain reaction, the velocity of the wind increased. Within minutes, vast amounts of topsoil were streaming in the direction of the chasm until the gorge was not only leveled, but transformed into a mound.

When all was still and the dust clouds had scattered, Dan glimpsed ovals of light leading the guests from the castle; the Pedwhips raced to the safety and reclaimed beauty of the forest. He peered closer. In the distance, within a forest clearing, he eyed Salvus trotting through the grassland and Ceremonia soaring above. Both friends were noticeably untroubled and unafraid.

The light within the marble statue's eye slowly faded, until it bore its previous state. What Dan had witnessed took just a few minutes, but he'd remember it for a lifetime.

Growing weaker, Sam asked, "Dan, are you ready to come down?"

"Yeah."

"What were you doing up there?" asked Jimmy, as his friend stepped from Sam's shoulders.

Suspecting Saint Michael intended that only he be allowed to view the great chastisement—or the archangel would have presented the opportunity to his co-travelers—Dan replied, "I was thinking about the forest creatures and the friends we left behind."

Dan was thinking about them, so he was true to his word; he hadn't lied.

As Jimmy and Dan reached to lift William to his feet, Cindy remarked, "I wonder how Salvus and Ceremonia are doing."

"I'm sure they're fine," declared Dan. "After all, they're now free to roam the entire forest unthreatened."

Turning from the statue, the travelers saw Father James, who remained standing ten feet behind the group. He was still captivated with the miracle of the sword.

After resting William in a pew, Dan neared the priest and greeted, "Good evening, Father."

Staring at the marble sword, Father James admitted, "I can't believe what I just witnessed." Escaping his upward gaze, he admitted, "You know, even priests need to be reminded of the power of prayer and the occurrence of miracles." With a genuine look of gratitude, he continued, "Thank you for sharing this with me. It's a gift I'll always treasure."

Since Father James was somewhat new to the parish, he had never met William. Stepping beside the pew, where the young man was seated, he introduced, "I'm Father James Roberts—and you are?"

Before he could respond, Dan interrupted, "Father, this is my brother, William."

The priest, in partial disbelief, exclaimed, "What?" Knowing he couldn't divulge any knowledge of the trip, since it was revealed to him by Dan in the confessional, he simply stated, "I don't understand."

"Father, I'm Cindy Somer."

"Nice to meet you, Cindy," replied the priest, as he extended his hand.

After greeting him, she explained, "The three of us took a journey with Dan to a parallel world to rescue William, who had been missing for thirteen years."

Father James was shocked and didn't know what to say, other than, "Well, welcome home, William."

"Thank you, Father," he replied.

"Actually, Father," informed Dan, "it's partly thanks to you we're standing here right now."

"I don't understand," replied the priest.

"Without going into a lot of detail," said Dan, "it was the votive candle that you blessed for me in this very church, before the trip, that defeated the sinister forces."

"Yeah," replied Jimmy.

Again, not knowing how to respond, the priest humbly offered, "I'm glad I could help." Diverting his glance to Sam, he admitted, "Yours is also a face I don't recognize."

Extending his hand to the priest, he replied, "I'm Sam White." Determined to keep his personal resolution, he admitted, "Um...look, Father, I haven't practiced the faith for a number of years and...well...I was wondering if you'd receive me back."

"Absolutely, Mr. White," voiced a delighted priest.

"Just Sam is fine," he corrected.

"Very well, Sam," he replied. "We'll start tomorrow, before the weekday Mass, by hearing your confession." Glancing at the three young men, whom he knew were Catholic, he urged, "And I'll hear your confessions, too."

"Yes, Father," replied Jimmy, William, and Dan in unenthusiastic tones.

"I'll meet you thirty minutes before the noon Mass in the confessional," he advised, "since you'll probably want to sleep beyond the early Mass." Looking at Cindy, he shared, "I was pleased to see your mother—" He eyed the other three young travelers, before adding, "Actually, all of your parents met below this statue every morning to offer prayers for your safe return."

"What?" exclaimed Cindy. "My mother was here every morning praying?"

"Oh, yes," confirmed the priest. "And you would do well to follow her example."

Glimpsing the sculpture overhead, Cindy halfheartedly consented, "Alright; I'll be here tomorrow for Mass."

"Good," said Father James, "and bring your mother."

After thanking the priest for his ongoing prayers, Dan and Jimmy raised William from the pew.

Observing a look of pain on William's face, Father James insisted, "Let me grab my car keys and I'll drive you home."

Offering an over-the-shoulder glance, while maintaining a firm grip around his brother, Dan graciously declined, explaining, "Thank you, Father; but I started my journey on foot and that's how I'll end it." Looking to his friends, he proposed, "But the others may take you up on the offer."

Before the priest could voice his charitable deed, Jimmy spoke for the group, "No thanks, Father. We'll also end our journey on foot."

After the priest made another attempt with his offer, the travelers declined, turned from the clergyman, and began the final leg of their journey home.

As Father James watched the worn-out group near the back doors, he suspected they'd been through hell and back. *After all,* he thought, *Saint Michael obviously felt their situation was dire enough to justify lending them his sword.*

Sadly, nothing could have prepared the priest for the unearthly adventures that would be secretly divulged in the confessional the next morning. He remained deep in thought, curious what evils the group battled, when he heard the church doors slam.

CHAPTER NINETEEN

Shattered Glass

Considering their extended hikes over the past thirty days, the walk from the church to Beacon Lane was a short distance. However, since William needed to ease the pain in his leg—and because Jimmy lived next door—the group headed to the Clay's house first. In no hurry to revisit the homeless shelter, Sam accompanied his friends.

Since 11:30 p.m. the night before, Nancy Clay maintained a vigil on her front porch, uncertain when, or if, her son would return.

As promised, Sara Somer arrived early the following morning and kept watch with Nancy throughout the day. Jeff remained close at hand to offer his wife and Sara moral support. The women passed the time with conversations and puzzles, while constantly peering up and down the street. At noon and again at 5:00, Jeff delivered meals to the ladies, since they refused to leave the porch for any reason, except to use the bathroom.

Later in the evening, after the sun had set and the full moon was brilliantly aglow, Sara glanced at her watch, announcing, "In three hours it'll be midnight."

Sensing her anxiety, Nancy rested her hand upon Sara's and urged, "We must remain hopeful. I'm sure Cindy will return soon."

The conversation ceased when the women heard the Parker's front door slam. Marie and Tom, who were restless to learn if Jimmy was with Dan, crossed the Clay's lawn and neared the porch steps.

"Good evening, Nancy," greeted Marie.

"Good evening, Marie…Tom," she replied.

Understandably uneasy with the uncertainty of whether or not her son would return that night, Marie remained at the base of the steps fidgeting.

Having lived through the same emotional unrest for the past thirty days, Nancy insisted, "Please, have a seat and make yourselves comfortable," as she pointed to an empty porch swing.

"Thank you," replied the Parkers.

After a few moments of deadly silence, Marie asked, "I know I keep asking you, Nancy, but have you received any more letters from Dan?"

"No, just the note from four weeks ago."

With a compassionate look directed toward Sara, Marie asked, "How are you holding up?"

Sara lowered her head; whimpering was heard.

Rising from her seat, Marie stepped alongside Sara, rested her arm across her shoulders, and whispered, "I'm sorry, I didn't mean to upset you."

Between sobs, Sara admitted, "I promised myself I wouldn't do this. You'd think the tears would eventually run dry. I just miss Cindy so much."

"Of course you do," consoled Nancy, before extending her hand again and placing it upon Sara's.

The screen door opened; Jeff joined the welcoming party on the front porch. After greetings were exchanged, he asked, "Can I get anyone something to drink?" After all declined the offer, he pulled up a chair and sat beside his wife.

There was another period of silence, as each parent glanced from face to face and then to the porch floor.

Jeff cleared his throat and assured, "We'll get through this—together. But we need to promise each other, right here and now, that we'll be there for one another until all children arrive safely."

After a unanimous agreement with his suggestion, Sara eased her growing anxieties by sharing with the group what she and Cindy enjoyed doing together. Thinking it would be practical therapy for her, the Clays and the Parkers listened attentively.

Seeing relief in Sara's eyes, after relating her stories, Marie and

Tom eased their worries by telling of their parental adventures with Jimmy; there were many.

For nearly two hours, tears and laughter were exchanged between the troubled parents.

The travelers turned the corner to Beacon Lane and noticed the porch light on the Clay's house, a couple hundred feet up the roadway, was lit. Dan and Jimmy continued supporting William between themselves; Cindy and Sam walked alongside.

The mood on the porch had taken a drastic turn from lightheartedness to despair, as the conversation switched from the preadolescent experiences of their children to what the parents would do if the unthinkable came to pass.

Nancy sat quietly in her chair, sipping from a glass of lemonade that Jeff had delivered with her dinner. From the corner of her eye she glimpsed movement in the distance. With her glass in hand, she rose from her seat, neared the porch railing, peered up the street, and attempted to identify the oncoming figures. As she rested her weight against the banister, the conversation in the background ended.

Though the evening was graced with a full moon, the travelers were barely recognizable from the porch. Still a hundred feet away, Nancy stared and prayed. Once the travelers stepped beneath a glowing streetlight, she dropped her glass to the porch. Amid the shattered glass, she whispered, "Dan? Dan?" As the travelers drew nearer, she clutched the railing and stammered, "Will…Will…?"

Jeff leaped to his wife's side.

She nearly fainted at the sight of her boys; thankfully, Jeff was nearby to support her. After pushing herself from her husband's grip, she jumped over the porch steps and dashed in the direction of the travelers, yelling, "William! Dan!"

Jeff and the other parents trailed Nancy up Beacon Lane to their children, screaming frantically.

Although she hadn't seen William in thirteen years, Nancy had always envisioned what he'd look like, so many years later. After all, Dan was the spitting image of his older brother.

The mother met her missing sons with such force, her boys and Jimmy nearly fell to the street. "William!" she screamed, before embracing and kissing him. Raising her head from his shoulder, she gave Dan an unrestrained hug and a kiss, followed by—to his surprise— "Thank you!"

Dan wondered if she somehow knew all along what he had set out to accomplish. His thoughts were interrupted by his dad giving him a death grip embrace and the clamor of Cindy and Jimmy's parents.

Nancy looked at Sam and immediately recognized him from the diner, a month earlier.

"Mom, dad," explained Dan, "if it wasn't for Sam, none of us would have made it back."

Nancy leaped into Sam's arms, thanking him for returning her sons.

"It's the least I could do," he joked, "since you treated me to a meal."

Nancy tried to laugh, but only wept; she embraced him a second time.

Jeff was next to offer his undying gratitude to Sam, followed by Sara and the Parkers.

Amid the noisy reunion, Jeff whistled to grab the group's attention. While he suggested they move off Beacon Lane to the safety of the sidewalk, Nancy abruptly interrupted and asked, "Where on earth have the five of you been? I mean, look at yourselves; your ragged clothes and—" Spotting William's ripped pant leg and a bloodstain, she exclaimed, "Oh my God, William, you're bleeding."

"He'll be fine," promised Jimmy.

Nancy and Jeff stooped to inspect the wound.

"How do you know he'll be fine?" asked Marie. "It looks pretty serious…even from this distance."

"Believe me, Mrs. Parker," interjected Cindy, "Dan, Jimmy, and Sam sustained worse injuries and they survived."

The group, fearing for their safety, eventually heeded Jeff's warning and stepped off the street to the Clay's driveway.

"You can't be serious," said Sara. Fearing her daughter's response, she, nonetheless, asked, "Do you mean the group suffered worse injuries than William's?"

"Mom," insisted Cindy, "it's nothing to worry about now; we're home."

"Cindy weathered a few wicked wounds herself," slipped from Jimmy's mouth.

"Sh," snapped Cindy.

William lost his balance and would have fallen to the driveway, if Dan and Jimmy hadn't caught him.

"I think," suggested Nancy to her husband, "we should get William to the emergency room."

Jeff squatted again for another look at his son's leg and ultimately declared, "It looks like it's already healing."

Dan seconded his father's observation, assuring, "Mom, he'll be fine."

"Heck," divulged Jimmy, "Dan suffered a worse injury than that on his leg; show 'em, Dan."

Jimmy was shushed again.

"What's he talking about?" asked Nancy.

"It's nothing, mom," replied Dan, "just a scratch."

"Let's have a look," ordered Jeff.

While Dan supported his brother, Nancy rested on her knees and raised her son's pant leg, revealing a few minor flesh wounds. "Thank goodness," she remarked, "it's not as bad as I feared."

Knowing his younger son only too well, Jeff continued, "Now the other leg."

Very carefully, Nancy lifted the second pant leg, exposing an unsightly scab from his calf to his ankle. Though his wound had obviously healed considerably, the physical disfigurement was still clearly visible.

"Oh my God!" she exclaimed, as she and the other parents witnessed the atrocity. "We need to get you to the emergency room now!"

"Mom, please," insisted Dan, "I'll be fine. If it hasn't killed me yet, I doubt it will."

Nancy looked at her husband, then back to her younger son and asked, "How long have you had this?"

"I don't know," he replied, "maybe a couple weeks or so."

"A couple weeks!" shouted Nancy. "Who did this to you?"

"It's not who, but what," escaped from Jimmy's mouth.

There was a deadly silence.

Dan broke the awkward stillness, "Look, we'll have plenty of time to explain what happened on our trip during the next few weeks. But for now—and I'm sure I speak for everyone—we could really use a warm meal and a hot shower."

Cindy stepped alongside Dan and whispered, "Sooner or later they'll learn where we were. We should probably tell them now. Besides, it might be easier telling them as a group."

Overhearing Cindy's poorly muffled comment, Jeff looked at Dan and warned, "Son, I want you to be honest with me, your mother, and the rest of the parents." Partly dreading his son's forthcoming response, he, nonetheless, asked, "Where have you and your friends been the last thirty days?"

Dan eyed his co-travelers, who all nodded. "We discovered a portal in an oak tree in the forest," he explained, "leaped through it and into a parallel world, where we rescued William."

"A parallel world?" questioned Nancy. "What's that?"

"Basically," explained Dan, "we left this world and entered a similar world."

As the remaining travelers supported Dan's story, the parents were speechless.

Nancy, who remained marginally skeptical, asked, "William, you've been missing for thirteen years. I trust you to give me an honest answer. Is this story your brother's telling about being in a parallel world the truth?"

William lowered his head, as if ashamed of his abduction thirteen years ago, but eventually raised his sights and replied, "I don't recall a tree's portal so many years ago, but I do remember being held prisoner in a demonic castle."

Another period of silence followed, as the parents tried to come to terms with the reality their children were in a savage world for thirty days and stalked by creatures they dare not imagine.

Sensing his time for departure had arrived, Sam exchanged farewells with the parents, before reminding his co-travelers, "I'll see you tomorrow morning at church."

Nancy, who was still recovering from the latest revelation, pulled herself from her thoughts and asked, "Sam, where will you be staying tonight?"

"Probably at the homeless shelter."

"Absolutely not," she insisted, "you're staying here with us. There's an extra bedroom in the basement with a full bath." Detecting an upcoming refusal, she reminded, "Sam, you brought my boys home. This is the very least Jeff and I can do to thank you."

Sam humbly accepted.

Nancy relieved Dan in upholding his brother. With her husband's assistance, she helped William into the house and lowered him to the couch.

Sara approached her daughter, gave her another hug, and suggested, "I think it's time we headed home also."

Looking down at Sam, Jimmy, and Dan, who had sat on the street curb moments earlier, she replied, "Mom, just a few more minutes with the guys."

Knowing the dangers and tragedies had brought the travelers closer together, Sara agreed, "Alright; I'll see if the Clays need help with William." After giving her daughter a peck on the cheek, she stepped to the sidewalk and ascended the porch steps.

After watching her mother enter the house, Cindy plopped to the curb.

Staring in the direction of the forest, though they couldn't see the woods with the town's obstructions, Dan admitted, "Considering the creatures and the amount of time we spent in the parallel world, it's still hard to believe we made it back."

"I know," seconded Sam. "I thought my first visit twenty years ago was hellish; and even then, I entered only the fringes of the forest."

Cindy kicked off her boots and confirmed, "Yeah; but it's mainly because we kept an eye out for one another. I mean, we took turns at night patrol, we conserved our food supplies, and—" She leaned forward on the curb, glared at Jimmy, and clarified, "At least eventually, and we put our lives on the line for one another."

Not removing his gaze from the direction of the forest, Dan replied, "That's true. But I'm afraid even that wouldn't have been enough without Saint Michael's help the moment we entered the parallel world."

"From the moment we entered the parallel world?" asked a bewildered Cindy. "What do you mean?"

Realizing he hadn't told his friends what he experienced before leaving the darkened forest, Dan said, "I guess I forgot to tell you."

"Tell us what?" asked Sam.

"Do you remember," he explained, "before we left and I was standing between Spiritus Malus and Saint Michael?"

"Yeah," replied Sam.

"Anyway," he continued, "when Saint Michael rested his hand on my shoulder, I felt the familiar warm touch, but that time it wasn't invisible."

Doubtful, Sam asked, "So, you think it was the same warm touch you felt from early on in the journey?"

"I know it was," declared Dan.

"Well, I'll be," mumbled Sam.

"But what about—" asked Cindy.

The conversation ended; the travelers spotted Kevin Sur and Tony Malice walking up the street.

As the two notorious bullies neared the group, Malice ignored Sam, stared at the three teenagers, and sarcastically remarked, "Oh, look, it's the three girls who skipped survival camp."

Looking at the ruffians standing overhead and then lowering his gaze to Dan, Sam asked, "Are these the two bullies?"

"Yeah," he confirmed, "but somehow they don't seem frightening anymore."

"It's just as well you three girls didn't come to camp," taunted Sur, "you never would have survived. There were snakes, poisonous spiders, and even a mountain lion was on the loose."

"Oh, my gosh," derided Jimmy, "you're right. I don't think we would have survived. It sounds horrible."

Disregarding Jimmy's sarcasm, Sur stared at Dan and remarked,

"I heard at camp that you and your pathetic friends went missing. Where were you…out saving the world?"

Dan glanced at his co-travelers, stretched his legs into the street, and confidently replied, "Yeah, something like that."

Humiliated for his friend, Malice kicked a rock from the street in Dan's direction, demanding, "Are you mocking Sur?"

Dan looked at Jimmy and grinned.

His neighbor returned the smirk, annoying the bullies even more.

"Get up, Clay!" ordered Malice.

Recalling Dan's valiant actions on the drawbridge with Judas and his daring rescue of Jimmy from the Oswagi nest, Sam, Jimmy, and Cindy refused to move a muscle. They knew he could handle his own.

Dan rose to his feet.

Malice threw a punch.

Dan swerved, missing the oncoming blow, and quickly nabbed his assailant's arm. Before the bully knew what had happened, Dan leveled him to his stomach upon the pavement and twisted his arm between his shoulder blades.

Malice let out a prolonged moan.

Sur had made only one step to free his unruly friend, when Dan— in a squat position over Malice—switched his weight and thrust a leg in Sur's direction, sending him to the street as well. Though he briefly enjoyed the long-awaited upper hand, he realized the bullies weren't worth it. To him, making up for lost time with his brother, parents, and friends was top priority. He released his grip on Malice and ordered, "Get out of here!"

Completely embarrassed, the thugs raised themselves from the pavement and walked up Beacon Lane at a fast pace.

After eyeing the bullies disappear into the darkness, Dan rose to check on his brother.

Jimmy headed next door, where his parents had entered several minutes earlier, allowing their son time with his friends; Cindy and Sam followed Dan into the Clay's house.

"Are you ready to go home, honey?" asked Sara, as her daughter stepped into the living room.

"Yeah," she replied. Glancing at Sam and Dan, she reminded, "I'll see you tomorrow in church."

"Church?" asked her mother.

"Yeah, mom," she answered. "We ran into Father James tonight at church and I promised him I'd be at Mass tomorrow. He also asked you to come along."

Remembering her daily trips to the church for morning prayers and the inner peace she experienced during the visits, she eventually welcomed her daughter's suggestion and admitted, "That's probably not a bad idea."

Before closing the front door behind her, Cindy offered a backward glimpse and announced, "See you tomorrow."

Nancy remained puzzled why the group visited Father James earlier that evening, but decided to inquire later; she had a guest to accommodate. She led Sam to the top of the basement steps, carrying clean sheets and towels.

"Mrs. Clay," began Sam, halfway down the steps.

"Please," she interrupted, "call me Nancy."

"Sure," he said. "Nancy, are you sure you want me to stay here?"

Stepping on the basement's bottom landing, she turned and explained, "Sam, for thirteen years, I've waited and prayed for William's return. Not only did you bring him back, but I have a strong feeling if it wasn't for you, Dan never would have returned." Handing him the bath towels, she insisted, "Yes, I want you to stay. Besides, you're now a member of this family."

"Thank you," he replied, while scratching his oily scalp.

As Nancy gave Sam a tour of his new quarters, Dan and his dad helped William up the steps to the boys' shared bedroom. Although Jeff knew it would be better for his older son to avoid the steps and sleep on the living room sofa, William demanded sleeping in the room with his brother.

By 2:00 a.m., the Clay household was asleep in the safety of their own beds, with no one assuming first watch.

CHAPTER TWENTY
The Dinner Party

THE NEXT MORNING, WITH THE FAMILY SEATED AROUND THE kitchen table, Nancy asked her sons and Sam why they needed to leave for the noon Mass at 11:15.

"We promised Father James last night," informed Dan, "we'd go to confession this morning."

Though Nancy was pleased with this act of humility, her son's comment provided the perfect opportunity for her to inquire, "Why did you see Father James last night?"

"We had to return something from the trip," answered Dan, before reaching for a piece of toast.

Jeff entered the kitchen, saying, "Good morning," to which everyone responded likewise, except Nancy.

Curious with her son's remark, before her husband entered the room, she asked, "What did you have to return?"

"Just something we thought Father James could use," said William, with a mouthful of eggs.

Suspecting it was a personal matter between her sons and the parish priest, Nancy downplayed the issue, mumbling, "Oh."

Watching the men eat, Jeff joked, "Didn't you guys eat while you were—wherever you were?"

"Oh, yeah," replied Sam, "mostly rabbit and fish, but never pancakes, eggs, and hash browns."

Jeff's remark regarding their whereabouts still troubled Nancy, who successfully changed the subject by suggesting, "Sam and William, I'm sure Jeff has some clothes which will fit that you can wear to church."

"Yes, ma'am," replied William and Sam in unison.

As Nancy sipped her coffee, she was in heaven. She hadn't seen her boys at the table enjoying a meal in more than a decade. Offering a passing glance to her husband, she noticed he, too, was staring at his sons devouring the food before them.

After the plates were emptied, the men headed upstairs to get dressed.

Arriving at church at 11:25, Dan looked to the confessional where a green light was aglow, indicating Father James was ready for a penitent. But this day was different. In addition to attending the noon weekday Mass, which the Clays seldom did, the young men decided to sit in a different pew, other than the fifth, where the family always sat.

The parents followed.

The brothers and Sam walked beyond the center aisle and entered a pew, ten rows back from the sanctuary and near the protective gaze of the sculpture of Saint Michael the Archangel.

Nancy couldn't explain it, but she knew, even during their drive to the church, that was where they'd kneel. She and Jeff happily agreed, since it was the area where they and the other parents spent their mornings in prayer for the travelers' safety.

Each man examined his conscience. Dan was the first to rise. En route to the confessional, he spotted Cindy and Sara at the back of the church.

Meeting in the center aisle, Cindy whispered, "Dan, I'm not Catholic; but do you think I could talk with Father James in the confessional? I think I'd feel better discussing a few things with him."

In an uneasy state, as most penitents are before confessing their sins, Dan replied, "Just tell him you're not Catholic and that you want to talk with him in private for guidance. I'm sure it's okay."

"Alright," replied Cindy, who followed her friend to the confessional.

Sara joined the Clays in their pew.

Dan entered the confessional, where he remained for nearly five minutes. During that time, the Parkers had arrived and joined the

Clays and Sara in their newly-assigned seating. As Marie and Tom entered the pew, Jimmy stepped aside and helped Sam walk William to the line of penitents.

Dan exited the confessional and Cindy entered, where she remained for several minutes.

At 11:50, once the travelers had left the confessional—and obviously digressed in telling the priest a few stories of their quest—Father James approached the sanctuary with a troubled look. *My God,* he thought, *what could I have done to prevent such an experience?* Amid his unwarranted feelings of guilt, he entered the sacristy and vested for Mass.

Within an hour, the liturgy had concluded and the five travelers were welcomed on the church lawn by a group of well-wishers, who pleaded for an answer to their whereabouts during the past month. To the parents' surprise, Sam and their children cleverly dodged the questions and offered only vague responses.

In celebration of their return, the Clays, the Somers, and the Parkers gathered at the local diner for lunch. Throughout their extended three-hour meal, the parents learned—much to their distress—of the demonic beings their children had encountered. Frequently, the accounts seemed so unreal that they questioned their children's honesty. But their visible scars ultimately supported their stories. At 4:00, the families left the restaurant and returned to their homes. For the Clays, the rest of the day was spent catching up, not simply on the last thirty days, but the past thirteen years.

Since the Clays enjoyed a late lunch, their evening meal was served later than usual.

Minutes after the kitchen was cleaned, Sam remarked, "Nancy, if it's alright, I think I'll call it a day."

"Absolutely," she replied. "I think we'll all be retiring soon. It's been a very busy and enlightening day."

Within an hour, the Clay household was asleep.

Over the next month, life slowly returned to normal. Nancy and Jeff qualified for a loan and hired a private tutor for William, Dan reviewed the results of his college applications that he submitted months earlier, and Sam gradually acclimated to his new family. As for Nancy and Jeff, they couldn't have been happier.

Shortly after their return from the parallel world, it was decided that once their daily schedules were commonplace, the Clays would host a homecoming meal for the returning travelers. Nancy and Jeff suggested the next full moon as the obvious night to celebrate. After all, they reasoned the moon was the means of transport which led their children home. The Parkers, Sara, and Father James agreed and accepted the invitation.

●

On July 30—the following full moon—at 4:30 in the evening, as Nancy was occupied with the homecoming feast preparations, there was a knock at the front door. Jeff, who had recently arrived home from work, crossed the living room floor.

"Hey, Mr. Clay," greeted Jimmy.

"Hello, Jimmy."

"Are Dan, William, and Sam around?" he asked.

"Yeah; they're downstairs. Go ahead…and tell them to bring up the extra leaves to the dining room table, like they promised."

"Sure," replied Jimmy, as he headed for the steps.

"Who was at the door?" asked Nancy, as her husband re-entered the kitchen.

"Jimmy; he's downstairs with Sam and the boys."

"Are the leaves to the dining room table in place?" she asked.

"I told Jimmy to remind the boys." He opened the refrigerator, grabbed a platter of produce, and volunteered, "I'll fix the vegetables and dip."

"That would be great, honey."

●

Downstairs, Jimmy was welcomed with a headlock from William and a punch in the arm from Dan. Sam simply rolled his eyes before inquiring, "Jimmy, I thought you said your parents had you doing chores today."

"Yeah," he answered, "but they're almost done." The teenager's month-old resolution to be more helpful around the house was clearly waning.

"What do you mean almost done?" asked Sam.

"I'll finish cleaning the bathrooms later tonight after our get-together," schemed Jimmy. "I was curious if you guys wanted to see a movie tonight."

"Jimmy," exclaimed William, "your parents and Father James are coming over tonight for our homecoming meal."

"I know," acknowledged Jimmy, "but there's still time to catch a movie and be back before the meal at 8:00."

"I don't know," replied a doubtful Dan, "mom and dad may not like the idea."

"Oh," blurted Jimmy, "I almost forgot. Your dad wants you and William to grab the leaves to the dining room table."

As the brothers neared the closet where the leaves were stored, Jimmy instructed, "After you place the leaves in the table, ask your parents about the movie. Maybe then they'll agree."

"Don't you think that's a bit devious?" said Sam.

"Maybe," replied Jimmy, "but it works in my house."

"Alright," agreed Dan, "but I'm asking them only once. If they think it's a bad idea, I'm not pushing the issue."

"Fair enough," said Jimmy. Without skipping a beat, he asked, "Can I use your phone?"

"Sure; why?" asked Dan.

"We have to invite Cindy," declared an obstinate teenager.

"Jimmy," reminded Dan, "first let's see if it's okay with my folks."

It was too late; Jimmy had Cindy on the line.

As Jimmy was prematurely inviting Cindy, the brothers lugged the cumbersome leaves to the dining room, removed the flower arrangement, and separated the table.

"Careful, don't scratch the floor," warned Nancy, who had just entered the room. As she spread a decorative tablecloth, she added, "So, what do you two have planned for the next few hours?"

Eyeing Sam and Jimmy at the basement entrance, Dan replied, "We were thinking about seeing a movie before the company arrives."

"A movie?" questioned Nancy. "But Jimmy's parents, Sara, and Father James will be here at 8:00."

"There's a 5:30 movie," blurted William, "and we'd be home before 8:00."

Jeff, who had just stepped into the room, overheard the proposed picture.

"I don't know," said Nancy, before glancing to her husband for his opinion.

Aware the travelers had spent a lot of time with their families over the past month, but little time with one another, Jeff stressed, "Are you sure you'll be back before 8:00?"

"Positive," replied William.

Jeff looked at his wife, who nodded slightly.

"Alright," permitted Jeff, "but I want you straight back here after the movie."

"Thanks," replied Dan, who was already nearing Sam and Jimmy.

"But, Dan and William," demanded Nancy, "I want you to wear nice clothes to the theater. When you come home from the movie, I want you ready to welcome our guests."

Dan and William reluctantly agreed. Sam, on the other hand, was already appropriately dressed for the evening's gathering.

"Jimmy," suggested Jeff, "you should probably change your clothes, too."

"Yes, Mr. Clay," mumbled Jimmy; he neared the front door.

In the kitchen, Jeff reassured his wife that the group would be fine and that a movie was a good idea, since they needed some time together.

Nancy was overjoyed having her sons home at last; but she still feared for their safety. Ironically, at the same time, she knew they'd be alright. *After all,* she thought, *it's just a movie in town.*

By 5:15, the Clay brothers and Sam darted from the house, caught up with Jimmy next door, and raced to the movie theater on Main Street.

Cindy had agreed to meet the men on Chelsea Avenue, since her mom had a last-minute errand to run and needed her help.

When the five met, no time was wasted on mindless chatter; they were already five minutes late.

Though the group enjoyed the horror flick, each one quickly realized it wasn't so much the movie they appreciated, as much as the company. As each gruesome scene flashed upon the wide screen, the travelers took turns whispering on its tameness.

●

In the Clay's house, Jeff and Nancy continued readying the house and preparing the meal for their guests. Nancy was basting a turkey and Jeff was putting the final touches on the hors d'oeuvres. After closing the oven door, she stepped into the living room and lit the scented candles.

"Honey," she yelled, "bring the vegetable dish and set it on the living room table."

Jeff, who lingered in the kitchen shoving three carrot slices in his mouth, only mumbled.

Nancy had lit the last candle atop one of the side tables, when a knock was heard at the font door. Rushing to the foyer, she glanced at the hallway clock; it was 7:45 p.m.

"Hello, Father," she welcomed.

"Good evening," replied the priest. "Am I the first one here?"

"Yes, Father; but the others will be here shortly."

Entering the living room, carrying his Bible, Father James greeted Jeff, who was having difficulty making room on the table for a platter overflowing with vegetables and dip.

"I'm glad you could make it, Father," said Jeff.

"I wouldn't miss this homecoming for anything," he declared.

Displaying his Bible, Father James asked if he could set it somewhere close by. "Since it might be a late night," he presumed, "I thought I'd bring it along to read Scripture later in the evening."

Jeff took the Good Book and placed it on a side table, next to a glowing candle.

Wiping her hands on a napkin from her apron pocket, Nancy asked, "Father, may I get you something to drink?"

"That would be nice. May I trouble you for a soda?"

"It's no trouble at all, Father," assured Nancy, who turned and re-entered the kitchen.

Father James sat on the sofa; Jeff joined him.

Noticing a new family portrait, which was taken several days prior and centered above the mantel, Father James asked if the boys and Sam were around.

"They'll be here in a few minutes," said Jeff. "They, Jimmy, and Cindy decided to take in a movie before the meal. But they promised they'd be back by 8:00."

"Here you are, Father," said Nancy, handing him his drink.

"Thank you. So, Jeff tells me your boys, Jimmy, Sam, and Cindy are at a movie."

"Yes," confirmed Nancy. "Jeff thought it would be a good idea for the five to spend time together."

"I think that's great," seconded Father James. "They need to relive their adventures. I'm sure talking about it will be very therapeutic."

Another knock was heard at the door.

"Excuse me, Father," said Nancy, as she rose from a wing chair.

The Parkers and Sara had arrived at the same time. After receiving her guests and accepting their platters of food, Nancy escorted them to the living room. Within minutes, the parents and the parish priest were enjoying a lively conversation and nibbling on hors d'oeuvres.

•

Stepping from the theater onto Main Street, the full moon hanging over the forest captured the attention of the travelers. To them, nothing was more spectacular or more pleasant than the celestial body.

For a few minutes, the group silently stared heavenward, until Cindy lowered her head to ease the strain in her neck and alerted, "We should probably head out." Looking at her watch, she blurted, "Oh, my gosh; we're ten minutes late."

Her four companions dropped their gaze and began their fifteen-minute walk to Beacon Lane.

●

Marie had just commented on how Dan's note in Nancy's Sunday missal provided the hope she desperately needed for her son's return. Sara supported her sentiment.

Nancy rose from her chair and hinted, "There's something else I think you should see." She left the living room and ascended the staircase. Moments later, she returned with a hand firmly clenched. "This is something Dan crammed in his pocket in the other world and forgot about it, until one day when I was washing his jeans."

All eyes were fixed on her tightened fist.

After opening her hand and unfolding the ancient parchment, she explained, "When I asked Dan about this, he told me it was a secret potion he ripped from the Reclaimers' book of elixirs. He believed, and still believes, they were attempting to relocate the portal to a well-traveled location."

The manuscript was handed to Tom, who studied the document closely. Marie accepted it from her husband and analyzed its drawings and ingredients. After Sara examined the parchment, she handed it to the parish priest.

"My gosh," admitted Father James, "I hardly recognize anything listed or pictured on this document. For example, this first ingredient—what's a manticore's claw?" Clearly expecting no one to answer, he placed the parchment on the side table, atop his Bible, since Nancy had her hands full carrying the empty vegetable dish to the kitchen.

Nearing the arched open doorway, Nancy turned and answered, "I couldn't tell you what a manticore is, Father, but I do know a Bozeman is a giant porcupine, according to Dan."

"Speaking of Dan," remarked Jeff, "where are the boys? They should have been here by now."

"Tom and I made Jimmy promise us," shared Marie, "he'd be here by 8:00, before we agreed to the movie."

"That's alright," interjected Father James, in defense of the travelers, "let them enjoy their night on the town. This gives you time to share with one another how you feel your children are adjusting since their return."

"Well," disclosed Sara, "I've found Cindy making extra efforts at being more sociable with her girlfriends. I mean, just the other day, she and Katie Bush went shopping together. I couldn't believe it; after all, Katie was one of her former classmates whom she constantly criticized."

As Nancy re-entered the living room from delivering the empty dish, Marie interrupted Sara's update on her daughter's social progress and said, "Excuse me, Nancy, if the children will be here soon, maybe I should warm my mashed potatoes in your oven."

"Let me help you," offered Nancy.

"Please," she insisted, "I'll be fine. Stay here and entertain your guests." Marie, joined by her husband, stepped into the kitchen.

Within moments, Sara also excused herself to prepare her fruit dessert, which Nancy had placed on the kitchen counter, upon her arrival.

From the living room, Nancy yelled, "If you need any help, let me know."

"Thanks, we're fine," was heard from the kitchen.

With the Clays entertaining Father James in the living room, Nancy began, "Father, I can't begin to tell you how happy Jeff and I are to have our boys home. I pray everyday this will be a happy home again."

No sooner had the priest promised the hosts their home life would be cheerful again, when the side table—upon which rested the priest's Bible and the ancient parchment—wobbled.

All sights were focused on the table, as Father James pressed a hand upon the furniture to end its erratic behavior.

A look of terror flooded Nancy's eyes before shouting, "The manuscript!"

The priest, Nancy, and Jeff were unaware that that the beams of the full moon had cleared the birch tree in the front yard; the life-giving rays met the cursed parchment.

Now standing and using both hands, the priest tried to overpower the table's shakes.

The furniture remained unrestrained.

Within seconds, the intensifying jolts threw Father James backwards, landing him on the living room carpet.

Nancy and Jeff dashed to his side.

Hearing a thud, Marie, Tom, and Sara rushed to the kitchen entryway, where they witnessed a flash of light leap from the parchment, bounce off the living room wall, and materialize a creature from one of the potion's ingredients. Between the Clays—who were sitting on the living room floor beside the priest—and the Parkers and Sara—who were trembling in the kitchen doorway—stood a manticore.

The unnatural creature boasted the body of a lion, the head of a man, and a slender tail, complete with poisonous quills that were released at predators and prey alike. Seeing potential victims in front and behind, it focused its deadly gaze on its closer targets near the living room fireplace. The Clays and the priest inched backwards, until they were pinned against the hearth. The manticore made a weak lunge, but was quickly repelled by the fireplace poker, which Jeff had snatched moments before the charge.

The Parkers and Sara grabbed the nearest weapons—three knives—and crept toward the manticore, hoping a distraction from behind would confuse the beast and prevent it from pouncing on the priest and the Clays.

Sadly, they had advanced only a few steps beyond the arched open doorway, when another blazing beam of light leaped from the parchment, ricocheted off the wall, and created a three-foot troll—the second element of the potion—between the manticore and themselves. On seeing the creature's single yellow eye in the center of its forehead, its jagged fangs, and its four-clawed hands and feet, Marie labored to breathe.

Unlike the manticore, the troll wasted no time in securing its next meal. It neared the three guests, who fearfully displayed their weapons, as they stepped backwards into the kitchen, until they were trapped against the sink.

With nowhere to retreat, the guests were forced to summon their dwindling courage and jab their weapons in the direction of the creature, hoping it would back away.

With three shiny blades now in clear view, the troll suspended its forward movement; it scrutinized the situation and its surroundings.

●

At a fast pace, since they were already late, Sam, Cindy, Jimmy, Dan, and William jumped onto the Clay's porch.

William gripped the screen door handle; Dan blurted, "Wait."

The older sibling lowered his hand and looked at Dan, who was peering through the parted curtains in the living room. He stepped alongside his younger brother and saw the unimaginable: the parish priest and their parents confined against the fireplace by a creature none of the travelers had encountered in the parallel world.

Noticing the family car, Cindy knew her mom was also in danger, though she couldn't see her.

The same fear for his parents haunted Jimmy.

The young travelers were prepared to storm through the front door and rescue their parents, when Sam reminded them if they did, they'd be in the same defenseless predicament. "Come on," he advised, "let's crawl through the basement window and grab the weapons." Detecting frustration and impatience on the faces of his companions, he warned, "If we burst through the front door now, we'll be useless and at the mercy of the four-legged beast."

As much as they hated delaying their surprise attack, the travelers knew Sam was right. With great speed, the party dashed off the porch and into the back yard, where Sam had left his bedroom window ajar.

Unsure how many creatures had invaded the house and whether any lurked in the lower level, Sam entered first. Although a tight squeeze, he eventually jumped to the basement floor with surprisingly little noise. He quickly scanned the area; no alien being was spotted. He turned and helped Cindy through the window. Once all were inside, he reached under his bed and grabbed five lances. "Alright," he ordered, "let's watch each other's backs, like we did in the forest."

The group sneaked up the basement steps, with Sam taking the lead.

●

In the living room, the manticore made three additional charges at the Clays and the priest, but was driven back with the poker. Unfortunately, on its final lunge, its claws grazed Jeff's arm and instantly drew blood.

On witnessing the clash, Father James grabbed the poker from Jeff and assumed a defensive posture.

The manticore retreated slightly, but only momentarily.

Nancy, who remained sitting on the floor beside her husband, was in near shock. Her heavy breathing provoked the beast.

The manticore lashed its tail at the group, hurling a venomous spine.

The priest dodged the oncoming quill that embedded itself in the fireplace. Yellow pus dripped down the bricks.

In the kitchen, the troll scanned the area and rushed at the cornered group.

Tom received a gash on the cheek, when deflecting the creature's lunge at Sara. Luckily, he inflicted a flesh wound on the troll's chest, though it wasn't life-threatening.

The troll took several steps back.

●

As Sam stepped upon the top basement step, a third beam of light burst from the ancient parchment and captured the attention of everyone in the living room and in the open kitchen—including the creatures. But nothing appeared with the latest surge of light.

The creatures resumed their assault.

Sam and his co-rescuers entered the main level and saw the creatures at close range. Instinctively, the Clay brothers and Sam darted toward the manticore; Cindy and Jimmy raced into the kitchen.

"Cindy," yelled Sara, "get back!"

"Not another disgusting troll," declared Cindy, with her lance raised.

The troll turned to its enemy and accused, "You—you and your friends killed a tribal member in the forest. For that unforgivable act, you'll pay—you'll pay with your life."

Jimmy, also with his weapon raised, crept along the periphery of the kitchen, attempting to place the troll between himself and Cindy.

"Think again," dared Cindy, before releasing her weapon.

The troll dropped to the floor.

In her agitated state, she overshot her target, sending her lance through the kitchen window, narrowly missing her mother and the Parkers.

The creature sprang so swiftly at its assailant that Jimmy failed to launch his spear.

Cindy immediately snatched a carving knife, which was resting on the counter beside her, and extended her arm.

The troll made contact with the blade and crashed upon Cindy's chest, knocking her to the kitchen floor. Amid the collision, the troll's claws punctured her neck.

Sara screamed and rushed to her daughter; Jimmy also dashed to his friend, reaching her first.

With diminishing strength, Cindy pushed the beast off, grabbed the counter, and struggled to her feet with Jimmy's assistance.

Sara insisted she remain on the floor; Cindy refused her suggestion.

With its last breath, the troll foretold, "You and your friends will soon—"

Recalling Sam's earlier warning that premonitions were a recipe for present worries, Cindy grabbed Jimmy's lance and drove it into the troll, while completing its prediction, "My friends and I will soon never see you or your kind again."

The troll closed its eyes forever.

Cindy was clutching the counter to steady herself, when she and the other kitchen occupants heard an uproar in the living room. Knowing her friends were still in danger, she stumbled to the adjoining room, strongly against her mother's wishes.

The manticore was now surrounded: a poker in front and three lances—held by William, Dan, and Sam—behind. Enraged at seeing his mother panting and his father's bloody arm, Dan waited until the beast's head was turned in his parents' direction before targeting the beast; William did likewise. In a split second, the brothers inflicted two lethal wounds to the manticore's back side. The creature roared, turned, and painfully limped in the men's direction.

The siblings quickly withdrew several feet.

During the assault and the resulting advance of the creature to their unarmed sons, Jeff and Nancy crawled to the foyer; the priest dashed to the cursed manuscript that had fallen to the floor during the table's prior unexplainable movements.

Father James knew the parchment must be destroyed or more creatures would flash into existence before their eyes. With the manuscript in hand, he was astounded. The initial three ingredients had vanished from the parchment. *What was the third ingredient?* he thought. *And where is it now?*

As Sam diverted the manticore's attention with aerial movements of his weapon, Dan and William guardedly circled around the beast, yanked their lances from the wounded creature, and sank them into the manticore a second time. Sam delivered the fatal blow to its neck. The lion creature howled, seconds before collapsing in a pool of blood. At the death roar, the guests, who had recently left the kitchen and were standing at the fringes of the living room, exhaled loudly.

Sara placed her arm around her daughter's waist and was helping her to the couch, when a Titan Spider fell from the ceiling and landed near the foyer. The female variety of the arachnid, though half the size of its male counterpart which the travelers had encountered in the parallel world, was just as deadly.

"The third ingredient," whispered Father James, while holding the manuscript over a lit candle. To his amazement, the parchment refused to burn; rather, it snuffed out the candle's flame. He tried to rip the manuscript, but even this proved impossible. The troublesome parchment seemed indestructible.

Surrounded by eleven predators—or so the Titan Spider imagined—it released several strands of entangling silk at its nearest victim, Nancy.

Jeff, who was sitting in the foyer beside his wife, not only failed in removing the fibers from her leg, but became tangled in the process. With a gummy web stuck to his neck, he glanced at eye level across the strand.

The Titan Spider unhinged its jaws and released hundreds of its young, which inched along the web toward Jeff's throat and Nancy's leg.

Jeff worked frantically to remove the fibers from his wife, but his efforts proved futile.

Nancy passed out.

Seeing the miniature Titan Spiders, Dan and William bolted to their parents' rescue, but were delayed by a Fury that instantly appeared between them and their parents, with a fourth explosion of light.

The Fury, a distant cousin of the winged flesh-eating Harpy, had no talons. Rather, she was disfigured with an oversize human mouth and reeked of decaying flesh. As the Clay brothers advanced, with their lances at shoulder height and their noses covered, the Fury spat in their direction. The brothers dodged the saliva before it hit the carpet. Upon impact, the drool burst into flames, which the young men and Sam quickly stamped out. The Fury's relentless spitting, however, kept the brothers, Sam, and the guests busy putting out fires and dispersing smoke. In the end, a clear shot at the latest unearthly arrival seemed hopeless.

After extinguishing a fire at her feet, Cindy darted to Nancy and Jeff, but lost consciousness en route and collapsed to the floor.

Sara raced to her daughter, dropped to her knees, and rested Cindy's head in her lap; Tom bolted to the kitchen, jumped over the dead troll, grabbed a moistened cloth, and returned to Sara's side.

Sara applied the damp towel to her daughter's bleeding neck, imploring, "Cindy, wake up; please, wake up." She wept bitterly.

Still handling the manuscript on the living room floor, behind the protection of the couch, the priest thought, *If these creatures are from the parallel world—and since this hellish manuscript was the means that transported them—then maybe...just maybe.* He reached for his Bible, placed the manuscript amid its pages, and slammed the book. The parchment smoldered and eventually was ablaze within the pages of the book. Quite unexpectedly, the diminutive spiders, the mother Titan Spider, the expired manticore, the dead troll, and the Fury vanished.

With no trace of silk on Nancy's leg or his neck, Jeff lifted her and carried her to the sofa.

Cindy jolted to consciousness.

Like the creatures, the battle scars which Cindy, Tom, and Jeff had sustained also disappeared.

A clanging sound echoed from the kitchen. Sara and Cindy looked beyond the open entryway and saw the carving knife and Jimmy's lance, which previously impaled the troll, tumble to the floor.

With Cindy's miraculous healing, Sara handed the wet cloth to Jeff, who placed it upon his wife's forehead. After a few moments of gently shaking her, she awoke. "They're gone," he assured.

Nancy simply nodded.

Father James opened his Bible to discover nothing remained of the parchment, not even ashes; the pages of his book were not the least bit scorched. "Amazing," he whispered to himself.

Astonishment consumed the Clays and their guests, as they scanned the former war zone: the living room carpet was free of burns and manticore blood. Not a trace of the quill remained embedded in the fireplace, nor was yellow pus dripping from the bricks. It was as if the unnatural events of the evening were ripped from the pages of time...but not from the minds of the Clays or their visitors.

As the families relaxed in the living room, regaining their strength and composure, the parents admitted to themselves they had previously entertained fleeting doubts about their children's outlandish stories in the other world. Their former skepticisms, much like the unusual creatures, evaporated into thin air.

For nearly thirty minutes, the eleven rested in the living room with hardly a word spoken. Eventually, Jimmy broke the silence, asking, "Well, now that that's over, can we eat? I'm starving."

Cindy, who was sitting on the floor beside him, had recovered enough strength to slap him across the chest. "Jimmy," she reproved, "after everything our families have been through, how can you think of food?"

"Cindy," interrupted her mother, "are these the kind of creatures you confronted in the parallel world?"

Realizing she would be overly concerned, Cindy reassured, "There's nothing to worry about; we're home."

Tom, however, was not so easily dissuaded. "Jimmy," he questioned, "did you run into beasts like these in the other world?"

Jimmy glanced to his companions, who nodded. "Yeah, dad," he admitted, "nearly every day for a month. And to be honest, I was usually scared to death. But we were in it together. Somehow, I knew I'd be safe with the others around."

Eager to change the frightful subject, Nancy rose from the couch, forewarning, "I hope everyone likes overcooked turkey," as she neared the kitchen, assisted by her husband.

Marie, Tom, and Sara followed their hosts into the kitchen, but stopped short of the entryway. The guests stared in disbelief at the kitchen window which was intact.

Removing the turkey from the oven and placing it on the counter, Nancy turned and saw a look of disbelief on her guests' faces. Thinking they were worried about the meal, she remarked, "It's burned, but it's still edible."

Within minutes, everyone was gathered around the dining room table, except Father James. Since the combustion of the parchment, he had been meditating in a wing chair in the living room. Of all the pages in the Bible to open randomly and shove the manuscript, he had flipped to Saint Matthew's narrative, "Expulsion of the Demons in Gadara."

Nearing her parish priest, Nancy asked, "Father, would you like to join us now?"

"If it's alright with you," he replied, "I'd like to read a passage or two; you go ahead and eat."

Confident Scripture would ease her anxieties, she sat on the sofa and remarked, "I feel like listening to a passage or two."

The priest glanced at his host, smiled, and began reading.

One by one, the guests entered the living room to hear the humble priest read. As the words of the Bible were pronounced, the parents held their children close, though they knew—beyond a doubt—they could protect themselves.

Nearly three hours after the guests' arrival, the meal was served, complete with a well-done turkey, mashed potatoes, corn, and a fruit dessert.

At precisely 11:50 p.m., the priest's cell phone rang. "Hello, this is Father James." There was a pause before he concluded, "I'll be there right away." Replacing the phone to his belt, he graciously thanked the Clays for their hospitality. "A parishioner," he informed, "is not expected to make it through the early morning hours at the hospital. I need to administer the last rites."

"Of course, Father," agreed Nancy. "Let me grab your Bible from the living room."

Within seconds of receiving his book, the priest approached the front door, escorted by the entire dinner party.

"Thanks, again, Nancy," said the priest.

"Thank you, Father," she replied. "And Father, please don't let tonight's unfortunate events discourage you from visiting us again soon."

The priest grinned before assuring, "No, I wouldn't dream of it." He stepped onto the porch and neared his parked car on the street.

Seconds after Father James turned the corner, Sara and the Parkers also exchanged farewells with the Clays. It was an exhausting evening and it was late.

After their personal items were gathered, the Parkers walked next door; the Clays and Sam accompanied Sara and Cindy to their car.

As the families talked near the street curb, Father James was driving up Main Street. Lost in his thoughts on the events that transpired during the homecoming celebration, he initially failed to recognize something most unusual on the church lawn, until he was beyond the building. Reducing his speed, he peered into the rearview mirror. His heart dropped to his stomach; a stately tree stood on the church grounds, only yards from the front doors. "What the—" he whispered. "It wasn't there this morning." Recalling the story of the oak's portal, he reached for his cell phone and dialed the Clays.

Since the Clays and Sam were engrossed in a conversation with Sara and Cindy outdoors, no one heard the phone ring.

Father James left a message, "Dan, William, I don't know how to explain it; it's kind of weird. I think you should come down—"

The priest's phone went dead.

With a parishioner at death's door, he hit the accelerator and continued up Main Street. *I'll check it out, once I return from the hospital,* he thought. Before turning the corner, he took one last look in the mirror and witnessed the church grounds fade into darkness.

A limb had shattered the nearby streetlight.

CHAPTER TWENTY-ONE

The Foreshadowing Dream

THE PRIEST'S THOUGHTS WERE DISRUPTED BY A LOUD BLAST. In his troubled state, thinking of what had appeared on the church lawn, he crossed the center of the road; an oncoming car had slammed on its brakes and blared its horn. The priest quickly veered back into his lane and reduced his speed. With no cars behind, he inched his way to the car in the opposite lane.

"I'm so sorry," apologized Father James, after opening the window. "I was preoccupied with something at the church."

Noticing the priestly collar, the middle-aged man abandoned his initial intent to admonish the careless driver and replied, "That's okay, Father. Are you alright?"

"Yes; and you?"

"Yeah, I'm fine," answered the driver, "just a little startled."

"I'm terribly sorry," restated the priest. Seeing headlights in his rearview mirror, he concluded, "God bless," before rolling up the window, touching the gas pedal, and heading to the medical center. Within minutes, he pulled into the hospital parking lot. Since it was nearly 12:30 a.m., parking spaces were ample and no waiting line lingered around the front desk.

"Good evening, Father," welcomed the nurse on duty, "I mean, good morning."

"Good morning."

"Who are you here to see?"

"Alice Schaeffer, one of my parishioners."

"Oh, yes," acknowledged the nurse. "She's in room 222, though it doesn't appear she'll make it through the early morning hours."

"Thank you," replied Father James, before turning and approaching the elevator. During his ride to the second floor, he made a deliberate effort to dismiss his recurring thoughts about the tree on the church's lawn and concentrate on administering the last rites to his elderly parishioner. After all, hearing a dying person's final confession, anointing them with holy oil, and sending them into the loving hands of the Almighty was one of the most sacred rituals he would perform as a priest.

The elevator door opened. Stepping out, he searched for room 222. His scan ended when he spotted Al Schaeffer entering a room, several feet ahead, carrying a glass of water. Within seconds, the priest was tapping on the door. With permission granted, he entered.

"Good morning, Father," said Al, who was understandably distraught.

"Good morning, Al."

"Thank you for coming on such short notice," he acknowledged, while shaking the priest's hand. "It means a lot to Alice and me."

"How's she doing?" asked the priest.

"Not too good. Her breathing is labored and her heartbeat is irregular."

Father James draped a stole over his shoulders and sat beside the patient's bed. "Alice," he whispered.

The elderly woman slowly opened her eyes and looked in the direction of the voice. "Father," she mumbled, with growing difficulty, "I think it's time."

Glancing to the opposite side of the bed, the priest requested, "Al, could Alice and I have a few minutes alone? I'd like to hear her confession."

"Sure, Father," he responded, before releasing his weak grip from his wife's hand and nearing the door. "I'll be waiting in the hall."

The priest nodded, before directing his attention to Alice. After making the sign of the cross, he began, "May the Lord be in your heart and in your soul to help you to confess your sins with true sorrow."

"Bless me, Father, for I have sinned," admitted Alice, "it's been one month since my last confession; these are my sins. I've gossiped, I've entertained unkind thoughts against my neighbor, I've been uncharitable, and I've fallen asleep during one of your homilies."

A noticeable grin emerged on the priest's face, as he consoled, "Falling asleep during one of my homilies isn't a sin."

After giving the penitent absolution, Alice whispered several prayers which the priest had imposed as her penance. He proceeded to anoint her forehead and palms with sacred oil and pronounced a few inaudible words. Minutes later, when the last rites had concluded, he reached for a tissue from a bedside table and wiped the blessed oil that had dripped to her nose.

As the priest neared the door to call the waiting husband, Alice requested, "Father, may I have a few more words with you in private?"

"Of course," he replied, as he withdrew from the closed door and returned to the chair. "What is it?"

"Before you arrived," began Alice, "I was sleeping."

"That's good; you must rest to regain your strength."

"No, Father," corrected Alice, "that's not it. It was the dream I had."

Curious, though also restless to return to the church to investigate the anomaly on the front lawn, the priest urged, "Go on."

"I was having a dream about you."

"Me?" questioned the priest.

Alice reached for her glass of water to wet her lips, but the priest intercepted and handed the glass to her, asking, "What about me?"

After taking a sip, she continued, "I don't know what to make of it. You were praying in the church late at night, when you were yanked from the Communion rail; you were yelling at someone."

The priest set his hand on her forearm and assured, "Alice, it was just a dream. We all have dreams that seem out of the ordinary; dreams we can't explain or understand. That's perfectly normal."

"But that's not the part that upset me the most," clarified Alice.

Sensing she wanted to unburden herself, the priest asked, "So, what upset you?"

Alice took another drink before continuing, "After you were dragged from the Communion rail, I noticed a pool of blood where you had been kneeling."

"It was just a dream, Alice," restated Father James. "There's no connection between it and reality; there's nothing to worry about."

Ignoring his attempt to ease her anxieties, she further explained, "In my dream, I saw the back side of two people, who were also praying—but in the fifth pew, where my husband and I always sit. Anyway, they also were yanked somewhere, but not before one bashed its head against the pew. Then there was near total darkness. I remember looking around the church and seeing several broken stained glass windows. The weird thing is—"

Father James steadied her hand, as she took another sip of water.

"The weird thing is," she continued, "I saw a large tree outside the broken windows." She closed her eyes, reliving her dream, and added, "That's what I can't explain. After many years tending the church grounds, I know there's no tree on the front lawn."

Father James sank into his chair, thinking, *Alice has been in the hospital for nearly a week. And it was only minutes ago when I first noticed the tree's unexplained appearance. How on earth could she know about it?*

His thoughts were interrupted by Alice asking, "Father, are you alright?"

Father James cleared his throat and replied, "Yes, I'm fine. Just lost in my thoughts, I suppose." Embarrassed with his mental distraction, he admitted, "I guess I'm still a bit tense from my drive to the hospital a little while ago."

"Why, of course," assured Alice. "Near-collisions will alarm anyone."

The priest, who was rising from his chair to call Al, plopped to his seat again and asked, "How did you know of my near-accident just a few minutes ago?"

"Oh," apologized Alice, "I guess I left it out; that was the first part of my dream." The patient detected a look of anxiety surfacing on the priest's face. "Father," she insisted, "here, have a drink," as she handed her half-empty water glass to him.

"No, thank you," he replied, "I'm fine." He rose from his chair again and approached the door.

With Al at his wife's bedside, the three talked until 2:00 a.m., before Alice drifted asleep.

With the patient resting comfortably, Father James gathered his personal belongings and prepared to return to the church. But Al's request that he stay a little longer precluded him from leaving.

As she slept, the priest listened to Al recount his life's story from the day he first met Alice. Suspecting it was comforting for him, the priest sat quietly, listening to the pre-World War II story, while offering repeated glances to the patient.

At 4:00 a.m., a distress signal was heard; Alice had gone into cardiac arrest. Two nurses and a doctor bolted through the door wheeling a defibrillator. After releasing Al's grip from his wife's hand, the doctor attempted to restore a normal heart rhythm. Quite abruptly, Alice opened her eyes, stared at the priest, and yelled, "Brad Blaze!" Within seconds, she was in the hands of the Almighty.

Father James was puzzled with her final words. Redirecting his attention to the situation at hand, he approached the recent widower. Giving him an embrace, he consoled, "I'm so sorry, Al."

The elderly man wept in his arms.

Father James offered counsel and conversation to the grieving man until 6:30, at which time he escorted Al from the hospital to the parking lot. Although he insisted driving his parishioner home, the elderly man was resolved on walking the ten blocks.

"I need some time alone," said Al.

"Of course," yielded the priest, "I understand."

Father James stepped into his car and drove from the parking lot. Though still determined to reach the church as quickly as possible, he knew it was more important that Al arrive home safely. With little traffic on the residential roads, he drove slowly, keeping an eye on his parishioner. After watching Al enter his home, he hit the gas pedal and sped to the church.

It was now 7:15 in the morning; the sun had already risen.

Upon his arrival at the parish, Father James was mystified at seeing three police cars and a Lawton Utility truck parked along the curb. Stepping from his car, he was greeted by Officer Moore.

"Good morning, Father," said the policewoman.

"Good morning," he replied. "Is there a problem?"

Ignoring his question, the officer asked, "Father, have you been away all morning?"

"Yes," he replied. "I had dinner late last night with a parish family; shortly before midnight, I received a phone call from the hospital, asking me to administer the last rites to a dying parishioner."

"May we search inside the church?" inquired the cop.

"Of course," replied the priest, as he reached into his pocket for his keys. "Is there a problem?" he asked again.

Advancing to the front doors, Officer Moore explained, "Earlier this morning, at precisely 3:47, a woman telephoned police headquarters to report a broken streetlight."

Without disrupting his stride, Father James visually followed the officer's gaze to the smashed light above her patrol car. "I see," he replied.

"Anyway," she continued, "Brad Blaze, of Lawton Utility, accepted the call from the police station."

"Brad Blaze?" blurted the priest.

"Yes, Father," she answered. "Do you know him?"

"Why, yes," replied the priest, while unlocking the front door. "He's a parishioner of mine."

The two entered the church.

"Apparently," clarified Officer Moore, "Mr. Blaze never phoned in when he arrived at the site, as all electricians are instructed to do; he hasn't been heard from or seen since."

Walking down the center aisle, the priest suggested, "Have you searched the perimeter of the building?"

"Yes," informed the officer, who quickly added, "by the way, in the years I've patrolled Lawton, I've never noticed the oak tree in front. What's up with that?" Before the priest could respond, the policewoman admitted, "Granted, we often get used to our surroundings and unknowingly become oblivious to certain things; but I could almost swear I've never seen that tree before."

Nervously rubbing his hands, the priest thought it was best not to divulge what he strongly suspected, for fear it would endanger local citizens, who would flock to the oddity. He gripped a pew, genuflected, and successfully dodged the tree's peculiarity by asking, "Was anyone else reported missing?"

"No," replied Officer Moore, "just Brad Blaze."

Extending his hand to excuse himself, the priest volunteered, "If there's anything I can do to assist in your investigation, please let me know."

"Thanks, Father," remarked the officer, while shaking his hand. "I'll be in touch."

After a two-hour search inside the church and parish buildings, Officer Moore approached Father James near the sanctuary, informing him there was no trace of the electrician.

The priest was not surprised.

"Tell me, Father," she asked, "does Brad Blaze have any family we should contact?"

"I'm afraid not," he answered. "He was unmarried, with no siblings, and his parents died of natural causes several years ago."

"Very well," she replied. "We'll post his name and picture at the station and around town, while we continue our search. But in the meantime, should you see him or discover anything unusual around the church in relation to his disappearance, give me a call."

"I will, officer," agreed the priest, who walked with her to the church doors.

Stepping outside, Father James and the policewoman observed a throng of curious onlookers gathering along the street curb. The Clays and Sam stood at the front of the group.

"Well, thanks again, Father," said Officer Moore. "I'll let you know if we unearth anything."

"Good day," replied the priest.

Passing in front of the crowd, the policewoman spotted the Clays. Drawing near the family, she greeted, "Good morning."

"Good morning, officer," replied Jeff.

Looking at Dan and William, she asked, "How are you two adjusting to life back in Lawton?"

"Fine," replied William. "It's great to be home."

The officer advanced two steps, but quickly retraced them. Placing her face within inches of Dan's, she declared, "For the record, I don't believe your story that you and your friends were camping in the forest for a month." She switched her glare to William, claiming, "Or that you were abducted and living in the town of Rising Meadows for the past thirteen years. But whenever you feel like telling me the truth, you know where to reach me." Glimpsing Sam, she maintained,

"And your story about living on the streets of Pleasantville is flimsy at best."

Shortly after the travelers' return from the parallel world, Officer Moore paid a home visit. Jeff and Nancy thought it was wise not to alert the police to the tree, especially since their sons told them the enchanted oak had been transformed into a dogwood tree and it was no longer a threat. The travelers' parents suspected that disclosing too much information about their children's adventure would encourage other youngsters to explore the forest, possibly putting their lives in danger—not to mention the flood of reporters from the neighboring towns, who would hound their children with endless questions.

Trying to hurry along the policewoman so she and her family could speak in private with the priest, Nancy stressed, "Thank you, officer. But for now, I'm happy they're home, safe and sound."

"Fine," replied a disgruntled cop, "if you can live with their tall tales." She directed a stern look at Dan and William, hoping they would come clean to the whereabouts during their absence. With no information forthcoming, she retreated to her patrol car, infuriated with the group's silence.

Moments after the police cars drove away, towing the Lawton Utility truck as potential evidence, the crowds slowly dispersed, except the Clays and Sam.

Descending the church steps, Father James neared the family.

"Father," exclaimed Dan, "we didn't get your message until this morning."

"Sh," mumbled the priest, as he eyed a few bystanders dawdling behind the family. "Follow me into the church," he directed. Once inside, he acknowledged, "Thank you for coming; this phenomenon is new to me."

"You mean the tree?" asked Dan.

"Of course."

"Father," interrupted Sam, "I don't remember a tree on the front lawn."

The priest offered no response.

"What were the police looking for?" asked Nancy, to divert the subject from the oak.

"It seems," informed Father James, "Brad Blaze—a parishioner and an electrician with Lawton Utility—was here early this morning repairing the streetlight near the church, when he went missing." Looking at the three travelers, he asked, "Do you suppose this is a similar tree to the one you leaped through?"

"I don't see how," blurted Dan.

"Do you remember anything strange," questioned the priest, "or out of the ordinary the night you crossed over and entered the church?"

"No," replied Dan.

"Well, actually—" mumbled Sam.

"What?" asked Father James.

"It's probably nothing," replied Sam.

"Sam," insisted the priest, "if there's something you know that may shed light on Brad's disappearance, I need to know."

Sam looked at Dan and related, "I remember scraping mud off our boots, before we entered the church, because we didn't want to track the filth inside."

"Yeah," admitted Dan. "So?"

"I know it's a long shot," admitted Sam, "but I suppose it's possible one of us transplanted a shoot from the parent oak to the church's front lawn on our boots."

"That's impossible," replied Dan, in a defensive tone.

"And," added a hesitant Sam, "you also cut your finger on a thorn that was stuck to the bottom of your boot."

Dan fell silent. As much as he hated to admit it, Sam's explanations made it possible.

Sensing his uneasiness, Father James rested his hand on Dan's shoulder and counseled, "Like Sam said, it's probably a long shot. But even if it happened as he described, you're not at fault; it was an accident."

"Father," maintained Jeff, "I still think it's pretty unlikely Dan carried a twig from the forest all the way to the church on his boots."

"Probably," interrupted Sam, "but then how do we explain the appearance of a towering oak on the church lawn—which wasn't there only days ago—and the disappearance of Brad Blaze—who was working on a streetlight within feet of the tree?"

The group remained silent weighing the evidence.

The priest, the Clays, and Sam failed to recognize the importance of Dan's blood. With the sprout having absorbed the life-giving fluid a month prior, all that remained for the oak shoot to reach its full stature and acquire its paranormal abilities was a thirty-day germination period and the beams of a full moon. On a cloudless night, when the moon's rays are most intense, the tree could reach its maximum height in a matter of hours.

In his heart, Father James feared the tree was the second generation of the spirited oak that once cursed the nearby forest. *Alice Schaeffer,* he thought, *must have witnessed Brad Blaze's entry into the tree in her final dream before she died—just as she envisioned my near-fatal car accident. But what about her dream of me praying at the Communion rail?* He decided to keep his thoughts private, since their revelation would needlessly worry Dan.

The priest's reflections were distracted by Nancy vowing, "We'll keep Brad Blaze in our prayers; he could be anywhere."

"Yes," encouraged the priest, "we all should pray for his safe return."

The Clays and Sam neared the church doors; Father James followed.

As the doors closed behind them, they were pleased the crowds had disbanded.

Stepping off the sidewalk, Dan neared the tree and cautiously touched its surface. As he had hoped, it was solid.

"How is it?" asked Jeff, from the sidewalk.

"It's fine," he answered.

All minds were eased, except the priest's.

Completely familiar with the qualities of the original oak—and secretly aware of Alice's visions—Father James was grateful the tree was fine for now. But he had a nagging feeling that on August 30, the next full moon, all hell would break loose on the steps of Saint Augustine of Canterbury Catholic Church.

"Don't worry, Father," assured Jeff. "I'm sure Brad Blaze will show up."

"I hope so," he replied.

As the Clays and Sam drove from the parking lot, Father James ascended the church steps to offer prayers for Brad Blaze's safe return—wherever he was.

During their drive home, the passengers scrutinized the facts: the tree had grown supernaturally to its full height in a short span of time, Dan and Sam had removed mud from their boots that fell to the church grounds, Dan or Sam may have transported a shoot from the enchanted oak to the church lawn, Dan had cut his finger on a thorn at the church, and another Lawton citizen had vanished without a trace. Sadly, all five came to the same conclusion, though no one voiced their verdict that the new oak was most likely a second generation.

Suspecting the thoughts were tormenting her son—and knowing he would do whatever was necessary to rectify the situation—Nancy declared, "Dan, there was nothing wrong with cleaning your boots. Nonetheless, I want you to promise me you won't investigate the tree any further…not now and definitely not during the next full moon."

Still mentally debating whether he was the indirect cause of Brad Blaze's mysterious disappearance, Dan only partly heard his mother's directive.

"Dan," snapped a worried mother, "are you listening?"

"Sorry. What?"

"I don't want you near that tree," she warned, "not today, not tomorrow, and certainly not next month."

The teenager remained silent.

"Dan," stressed his mother, "I want you to promise me."

"Okay, mom," he grumbled.

Looking at her older son, she added, "And William, I also want you to promise me."

"Sure, mom."

Sam, who was visually lost outside the car window thinking of the tree, received a nudge from William.

"Mom wants you to promise her, too," he said.

"Sorry," replied Sam, once his attention was directed to Nancy.

"Sam, as the oldest of the travelers," she reminded, "I want you also to promise me you won't go near the oak tree on the church lawn and you'll make certain Dan and William never venture too closely either."

"Yes, ma'am," agreed Sam.

Though only mildly satisfied with their forced responses, Nancy turned and sat squarely in the front passenger's seat, after offering a passing glance to her husband behind the wheel. Both parents knew they'd need to keep a watchful eye and an attentive ear on their sons during the next month.

No additional words were spoken until the family pulled into the driveway. On entering the house, Nancy suggested, "Since we rushed out the door this morning to see Father James, I'll fix us some breakfast."

Attempting to block out—if just momentarily—the oak from his sons' thoughts, Jeff agreed, "That sounds great; boys, let's set the table."

Within an hour, the family was enjoying a hot breakfast. Halfway through the meal, a knock was heard at the front door. Setting his napkin aside, Jeff neared the foyer.

"Good morning, Jimmy," he greeted.

"Morning, Mr. Clay," replied the neighbor, who was soon darting through the living room on his approach to the kitchen. Obviously, he had something significant to share with his former co-travelers.

Jeff re-entered the kitchen, where he overheard Jimmy ask, "Did you hear about the oak tree on the church lawn?"

"Yes, we heard," said Nancy, "but don't let your thoughts stray, Jimmy. It's just an oak tree. There's nothing eerie about it."

"Of course there is," challenged Jimmy. "It shot up in practically no time!"

"Jimmy," warned Jeff, "don't get any wild ideas about checking it out. Like Mrs. Clay said, there's nothing eerie about it."

Fearing Jimmy might explore the church grounds, Sam minimized, "I saw it this morning and it doesn't seem to bear the traits of the other oak."

"You saw it?" blurted Jimmy.

Realizing he had accidentally disclosed too much information, Sam downplayed his encounter with the tree, stating, "Yeah, I was out earlier this morning and noticed it. But it seems like any other tree."

"But I didn't see it on the church lawn," declared Jimmy, "even last week."

"Jimmy," reminded Jeff, "just because it matured in a short span of time doesn't make it a tree with a portal."

"But what about—"

"Jimmy!" shouted Nancy. "That's enough!" Regretting she had been excessively harsh with her neighbor, she apologized and offered, "How about some breakfast?"

With the simple mention of food, he forgot what he was about to ask.

During the meal, Jeff and Nancy were grateful the topic of conversation quickly drifted from the oak to basketball. The parents were also pleasantly surprised Jimmy was unaware of Brad Blaze's disappearance...though they suspected it would be only a matter of hours before he heard of it through town gossip or through the police postings around town.

The moment the plates were emptied, Dan, William, and Jimmy were out the back kitchen door and soon arguing about an out-of-bounds shot.

As the young men enjoyed themselves, Sam helped the Clays clean the kitchen, promising, "I'll keep a close eye on Jimmy, too."

"That's not a bad idea," replied Nancy.

"Um, Nancy," mumbled Sam, "I'm afraid I have to go back on my word to you earlier this morning."

She raised her hands from the dishwater, turned to the newest family member, and asked, "What word is that?"

"I have to leap through the tree during the next full moon," he replied.

Jeff, who was helping Sam dry the dishes, insisted, "Why on earth do you need to make another journey?"

Sam walked to the table and took a seat. "You see," he explained, "in the time I've known Dan, I've learned a great deal about him. For example, I can promise you he's troubled about Brad Blaze; I can see it in his eyes. I also know he feels responsible for his disappearance, even though the transported shoot could have come from my boot." He paused to study Nancy and Jeff's facial expressions. "You both sense he blames himself, too," he continued, "and you also know he won't let it rest. One way or another, he'll be at the tree—if not next month, then the month after."

The Clays joined Sam at the table.

"Yes, Sam," admitted Nancy, "I do sense he harbors feelings of guilt and fears for Brad Blaze's safety." She rested her chin atop her folded hands and admitted, "And you're probably right; he will seek out the tree sooner or later. But what can we do?"

Sam leaned in, placed his elbows on the table, and suggested, "We'll tell your sons I'll enter the tree during the next full moon. I'll find Brad Blaze and bring him back. This way, Dan's conscience will be eased, without either of your sons stepping into the tree."

"Sam, are you sure it's wise to go alone?" asked Jeff. "Maybe I should join you."

Nancy remained silent.

"Don't worry, Jeff," said Sam. "Even though I never actually witnessed the wrath of God, I'm sure the Reclaimers have been incapacitated and the parallel world is now a peaceful place with no savage animals. Brad Blaze is fine and I will be, too."

"But what if you don't find him before the sun rises the next morning?" proposed Jeff. Before Sam could respond, Jeff voiced the unthinkable, "And what if the Reclaimers were successful in relocating the portal to another location after you left? If they did, you could enter virtually anywhere in their world."

"Like I said," restated Sam, "I'm certain the Reclaimers have been put out of action. It's impossible for them to relocate the portal." Glancing to Nancy, he promised, "I'll find Brad Blaze in time, since he's probably somewhere in their town." He crossed his arms, stretched back in the chair, and cautioned, "And if for some reason I don't find him right away, then I'll return the following full moon." Recalling the oak, he forewarned, "Just make sure no one cuts down the tree, until I return with Brad."

"Fair enough," said Jeff, "we'll discuss the issue with Father James."

Sam rose from his chair, stared out the kitchen window at the men playing basketball, and asked, "So, do I have your blessing on this one last adventure?"

"Yes," replied Jeff. "We'll inform the boys tonight."

Though the full moon wouldn't rise for another twenty-nine days, Sam left the kitchen, descended the basement steps, and began sharpening his lances and cleaning his revolver, in the unlikely event he'd need weapons in the transformed parallel world.

At the dinner table that night, Nancy opened the uncomfortable conversation by announcing, "Dan and William, your father and I have something we'd like to discuss with you."

By her tone of voice, the sons guessed they were in trouble for something they did or failed to do.

"What's that, mom?" asked Dan.

Knowing his wife's uneasiness with the subject, Jeff immediately spoke up, "Dan, your mother and I know you feel responsible for the oak tree on the church's lawn. We also believe you'll probably attempt another journey sometime, even though you promised us you wouldn't."

"Dad," he explained, "it's just that if it wasn't for me carrying a twig from the parallel world on my boot and then cutting my finger—"

"So," interrupted his father, "Sam has volunteered to travel alone through the tree during the next full moon to find Brad Blaze—if that's where he is."

Dan looked across the table at Sam and reminded, "But you'll need help finding Mr. Blaze; you don't know what he looks like."

Swallowing a piece of chicken, Sam replied, "I've already planned on grabbing a police posting from town. After I've crossed over, I'll check with Doctor O'Brien first. The chances of Brad being at his house are pretty good."

"But what if he's not at the doctor's house," challenged William, "and you don't find him before sunrise?"

"That's doubtful," answered Sam. "But if, by some quirk, I don't find him right away and I miss the full moon, I'll return during the next one." He took a gulp of milk before confiding, "After all, it would be nice to visit with Doctor O'Brien and tell him of our adventures, not to mention hunting in the peaceful forest and possibly meeting up with Salvus and Ceremonia."

The brothers also missed their two woodland friends and hoped someday—somehow—their paths would cross. But since the transformation of the original oak into a dogwood, their secret aspirations were dashed...until now.

"Mom, dad," said Dan, "since the parallel world is peaceful now, can William and I travel with Sam to help find Mr. Blaze and maybe spend some time with Salvus and Ceremonia?"

Nancy slammed her glass on the kitchen table and shouted, "Absolutely not! In the month since your departure from that accursed place, not to mention another month from now, anything and everything could have changed in that world. My gosh, just look how fast the oak tree grew." Realizing she had been annoyingly blunt, she directed her sights to Sam and apologized, "I'm sorry," and then poorly convinced, "I'm sure it's fine."

Sadly, Nancy had not revealed anything Sam had not previously questioned. He, like she, knew there was a distinct possibility the parallel world was not how the travelers had left it. He had a gut feeling she was right; dire events could have befallen the parallel world since the group's departure. But Dan's mental anguish on whether he was responsible for the second generation oak demanded he make the leap and rescue Brad Blaze.

The remainder of the meal and dessert were taken in near silence.

Now, like never before, Sam, Jeff, and Nancy knew the young men had to be watched closely.

To ease her growing worries, Nancy insisted her sons give their word of honor again that they would not explore the oak during the next full moon.

After a lengthy pause, the brothers promised.

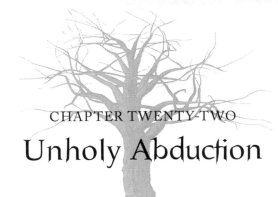

CHAPTER TWENTY-TWO
Unholy Abduction

The following weeks were routine. William met daily with his personal tutor; Dan enjoyed summer activities with his closest friends, Jimmy and Cindy; while Sam mentally prepared for his upcoming leap.

As the date of the August full moon drew closer, Sam came to view his imminent trip with greater apprehension. He knew anything could have deteriorated in the parallel world since the travelers' exodus.

With August 30 less than a week away, Dan and William had become increasingly annoyed they wouldn't be joining Sam. They secretly feared for his safety.

Though the Clay brothers and Sam never mentioned the story of Brad Blaze's unexplained disappearance to Jimmy and Cindy, it was only a matter of hours after the unfortunate incident before the two teenagers learned the sketchy details, thanks to the police postings around town.

"Do you think the oak on the church lawn is another portal?" asked Cindy, as the four travelers enjoyed a burger at the local diner.

"We're not sure," replied Dan. "Sam's going to check it out on Friday night."

"Are you and William going with him?" asked Jimmy.

"No," answered Dan. "Our parents made us promise we'd stay behind."

Sensing the wheels turning in Jimmy's sluggish brain, William warned, "Don't even think about it, Jimmy. There's no need for you or any of us to go with Sam. The parallel world is peaceful now; he'll be fine. He's simply traveling to find Mr. Blaze—presuming that's where he went—and returning that night or early the next morning."

Cindy grabbed a napkin from the greasy dispenser and commented it would be nice to see Ceremonia and Salvus again.

"Yeah," seconded Jimmy. "I wonder if Ceremonia still thinks of me."

The arrogant teenager received a slap across the chest from Cindy, who ridiculed, "Honestly, Jimmy, would you leave her alone? She was never interested in you in the first place; she just felt sorry for you."

Rubbing his chest, he glanced across the untidy booth at the brothers and asked, "So, you're really not leaping through the tree this full moon?"

"No," answered William, "and neither are you two," as he stared at Jimmy and Cindy.

"Alright…alright," mumbled Jimmy. "I won't; I promise, especially since Ceremonia just felt sorry for me."

The group finished their meal and visited the movie theater, after which they headed to the Clay's house. Descending the basement steps, the four friends eyed Sam arranging several items he'd be taking on his transworld trip.

"Sam," questioned Cindy, "if the parallel world is peaceful, why are you packing the lances and your revolver?"

Attempting to dispel any notions she might have of joining him, he explained, "Just out of habit, I suppose. And if, for some reason, I don't find Brad Blaze right away and have to wait for the next full moon, I wouldn't mind getting in some hunting. Besides, experience has taught me it's always best to be overly prepared."

"Sam," interjected Jimmy, "maybe I should go with you…you know…in case you need help finding Mr. Blaze."

Sam dropped his backpack to the floor, reprimanding, "Absolutely not! Your parents would be worried sick about you."

"What's the big deal?" challenged Jimmy. "If we left a couple hours after the full moon rose, when my folks are asleep, they'd never know I was missing."

"No, Jimmy," reiterated Sam. "This is a one-man trip." Looking at his friends' long faces, he predicted, "Look, guys, I'll probably be gone just a few hours and I more than likely won't venture deep in the forest. So, I can promise you I won't see Salvus or Ceremonia. This is going to be a boring leap, trust me."

Watching Sam snatch his backpack from the floor, Dan noticed his hand tremble, ever so slightly. As he suspected, his friend was more worried than he let on. *I wish I could join him somehow,* he thought, *without my parents finding out.*

Dan's attention was directed to Cindy, disclosing, "Sam, my mom will be out of town from Friday through Sunday on a business trip."

"So," replied Sam.

"So," clarified Cindy, "that means I can travel with you and she'll never know."

"Forget it," snapped Sam. "How can I make it any clearer to all of you? I appreciate your concern, but this is a trip I must take alone."

Dan attempted to justify a reason for traveling, when Sam interrupted, "No exceptions."

Abandoning their ambitious transworld plans, the four travelers climbed the basement steps. To their surprise, Nancy and Jeff were sitting at the kitchen table and had overheard their conversation.

"Good evening, Mr. and Mrs. Clay," greeted Cindy.

"Hello, Cindy," replied the Clays.

Cindy and Jimmy neared the back kitchen door, but stopped in their tracks when Nancy remarked, "We couldn't help but overhear your discussion downstairs about Sam's trip on Friday."

The teenagers turned and neared the table.

"I just thought since my mom will be out of town this weekend," reasoned Cindy, "I could help Sam find Mr. Blaze."

Jimmy had no convincing motive to support an upcoming trip other than to see Ceremonia.

"Look, guys," explained Nancy, "Sam will be gone just a few hours. He won't encounter any wild creatures—since they were annihilated nearly two months ago—and he won't be gone long enough to visit Ceremonia and Salvus." After resting against the back of her chair, she concluded, "Compared to your last trip, this one's going to be pretty dull." Though she retained serious doubts about the safety of the trip, she never voiced her fears, lest the teenagers worry excessively for Sam and attempt the leap.

Jeff rose from his seat, rested both hands on the table, and added, "There's no need to upset your parents." Glancing to his sons, he stressed, "Our boys have promised to stay behind. I think you owe your parents the same courtesy."

"I suppose," replied Jimmy.

Cindy echoed the same sentiment.

"Very well then," said Nancy, "now get home and tell your parents hello for us."

As the door closed behind them, Nancy sensed that without her mother around the coming weekend, Cindy would take the trip. *How on earth can Jeff and I keep an eye on William, Dan, Jimmy, and Cindy?* she thought. She resigned herself to the fact that Sam might have a resourceful young lady as a companion on his journey.

On Thursday morning, Sam slept in; the Clays drove to the weekday Mass. Once in the church parking lot, they noticed members of the Saint Joseph Grounds Crew standing on the front lawn inspecting the oak.

"Good morning," said the Clays.

The workers were too engrossed with the tree to respond.

As was typical, Father James greeted his parishioners after Mass at the back of the church. The Clays stayed a few minutes after the service, offering prayers for Sam's upcoming trip. As a result, they were the last to leave.

"Good morning, Father," said Nancy.

"Good morning," he replied. After glancing around to verify no one was nearby, he continued, "I guess you've heard there haven't been any developments on Brad Blaze's disappearance."

"Yes, Father," replied Jeff, "which is what we wanted to speak with you about."

"What's that?" he asked.

"Remember us telling you that Sam offered to take the trip during the next full moon?" asked Jeff.

"Yes, how could I forget?" replied Father James.

"Well," reminded Nancy, "that's tomorrow night."

"I hope he's doing the right thing," expressed a worried priest.

"Sam thinks it will be a brief trip," replied Jeff, "and that he'll return within a few hours. Although no one knows for sure if the world has relapsed to its previous state during the past two months, chances are it's still peaceful."

"And if it's not?" asked the priest.

The Clays had no response.

Stepping outdoors, the priest spotted four volunteers standing near the oak, with one worker revving a chain saw.

The priest dashed to the lone lumberjack, yelling, "Turn it off!" Immediately upon the saw falling silent, he ordered, "This tree is not to be cut down!"

"But, Father," alerted Frank Thomas, the head volunteer, "being only feet from the building, it's simply a matter of time before the sidewalk buckles and the church foundation cracks. Besides, its limbs reach dangerously close to the stained glass windows; it's an accident waiting to happen."

"Like I said before," replied the priest, "I appreciate your concerns; really, I do. But I want the tree to remain."

"You're the boss," replied Frank, before he and his fellow volunteers left the area for the parish garage.

"Whew, that was too close," remarked a mortified priest. "After I learned of Brad Blaze's disappearance from the police, I made it clear to the volunteers I wanted the tree to stay, since I thought it would be Brad's only way home…presuming he stepped into it. As it turns out, it's also Sam's only entrance into the parallel world."

After a visual sweep of the parish grounds to confirm no one was approaching, Jeff continued, "Anyway, Sam thinks it will be safe to travel tomorrow night." Looking at his sons, he stressed, "Dan and William have promised they won't step foot inside the tree."

Looking at his young parishioners, Father James advised, "I think it's best you stay behind this time." Since he wasn't totally convinced the parallel world was tranquil—much like Nancy and Jeff suspected—he kept his doubts to himself, so as not to worry the young men. "Sam's a clever and competent man," he shared. "I'm sure he'll be fine." He concluded his remarks, however, by suggesting, "But let's keep him in our prayers."

"Sure, Father," responded the two brothers.

Sadly, Dan was already entertaining serious doubts about honoring his promise to his parents, especially after witnessing Sam's trembles with his upcoming leap.

After parting from the priest, the family headed home.

The following morning, the Clays awoke early, primarily out of anxiety for Sam's trip that night. Over a hot breakfast, Nancy asked if there was a need to pack food for the journey.

"No, thanks," replied Sam. "Brad Blaze and I will be back before you awake tomorrow morning. And if for some reason we're late in returning, I'm sure the O'Briens will house and feed us."

"Nevertheless," insisted Nancy, "I'll prepare a few snacks, just in case."

William and Dan made several attempts that day—in private—to convince Sam they also should make the journey. As much as Sam knew he'd enjoy their company, he couldn't shake the feeling that danger awaited him. He vehemently denied them permission.

By 6:00 p.m., Sam was packed and lugging his backpack up the basement steps to the kitchen. Since the sun wasn't forecast to set until 8:12, Nancy prevailed on him to rest awhile and to enjoy a cup of coffee.

Sam took a seat.

"Do you have everything?" asked Jeff.

Opening his knapsack and taking a final inventory, he confirmed, "Yeah, I think so."

Rising from her chair, Nancy grabbed a bag from a lower cabinet and retraced her steps to the table. "You better pack this, too," she remarked.

"What's this?" asked Sam, before opening the bag.

Inside were juice, cookies, crackers, and breakfast bars.

"I appreciate it, Nancy," said Sam, "but I'll be gone just a few hours."

"Be that as it may," she replied, "you should take it along."

"Thank you," he acknowledged, before cramming the snacks into his oversize backpack.

At 7:00, Jeff offered the traveler a ride to the church.

Sam respectfully declined, explaining, "I'd rather walk to clear my mind." After setting his coffee cup in the sink, he proposed, "If it's alright with you, I'd like to leave now, so I can visit with Father James for a few minutes before my trip."

"We understand," said Nancy, as she rose and gave him a hug.

As Sam walked through the front door, Dan, once again, witnessed his shakes, though more pronounced than before. As much as he longed to join his friend on the journey, he made a promise to his parents, who were now watching his every movement and every facial expression.

Jeff and Nancy knew their younger son through and through and shuddered at what they suspected he was thinking.

"Mom, dad," implored Dan, "can William and I walk with Sam to the church, if we promise to come back after he's entered the tree?"

As helpful as both parents thought it would be for Sam, they also knew curiosity could get the better of their sons and they'd make the leap. Ultimately, Jeff decided, "Son, I'm afraid not; Sam wants some time to himself."

After a firm handshake between Jeff and Sam, the traveler resumed his walk across the porch and stepped onto the Clay's front lawn.

Bolting off the porch, Dan and William gave Sam a slap on the back, followed by a warning, "Be careful."

"That's my plan," he replied. "Now get back in the house."

The men turned and jumped over the porch railing, joining their parents. The family watched the lone traveler, until he turned the street corner.

The Clays stepped inside and locked the door.

All were nearing the kitchen, when the phone rang.

"Hello," said Dan. Seconds later, he continued, "Yeah, Jimmy, he just left." A moment of silence followed, which ended with Dan saying, "No, thanks; William and I are in for the night." He hung up the phone and sat at the table.

"What did he want?" asked Nancy.

"He and Cindy are going to a 9:30 movie," answered Dan, "and wanted to know if William and I could come along."

"That's nice of them to invite you," replied Nancy, "but isn't that rather late—even for a Friday night?"

Dan shrugged his shoulders.

At the church, Sam glanced to the oak on the lawn, climbed the steps, and entered the House of God. With only two rows of lights aglow near the sanctuary, he peered up the center aisle and saw Father James offering Evening Prayer. Quietly approaching the priest, he genuflected and knelt beside him.

"Good evening, Father," he whispered.

"Good evening, Sam," he replied. "Are you ready for your journey?"

"Almost," said the traveler. Gazing at the crucifix overhead, he asked, "Father, before I take my trip, would you have time to hear my confession, just in case I don't return?"

"Of course," replied the priest, "but do you think this rescue mission will be as perilous as the last?"

"Actually, Father," he admitted, "I don't know what to expect. I'm hoping the world is still peaceful; but I won't know until I arrive."

Father James placed a stole over his shoulders and made the sign of the cross above the penitent's head. Sam confessed his misdeeds. After the absolution and penance, the priest escorted the traveler to the church doors.

Outside, Sam experienced a bitter chill in the air; he shivered.

Seeing him shake, Father James gripped the straps on his backpack and warned, "Are you sure you want to go through with this?"

Before responding, he recalled his two-month-old resolution never to revisit the parallel world again. "Yes, Father," he eventually replied. "I need to do it for Dan and Brad Blaze." After verifying the absence of onlookers, he neared the oak.

The priest remained on the church steps.

Cautiously, Sam extended his hand. "It's soft," he yelled.

"May God be with you," whispered the priest.

After tightening his knapsack for the leap, he stepped several feet back and then ran into the tree. His third transworld journey in twenty years had begun.

The priest re-entered the church, where he offered prayers for a safe and successful journey.

Discovering that waiting for Sam's return was unbearably difficult, Dan and William retired at 10:00; their parents turned in shortly thereafter.

Dan also realized that sleeping would not come easily or naturally; William experienced the same frustration.

Glancing at the clock on the nightstand, Dan noticed it was 11:10. In the midst of tossing and turning, he rolled out of bed, concealed blankets and a pillow under his covers—mimicking a person in bed—got dressed, grabbed his flashlight and house key, and headed for the bedroom dormer. Opening the window, a faint squeak was heard, which drew William's attention, who also was wide-awake, but with his back facing his brother.

Turning in the direction of the shrill sound, William spied his brother sitting on the windowsill, with one leg resting on the roof.

"Dan," he whispered, "what are you doing?"

"Sh," ordered Dan, "you'll wake up mom and dad."

Climbing out of bed, William neared his sibling, reminding, "We promised them we wouldn't make the leap."

"I know," admitted Dan, "but I never promised I wouldn't be in the church praying and waiting for Sam and Mr. Blaze. Besides, I'm not going to get any sleep tonight. This way, when they return in a few hours, I'll be in the church waiting for them."

Defending his escape by thinking Sam and Brad Blaze could use the extra prayers and would appreciate the welcoming party, William demanded, "Wait for me." After creating a similar disguise in his bed, he slipped on a pair of jeans and neared his brother, who remained seated upon the window's ledge.

Suspecting the streetlight at the church might be smashed, Dan directed, "Grab your flashlight…just in case."

Placing the flashlight in his back pocket, William followed his brother onto the roof. Moments after closing the window behind them, they jumped from the second floor and landed painlessly on the front lawn.

The men had been away barely several minutes when Jeff—in

an effort to quell his nagging thoughts—rose from his bed to check on his sons. He opened their bedroom door, only slightly, and poked his head inside. Not wishing to stir them, he left the light out. From the poorly lit hallway, he was grateful seeing his sons in bed…or so it appeared. With his mind at ease, he returned to his room.

During their walk to the church, reality quickly set in; the brothers knew they were in for a heap of trouble upon their return at daybreak. But they remained hopeful their parents would not be too upset, since they were in the church praying for Brad Blaze and Sam's safe return—presuming the church was open.

To their relief, the doors were unlocked. As tempting as it was, Dan avoided the tree, which stood near the corner of the building, and stepped inside. In addition to the open doors, the brothers were amazed at seeing a few lights on and their parish priest kneeling near the sanctuary. Not wanting to disturb him, the men entered the fifth pew.

●

At that precise moment, 11:35 p.m., Cindy and Jimmy exited the movie theater.

"Wow," exclaimed Jimmy, "I have to see that again!"

"I'm not surprised," replied Cindy, "since you talked through most of it."

"I wasn't talking," defended Jimmy, "I was merely thinking out loud."

Before Cindy could deliver another insult, the teenagers turned the street corner and saw the church steeples in the distance; the full moon loomed overhead. Both stopped in their tracks, thought about Sam, and wished they'd been permitted to join him.

Tapping Cindy on the shoulder, Jimmy suggested, "Hey, let's check out the tree to see if it's soft."

"I don't think that's a good idea," she replied.

"Oh, come on," urged Jimmy, "there's no harm in just touching it. Besides, we have to walk past the church to get home."

Cindy bent over and tied her bootlace before yielding, "I suppose it's okay, since it's on our way home. But we're not jumping into the tree."

"I know," promised Jimmy, "I just want to touch it. If it's hard, then we know Sam never took the trip and the oak is just an ordinary tree. I'm just curious."

The two began their seven-block hike to the parish.

●

Inside the church, Father James was so absorbed in prayer he failed to hear or see the Clay brothers enter. Within minutes, the young men—like their parish priest—were making petitions to God. Without warning, two stained glass windows exploded; two oak limbs had plunged from their lofty heights and burst through the windows. Unlike the first generation oak, the tree had ascended a rung on the evolutionary ladder; the limbs had assumed lives of their own.

Before the three men could react to the unholy entry, the first aggressive limb seized Father James' leg. The second branch wrapped itself around his waist with such force, a gash was ripped in his side; blood immediately flowed. He grasped a vertical post on the Communion rail for dear life. Unfortunately, he was twisted so savagely the support broke free. He was dragged across the church floor—clutching his prayer book in one hand and fumbling for an immovable object with the other. Recalling Alice Schaeffer's dream of two worshipers, he looked to the pews, where he saw the brothers dashing to his rescue. "Get out of here!" he yelled.

As the priest was lifted from the floor and pulled through a window opening, four more violent limbs crashed through the stained glass windows and captured the brothers, tumbling Dan and bashing his head against a pew. In the struggle, his house key flew from his shirt pocket and fell to the floor.

Dan was ensnared around his thighs and chest; William was grasped around the neck and waist. Both fought valiantly to escape the tightening grip of the branches, but their efforts were in vain. As the brothers were pulled toward the window openings—and ultimately lifted above their ledges—Dan saw Father James pitched into the base of the tree.

●

A couple hundred feet from the church, Jimmy and Cindy froze; they witnessed the wild and brutal movements of the oak limbs inside the window openings.

Jimmy raced to the church. Cindy remained behind, but only for a moment. After she saw Dan tossed into the tree, she also dashed to the church.

Jimmy halted, once again, just yards from the building, in complete disbelief of the tree's supernatural abilities.

Cindy remained several feet behind her friend.

Seconds later, William was flung into the tree.

After releasing William, the two limbs hovered in midair; they detected a presence close by. Before Jimmy could escape, a limb darted in his direction, seized the teenager, and cast him into the oak's base. However, unlike his companions, he was hurled backwards into the tree.

On witnessing his disappearance, Cindy was panic-stricken. She bolted in the opposite direction for help; but her sprint proved no match for the second limb.

The branch, resuming its violent and unpredictable movements, crashed into the church building in its hunt for the fleeing teenager.

Within seconds, Cindy vanished into the tree.

●

At 6:00 a.m., the Clay's alarm rang. The night before, Nancy set the timer earlier than normal, so she could prepare a bountiful breakfast for Sam, Brad Blaze, and her family. Rolling out of bed, ever so slowly, she headed to the kitchen; Jeff remained in bed. Staggering down the stairs several minutes later, he met his wife near the warm oven.

"Good morning," greeted Nancy. "Why don't you check on Sam in the basement?"

"Sure," he agreed, "though I'm sure it's too early, even for him, to have an appetite."

In the lower level, he was troubled at seeing an empty bed. Although he and Nancy knew there was a possibility he would not return until the next full moon, they were hopeful he'd find and deliver Brad Blaze within a few hours. Returning to the kitchen, he informed, "Honey, you better not cook too much breakfast."

Nancy rested the spatula in the pan, turned to her husband, and surmised, "He never made it back?"

"I'm afraid not," he replied. "But we knew there was a chance he'd not return until next month." Seeing Nancy's unsettling reaction, he neared his wife, placed his arm around her, and promised, "He'll be alright. I'm sure he's in a peaceful world enjoying some hunting. He'll return during September's full moon."

"Do you really think so?" asked Nancy.

Jeff nodded and gave her a kiss on the cheek.

Returning her gaze to the oven, she remarked, "Well, I guess there's more for us and the boys. Speaking of which, why don't you wake them. It might be a good idea to tell them about Sam's delay over a hot breakfast."

Jeff sauntered to the boys' bedroom. Once inside, he switched on the light. On seeing his sons under the covers, he ordered, "Alright you two, rise and shine." He had just turned to leave the room, when he noticed that neither boy stirred, which was most unusual, especially for Dan, who was a light sleeper. Approaching his younger son's bed, he reached to rouse Dan, when a pillow and blanket dropped to the floor. "God, no," he whispered, before dashing to William's bed and discovering the same deceptive scenario. Then it hit him. *How on earth do I tell Nancy?* he thought, while staring at the slightly open window. Struggling with how to tell his wife, he left the bedroom, but delayed his entrance into the kitchen. He sat upon the living room sofa.

Nancy, who was nearing the kitchen entryway to grab milk from the refrigerator, noticed him sitting in the living room, but with his back facing her; she knew something was wrong. She entered the room, sat beside him, and instead of asking what was wrong—like she intended—she inadvertently asked, "They're not here, are they?"

Jeff was stunned with his wife's perception. *But then again,* he thought, *she's seen this look in the recent past—when I told her about Dan's first disappearance.*

Jeff rested his hand on Nancy's and promised, "I'm sure they're fine." Before his wife could respond, he blurted, "Maybe they're at the church."

"Of course," replied a hopeful Nancy, "maybe they're with Father James."

Within minutes, they were dressed and racing out the front door.

Jeff was opening the passenger's door for his wife, when Tom and Marie bolted across their lawn, yelling, "Jimmy never came home last night after the movie! Are William and Dan around?"

Nancy grabbed her husband's waist and lowered herself, until she was kneeling on the driveway, imploring, "Oh, God…please…not again."

Jeff raised his wife and helped her into the car, while explaining to Tom and Marie they were heading to the church, trusting William and Dan were with Father James. "Get in," he ordered, "maybe Jimmy's there, too."

The drive to the church was absolute hell for the parents, as they dared to imagine the unthinkable.

Before the car entered the church lot, the passengers saw two police cars parked alongside the curb with their lights flashing.

Dashing from the car, before it came to a complete stop, Nancy ran to the front doors. She was attempting to crawl beneath the yellow police tape, when Officer Moore foiled her advance.

"Mrs. Clay," she ordered, "the church is off limits."

"Why?" she yelled.

"Judging from the broken stained glass windows," said the officer, "I'm afraid there's been a burglary."

Jeff, Tom, and Marie had reached the church steps and overheard the cop's theory.

"Has there been any sign of teenagers?" asked Jeff.

Officer Moore looked at him, then Tom and Marie, and remarked, "Have you lost your children again?" Switching to a sarcastic tone, she replied, "Maybe they're camping in the forest again."

Ignoring the policewoman's spiteful remark, Marie related, "Jimmy never came home last night after a movie; we thought maybe he, Dan, and William were visiting Father James, since they've become good friends."

As the policewoman took two steps nearer the church, she confided, "Apparently, Father James is missing."

"Father James?" blurted Nancy.

The officer turned and explained, "Yes, his car is still in the garage and—"

"And what?" demanded Nancy. "What?"

"A Communion rail post is resting in a small pool of blood," revealed the officer, "and drops of blood lead to the smashed windows."

Nancy and Marie fell into their husbands' arms.

After ordering the parents not to trespass, the cop entered the church.

Sara, who returned earlier that morning from a business trip that ended ahead of schedule, raced from her parked car to the church steps. On spotting the Clays and the Parkers, she cried out, "Cindy's not around! Have you seen her?"

Nancy broke from her husband's grip and put her arm around Sara, who recalled a similar display of emotional support in the recent past; she wept.

"It'll be alright," promised Nancy. To calm Sara and the Parkers—not to mention herself and Jeff—she insisted, "We must believe they're in a peaceful world for the next month and not in a merciless place like before." Knowing Sara was in no condition to drive, Nancy assisted her from the church steps, while inviting her and the Parkers, "Come home with us; I have breakfast waiting. Jeff and I will update you over the meal."

Arm in arm, Nancy and Sara neared the Clay's car.

During their short walk across the church lawn, a sudden gale forced a low-hanging oak limb to strike Nancy's back. Startled, she spun, glanced at the majestic tree, and clearly detected a demonic face—perfectly disguised—at its base. A diabolic chill consumed her entire being.